Praise for the Books of T. C. LoTempio

"Nick and Nora are a winning team!"
—Rebecca Hale, *New York Times* Bestselling author

"A fast-paced cozy mystery spiced with a dash of romance and topped with a big slice of 'cat-titude.'"
—Ali Brandon, *New York Times* Bestselling author

"Nick and Nora are the purr-fect sleuth duo!"
—Victoria Laurie, *New York Times* Bestselling author

"A page-turner with an endearing heroine."
—*Richmond Times Dispatch*

"Excellently plotted and executed—five paws and a tail up for this tale."
—*Open Book Society*

"Nick brims with street smarts and feline charisma, you'd think he was human . . . an exciting new series."
—Carole Nelson Douglas, *New York Times* notable author of the Midnight Louie mysteries

"I love this series and each new story quickly becomes my favorite. Cannot wait for the next!"
—*Escape With Dollycas Into a Good Book*

"I totally loved this lighthearted and engagingly entertaining whodunit featuring new amateur sleuth Nora Charles and Nick, her feline companion."
—*Dru's Cozy Report*

Books by T. C. LoTempio

Nick and Nora Mysteries

Meow If It's Murder
Claws for Alarm
Crime and Catnip
Hiss H for Homicide
Murder Faux Paws

Urban Tails Pet Shop Mysteries

The Time for Murder Is Meow
Killers of a Feather

Cat Rescue Mysteries

Purr M for Murder
Death by a Whisker

Killers of a Feather

Urban Tails Pet Shop Mysteries

T. C. LoTempio

Killers of a Feather
T. C. LoTempio
Copyright © 2022 by T. C. LoTempio.
Cover design and illustration by Dar Albert, Wicked Smart Designs

Beyond the Page Books
are published by
Beyond the Page Publishing
www.beyondthepagepub.com

ISBN: 978-1-958384-02-2

All rights reserved under International and Pan-American Copyright Conventions. By payment of required fees, you have been granted the non-exclusive, non-transferable right to access and read the text of this book. No part of this text may be reproduced, transmitted, downloaded, decompiled, reverse engineered, or stored in or introduced into any information storage and retrieval system, in any form or by any means, whether electronic or mechanical, now known or hereinafter invented without the express written permission of both the copyright holder and the publisher.

This is a work of fiction. Names, characters, places, and incidents either are the product of the author's imagination or are used fictitiously, and any resemblance to actual persons, living or dead, business establishments, events or locales is entirely coincidental. The publisher does not have any control over and does not assume any responsibility for author or third-party websites or their content.

The scanning, uploading, and distribution of this book via the Internet or via any other means without the permission of the publisher is illegal and punishable by law. Your support of the author's rights is appreciated.

To Rob White . . . and he knows why!

One

"You know you've put me in a very awkward position . . . this is extremely short notice. Yes, of course I understand. I know it can't be helped . . . okay, fine. Yeah, yeah. I'll be on the lookout for it."

Had I been on a landline, I'd have slammed the receiver down with a satisfying crash. But since I'd taken the call on my cell, I had to settle for hitting the End key and dropping the phone on the desk with a bit more force than necessary. Across the room, my big, beautiful fluffy white Persian cat, Purrday, gave me a look—as much as a feline can—that said *What's wrong?*

I looked the cat straight in his one clear blue eye. "Guess what! The singer I hired canceled!"

Purrday cocked his head. "Merow?"

"You heard me right. He canceled. Apparently his grandmother, who's in a nursing home in Florida, suffered a bad fall. She has no other relatives so he's got to fly down immediately." I ran my hand through my mass of blonde curls and gave one of them a sharp tug. "Oh, I know it's a valid excuse, but it puts us in a heck of a position. The grand opening's Saturday. That's forty-eight hours away. Where am I going to find another singer on such short notice?"

Purrday jumped down from his perch on the wide sill of the window in the back room of my store. He padded over to my chair, leapt onto my lap, and nuzzled his nose against my chin.

I stroked the cat's back. "I know, I know. I'm from Hollywood. I should be used to rejection, right? Let me tell you, it never gets any easier."

My name is Shell McMillan. Up until a few months ago, I'd been better known as Shell Marlowe, the star of *Spy Anyone*, a popular cable TV show. When it had been canceled (to make way for a game show starring the irrepressible Alec Baldwin) I'd looked on it as a chance to get a fresh start in life. As fate would have it, my Aunt Tillie passed away a few days later, leaving me her Victorian mansion, a healthy financial portfolio, her cat Purrday—and her business, the Urban Tails Pet Shop.

Urban Tails had been a favorite with the residents of Fox Hollow, Connecticut. The citizens of the sleepy village loved their pets, and they loved the personal services my aunt used to provide for them even more. In the past week I'd received many phone calls and letters saying how much everyone was looking forward to having the shop open again. Truthfully, I was looking forward to it myself, so much so that I might have gotten a bit carried away with preparations. I'd secured an ordinance from the town to have the block closed to traffic from ten a.m. till six in the evening, and enlisted the cooperation of the other merchants, who were all more than willing to help. It was going to be one huge block party. In addition to the food trucks I'd hired and the vocalist that I now didn't have, I'd booked some other local entertainment as well. All the merchants would have displays out in front of their stores, and Rita Sakowski, who ran the local café, Sweet Perks, had promised to serve free coffee and doughnuts all day long. Everything had been running like clockwork, maybe too much so, until now.

The back door opened and my pal Olivia Niven, her arms laden with bags, sailed through. Purrday jumped off my lap and padded over to rub his portly body against Olivia's legs. My cat loved Olivia, as did most men. She was tall, with a lithe dancer's body, which was appropriate since she ran the local dance studio. Her thick dark hair was done up in a casual ponytail and her face, scrubbed clean of makeup, looked fresh and dewy. She looked more like one of the teens in her dance class than their thirty-five-year-old teacher. Her ponytail flipped over one shoulder as she laid the bags down and bent to pet Purrday. "Hey there, handsome," she cooed. "All excited about the grand opening?"

"He's probably more excited than I am right now," I said glumly. "Right now I'm extremely annoyed."

Olivia looked up from giving Purrday a chuck under his chin. "Uh-oh. What's wrong? Something happen with the Rialto? Don't tell me Buck backed out after all?"

The Rialto was one of Fox Hollow's staples, a small theater that specialized in running classic films. The manager, Buck Adams, had been a tad reluctant to participate at first. He'd had a few bad experiences with events like this in the past, but I finally managed to convince him to participate in this one by a) telling him every other merchant was in, and he'd look really dumb refusing, and b) offering him freebies for his two pugs, Tracey and Hepburn. He promised to have a sidewalk concession stand offering fairly simple stuff—caramel apples, popcorn, cookies, and some light beverages. After some arm-twisting (and monogrammed ceramic bowls for Tracey and Hepburn), he'd also agreed to a raffle for two movie tickets. "Nope, Buck's fine. It's Elvin

Scraggs. He's bugged out on me. His grandmother in Florida took a bad fall."

Olivia coughed lightly. "His granny, huh?"

Something in the tone of her voice made me glance up sharply. "Don't tell me he doesn't have one," I moaned.

"Oh, he's got a granny in Florida, all right," Olivia said with a chuckle. "Viola Scraggs is pushing ninety but she's got more energy than both you and me combined. The woman power-walks every morning. Elvin's more likely to take a spill than her."

I set my jaw. "I knew it!"

Olivia leaned in a bit closer to me. "I happened to be in the Bottoms Up Tavern yesterday and overheard Elvin talking to his buddies, Justin McAfee and Harvey Blunt, about taking a fishing trip. I also noticed he shut up pretty quick when he noticed me."

I reached for my phone. "Of all the nerve. I'm going to call him back and give him a piece of my mind. Gary will never let me live this down. He told me to get a signed contract."

Olivia reached out, plucked the phone from my outstretched hand and set it down on the counter. "Don't feel bad. It wouldn't be the first time he pulled a stunt like this because someone told him the bass were running."

"Amazing. I'm surprised no one's sued him yet."

Olivia let out a hearty laugh. "Sue Elvin? For what? The guy's got no money, and the property he owns is mortgaged to the hilt. He lives like a hermit out there in the woods, doing odd jobs to make ends meet. Last week I heard he offered to help Mitch Frey fix some security cameras that weren't recording the time correctly. Everyone knows what he's like. The guy came out of the womb with a fishing pole in his hands. Given the chance, he'd spend all his time in that ramshackle canoe rather than doing any real work. He's just biding his time, waiting for dear old Granny to kick the bucket and leave him all her money. Did you give him a deposit?"

"Fifty bucks. He said he'd send me a check."

"Make sure you get it," Olivia cautioned. "Elvin always suffers from selective memory lapses when it comes to that little detail."

"Well, if it doesn't turn up by next week, I will give him a call. But right now what I need is another singer. Any suggestions?"

"Do you really need one? You've got the boom boxes and CDs, after all. They'll provide a wider range of tunes."

"I know, but I was looking forward to the live interaction. Elvin was slated to perform for an hour at the gazebo. I thought it would be fun. He could interact with the audience, do requests. Can't do that with boom boxes."

"Maybe Gary could pull a few strings," Olivia suggested. "He's always talking about his Hollywood connections."

I fought the impulse to roll my eyes at my friend. Olivia was referring to Gary Presser, my former costar on *Spy Anyone*. He'd come to Fox Hollow to help out when I'd been suspected of murder a short time ago. (A long story, recounted elsewhere for those who are interested.) I'd thought he'd return to LA once the culprit was behind bars; instead, he declared he'd been won over by the town and a simpler way of life and had decided to stay on. I was more inclined to think his attraction to Olivia, and hers to him, had more to do with it. He was currently searching for an apartment, and Olivia was helping him. In the interim, he was staying with me. Fortunately, my Victorian mansion is large enough so I could go for days without seeing him. Now, don't get me wrong. I love Gary like a brother, but . . . sometimes he can be a bit much, what with his oversized ego and all. He does have his good points, though, the main one being his remarkable cooking skills, which were much appreciated not only by me but by the kitties. Purrday was fond of Gary and lately my Siamese cat, Kahlua, even seemed to tolerate him, probably due to the treats he slipped them when he thought I wasn't looking.

As if on cue, the back door banged open again and the man in question breezed through. "Hello, there," he said. "How are the two loveliest ladies in Fox Hollow today?"

Olivia's cheeks flushed a delicate shade of pink and she murmured something in response. I, however, stood, feet apart, arms crossed over my chest, and glared at him. "Not so great," I announced. "There's been a last-minute cancellation. Our singer punked out."

"Singer? You mean Elvis?"

"Elvin," I corrected.

Gary frowned. "What happened? He got a better offer?"

"His grannie took a spill, or so he says," Olivia informed Gary with a broad wink.

Gary shrugged. "So he played the granny card, eh? No loss. I didn't much care for him anyway. He seemed a bit too slick." He looked at me and jabbed his finger in the air. "Make sure you get that deposit back. Fifty bucks is fifty bucks."

I bit down hard on my lower lip and mentally counted to ten before I spoke. "Is there a particular reason you're gracing me with your presence now? I was under the impression you were spending the day finalizing details with our live entertainers?"

"I was, until I ran into a bit of a snag."

I arched a brow. "A snag. Don't tell me it's another cancellation?"

He ran his hand through his mass of black hair, mussing up the sides just a bit. "In a manner of speaking. It's Captain Snaggle."

"The parrot?" I cried. At my feet, I heard Purrday give a soft hiss. "What's happened to him? He didn't . . . he isn't . . ."

"No, Captain Snaggle is fine. It's just, well, he's MIA."

I stared at him. "MIA?"

Gary pulled a face. "He flew the coop—literally. One of the high school kids was cleaning his cage and forgot to secure the latch. Captain Snaggle opened the door with his beak and, well, he took off."

Olivia barely suppressed a chuckle. "Now that's a smart bird, all right. Refresh my memory. Just what was the parrot supposed to do, exactly?"

"Tell fortunes," Gary and I chorused. "He was a tad restless, but once he got going he was very entertaining," Gary added. "He'd hold a little conversation with you, then pull your fortune out of a box."

"You don't say?" Olivia slid a glance Gary's way. "Did he tell your fortune?"

Gary leaned over and graced Olivia with one of his super hundred-watt mega-smiles. "Yes, he did. He told me a really pretty brunette was in my future."

As Olivia dissolved into a girlish giggle, I remarked, "Maybe it's not as big a loss as you think. After all, we already have a fortune-teller."

Gary's gaze snapped from Olivia to me. "We do? And who might that be?"

"I told you at dinner the other night. Rita's neighbor, Mae Barker."

"Rita recommended Mae? That's a hoot," Olivia said with a chuckle. "I didn't think Rita liked Mae that much. She's always telling me what a nosy busybody she is."

"I did get the impression Rita recommended her to get her off her back," I admitted. "Mae works at the Wegmans but dabbles in the Tarot and palm reading in her spare time. Rita did say—albeit a bit grudgingly—that she's pretty good, and some of the stuff she's predicted has actually come true."

Olivia cocked her head, considering. "There's probably room for both of 'em," she said at last. "Mae would no doubt appeal to the adults, and the kids would really go for the parrot."

"That's what I thought," I said and sighed. "It's moot now. No Captain Snaggle. And I'd planned to put him right in front of the shop, too, as a sort of enticement."

"I'm glad to hear you say that." Gary cleared his throat. "Because I've got another parrot all lined up and ready to go."

I stared at him. "You're kidding! You found another fortune-telling parrot? Where?"

"The same breeder, actually. Honey Belle is Captain Snaggle's sister."

"Honey Belle! What an adorable name!" Olivia clapped her hands. "And she tells fortunes too?"

"Yep, pulls 'em out of a box just like the captain. Only thing is, she's not as vocal as the other parrot, but maybe that's a good thing." Gary turned to me. "So, what do you think, Shell? Shall I lock down Honey Belle? Adrian even agreed to take a ten percent cut on the fee."

"That's surprising, considering he haggled over Captain Snaggle's to begin with." Adrian Arnold was a parrot breeder/trainer who lived in nearby Franklin. He'd boasted that some of his birds had appeared on television and commercials, although I'd yet to find evidence of that. He'd wanted five hundred dollars for Captain Snaggle's appearance, which had seemed unduly high to me. It had taken all of mine and Gary's charm combined to get him to agree to half that. Needless to say, I'd been less than impressed with the man.

"I think he feels bad about what happened. He said he'd take one seventy-five, but I've got to let him know"—Gary glanced at his watch—"in an hour."

I arched my eyebrow at him. "Why? Does the bird have another gig lined up?"

"Adrian said something about a kid's birthday party. I got the impression, though, that he'd rather do our gig. And whether you believe it or not, the guy did feel bad about what happened with the captain."

I had the feeling Arnold was more upset about losing a potential income source than about disappointing us, but I'd learned over the years it was best to pick your battles, especially where Gary was concerned. I might not like or trust Arnold, but I knew, despite what I'd said about not needing two fortune-tellers, that the bird would undoubtedly be the bigger hit. "Sure, why not. I admit, I'm curious to see how good this parrot is at predicting the future. Maybe we should consult her now. Maybe she can tell us where we can get another vocalist."

Olivia looked at Gary. "I told her the boom boxes were good enough. Most people won't care about a live singer anyway. They'll be having too good a time—I hope."

Gary nodded. "I agree with Olivia," he said, and then held up his hand, traffic-cop style. "You could probably get away without music entirely. They'll just be jazzed Urban Tails will be open again."

"I know," I conceded, "but it would have been nice. And the flyers do advertise a live vocalist."

He slid his arm around my shoulders. "I know how you are when you get your heart set on something. Tell you what, I'll ask around when I'm out and about."

"That's very kind of you."

"Worst-case scenario, I could always be persuaded to perform a few numbers."

I threw up both hands. "No. Absolutely not."

"Oh, come on. You know I have a pretty good voice."

"I've passed by the guest bathroom and heard you several times. I'd prefer that your singing remain in the shower, if it's all the same to you."

Gary glanced over at Purrday. "Purrday's heard me. What do you think, fella?"

Purrday stretched out on the floor and put his paws up to his ears.

"Thanks a lot. Say, aren't blue-eyed white cats supposed to be deaf, anyway?"

Olivia drew in a breath. "Oh my goodness. Is that really true? I thought it was just a myth."

"No, it's true," I said. "It's a condition called congenital sensorineural deafness. It occurs in domestic cats with a white coat, and is most likely to appear in cats with blue irises." I'd always harbored a secret desire to be a veterinarian, and after I'd adopted Purrday, I had looked it up. "It doesn't mean that every blue-eyed white cat is deaf, though. If you ask me, Purrday can hear just fine."

Gary laughed. "Or he reads lips."

Purrday let out a loud *merow* and glared at Gary with his one good eye.

Gary threw up both hands. "Okay, okay. I'm going." He started for the door, paused. "I forgot to take something out for dinner. How about meeting at the Bottoms Up at five thirty instead? My treat."

"You really like that place, don't you?" The pub-style eatery was new in town, only having opened two weeks ago, and was fast becoming a town favorite. Both Gary and Olivia had become regulars. I'd been so busy the past few weeks with plans for the reopening that I'd had yet to try it.

"Their cooking is almost as good as mine," Gary said solemnly. "Plus, who can resist that name?" When I didn't laugh at his lame joke he added, "Seriously, you should try their macaroni and cheese, Shell. You'd love it." He looked at Olivia. "You're invited too, of course. And Rita and Ron too, if they're available. We can have a little pre-opening celebration." Rita Sakowski owned the local coffee shop, of course, and Ron Webb was the local florist. They, along with Olivia, had taken me under their wings when I'd moved to Fox Hollow.

"That sounds great," Olivia said. "Count me in. I'll call Rita and Ron too."

Gary looked at me. "How about it, Shell?"

I sighed. "Sure. Why not. I've got to eat, and who knows? Maybe a miracle will happen and I'll land a great singer by five."

"Stranger things have happened," Gary called over his shoulder as he ushered Olivia out the door.

Purrday blinked his good eye. "Merow."

Once they'd gone, I plucked a thick sheaf of papers from my desk and started going down the neat rows, looking at stock and making sure we had enough of everything for the big day. I'd ordered plenty of pet food of all sorts—for cats, dogs, birds, hamsters, rabbits. I had two rows of bowls and eating accessories, and three full of toys. Brightly colored pet carriers covered one side of the far wall. The only thing lacking at the moment was livestock. Adrian Arnold had left me one of his brochures in the hopes I'd take on some of his parrots, but I'd put him off. There were a few other reputable breeders I wanted to consult with before I made a decision. So far I'd contracted with a parakeet and canary breeder, as well as one for hamsters, rabbits, and fish, but nothing could be delivered until next month. I planned in the interim, however, to contact the local animal shelter to see if I could arrange some dog and cat adoption days over the next few weeks. My eyes teared up for a brief instant, thinking how proud my aunt would be to see Urban Tails hosting events like those.

I tucked the papers underneath one arm and started to turn toward the back room, which doubled as a combination storeroom/office. As I passed the front door, I saw movement out of the corner of my eye and whirled around to see a face pressed up close against the glass. I took a step backward and halted the involuntary shriek that rose to my lips as I realized the face belonged to a boy—a teenaged boy. He raised a hand, tapped two fingers against the glass. I pointed to the sign on the door marked *Closed*. He shook his head and tapped again, more urgently this time.

I twisted the lock and opened the door a quarter of an inch, just enough to stick my nose out. "I'm sorry, but we're not officially open for business yet. The grand opening is this Saturday."

The boy nodded. "I know. I'm here about the job."

"Job?" My forehead wrinkled, then cleared. "Oh, if you mean the clerk positions, I hired two people yesterday."

The boy shook his head, making the gelled spikes on top wiggle just a tad. "No, not the clerk job. The assistant manager position."

I rubbed absently at my forehead. I was looking for someone I could trust to run the store in my absence, but I'd determined the ideal candidate would be older, with some experience with animals. "Ah, my associate, Gary Presser, has been conducting the interviews for that."

The boy's face split in a wide grin. "I know. I spoke with him yesterday. He told me to come by today around three. He said that you would want to interview me yourself."

"He did, did he?" I sighed, then opened the door all the way. "Why don't you come in. I just have to make a quick phone call."

"Thanks."

He ambled past me, and I took a moment to study him. He was probably somewhere around fifteen or sixteen, and resembled any number of young boys that same age with his spiky haircut, black T-shirt and jeans. He seemed more fastidious about his appearance than some of the other applicants Gary'd brought in, though. His shirt was tucked in and his pants weren't overly baggy.

I snatched my cell phone up and hit the speed dial number for Gary. He answered on the second ring. "Hey, good-lookin'. Miss me already?"

"In your dreams. Say, Gary, did you forget to tell me something when you were here earlier?"

"No, I don't think so."

"Are you sure? Nothing about someone who'd be stopping by? A young man?"

"Aw, geez!" I heard a loud slapping sound. "Is he there?"

"Yes," I hissed into the phone. "Would you mind telling me just who he is?"

"Your new assistant manager, or at least, the best candidate for the job I've seen so far," Gary answered. "His name is Robert Grant, but he prefers to go by Robbie."

"But he's just a kid," I protested. "I wanted someone older."

"He's eighteen," Gary replied. "Graduated Fox Hollow High two weeks ago and he's starting college in September."

"Oh, great, so he'll be working here, what, two months and then he's off to college?"

"No," Gary said. "He's going local. Going to study animal science at UConn. He might want to go on to veterinary school, but that's a few years off."

He had my attention now, and he knew it. "Animal science, huh?"

"Yep. He lives in Douglass, just outside Fox Hollow. His parents have a farm. His mother raises chickens and sells eggs. I think they've got a few cows, too. Maybe a horse. Anyway, the point is the kid's got experience with animals, which none of the other applicants had. I didn't promise him the job, I just said I thought you'd like to interview him. Don't forget, Bottoms Up at five thirty, unless I catch you at home before then."

Gary rang off and I tapped my cell against my chin. I looked back at Robbie, who sat slouched in the chair next to the counter. I sucked in my breath, squared my shoulders and walked over to him. I looked down at him with what I hoped was a pleasant smile and said, "Gary tells me you're college-bound. You're interested in animal science?"

Robbie's face lit up. "Oh, yes, ma'am. I love animals. It's natural, I guess. My parents have a farm, and my mother has a little egg business that I help her with."

"So your dad is a farmer?"

Robbie laughed. "Oh, no, ma'am. My dad's an accountant. He inherited the farm from his mother—my grandmother. But he does breed dogs on the side."

I lowered myself into the chair opposite Robbie. The kid had a genuine interest in animals, I could see that. His face practically glowed. "Tell me a bit about that," I encouraged him.

"He breeds bloodhounds. You've heard of Broadway Symposium's Summer Lovin'?" As I shook my head he went on, "He's a mighty fine bloodhound. Won the AKC best of breed at the Connecticut Pet Show twice and came in second in best of breed at Westminster two years ago. Came out of one of our litters. We used to breed cocker spaniels, too, but the hounds are more popular around these parts." He grinned at me, showing off even white teeth. "I'm pretty good with dogs and cats too, if I do say so myself. My girlfriend has two cats."

"Really? I do too. They'll probably be hanging around the store a lot. As a matter of fact, if I'm not mistaken, here comes one now."

As if on cue, Purrday emerged from his corner. He ambled over to where Robbie sat and fixed him with his one-eyed stare.

Robbie appeared totally unruffled. He bent over to give Purrday a scratch under his chin. "Well, aren't you a fine-looking fellow." His hand reached out, brushed against Purrday's fluffy white tail. "Pedigree," he said.

"That's right. This is Purrday. He belonged to my aunt, who originally owned this store."

Robbie scratched Purrday under his chin, and Purrday purred like a locomotive. "He seems very gentle. How'd he lose the eye?"

"I heard it was in a fight. And the other cat walked off looking much worse."

Robbie laughed. I watched the cat closely. Purrday raised his large white paw in the teen's direction. Robbie laughed and lightly touched his knuckles to Purrday's raised foot.

"Kitty high five," he said.

Purrday let out a loud, rumbling purr, then turned around and padded back to his corner. He turned around twice and looked at me, as if to say, *I've given him my seal of approval. Now it's up to you.*

Robbie shot me a triumphant look. "See, like I said, I get along swell with cats."

"It would appear so," I said. "I take it you'd have no problem giving dogs a bath, or clipping cats' claws? Those are things that I want to start doing here at the pet shop."

Robbie stretched his long legs out in front of him. "No, ma'am, not at all. I've given baths to plenty of dogs in my time, and I just clipped my girlfriend's cats' claws the other night. I figure this is all good practice for when I open my own vet practice someday." He bent over, and I noticed the black backpack at his feet for the first time. He unzipped the top, riffled through the contents and finally whipped out a manila file folder, which he passed over to me. "There's a copy of my application, along with some letters of recommendation."

I took the folder and flipped through it. Sure enough, there was the form, neatly filled out, along with two neatly typed letters. I scanned the application quickly, then turned my attention to the letters. I glanced at the signature on the first one and looked up in surprise. "I see you worked at Sweet Perks?"

Robbie nodded. "Yep. Last year, during the summer. I did deliveries for the store." He grinned. "Mrs. Sakowski always said she'd hire me back in a nanosecond. She thinks I'd be a big asset to you."

I scanned Rita's letter and then moved onto the second. It was from Harlan Grace, the Fox Hollow High principal. Both gave the youth high praise. I set the paperwork aside and looked him straight in the eye. "To start, I'd need you full-time four days a week and alternate Saturdays and Sundays. When you start college we can discuss a lighter schedule. Would you have a problem with that?"

He shook his head emphatically. "Like I told Mr. Presser, it would be an honor to work with the both of you."

I had to fight hard to keep from choking at the worshipful way he said *Mr. Presser*. "Gary doesn't work here on a regular basis," I said. "He's just helping me out temporarily."

"Oh. Well, I'd still love to work with you, Ms. McMillan." He lowered his voice to a hushed whisper. "I was a big *Spy Anyone* fan. I cried when they canceled it."

I choked back a laugh, remembering Gary doing the same thing. I held out my hand. "You've got the job, Robbie, if you want it."

The teen shot out of the chair and grabbed my proffered hand. "I sure do. Thanks so much, Ms. McMillan. I can start right now, if you want." His gaze darted around the store. "I could help you finish setting up, although it seems like you've already got that under control."

"Saturday's fine." I clapped him on the shoulder. His youthful enthusiasm was refreshing, to say the least. "Be sure to get here at nine a.m. Saturday. Opening day's going to be a long one. We can take care of the necessary paperwork then."

His eyes lit up. "I can't wait."

I walked him to the door. "I don't suppose you know of any singers who are free Saturday?"

Robbie, in the middle of adjusting his backpack, paused. "No, I'm sorry, I don't. Why?"

I explained my predicament. When I'd finished, Robbie nodded. "I know what you mean. Boom boxes are nice, but there's just something about live entertainment." He paused and then added, "There was a guy who rented an apartment from one of our neighbors some years back. His name was Johnny Draco. He had a terrific voice."

I looked up with interest. "Yeah? Is this Johnnie guy still around?"

Robbie gave his head an emphatic shake. "No. He left town." He paused again. "You probably wouldn't have wanted to hire him anyway," he said.

"No? Why not?"

Robbie shuffled his weight from one foot to the other, studiously avoiding my gaze. Finally he looked at me. "I'm not one hundred percent certain, you understand," he said, "but there's a good chance Johnny might have spent the last few years in prison."

Two

"Prison!" I cried out. "Oh my goodness! What did he do?"

Robbie's cheeks reddened and he shoved his hands into his pockets. "Oh, gee, Ms. McMillan, I probably shouldn't have said anything. My mother always told me it's not polite to gossip."

"Your mother is very wise. Did she also tell you it's not polite to tease people with dramatic statements?"

He managed a small grin at that. "I really don't know the details, because I was in junior high when it happened. My parents used to talk a bit about it at the dinner table. As near as I can recall, he was suspected of swindling some folks out of money but nothing could be proven. And then, one night, he just vanished—poof! Into thin air. And was never heard from again."

"Like a thief in the night," I murmured.

"That's a good analogy," said Robbie. "I guess in this case it could be true. It sure made him look guilty. My parents thought maybe he tried to pull something somewhere else and got caught." He shifted his backpack to his other shoulder. "I probably should get going. I'll see you Saturday, Ms. McMillan."

Robbie left and I locked the door behind him. I glanced down at Purrday, who was at my feet, looking up at me. "Meower," he said.

"Yes, I know. That was an interesting story Robbie told us. It happened a long time ago, though. None of our concern."

"Meower," Purrday said again. He turned and stalked off to his corner, white tail waving like a plume.

I tried to concentrate on finalizing my inventory, but I couldn't turn my thoughts away from the mysterious Johnny. Finally I set down my list, reached for my phone and punched in a number. A few seconds later a feminine voice came over the wire. "Secondhand Sue's. How can I help you?"

"Hey, Sue, it's Shell."

"Shell! How are you? Getting all excited for Saturday, I bet."

"I'll admit, the butterflies are churning. You're planning on coming, right?"

"Oh, absolutely. And don't worry, I've got a pet sitter for Rocco. My neighbor said she'd watch him." Rocco was Sue's dog, a giant pit bull-retriever mix that was more playful than predatory. The dog would lick you to death if you'd let him. I detected a bit of a smile in her voice as she added, "I don't know if Josh mentioned it to you yet, but he managed to get Saturday off."

"The whole day? How on earth did he manage that?" I knew Josh had been putting in a lot of overtime the past two weeks, since two of his men were down with the flu.

"He managed to get a recruit over from Hartford. Name's Riser, I think. Came highly recommended. Anyway, he's going to spell me for a bit here, then head on down to your shop."

I couldn't stop the smile that spread across my face at those words. Sue Bloodgood was not only the proprietor of Fox Hollow's only thrift shop, she was also the sister of Josh Bloodgood, a homicide detective I'd recently started dating. Thanks to his overtime and my preoccupation with the store opening, we'd only managed one date, but it had been a highly satisfactory event. "That's excellent news," I said.

"Yep. Now let's just hope there are no homicides that will demand his attention Saturday."

"Amen to that. I don't know how he does it. I had enough drama with Amelia's murder to last me a lifetime."

"Josh has done it for so long it's like second nature." She laughed. "Besides, you were on the wrong end for that one, Shell. It's different when you're the investigator and not the suspect."

"Can't fault that logic. I should actually have some time to spend with him at the festivities too, seeing as I just hired an assistant manager."

Sue let out an excited squeal. "Oh, good! So you hired Robbie Grant!"

I couldn't keep the surprise out of my voice. "How did you know?"

"I saw him go into your shop a while ago," Sue confessed. "Rita told me she wrote a nice letter of recommendation for him. He's a good kid, Shell. His dad raises pedigreed bloodhounds, you know."

"So he said."

"They've got one on the force with the K-9 squad. You can ask Josh about him. I think Robbie is the one who brought the dog over and helped train him. He's a hard worker. Rita said she'd have hired him back in a heartbeat, and to tell you the truth, I considered hiring him, too. You've got a good one there, believe me."

"I agree." I paused and then said, "My singer punked out."

"Elvin? When?"

"About two hours ago."

"I can't say I'm surprised. He's got a habit of doing that. I hoped for your sake it'd be different this time, though."

I groaned inwardly. It seemed everyone knew about Elvin's proclivity for backing out of commitments except me. I said, "Thanks, Sue. I don't suppose you know any singers who'd like to make some extra money Saturday?"

"There are a few girls from the church choir, but they always have their practice Saturday afternoon. It's pretty short notice."

"I know." I hesitated, then plunged right in. "Robbie was telling me about some guy who used to live near him that had a nice voice. Some guy named Johnny Draco?"

"Johnny Draco," Sue murmured. "Gee, I haven't heard that name in a long time. Now that I think about it, he did rent an apartment from one of Robbie's neighbors. I didn't realize he knew him."

"Knew *of* him is more like it. He said that his parents suspected Draco might have done some prison time."

"Yeah? That would make a lot of folks around here pretty happy," Sue said. "If it's true, which it probably isn't."

"Why do you say that?"

"Oh, no particular reason. The guy had the gift of gab, and he led a charmed life. He was never charged with any crime, although the way he just up and took off made people wonder."

My curiosity was now officially aroused. Before I could question Sue further, though, she said, "Oh, a customer just walked in. We'll talk later."

Sue disconnected, and I frowned at my phone. I was too antsy to wait until later. My laptop was at home, so I called up my favorite search engine on my phone. I was just about to type in Draco's name when the phone chirped, indicating an incoming call. I looked at the name on the Caller ID and suppressed a groan when I saw "Mother" pop up on the screen. Swell. I was tempted to press the Ignore button, but knowing my mother, she'd keep blowing up my phone line until I answered. With a sigh, I depressed the Answer button. "Hello, Mother."

"Crishell." My mother, Clarissa McMillan, is a classically trained actress who'd enjoyed a long, satisfying stage career, mostly performing in Shakespearean productions. She always had something to say about my career, and had never approved of my role choices. And she was even less thrilled now about my decision to give up show business to sell, as she put it, "dog food and kitty litter." She also continued to refer to me by my given name, even though she knew I hated it. "I just called to find out if you are still planning on making the biggest mistake of your entire life." Oh, and did I mention she doesn't mince words?

"If you're referring to my reopening Urban Tails, Mother, the answer is yes. It's set for this Saturday, as a matter of fact."

My mother let out a long-drawn-out Academy Award–winning sigh. "Your aunt is turning over in her grave, trust me. Matilda would never have wanted you to throw away your career on the business she built up."

"Aunt Tillie knew how much I loved animals. I know how much this store meant to Aunt Tillie. If you ask me, Mother, she knew exactly what she was doing, and what I would do as well." I waited a moment, but there was no reaction whatsoever to my statement. If it wasn't for the fact I could hear her breathing, I'd have sworn we were disconnected. "If that's all," I said at last, "I've got a lot to do here."

"Since it seems nothing I say will convince you, I may as well stop talking about it." This statement was followed by another long-drawn-out sigh, and then my mother added, "I hear they canceled the plans for the *Spy Anyone* reboot."

"That's a shame," I said, although I truly didn't care. "What happened? Patrick bowed out again?" My ex-fiancé, Patrick Hanratty, had originally been tapped to direct the reboot, but then bowed out over a salary dispute. That news didn't surprise me one bit. Patrick had always been overly . . . frugal . . . during our relationship. Apparently, though, the matter had been resolved because the last I'd heard, he was back in. My mother refused to accept the fact that I had zero interest in doing this reboot, and especially not with Pat at the helm. Our breakup had been less than amicable, and publicized in every gossip rag imaginable.

My mother sniffed. "No, the backers did. They didn't want to chance a reboot with an entirely new cast. You dropped out, after all, and it seems Gary Presser has also exited the Hollywood scene. Max hasn't heard from him in weeks."

"I know. He's here in Fox Hollow."

"What!" Now there was more animation in her voice. "What is he doing there, for goodness sakes?"

"Well, he originally came to help me out of my predicament—"

"You mean when you were accused of murdering that woman!"

"Suspected, mother. I was never actually accused. Once everything was resolved he decided to stay on."

"Hmpf. I bet he jumped at that chance."

"What's that supposed to mean?"

"Oh, Crishell. I don't really have to spell it out for you, do I? The man's always been attracted to you."

"Mother, there's nothing between Gary and me. We're more like brother and sister. Besides, I'm not his type."

"Darling, anything who wears a skirt and has a pulse is Gary's type."

"You're wrong." And then, just because I knew it would irritate her, I added, "He's here because he decided he preferred the quiet life to Hollywood too."

"What is that, catching? Should I be inoculated or something before I fly in?"

I'd started to straighten a row of bowls, but at her words my hand froze midair. "Wh-what did you just say? You're flying in?"

Clarissa McMillan sniffed. "That's what I said. You seem determined to ruin your life, but that doesn't mean I can't be by your side while you do it. After all, dear, isn't that what a mother is for?"

My brain was struggling to process this highly upsetting new development. "Yo-you're coming to Fox Hollow? For the grand reopening?"

"Are you going deaf, Crishell? Isn't that what I just said?"

"Yes, but you didn't mention coming before," I sputtered. "I thought you had plans this weekend?"

"They fell through, so I decided to lend you my support instead." She paused and I could hear the familiar hurt tone as she said, "Why, don't you want me to come?"

Oh, boy, was that a loaded question. "Of course I want you to come, Mother, but it is the day after tomorrow. You can get a flight on such short notice?"

"A friend of mine has a private jet and offered me its use. I should arrive sometime Saturday morning. Now, are there any good hotels in the area you can recommend, or do I have to call Celestine?" Celestine Connors had been my mother's travel agent for years. They'd been on the outs for a while after

Celestine had helped my father arrange his elopement with my mother's best friend, but had since kissed and made up.

I knew darn well there were no hotels in or around Fox Hollow of the caliber my mother was used to. The nearest Hyatt Regency was fifty miles away. I also knew that if I referred her to one of the cozy bed-and-breakfast inns both she and the inn's owners would never let me forget it. So, I uttered words that I knew I'd regret for the rest of my natural life.

"Don't be silly, Mother. You know you're more than welcome to stay with me at my house. There's plenty of room."

"Well, isn't that generous of you." My mother's tone indicated that she was wondering what had taken me so long to make the offer. "If you're sure it's no bother. I imagine you'll be happy to have company. It must get lonely, rattling around in that big old dusty house all alone."

"It's not dusty, Mother. And I'm not alone. I have Kahlua and Purrday." Kahlua had been a birthday gift from my mother. When she'd learned I was going to adopt a cat from the local shelter in LA, she'd promptly secured me a pedigreed Siamese, declaring that no daughter of hers was going to own a half-breed animal.

I could hear the suspicion in her tone as she asked, "Kahlua I know, but who on earth is Percy?"

"Purrday, Mother. He's Aunt Tillie's cat. She left him to me. And before you say one word, he's a pedigree. A Persian." I'd deal with the whole one-eyed thing later. Maybe if I was lucky she'd up and leave before she noticed it.

"A Persian, hm? They're beautiful cats." My feeling of relief was short-lived as she added, "They have such long hair, though. It must be all over your furniture."

"Gary does a good job sweeping up after the pets." The words tumbled out before I thought, and I involuntarily clapped a hand over my mouth.

"Gary? You can't possibly mean Gary Presser?"

I took a deep breath. "Actually, yes, I do."

"*What!*" I had to hold the phone away from my ear. "He's there? Freeloading off you, no doubt! Crishell, what on earth are you thinking? You should know better! Unless . . . heaven help me, you're not attracted to him, are you?"

I set my jaw. I was *not* having this conversation with her. "Oops, Mom, there's a lot of static on the line." I . . . hear . . . go. See . . . Saturday." I tapped at the phone a few times and then disconnected. Knowing my mother, she hadn't fallen for that old trick. Another thing I'd be hearing about, I was sure.

I glanced at my watch. It was four thirty. Darn, where had the day gone? I'd have just enough time to go home, change and meet Gary and Olivia at Bottoms Up. I looked longingly at my phone. I hated to stop my research, but maybe Olivia would know something about this Johnny Draco, or maybe Rita or Ron. Definitely Rita. As the proprietor of the local coffee shop, she heard a lot of gossip.

I started for the back room to gather up my things and Purrday, when I heard an insistent *tap tap tap* at the front door. I walked back and peered out the side curtain. A man wearing a gray hoodie, his hands stuffed in the pockets of his sweatpants, stood on the stoop. I sighed, walked over to the door, made sure the safety chain was on and then fumbled my phone into my left hand as I opened the door a crack with my right. "I'm sorry," I said in a pleasant tone. "We're not officially open for business until after the grand opening Saturday." I pointed to the poster in the window advertising the event.

"Grand opening?" He looked quizzically at the poster and then turned back to me. He had a rough voice with a trace of an accent—Boston, perhaps? He removed his sunglasses and I could see his eyes were a muddy brown underneath shaggy brows. He had even, regular features and he smiled pleasantly, revealing white, even teeth. "I'm sorry. I thought this was Matilda Washburn's store?"

"It used to be. She passed away a few months ago and left it to me. I'm her niece."

The corners of the man's lips drooped down. He looked disappointed. "So Matilda's gone," he murmured.

"Yes. Did you know her?"

He pushed the hoodie off his head, revealing a shock of thick, curly, bright red hair. "Yes, I did. It was a long time ago."

I hesitated, then removed the chain and opened the door. "I'm sorry. Would you like to come in for a minute?"

"Thanks." He stepped inside and shut the door behind him. "I'm sorry to hear about Ms. Washburn. She always seemed so indestructible, and she gave such good advice. It never crossed my mind that she was . . . deceased." He leaned in and peered at me more closely. "You look familiar," he said. "Have we met somewhere?"

"No, but it's possible you've seen me on television," I said.

"Television . . . hey, wait." He snapped his fingers. "Matilda was always talking about her niece, the actress. That's you! You're Shell Marlowe!"

"McMillan," I amended. "I'm retired from show business. I go by my real name now."

He arched a brow. "You look way too young to be retired."

"Thanks, but not by Hollywood standards."

He chuckled, then jabbed a finger in the air. "You were on that spy show. *Spies for Sale*, or something like that?"

"*Spy Anyone.*"

"Yeah, that's it. I liked it, a lot. Too bad it got canceled." He turned, glanced around the store. "So you're taking over Urban Tails," he murmured. "I imagine your aunt would be proud." He glanced again at the poster. "You set all this up?"

"Yes. I wanted to make it a big town event. If you're around Saturday, please feel free to stop by. All the merchants are setting up tables and offering free services."

"Yes, the merchants." His hand scrubbed over his chin as his eyes darted up the block, then back to me. "How about the coffee shop? Does Rita Sakowski still own it?"

"Yes, she does. And she'll be serving coffee and doughnuts all day."

He reached up to scratch behind one ear. "I suppose Quentin Watson still runs the *Fox Hollow Gazette*? And Stanley Sheer still has his barbershop?"

"Yes and yes." My curiosity had reached epic proportions. "It sounds as if you're from around here."

"I lived here a long time ago," he said in a soft voice. His gaze wandered back to the poster. "Live entertainment, huh? Dancing, singing . . . that sounds pretty good."

"Thanks. The dancers are still on target, but unfortunately, my vocalist had to bow out."

"I always enjoyed singing." He reached behind him, and I noticed the bulging gray backpack strapped there for the first time. He lowered the backpack to his feet and unzipped it. He rummaged through it, finally pulling out a long, black-and-white rectangular bar. He held it up. "This is what's called a digital instrument." He pointed to a long black area. "These are digital strings. These black and white things are digital piano keys."

I looked at it, fascinated. "I've never heard of anything like that."

"It's been out a few years. I connect it to my tablet and I can use it with several virtual instrument apps. I can make it play any instrument, even several at one time. Let me demonstrate."

The man pulled a thin, collapsible stand from his backpack and set the instrument on it. He pulled out his tablet, plugged it into the side of the instrument and fiddled with it for a few moments. Then he ran his hand across the black area. The sweet strains of "Eleanor Rigby" burst into life.

"That's amazing," I cried.

He started to sing the song. I had to admit, the man had a marvelous voice. He sang the entire first chorus of the song. When he finished, I applauded. He grinned at me. The act made his whole face seem boyish, although I suspected he was close to or at least forty years old. "Are you going to be around Saturday?" I asked impulsively. "If so, how would you like a job singing at my grand opening?"

An odd look passed across his face, but it was gone in an instant. "I'm flattered, Ms. McMillan," he said, "but I don't think it's a good idea."

"Why not? You've a marvelous voice."

He hefted up his backpack, started to shove his instrument back inside. "I, ah, get nervous in crowds. I guess you could say I get stage fright. I'd hate to choke in the middle of a song and ruin things for you."

"If crowds aren't your thing, maybe we could set a mic up here inside the shop and just pump your voice outside. You could perform from my storeroom." I laid a hand on his arm. "I'm sure we could work something out," I said. "Could you come back tomorrow, around ten? I'd like to have my associate hear you."

His tongue snaked out, swiped at his lower lip. "I don't know," he murmured. "I have a lot of appointments tomorrow, things I have to catch up on."

"It'll be fun," I said. "I've even got an animal act lined up. A fortune-telling parrot. My associate got the bird on the recommendation of Quentin Watson. This man, Adrian Arnold, supposedly has trained birds that have appeared in movies and on commercials."

The stranger's head jerked up and his eyes narrowed. His fingers dug into the backpack. "A bird trainer? What sort of birds?"

"Parrots, mostly. He has a fortune-telling parrot act."

"A fortune-telling parrot, you say?" He looked at the poster again and stroked at his chin. "Might be worth showing up just to see that."

"Yes, it would. And I hope you'll consider my offer."

His gaze slid from the poster back to me. "I'll think about it."

He zipped up his backpack, slid it over one shoulder. "That looks pretty heavy," I said.

He shifted it on his arm. "I can manage."

I pointed to a long jagged tear on one side of the bag that looked to be clumsily sewn. "It's pretty worn. I think I might have a nice nylon tote somewhere in the back, if you'd like it."

His fingers curled around the bag. "Not necessary," he said softly. "This one does me just fine, but thanks for the kind offer." He shifted the bag to his other arm. "I've got to get going."

"Okay." He turned to leave and I reached out and touched his arm. "I'm sorry. I didn't get your name."

"Ira," he said after a moment's hesitation. "You can call me Ira."

He walked swiftly away, and I closed the door again and locked it. Purrday came over, rubbed against my legs. I bent down and chucked him under his chin. "What do you think, Purrday? I hope he changes his mind. He's got a great voice. I think if we could get some sort of mic hookup to pipe his voice out so he could stay indoors, he'd do just fine."

Purrday turned his head as if he were bored with the conversation. I looked down at my phone and gasped. Ira's face stared back at me. "Look," I said, brandishing the phone in front of Purrday. "I must have accidentally clicked on the camera app and taken his picture when I opened the door."

Purrday looked at the photo, then let out a soft growl and turned his face away. I slid the phone back into my purse. I'd show it to the others at dinner. He'd said he lived here a while ago. Maybe one of them might remember the mysterious Ira.

Three

My Siamese cat, Kahlua, greeted me as I let myself in the back door of my Victorian mansion a few minutes after five. I bent down and gave the chocolate brown Siamese a pat on the head. "Hello, girl. Miss us?"

Kahlua let out the high-pitched yowl typical of the breed. She danced around my feet until I set Purrday's carrier down and opened the wire door to set him free. She immediately began licking the Persian's flat face. Purrday gave a rumbling purr and lay down to accept her ministrations.

I regarded the two of them with a sly smile. "And here I thought the two of you wouldn't get along." Actually, they hadn't at first, but Purrday had worn the fussy Siamese down. He had that way about him. A charmer, just like Gary. I tossed my jacket and purse over one of the kitchen chairs. There was a note pinned to the bulletin board I'd set up over the area where the cats' bowls were located. I walked over and plucked the note from the board and read it:

You're late! See you at Bottoms Up! G.
PS: Don't forget to feed the children.

"Hah," I said. "Like you guys would let me forget to feed you." I crumpled the note and tossed it into the trash, then I opened the cabinet where the cat food was kept and selected a can. Purrday and Kahlua both cocked their heads, looking at me expectantly.

"I know Gary's cooking has spoiled the two of you rotten, but you both used to like this brand's chicken and tuna." I opened the can and started to spoon it into their bowls. They immediately hunkered down, and a few minutes later the sound of contented slurping reached my ears. I chuckled and headed upstairs to change. I could feel a few butterflies flying around in my stomach, and wasn't sure if it was because I was nervous about Ira, or because I couldn't wait to see Gary's reaction to the news that he'd be sharing the house with—and cooking for, most likely—my mother this weekend. In the end I decided it was probably a bit of both.

• • •

A hour later I was lucky enough to find a parking spot directly across the street from the tavern. Formerly an Italian pizzeria known as Guido's, Guido

DiPiazza, the owner, had opted to retire to sunny Orlando and had sold the business to a young married couple who were originally from Detroit. The new owners had redesigned the entire interior, modeling it after an English pub they'd visited, then giving it a cheeky American name.

Gone were the stark white walls and framed artwork depicting Italy and the Leaning Tower of Pisa. In its place were dark pine walls on which were trendy posters of movie stars, both vintage and current, singing groups, and the like, and pine-plank floors that were covered most nights in peanut shells from the complimentary bowls of shelled peanuts that graced the bar and all of the tables. The tables themselves were also carved out of dark pine. An old-time jukebox, loaded with both current tunes and oldies, was positioned near a postage-stamp-sized dance floor. Probably the tavern's most arresting feature, though, was its large cherrywood bar, which took up one entire side of the room. I'd only been in the new place once, and it was to pick up a take-out cheeseburger, which had been quite good, if memory served. I'd yet to try anything else on the menu, but both Gary and Olivia seemed to think it deserved to be on Zagat's best restaurant list, so who was I to argue?

I stepped inside and stood in the doorway for a moment to get my bearings. I swung my gaze first in the direction of the bar. A man in a suit sat at the very end, sipping a mug of beer. A bit further down, two rough-looking guys in sweats also sat with frosty mugs in front of them, their eyes glued to the baseball game unfolding on the forty-two-inch flatscreen behind the bar. I turned toward the tables and saw a hand waving to me from the very back of the room. I headed in that direction and saw that the hand did indeed belong to Gary. Olivia sat right next to him, and they weren't alone. Also squeezed into the booth were Rita Sakowski and Ron Webb. Ron rose as I approached the table.

"Shell," he boomed out. He waited until I was seated and then leaned back, stroking his brown beard shot with flecks of gray. His eyes, peering out from behind his large tortoiseshell glasses, twinkled merrily. "Good to see you. I hear you've had rather a rough time of it today?"

I shot Gary a look. He spread his hands. "Hey, they asked."

I reached over, grabbed Gary's mug of Coors, and took a long sip before setting it back down. I wiped at my lips with the back of my hand. "You don't know the half of it," I said. "There was a bright spot, though. I took Gary's recommendation and hired an assistant manager."

"You hired Robbie!" Rita clapped both hands. "That's great, Shell. He's a good kid and a hard worker. You could do much worse."

I pulled a face. "Tell me about it. I'd like to wring Elvin Scraggs's neck."

"Well, I can believe Elvin Scraggs would back out at the last minute to go fishing. He's a tool!" Rita slapped her pudgy hand down on the black-and-white checked tablecloth for emphasis, causing the candle in the middle of the table to flicker. Short and stout with flame-colored hair that rivaled Raggedy Anne's, Rita had a temper. She tugged at the sides of her overflowing pink and orange caftan as she added, "It's not the first time that worm has backed out of a deal, believe me. He did it to Sissy Arnold, too, last year. Was supposed to sing at her wedding, canceled a week before. Told her some story about a relative dying in Florida. I tell you, that man has more imaginary relatives in Florida than Carter has pills."

"Not all of 'em are imaginary," Ron said with a chuckle. "Granny Viola's still going strong. He tries to act indifferent, but Elvin does really care about her."

"More like her money," Rita said with a snort. "I tell you, the man's a tool. He's lucky no one's cared enough so far to sue the pants off him. But someday, mark my words, he'll meet his match."

"Elvin is a bit of a louse, but his cancellation might have been a blessing in disguise," I began, but then was interrupted as a perky brunette wearing a white dress, pink apron, and bearing a gold name tag that said *Cecily* bounded over to our table.

"Good evening, everyone," she said. I noticed her gaze lingered a bit longer on Gary. "We've got some great specials tonight, in addition to our regular fare. Would you care to hear them?"

Gary leaned back and flashed the girl his patented, super-colossal charming smile. "Sure. Let 'er rip."

Cecily colored prettily and then began rattling off the list of specials: the Broadway Babe Burger, an eight-ounce Angus burger smothered in jalapeños and barbecue sauce, accompanied by homemade slaw and sweet potato fries, a shepherd's pie, and fish and chips. Gary and Ron both opted for the Broadway Babe Burger, while Rita and Olivia ordered the shepherd's pie. "I'll have the Old English Macaroni Cheese," I said, pointing to it on the menu. I looked right at Gary as I added, "It comes highly recommended."

The waitress's head bobbed up and down. "It is very good," she agreed.

"They use only three ingredients, add a sprinkle of Parmesan, and bake it in the oven till it's nice and bubbly." She licked her lips as she gathered up the menus. "I'll be right back with your refills, and a Coors for you," she added, but her bright smile was aimed at Gary, not me.

Olivia waited until Cecily had disappeared and then gave Gary a playful poke in the ribs. "The Presser charm has made another convert," she said.

"Yep. I'm still not sure whether it's a blessing or a curse."

I cocked an eyebrow. "You know which one I'd choose."

"Of course. Blessing." He laughed when I made a motion of throwing something at him. "Or was that Elvin's cancellation?"

"Don't laugh. It could very well be. A man came by the shop just as I was about to close. We got to talking and I told him my singer punked out. He has some sort of device that plays all sorts of instruments, and he's a regular one-man band. He's got an excellent voice, too. He seemed a bit on the reluctant side, but I think I convinced him to come back tomorrow so you could hear him. I'd really like to hire him."

"Wow, he sounds perfect," Olivia remarked.

"Indeed." Gary crossed his arms over his chest. "You don't think it was just a little too fortuitous, this singer just dropping around out of the blue?"

"It wasn't exactly out of the blue," I protested. "He was looking for Aunt Tillie. He wasn't aware she'd passed." I turned to Rita. "Funny thing, he asked about you, too."

Rita's hand turned inward so that she pointed at her chest. "Me?"

"Yep. He wanted to know if you still owned Sweet Perks. And you're not the only one. He also asked about Stanley Sheer and Quentin Watson. Asked specifically if Quentin was still the editor of the *Fox Hollow Gazette*."

"That is odd," Rita mused. "Why would a stranger ask about all of us?"

"I don't think he's a complete stranger. He said he lived here a long time ago."

Rita's perfectly penciled red eyebrows drew together. "What's his name?"

"Ira. He didn't offer a last name."

"You didn't push him for it?" Gary let out a moan. "Geez, Shell."

"Ira, you say?" Rita leaned forward, eyes narrowed. "What did he look like?"

"Hm, in his forties, I'd say, solidly built. He had on a hoodie and sunglasses—oh, wait, I can show you. I accidentally snapped his picture."

I retrieved my phone and passed it to Gary. "He doesn't look much like a singer," he said after studying the picture. "That can't possibly be his natural hair color."

"Let us see," Olivia demanded, holding out her hand. Gary passed her the phone and she held it out so Rita and Ron could see. "Something about him seems familiar," Olivia said after a moment. "I can't quite place him but—"

"I can." Rita's lips drew into a straight line, and her eyes flashed sparks. Her hand shot out, and a long nail tapped at the phone. "That's Johnny Draco. He's put on some pounds, and dyed his hair, but . . . it's him. I'd know him anywhere."

"Johnny Draco? The Johnny Draco everyone thinks swindled people?" I asked.

Everyone turned to look at me. "How do you know about that?" Rita demanded. "You weren't living here when this all went down."

"Robbie told me something about it," I confessed. "I asked if he knew anyone who could sing, and he mentioned this Johnny Draco."

"Johnny did have a nice voice," said Rita, "but that was the only nice thing about him." She raised her head and fixed me with a steely gaze. "If you hire him, Shell McMillan, you'll be asking for trouble." She leaned back in her seat and started to fan herself with her hand. "Oh my gosh, I bet my blood pressure has gone up a mile."

"Calm down, Rita." Olivia handed Rita her glass of water and watched as the other woman took a sip. "This can't be Draco. Shell said his name was Ira."

"Oh, it's him, all right. Y'all forget that Ira was his middle name," Rita said. "I'll never forget that face as long as I live. If he were here right now, why, it would be all I could do to keep from strangling him with my bare hands." She flexed her hands in front of her, and for a brief moment the expression on her face morphed into one of pure hatred. I shivered as a chill nicked up my spine.

"Now, now." Ron reached out and covered Rita's hands with his own. "You know what the doctor told you about your blood pressure, Rita. Besides, you've no conclusive proof this Ira is Johnny Draco. Why get so upset?"

"Ron's right, Rita," Olivia chimed in. "Your health is more important."

"Easy for you two to say," Rita burst out. "You guys weren't taken in by that silver-tongued devil." Her voice choked up and she reached for the voluminous orange striped tote bag that lay on the bench beside her. She reached inside, fished out a twenty and slapped it on the table. "I've got to get out of here," she murmured. "If you can't cancel my dinner, this should cover it, as well as my drink."

Olivia reached for the bill. "We'll get your food to go, hon," she said.

"Don't bother. I've lost my appetite." She made a shooing motion with her hand at Ron. He slid obligingly out of the booth so she could exit.

As she started to walk past me, I put out my hand to stop her. "Wait, Rita. I didn't mean to ruin your evening. Please sit back down."

Rita's eyes were overbright, and I could see tears start to form. She reached out and gave my hand a pat. "It's not you, dear. It's the idea that man is back and running around scot-free that's got my knickers all up in a twist. After what he did . . . I'm sorry. I've got to go."

She hurried out of the restaurant and narrowly missed bumping right into a waitress carrying a large pitcher of ice water. I looked at Olivia and Ron. "Okay, Robbie told me that this Draco was suspected of swindling people out of money. I'm guessing Rita was one of them?"

"Yep," Ron said. "Draco used to be an investment counselor, and a darn good one, by all accounts. He seemed to be a model, upstanding citizen. Anyway, about five years ago Draco was looking for investors. He had a sure thing, he said, and anyone who participated was certain to double, maybe even triple their investment."

"Sounds a bit risky to me," Gary commented.

"It was a gamble. Draco was up front about that right from the start. Despite that warning, though, quite a few people gave Draco money to invest, including Wesley Sakowski. He withdrew his entire pension fund, and Rita's retirement savings account."

"Ouch," I said. "I can guess how this ends."

"Yep. Long story short, the investment went belly up and they lost their entire retirement savings. At first everyone just thought it was an investment gone horribly wrong. After all, Draco did warn everyone before he took their money that it was a huge risk, and he even put in some of his own money. What made everyone suspicious was what happened afterward. Draco just up and quit the firm he was working for without giving any notice, and moved out of his apartment overnight. It made everyone have second thoughts, and everyone became convinced he'd run off with their money."

"Wow," I said. "I can see why Rita reacted the way she did."

"Yep." Ron scrubbed his hand along the side of his jaw. "Rita hired a PI to try and find him but it was like the guy vanished into thin air. He's stayed under the radar and away from Fox Hollow, until now, I guess."

"That does pose an interesting question. Why on earth did he come back after all this time?" mused Olivia. "To see how his marks were making out? He asked about practically all of them: Rita, Stanley, Quentin."

"Oh my God," I cried. "He asked about Aunt Tillie. He called her Matilda and seemed very upset at her passing. He called her indestructible. Did he cheat her too?"

Olivia let out a shaky laugh. "Your aunt never invested any money with him, dear. Tillie took care of her own investments. But they met at some charity function, and she took a liking to him."

"They were friends?"

"I wouldn't say friends exactly. But Tillie was fond of him. She never believed Johnny was guilty, although if I had to hazard a guess I'd say she second-guessed that opinion after he took off without so much as a goodbye to anyone."

"Maybe his reason for leaving had nothing to do with money," suggested Gary. "Maybe he was having woman troubles or something."

"He had a steady girl," Ron volunteered. "Krissa Tidwell. They weren't having any problems, though, at least as far as I know."

"Krissa Tidwell? You mean the woman who owns that lovely boutique, Ages Past?" Krissa was a pleasant woman who I judged to be somewhere in her early fifties. I'd pegged her as the spinster type. Apparently I was wrong.

"Yep. She gave Johnny a good deal of money to invest as well."

"Just how much are we talking here?" I asked.

"The amounts from each person varied, but my best guess is it was somewhere in the neighborhood of a quarter of a million—maybe a bit more. I know Quentin lost the most."

"Ouch," said Gary. "That had to hurt, especially Quentin. Was it birthday or communion money?" It was a well-known fact that the newspaper owner was a tightwad.

"This guy seemed to be a bit down on his luck," I said. "As an investment counselor, you'd think he'd know how to hold on to money. Let's assume, though, for the sake of argument, that Ira is Johnny and he's blown through all the cash. I agree with Olivia. Why return to the scene of his crime, a place where he's hated, and ask about his victims? It doesn't make sense."

"Maybe he came back to make amends," suggested Gary. "Or maybe he's missed Krissa all these years and come back for her."

"If that's the reason then Draco's stupider than I thought," snorted Olivia. "Krissa wouldn't touch him anymore with a fifty-foot pole."

Gary'd been fiddling with his phone while we talked, and now he handed it to me. "I've called up images of Johnny Draco. Take a look."

I took the phone, studied the images. They depicted a short, well-dressed man with brown hair and eyes in various poses—at a formal dinner, at a fundraiser, signing a contract. While I couldn't say he wasn't the Johnny who'd come by the store, I couldn't say with any certainty that he was, either. Finally I handed the phone back to Gary and shook my head. "I can't say. It could be the same man, then again, it might not. I just can't tell." I snapped my fingers. "The guy in my shop spoke with a slight accent. It sounded a bit Boston to me."

"Draco was from Massachusetts, the Salem area, I think," Olivia said. "He'd lost most of his accent when he lived here though."

"I know a way to solve this entire mystery," I said. "I'll just ask him when he comes to the shop tomorrow."

"*If* he shows at all," Olivia huffed.

"Olivia's got a point," Gary said. "The guy probably won't come back. You said he was reluctant, right?"

"He said he suffered from stage fright," I mumbled. "Crowds made him nervous."

"I bet," Gary muttered. "Did he happen to mention where he was staying?"

I shook my head. "Nope. He just said he'd think about my offer. I assumed he was staying at the inn in town."

Olivia shook her head. "I doubt that, not if he's trying to be incognito. If Rita recognized him, I bet others like Quentin would too."

Gary pushed his mug off to one side and propped his elbows on the table. "For the sake of argument, let's say the dude did come back. You're going to just come right out and ask him if he's the same Johnny Draco who left under a cloud of suspicion of larceny? Do you really think that's a good idea?" He reached out and patted my hand. "Perhaps I should handle this."

I fought the impulse to clock him right between the eyes, and it was tough, let me tell you. "If you want to, but I think your time might be better spent brushing up on your gourmet recipes."

"Gourmet?" His lower lip jutted out, something that happened when he was annoyed. "Why gourmet? What's wrong with my regular cooking? You always rave about it."

"Rave is rather a strong word. I do enjoy your cooking, Gary, but I'm not sure our houseguest will share my enthusiasm for it."

Both Gary's eyebrows rose. "Houseguest?"

"Yes. Didn't I mention it?" I said innocently. "This person is coming down for the grand opening, isn't that nice? I offered the use of the house. There are certainly enough rooms."

"Hm. So, who is it? It's someone fussy, apparently, so . . . wait, don't tell me. Max?" Max Molenaro, our agent, was the personification of fussy. "It's Max, isn't it? Swell." He laced his hands behind his neck. "He'll be bringing scripts with him for us to look at too, no doubt. Max never could take no for an answer."

"Relax, Gary. It's not Max."

"It's not?"

Cecily appeared just then, carrying a large tray with our drinks. As she set Gary's beer mug down in front of him, I reached out and touched her arm. "I think he's going to need something stronger, like a double Scotch."

"No, I don't." Gary cupped the mug possessively. "Just spit it out, Shell. Who's the houseguest?"

I looked him straight in the eye. "My mother."

"Clarissa! Snap!" Gary held out his mug to Cecily, pointed at me with his other hand. "She was right. Between dealing with a possible larcenist and Shell's mother, I definitely need something stronger. Take this back and get me a double, no wait, make that a triple Scotch. Macallan single malt, if you have it."

Olivia looked at Ron. "Wow, the good stuff. Shell, your mother must really be something else."

I raised my mug of Coors and smiled devilishly at Gary. "You have no idea," I said demurely.

Cecily returned with Gary's Scotch and our food. When she departed, Olivia picked up her fork. "Oh, I just remembered another of Johnny's victims. She didn't lose as much as the others, but it was a blow just the same."

I forked up some macaroni and cheese. "Yeah? Who is it?"

Olivia took a bite of her shepherd's pie and a sip of her beer before answering. "Josh's sister, Sue Bloodgood."

Four

We tabled the Johnny Draco conversation after that little reveal and spent the remainder of the evening discussing the plans for Saturday, then capped it off with another round of drinks at the bar. When Gary and I arrived back home a few minutes after nine, we were greeted at the back door by two indignant cats.

"*Er-owl,*" screeched Kahlua.

"Meower," said Purrday.

Gary looked at me. "If I didn't know better," he said, "I'd say they were hungry. You did leave them dry food before you went out, right?"

"Ouch!" I slapped my forehead with my palm, hard. I'd given them wet food but had completely forgotten to fill the dry food bowls. I slapped both my wrists. "Bad mommie," I said. I knelt down in front of the cats. "Can you forgive me?"

Both turned their heads in the direction of their bowls. I got up, went to the cupboard and got out the kibble. They wound around my legs as I filled the bowls, and when I'd finished, Purrday's tongue snaked out to lick at my ankle.

"All is forgiven," said Gary. "The power of food. Speaking of which—what is it your mother likes for breakfast again?"

"She likes maple-walnut kringle and semolina pancakes, but she's also been known to scarf down a good Bacon-Leek Quiche too."

Gary pulled a face. "Great. So it's safe to assume my world-renowned eggs Benedict won't be good enough."

"*World-renowned* is pushing it a bit, but whatever." I reached out to pat his cheek. "You'll think of something, I have no doubt. Just remember, she eats breakfast around the time normal people eat lunch."

"Swell." He leaned across the counter and cupped his chin in one hand. "Do you want to talk about it?"

"About my mother? There's really nothing left to say. We'll just have to play it by ear."

"No, not Clarissa. About this Johnny Draco. I know how you love a good puzzle, and this guy fills that bill to a T."

"It is a puzzle," I agreed. "To listen to Rita, this Draco is public enemy number one. He didn't seem like a con man to me. He was genuinely disappointed to learn my aunt had passed."

"Maybe he was disappointed because he was going to hit your aunt up for a place to stay."

"I didn't think of that," I admitted. "Aunt Tillie would have put him up, too. What really puzzles me is why he returned after all this time. There's got to be more to this story. Remember, no one's ever heard Draco's side."

"Because he wasn't here to tell it, and that's what makes him look guilty," Gary said. "Of course, there is always the possibility that maybe after that bad investment he decided it was time for a change. We did pretty much the same thing, after all. We got tired of the Hollywood scene, so we came here and put down roots in small-town America, rather abruptly, I might add."

"I'm actually the one who did that. You were more of a copycat." I shot him an impish grin. "Who knows, maybe my mother will end up doing the same."

Gary's jaw went slack. "Just had to ruin my good mood, didn't you?"

I chuckled and went over to make sure the cats had enough water. I left Gary poring over his collection of gourmet cookbooks in the kitchen and went into my den. It was my turn to do some research now. I called up Google and typed in "Johnny Draco investment scandal" and hit Enter. A few seconds later I was rewarded with two pages of stories. I selected the top article, by none other than Quentin Watson, and clicked on it.

> Fox Hollow, CT: Police are looking for John Ira Draco, 37, as a person of interest in a fraudulent investment scheme that bilked several prominent Fox Hollow inhabitants out of their savings.
>
> Police say that Draco, an investment counselor with Benson, O'Toole and McShay, took it upon himself to urge several of his clients to invest independently along with himself in a private investment in Tandor Industries, claiming that it was a "rising star" in the world of business and he could double their investments in a short period of time. Draco later claimed that the company had gone "belly up" unexpectedly and everyone, including himself, lost their initial investment. Investors were not alarmed at

first, since they understood there was a certain amount of risk associated with the undertaking. They became concerned, however, when Draco suddenly quit his position at Benson, O'Toole and McShay and left Fox Hollow overnight, without a word to anyone, including his companion for the past four years, Krissa Tidwell.

Police are of the opinion that the fact Draco required the participants to give him their share in cash should have been a red flag. He claimed that doing it that way cut through a lot of red tape and would enable him to "get in on the ground floor" faster. However, the investigation thus far has revealed that Tandor Industries did indeed close its doors, as Mr. Draco said. So far there is no conclusive proof that Draco did not invest the monies as he said, or that a swindle was perpetrated. The investigation is ongoing and Mr. Draco continues to be a person of interest.

The other articles I clicked on were all pretty much the same—while Draco's actions appeared suspicious, there was no real evidence a crime had been committed. Next I typed in "Tandor Industries." The articles that came up were all short and to the point. Tandor was a small commodity trading company that had branched out into several different areas in a short span of time and lost money just as quickly. Their last-ditch venture involving broadband management suffered greatly when it was revealed the executives had attempted to hide huge losses under dummy corporations. This negated their big comeback and the company filed for bankruptcy five years ago.

"Hm," I said with a frown. "I wonder if Draco did any research on this company before he urged people to invest in it. It seems to me that a savvy investment counselor would have definitely known this wasn't a good investment from the get-go."

I looked over at the cats. Neither seemed overly impressed. Both of them opened their mouths in large, unlovely cat yawns, then they returned to their ablutions.

"So sorry to bore you," I murmured. On an impulse, I fished my phone out of my tote bag and scrolled through my directory. I'd put Robbie's number in there earlier. I'd just found it when my phone buzzed, indicating I had an incoming text. My heart started to pound faster as I noted the sender's name: Josh Bloodgood.

Hey Shell—U got a minute? I'm almost at your house.

I texted back: *Sure thing. Meet U on the porch in five.*

I smiled when I got a smiley face in return. I closed my laptop and hurried out of the den, leaving the cats still doing their ablutions on my desk. A quick look into the kitchen told me that Gary had gone upstairs to bed. I slipped on a light sweater, as the evenings could get chilly in late June, and slipped out onto the porch just as Josh pulled his car into my driveway. I watched as he exited the car and strode toward me. He had on khaki pants and a light beige jacket that came to just above his hips. The pants were stretched taut against his firm, muscular body. His shock of dark hair wasn't quite as thick as Gary's, but it came darn close, and I yearned to brush that errant curl off his forehead. He bounded up the porch steps and stood next to me. I looked straight into his hazel eyes and smiled.

"This is a nice surprise."

He shot me a boyish grin. "I happened to be in the neighborhood," he said. He leaned casually against my porch railing. "I meant to call you after our date last week, but it's been crazy down at the station."

I eased my own hip against the railing. "No homicides, I hope."

He waved a hand. "Oh, nothing like that. It's just there's always a ton of paperwork on something, and just when you think you're finished . . ." He spread his hands. "I wanted to check in with you, see how the plans for the grand opening were coming."

"Not bad, considering. You'll be there, right? Sue said you had the day off, that you'd called in the calvary."

"She blabbed, huh?" He shook his head. "I wanted to surprise you, but yeah, I've got the whole day off. From what I've heard, Riser should be able to handle just about anything that comes up."

"Even murder?" I murmured.

Josh's eyes narrowed. "What makes you say that?"

"No particular reason. But it's been a heckuva strange day." I filled Josh in on what happened with Elvin, and with Captain Snaggle. I finished up with the story of Ira arriving at my door for an impromptu audition, and Rita and company's reaction to the photo of him I'd inadvertently snapped and Rita's belief that Ira was actually Johnny Draco. "Of course, this is all speculation," I finished. "I don't know for certain, and they don't either, that it is indeed the same man. Although Rita seemed to think he was, and she's plenty upset over it."

Josh stroked at the stubble on his chin with his long fingers. "It would be a pretty fantastic coincidence. I wasn't around when all this went down, but I have read the case file. You know that my sister Sue was one of the victims."

"I did hear that, yes."

"She didn't lose much, thank God. An aunt of ours passed and left us each a few thousand dollars, and Sue figured that if the investment was a success, it was more money she could pour into her business. Her loss wasn't as big as some of the others."

"You mean like Quentin Watson?"

Josh grimaced. "It wasn't his entire life's savings, but to a self-employed guy it was a nice chunk. Wesley Sakowski's pension fund took a hard hit too. He and Rita survived some rocky financial times after that."

"I did some checking online," I admitted. "It does seem as if a responsible investment counselor would have known that company was a risk from the get-go."

"He did, though. He did advise everyone there was a certain amount of risk, but he firmly believed that the company could be a success. It seemed as if he were hoodwinked along with everyone else."

"Until he took off," I murmured. "But if the guy's truly guilty, why come back at all. And would a swindler show concern for his victims? He asked about Rita, Stanley Sheer and Quentin, wanted to know how they were doing." I paused. "He also asked about my aunt. Apparently they were friendly, but not to the point where Aunt Tillie invested anything with him."

"Matilda Washburn was her own woman," Josh said. "She probably just didn't think it was a good investment. Or she had her fingers in other pies."

"Gary thought maybe he was hoping Aunt Tillie would let him stay at the house."

"He might be right. If the guy is Draco, he surely wouldn't check into the inn. And I don't recall him having many friends." Josh reached out and pulled me against his chest. "You know, if you're feeling apprehensive about his coming here tomorrow, I could send one of my men over to your shop to keep an eye on things, you know, just in case."

My eyes twinkled. "You don't think having the police there wouldn't be a deterrent?"

Josh smiled. "Not if he's innocent."

I leaned into him. I liked the feel of his arms around my waist. "Robbie said that his parents speculated Draco might have done time in prison."

"Could have, but I doubt it. If he'd been arrested for anything anywhere in Connecticut, I'd have heard."

"What if he wasn't in Connecticut?"

"Hm, you've got a point there. Then probably not." His grip around my shoulders tightened. "Just promise me you won't see him alone."

"Not to worry." I held up my finger and tapped it lightly against my chin. "Gary will be with me."

Josh cut me an eye roll. "Somehow that doesn't make me feel much better, but seeing as I'm pretty busy tomorrow, it'll have to do."

I wrapped my arms around his waist. "Wrapping up loose ends so nothing interferes with Saturday?"

"Something like that. I told you, nothing short of murder will make me miss this event."

"That's good. I could use your support, especially since my mother decided to come down and attend the grand opening."

"Your mother, eh?" He put his thumb under my chin and raised my head so he could look into my eyes. "Why do I get the feeling that's not a good thing?"

"Because it's not. My mother is an acquired taste."

"Hm, I could say that about her daughter. But I mean it in a good way."

He looked deeply into my eyes and I felt my toes start to tingle. I leaned in toward him, closed my eyes—and then they snapped open as the porch light came on.

"Shell?" Gary called. "Is that you out there?" The door opened, and Gary, clad in pajamas (OMG, was that penguins on them?) stood framed in the doorway. He saw Josh and his hand went to his mouth. "Oh . . . sorry."

I shot him a look. He didn't look sorry at all, if you asked me. He looked pretty pleased with himself.

Josh released me and took a step back. "No problem. I was just telling Shell that she shouldn't interview that singer alone tomorrow, just in case . . ."

"He turns out to be this infamous Johnny Draco?" Gary moved closer to me and grinned. "Not to worry, I'll be with her."

Josh hesitated, then leaned over and gave me a quick peck on the cheek. "I'll try and give you a call tomorrow, see how it went. And I'll definitely see you Saturday." He gave Gary a cursory nod and then bounded down the steps and over to his car.

Gary watched him get into the car and back out of the driveway before giving me a hangdog look. "You know, I don't think Joshy likes me very much."

I tossed him a withering glance. "Gee, I wonder why."

Gary couldn't resist a chuckle as I swept past him into the house. "I am sorry," he said. "I was going to the kitchen for a glass of milk and I saw shadows out on the porch. I wanted to make sure you were all right."

"Uh-huh," I said. I waved my finger under his nose. "You knew darn well I was."

He looked affronted. "I beg your pardon. I knew no such thing."

"Oh, spare me. You know Josh's car and you could see it perfectly well from the window."

"I couldn't be absolutely certain it was Joshy's car," Gary protested. "It doesn't say 'Police' or 'Homicide Division' on it in big black letters, you know. You're just upset because the sloppy good-night kiss you'd been hoping for turned into a chaste peck on the cheek."

I growled, because he was exactly right. "You just wait until one night when you're getting all cozy with Olivia. I'll get even," I hissed. "And his name is Josh, not Joshy." I turned on my heel and made a beeline for the stairway.

"Nighty-night, Shell. Pleasant dreams," Gary called after me.

"You too," I sang out. "After all, my mother will be here in less than forty-eight hours." A cheap shot, I knew, but Gary deserved it. I was halfway up the stairs when I remembered what I'd originally intended to do. I called up my photo app, found the photo of Ira that I'd snapped and forwarded it to Robbie along with a short message: *Does this look like Johnny Draco?*

I went into my bedroom, undressed and put on a nice pair of pajamas. I sat down at my dressing table and had just started to brush my hair when my phone vibrated. I snatched it up and read the text from Robbie.

Not one hundred percent positive, but it looks like him, except for that red hair.

I set the phone back on the dresser and turned to regard Purrday and Kahlua, who were sprawled across my bed. "Jury's still out, kitties," I told them. "Tomorrow is another day, though."

I had to admit I was kind of anxious to see what Ira slash Johnny would say. My gut told me, though, that the chances of him showing up were getting slimmer by the minute.

Five

Ten a.m. Friday came and went and, big surprise, no Ira.

"I told you he'd be a no-show," said Gary. He and I had been working on the window display since eight thirty that morning. He set down the two kitty scratching posts he'd been arranging. "Look, I know you're disappointed, Shell. I know you really wanted to have a vocalist, but I have to admit I'm relieved we don't have to deal with the possibility of the guy being a con artist and people we know blaming us for hiring him and maybe coming after him seeking revenge."

"I kind of figured he wouldn't show, but I must say, I'm disappointed," I said. "I wanted a crack at getting some answers. Maybe something, or someone, scared him off. Maybe after he left me, he went around to see some of those people and didn't get the warm and fuzzy reaction he hoped for."

"It's possible. In any event, we're better off." Gary set the scratch post down in between two cat tunnels and stepped back to study his handiwork. "Looking good."

I reached for my phone, which I'd tossed on the front counter. "That reminds me, I want to text Robbie, see if he can pick up more sweaters and hats from Kathleen Power and bring them over today. I've got a feeling the two dozen she brought over are going to go like hotcakes."

I glanced over at the display I'd arranged in the middle of the store. A stuffed bulldog and a stuffed gold tabby sat on a raised dais. The bulldog wore a blue-and-white-striped knit sweater with matching booties; the kitty had on a pink-and-gold sweater. Beneath them on a low shelf were various sweaters, hats and booties in gay colors, neatly folded. Olivia had mentioned that the few times Aunt Tillie had featured Kathleen's items in the shop, they had sold out. I could see why. The craftsmanship was excellent.

I texted Robbie and got a fast *Sure, no problem* back as answer. I texted him Kathleen's address and then noticed Gary glance pointedly at the clock on the wall. He saw me looking at him and shot me a sheepish grin. "It's almost noon," he said. "Want to break for lunch?"

"Wow, is it that late already?" I brushed a hand across my forehead. "I thought maybe we could order in. I'd like to finish up these interior displays and then bring out that big table from the storeroom. It'll be perfect to put the refreshments on."

Gary shrugged. "Okay. How about I order us some burgers from Bottoms Up?" As I rolled my eyes he added hastily, "Or maybe you'd prefer a pizza with everything from Angelo's."

I shot him a broad grin. "Now you're talking. There's a take-out menu on the counter next to the register."

Gary went to order the pizza and I returned to putting the finishing touches on the display in the window. As I worked, my thoughts kept circling back to yesterday's events. Draco showing up and then seemingly vanishing into thin air certainly seemed like history repeating itself. I had to ask myself, though, what had made the man come back here in the first place?

"The criminal always returns to the scene of the crime," I murmured. I knew that was a standard plot device of television detective shows and movies. I remembered reading somewhere that law enforcement officials believed that perpetrators of certain crimes often returned to witness their handiwork. Had Johnny Draco returned to see how his victims had fared after the loss of their savings? He'd certainly seemed interested in them. I shook my head. There had to be a more compelling reason for his return after so long.

Perhaps a better question was, where had he been during the time he was away from Fox Hollow. If he had spent time in prison, what for?

"Maybe if he had, it might make Rita feel better."

"What would make Rita feel better?"

I didn't realize I'd spoken the words aloud until Gary appeared at my elbow. I waved my hand in the air. "I was just thinking out loud."

He cocked his head at me. "You were thinking about Johnny Draco. Still."

"Guilty." I glanced out the large picture window at Sweet Perks. "I called Rita earlier, but the call went to voicemail. I thought she might call, but so far nothing."

"She still might be upset. His presence seemed to stir up quite a few unpleasant memories, and it's understandable. Olivia says that's the way Rita is. She bottles everything up, stews over it till it gets to a simmer and then *poof!* She's over it. You watch! She'll be around today, back to her usual perky self."

"I hope so." But deep down, something told me that wasn't the case.

Gary gave his stomach a pat. "Getting back to lunch, Angelo's is slammed, so I'm going to run over and pick up the pizza. I'll be back in a jiff." Angelo's was located at the end of Main Street, but it was a long block. Gary grinned. "I know how you hate cold pizza, so I'll walk fast."

He sailed out the door. I locked it behind him and then went behind the counter. I picked up one of the flyers that had the schedule of events on it and studied it. Elvin Scraggs had been up first, scheduled to give his concert at the gazebo following lunch—well, that was out now. Olivia's dance class was scheduled for their recital at two, and there were various acts aimed at the younger crowd from three to five: a marionette show, a clown with a juggling act, and a mime. I nibbled absently at my lower lip. So the live entertainment would start at two instead of one, was that really such a big deal? All the people I'd spoken with this week had said how glad they were that Urban Tails was reopening. They'd seemed more focused on that than anything else.

I thought about the other merchants. They all knew what a boon the successful pet shop had been to everyone and were going all out to ensure its continued success. Their loyalty to my aunt's lifelong work made a tear come to my eye. I brushed it away quickly. My aunt wouldn't have wanted to see me blubbering.

My phone buzzed and I snatched it up. I saw the *Fox Hollow Gazette*'s name on the screen and hesitated, then hit the Answer button. "Urban Tails, Shell speaking."

"How excited you must be that this is finally happening." Quentin Watson's voice sounded cheerful enough, but it had an undercurrent, an edge to it.

"Supremely. I imagine I can count on you for a full feature article?"

"Absolutely." A pause and then: "I heard you were hiring Johnny Draco to replace Elvin Scraggs."

It never amazed me how that man got hold of information. He had to have informants and snitches lined up all over town. "Who told you that?"

A dry chuckle. "Ah, Shell, you know a good newspaperman never reveals his sources."

"Yeah, well, in this instance your source has it all wrong. I have no vocalist. I didn't hire the man, and he said his name was Ira, by the way."

"Ira was Johnny's middle name, but I'm betting you know that. I'm betting you've already researched Draco and the scandal of five years ago."

"I know enough to know he allegedly swindled a lot of people, you included," I said.

"Allegedly nothing. The man's guilty as sin," Watson snapped.

"I see. And you know that because..."

"Because he is. Come on, Shell. The man took off in the middle of the night without a word to anyone, not even the woman he was involved with. Are those the actions of an innocent man?"

"They could be considered the actions of a troubled one. He lost money himself, didn't he?"

"I'll forgive you for taking his side, since you weren't around at the time. But if you should see him today, give him a message from me. Tell him not to be such a coward and come and face me. I have a few things I want to say to him."

"I'm sure that he'll come and see you, Quentin, when he's ready. He asked about quite a few people, my aunt for one... and you."

"He did, did he?" Watson snorted. "Doesn't surprise me he inquired about your aunt. She always did stick up for the underdog. Personally, if I were him, I'd think seriously about getting the heck out of Dodge before something... unfortunate happens." He paused. "If you see him, you might pass along that message."

"I told you, I'm not going to see—"

I sighed. I was talking to air. Quentin Watson had hung up. I paused, mulling over his last words. Something unfortunate, he'd said. Like what? An accident? Or worse?

I shrugged off thoughts of Watson and Draco and went back to my work. I noticed that there was room on the lower shelf on the far wall and decided to put out some of the airline travel carriers I'd found in the storeroom. They weren't where I'd last seen them, of course. No doubt Gary had moved them somewhere when he was rummaging around. I finally located them in the far corner and had just picked one up when I heard an insistent tapping at the back door. Gary, no doubt, had forgotten the key I'd given him. I set the travel case back down and hurried over to the door. I didn't even bother to look out, just pulled it open, and then I gasped in surprise.

Perched on the lowest branch of the tree that stood just outside the door was a large bright red parrot with a black beak. The parrot stared at me for a minute and then said in a high-pitched voice, "Honey is a good bird. Honey is a smart bird. Honey sees all, knows all."

I stared right back at the bird. "You must be Honey Belle," I said. "Did you tap at the door with your beak?"

"No, but that sounds like a good trick to teach her."

I glanced up and saw Adrian Arnold hurrying toward me. He held a large box in both hands. As he approached, I saw that the box was filled to the brim with individual slips of brightly colored paper. The swarthy man gave me a smile as he approached.

"I tapped on the door, but I forgot the box so I had to go back to the car."

"Oh," I said. I looked from Adrian to Honey Belle and then back to Adrian again. "I'm sorry, I wasn't expecting you until tomorrow."

Adrian's bushy eyebrows drew together in a frown. "Didn't Gary mention I'd be stopping by? I wanted to leave Honey's fortune box here, and Gary was also going to have you sign the contract I gave him yesterday. I had to make a new one up for Honey."

"He must have forgotten." I hesitated, then swung the door wide. "He'll be back shortly. Why don't you come in and wait?"

"Thank you." He held out his arm. "Honey Belle. We're going inside."

The parrot hopped off the branch and right onto Adrian's arm and they followed me inside. I shut the door behind us and said, "It's good you dropped by, it saves me a call. I wanted to go over the itinerary for tomorrow with you."

"Sure." Adrian set the box down on the counter and eased his frame into one of the well-worn chairs. Honey Belle remained placidly on his arm the whole time, but when he was seated, the bird hopped onto his shoulder. "Gary said we could set up right in front of your shop."

"That's right. I thought having Honey Belle perform outside might encourage more people to stop in."

Adrian laughed. "I don't think these people need much encouragement for that, Ms. McMillan. It's all anyone's talked about this past month. They can't wait for Urban Tails to be open again."

"That's kind of you to say."

"It's not kind, it's the truth."

"Did you know my aunt?" I asked.

"We met a few times. I bought a few supplies for my birds here."

Honey Belle let out a loud squawk. "Aunt Tillie. One sharp cookie."

Adrian's cheeks flamed, but I laughed. "Yes, she was. Honey is a good judge of character."

"Unfortunately Honey Belle never met your aunt," Adrian said. "She only knows what I and Captain Snaggle have told her." He paused and then added,

"The captain performed at some charity events that your aunt chaired. Ms. Washburn was very fond of the captain."

"I'm sure. My aunt loved all animals. I take after her in that respect. Speaking of the captain, did you ever find him?"

Adrian raised his hand and pulled absently at his ear. "No, and I have to admit it's got me pretty upset. I spent a lot of time and money training that bird. He's a yellow-naped amazon."

"I never heard of that breed."

"They're native to southern Mexico, Central America and northern South America. They're on the smaller side, fifteen inches from the beak to the tip of the tail. They're very intelligent, though, and emotional as a human toddler. Why, those birds can live more than seventy years with the proper care."

"Goodness." I looked at the other parrot, still perched on Adrian's shoulder. "And what breed is Honey Belle? Obviously she's not a yellow-naped amazon."

"No, she's not," Adrian said and chuckled. "I just called her the captain's sister because I got 'em both on the same day. Honey Belle is an eclectus parrot. She's bigger than the captain, measures twenty inches from beak to tail. Her life span's a bit shorter though. Eclectus usually live between thirty to fifty years. They thrive in tropical rain forests, and are usually found in Australia and New Guinea. I bought her from a breeder from Australia."

I inched a bit closer to peer at the parrot, who sat complacently on Adrian's shoulder, watching me with her bright black eyes. "Her coloring is beautiful," I murmured.

"With eclectus parrots, you can tell the sex of the bird by the color of its feathers. Males are a brilliant emerald green with bright orange beaks, and the females are mostly bright red, with black beaks and deep purple markings on the chest and tail."

"You certainly know a lot about birds," I said. "Have you been doing this long?"

He shrugged. "It started as a hobby, then I went into it full-time a few years ago."

Honey Belle suddenly let out a loud honk. I jumped.

Adrian let out a laugh. "I should have warned you—that loud honk is distinctive of the breed. She's just as intelligent as Captain Snaggle, though, maybe even more so. She's just quieter."

"I'm sure she is." I looked over at the box. "Just how does she tell fortunes? Gary didn't really explain it."

"Pretty much the same as the captain, although he would actually engage the subject in conversation. What you heard Honey Belle say before is pretty much it." He turned his head and lifted a finger toward the parrot. Honey Belle bent her head and nibbled at Adrian's finger. "Honey Belle, this nice lady would like her fortune told."

Honey Belle lifted her head to look at me. Then she repeated what I'd already heard her say. "Honey is a good bird. Honey is a smart bird. Honey sees all, knows all." The bird hopped off of Adrian's shoulder and over to the box on the counter. She bent down and pecked at the different squares of paper. She did this for a few moments before finally selecting one in a bright pink color. She hopped back on Adrian's shoulder and extended the paper in her beak to me.

Even I had to admit it was pretty impressive. I reached out and took the paper. "Thank you, Honey Belle."

The bird let out another loud honk then lifted up one foot. "Cross my claw with silver," she said.

Adrian's cheeks reddened slightly. "She got that phrase from her brother too." He looked at me. "I usually have a tip jar on the side. Anything I get, I usually donate to the animal shelter."

Somehow I doubted that, but I wasn't going to argue the point. I wasn't particularly fond of Adrian but I knew the birds were expensive and that their feeding and care could run into large sums of money. "Feel free to have your jar at the ready," I told him. "I imagine the children will love to give Honey Belle a dollar or two for their fortune."

Adrian inclined his head. "Thanks so kindly." He pointed to the paper. "Well, aren't you going to have a look? Honey Belle's pretty good at picking out fortunes that suit her customers."

"Sure." I unfolded the pink paper and read the words that were printed in large, black block letters: "You will solve a complex problem."

"Really? That's the fortune?" Adrian came over to peer over my shoulder. "Hm. I had some of the high school kids print up a whole batch of fortunes. I guess I should have gone through them before I put them in the box. This is an odd one. Obviously some kid isn't doing well in algebra and it's their idea of a joke. Would you like a do-over?"

"Not necessary," I said. I slid the paper into my pocket. "Besides, I don't take this kind of thing seriously."

"Suit yourself. Still, I probably should take the box back home and go through these, make sure they all make sense." When he spoke, I noted an impatient edge to his tone. He stole a glance at his watch. "Will Gary be back soon? I, ah, almost forgot, I have another appointment I must get to."

"I honestly thought he'd be back by now. He did say Angelo's was slammed, though. He's probably still waiting for our lunch."

Adrian walked over to the window next to the door. Suddenly he reached in his pocket, pulled out his cell phone. He glanced at the screen, and his whole body tensed. He slid the phone back into his pocket and turned to me. "You know, the contract can wait," he said. "I'll just pick it up tomorrow when I report in—he said you'd like us here by nine thirty?"

"Yes, to set up. The festivities begin at ten, when the shop's officially open for business."

"Fine. Honey Belle and I will see you at nine thirty, then."

Adrian snatched up the box and then he and the parrot hustled out the back door without a backward glance. I walked over to the window and glanced out. Adrian paused at the corner, looked around, and then ducked into the back alley behind the coffee shop.

"Well, that's curious," I murmured. "I thought he was anxious to get to his appointment. Why is he going back there? There's nothing there but dumpsters. His appointment can't be there—or can it?" I paused as I realized that neither Purrday nor Kahlua were around to answer me, as they usually did. I'd left them home today, and it was probably a good thing. I certainly hadn't planned on seeing either Adrian or his parrot, and I still wasn't quite sure how either cat would react when they saw the bird tomorrow. Fortunately, they'd be inside and Honey Belle outside. I started to turn away when a flash of something black caught my eye. I pressed my nose against the window for a better look.

Adrian, sans parrot, had emerged from the alley and now stood, deep in discussion with a slightly shorter figure dressed in black hoodie and slacks. Adrian's face was red, and the shorter person waved his arms about like a windmill. The conversation seemed pretty intense. The shorter man's arm came up, knocking back his hood. I gasped as I recognized the shock of red curly hair.

Adrian's companion was Ira, or rather, Johnny Draco. The two men stood for a minute, glaring at each other, and then both turned and walked off in opposite directions. I frowned. Two questions came immediately to mind: Did they know each other? And what were the two of them discussing so intensely?

Six

"And you're certain it was Johnny Draco?"

It was a little after nine on Saturday morning. The police had arrived promptly at eight thirty and begun shutting down the three-block area where the event was being held. Olivia had organized a group of her students to act as a decorating committee. The girls had been hard at work since six a.m., hanging streamers from poles and awnings, and erecting canopies up and down the blocks. Shop owners were busy, setting up tables or booths in which to showcase their wares and services. Robbie had arrived right on time, as did the two high school girls I'd hired as part-time clerks, Janine Dowd and Sunny Sloane. As it turned out, the girls, who were both juniors, knew Robbie. Judging from the worshipful looks they cast his way, I fancied they both had a bit of a crush on him, too. They all seemed enthusiastic, though, and ready to do whatever it took to make the opening a success.

The smell of Bolivian Extra Bold wafted in through the window, mingled with the aroma of freshly baked doughnuts. Sweet Perks had already set up their booth and I sniffed the enticing air, taking it as a good sign all was now well with Rita even though she had yet to return one of my calls or texts.

I finished putting the finishing touches on the display of Kathleen Power's knitted sweaters and turned to face Gary. I hadn't had a chance to talk to him yesterday. We'd worked nonstop till nine at night getting the store ready, and then Gary had taken Olivia out for a late supper. I'd been in dreamland when he finally got home. "I'm positive," I said. "There was no mistaking that red hair."

"I'm surprised you didn't run out and ask him why he never showed up to audition."

"I considered doing just that, but their conversation ended rather abruptly." I put a finger to my lips. "I can't help but wonder what they could have been discussing so heatedly. Is it possible Arnold was another of Draco's so-called victims?"

Gary shrugged. "I suppose anything's possible, but why do you care?"

I reached into the pocket of the beige twill pants I wore and withdrew the slip of paper Honey Belle had given me yesterday. I handed it to Gary. "Maybe I'm meant to solve the mystery of why Johnny Draco's back in town."

Gary looked at the paper then gave it back to me. "You know, just because you lucked out solving one mystery . . ."

I threw my shoulders back. "I beg your pardon. Luck had nothing to do with it." As Gary continued to give me the evil eye, I added, "Well, okay, maybe luck had a teeny bit to do with it. But this is personal. Draco may have swindled some of our friends. I for one would like to find out if that's true, and if it is, justice should be served."

"Granted, but that doesn't mean you have to be the one to do it. What the heck?"

We heard a loud screech and a meow, and then Purrday and Kahlua came racing out of the back room and dashed madly around the store. I turned around and clapped my hands. "Hey, hey, no kitty hijinks today. You two are gonna be on your best behavior, right?"

The two cats stopped, cocked their heads and stared at me for a full minute before taking off on another mad dash.

I tossed Gary a black look. "I knew giving them those catnip sticks to play with was a bad idea," I muttered.

"Oh, don't be such a worrywart," Gary grumbled. "They'll wear themselves out and be quiet as mice the rest of the day."

"Ssh," I cautioned. "Don't bandy the *m* word around when they're in this state."

Gary had turned to look out the window while I was speaking, and now he let out a low whistle. "Uh-oh. Will you look at this."

I walked over to stand beside him and peer out the window. A large coral-colored tent was set up a few doors down. A woman stood in front of the tent. She wore printed pants the same color as the tent, a long white tunic with gay flowers splashed all over it, and a turban of bright orange wrapped around her head. A large hobo bag in tones of orange and coral was slung over one shoulder. She paused to speak to the man setting up the tent next to hers, then turned and strode purposefully toward the pet shop.

"OMG, she's coming here," he cried. He raised his hand and pointed out the window at her. "Who is she?"

"That's Mae Barker, our second fortune-teller," I replied. "And if I'm not mistaken, here comes our other fortune-teller and her owner." I pointed across the street. Adrian, Honey Belle perched on his shoulder, was also heading toward the shop. I hurried over to the desk, snatched up the contract I'd signed earlier and pressed it into Gary's hand. "He's early. Can you meet him outside and give him this? I really don't want a loose p-a-r-r-o-t in here with the cats."

The cats whizzed by just then. As I spelled out the word, they both stopped and cocked their heads. Then both let out low growls and scampered back into the storeroom.

Gary choked back a laugh. "I always knew Purrday could spell."

A loud meow of assent came from the storeroom. Gary snatched up the contract. "I'll just go out the back." He beat feet out of there as I opened the door to admit Mae.

"Good morning, Shell," Mae said. She was a plump woman in her mid-fifties, who liked to use her hands expressively when she spoke. She put a hand to her breast, and I noticed there was a ring on every finger and each ring had a different colored stone set in it. About a dozen bracelets that matched the stones on the rings graced her wrist. "How excited you must be, to finally be reopening your aunt's cherished store."

I nodded. "Yes, I confess to a few butterflies, but other than that, I'm really jazzed about today. You couldn't ask for more perfect weather."

"True." Mae glanced around the shop. "Everything looks wonderful. I'll have to try and make time to stop in later." She inclined her head toward the sweater display. "I'd love to get one of those for Brutus." Her hand dove into the pocket of her caftan and she removed a photograph, which she handed to me. "His birthday is next week."

Brutus was a French bulldog who apparently liked to dress up. In the photo he was wearing a sailor cap. A red bow tie was knotted around his neck. I handed her back the photo and waved her toward the display. "Why don't you do it now?" I suggested. "You can have first pick before the opening. On the house, for Brutus's birthday."

Mae's face brightened. "Aren't you a dear." She walked right over to the display and started to paw through the sweaters. "It's something, isn't it, about Johnny Draco being back in town? Rita was *so* upset to think you might have actually hired him. That man had best be careful. Lots of people would like to tan his hide. He was a charmer, though. Just ask Krissa. She nearly blew a blood vessel when I told her." She held up a green-and-white-striped sweater. "Isn't this one darling," she cried. She held it out, examined it, then shook her head. Too much green." Mae refolded the sweater and picked up another.

"The man who came here said his name was Ira. He did ask about some locals, though," I said, hoping to draw more out of Mae. "My aunt, for one. And Quentin and Rita and Stanley Sheer."

"He didn't ask after Krissa?" Mae clucked her tongue. "Isn't that just like a man. Well, if Rita gets her hands on him, he'll wish he'd never been born."

"Well, as you already pointed out, there are others who have issues with him."

"True. Who knows, maybe he pitched a tent in the woods. He wouldn't take a chance staying at the inn. Lester Babcock was another of his victims."

"Just how many people were in on this investment?" I asked.

Mae frowned. "Well, Rita and Wesley, and Lester Babcock, Quentin Watson, Stanley Sheer, Krissa . . . there were a few others too, I think, but offhand I can't recall their names."

"I don't suppose you'd know if Adrian Arnold was one?"

Mae's eyebrows drew together. "Adrian Arnold? Doesn't sound familiar, but of course I don't know everyone that was involved. If you're really that interested, Shell, ask Quentin Watson. I'm sure he knows."

Mae turned back to riffling through the sweaters, and I glanced out the window. There was no sign of Gary or Adrian, but Rita was just exiting the side door of Sweet Perks. She stood uncertainly for a moment, then turned and started toward the back alley. I decided this might be a good time to talk to her. "Mae, I've got to run out for a sec."

Mae now held up a pink and purple sweater. "This is nice. Oh, fine, sweetie. No worries." She raised her hand, moved it in a lazy circle. "If anyone tries to get in, I'll chase 'em away."

I hurried out the door and moved swiftly in the direction of the back alley. I reached the alley entrance just in time to see Rita turn the corner at the far end. I frowned. It was a dead end back there, nothing but dumpsters. Why was she going there? As I debated following her, a hand came down on my shoulder. I gasped and whirled around.

"Shell? What are you doing out here? Shouldn't you be readying your shop for the hoard of customers?"

I met Stanley Sheer's intense gaze. The barber was a short but powerfully built man. Not bad-looking either, if one could overlook that bad comb-over. I gave him what I hoped was a bright smile. "Stanley, hi. I . . . ah . . . thought I saw a cat go back there."

"Not one of yours, I hope."

"Oh, no. Purrday and Kahlua are at the shop."

Stanley flexed his muscular fingers, then shoved his hands into the pockets of the baseball jacket he wore. "I wouldn't worry. There are a few stray cats that we merchants feed on a regular basis. They help keep the rodent population under control." He paused. "Speaking of rodents, I hear you nearly hired Johnny Draco yesterday."

I bit down hard on my lower lip and counted to ten before responding. "I had no idea who he was. He said his name was Ira."

"Yeah, well, it figures the coward would come back in disguise. I wonder why he's here. Come back to gloat over our misfortune, no doubt. All I can say is he'd better steer clear of me." He glanced at his watch. "Well, I have to get back to my tent. It's almost time for the festivities to begin." The words *and you should too* were clearly implied in his tone.

He turned and walked off. I hesitated for only a split second before turning and walking into the alley. As I approached the corner where I'd last seen Rita, angry voices reached my ears.

"I can't believe you intend to do this," Rita shrilled. "And with stolen money."

"I told you, it's not stolen, it's my money, money I earned honestly," rumbled a male voice. "I went away to make a fresh start where no one knew me, and I saved my pennies to come back here. I'm tired of being blamed for something I didn't do. You know, I lost money too. I'm as much a victim as you."

"How dare you say that!"

And then I heard the sound of a loud slap, and then footsteps. I barely had time to slip behind a nearby dumpster when Rita emerged from the alley, rubbing her hand. She stalked off, her chin held high. I was about to follow her when I heard more footsteps, so I ducked back behind the dumpster. A few minutes later a figure dressed all in black appeared. Johnny Draco was dressed in the same outfit he'd had on yesterday when I'd seen him arguing with Adrian Arnold. He was rubbing the side of his face and I could see a large red welt starting to form. He walked off, mumbling, in the opposite direction.

What had gone on back there? I craned my neck, trying to keep track of Draco, who was now walking swiftly. He was almost at the center of town, not far from Krissa's store. Was he planning on visiting her? I'd just decided to head on over to Sweet Perks in the hopes of corralling Rita when I caught a movement out of the corner of my eye. I looked up just in time to see another figure detach itself from the shadows and start off after Draco. Unfortunately, I was too far away to get a clear look at whoever it was.

I started to make my way over to the coffee shop but a swift glance in the direction of Urban Tails changed my mind. A long line was starting to form, and I could see Robbie and the girls bustling around inside. It wasn't fair to leave them to open up so I could play detective. I'd have to find a spare moment later to speak with Rita about what I'd seen and heard.

• • •

The steady stream of customers started at ten and only started to thin out around noon. We were so busy that I had scarcely a moment to reflect on Rita, Draco, or anything else, for that matter. Kathleen Power's beautiful sweaters, hats and blankets sold out almost immediately, and Gary set up an order sheet so those who'd missed out could put in an order for a sweater or a blanket in their favorite color. Dog and kitty supplies fairly flew off the shelves, and I noticed with some pride that I'd have to call my suppliers on Monday for a restock on several items, including the animal travel carriers. At least ten people inquired when the advertised doggie grooming would begin. One woman who had her teacup French poodle in her tote bag was especially enthusiastic. "Make sure that they can do manicures," she said. She scratched the top of the dog's head and her eyes widened and she let out a pleased yip. "Arabella hasn't had a decent manicure since your aunt closed up shop."

I noticed Arabella's blue-tinted nails were indeed chipped. I promised to do my best.

Around twelve thirty the crowd had thinned enough so that I didn't feel guilty taking a short break. I was eager to check out the other tents and displays, and possibly track down Rita and/or Draco. Gary and Robbie both waved me off with confident assurances that they'd be just fine. I decided to believe them and strolled leisurely outside. My first stop was Sweet Perks. The café was crowded to capacity, and there was a long line at the register. I didn't see Rita anywhere around, so I figured I'd have to catch her later and went back outside.

A large crowd had gathered to the right of my store entrance where Adrian and Honey Belle had set up shop. I spotted Buck Adams, wearing a white cap that said *Rialto* in bright red letters, standing on the fringe of the crowd and made my way over to him. He jumped as I tapped his shoulder. "Shell. You startled me," he said with a laugh. "I guess I was getting all caught up in the parrot act."

"How are they doing?" I asked as a teenaged girl slipped a dollar bill into the glass jar that hung off the side of the large wooden box.

"It's interesting," Buck replied. "Arnold certainly has that bird trained well."

We watched as Adrian turned to the bird sitting on his shoulder. "Honey Belle, this nice young lady wants to know what her future holds," he said.

The parrot cocked its head to one side and its black beady eyes fastened on the girl. Then the parrot let loose its familiar spiel, "Honey is a good bird. Honey is a smart bird. Honey sees all, knows all," before dipping its head down and plucking a slip of blue paper from the box. Honey Belle extended her beak, and the giggling girl took the paper and unfolded it.

"Ooh, this says my secret wish will come true," she squealed. "I hope that means Rodney Biggerman's going to ask me on a date."

"Honey sees all, knows all," the bird chirped again, and the crowd broke into laughter and applause. I grinned at Buck. "I've got to agree with you. He's done a remarkable job with that parrot."

"Yeah, pretty good, considering he's only been doing it a few years. He had some other fancy job before he got into this line of work."

"Really? What did he do?"

Buck pushed his cap up on his forehead. "To tell you the truth, I'm not exactly sure. It had something to do with banking, or investments, I think."

Investments? A little bell pinged in my head. "Do you think he knew Johnny Draco?" I asked.

Buck shrugged. "I doubt it. Johnny was local, and Arnold worked somewhere in New York, I think." He glanced at his watch. "Oops, I'd better get back to my table," he said. "We'll be having the grand prize drawing around three. You should stop by, Shell."

"Maybe I will."

Buck hurried off and I made a mental note to follow up on Adrian Arnold's former occupation. I watched Honey Belle deliver another fortune to a gray-haired woman dressed in a shocking pink running suit. As the parrot homed in on the next client, another teen girl, I left and sauntered down the block, checking out the various tables, tents and canopies. I saw Mae inside her tent, laying out cards in front of Mimi Monaco, who ran the information desk at the library. The tent being hosted by City Hall was pretty packed. Volunteers were handing out flyers from the participating shops and restaurants, various pamphlets on civic activities, even job applications. The local realtors association had a tent too, and the various realtors were wasting no time in flagging down prospective clients. One, a middle-aged dyed blonde in her late fifties wearing a yellow jacket and navy skirt, waved a colorful brochure under my nose as I passed. "Looking to sell your home?" she inquired. When I shook my head no, she pressed the brochure into my hand anyway, along with her business card. "Maybe you know someone who is."

I strolled past some more tents, the mime doing his thing, and a hot dog cart. I'd been keeping a sharp eye out, but so far no sign of Draco. I wondered if maybe he'd decided to skip town again. Before I knew it, I was standing in front of the gazebo. The seating area was nearly filled and I realized that it was nearly time for Olivia's girls to give their first performance. Olivia, bless her heart, had added an extra number from *Annie* to help fill the gap left by Elvin. I walked around to the back of the gazebo and saw Olivia straightening the skirt of one of the dancers. She glanced up as I approached.

"All set," she said to the girl, then offered me a large smile. "Shell! How nice. Did you come to watch?"

I shook my head regretfully. "I can't stay too long. I left Gary in charge. Plus, my mother is due to show up any second now."

"Uh-oh, you'd better hurry back then." Olivia's laugh tinkled out. "Don't worry, Stella Fein's taking a video. Her daughter is playing Annie. She promised to send me a copy so we can all enjoy it later."

One of the girls hurried up to Olivia. She wore a curly red wig, so I imagined that she must be playing the role of Annie. "Miss Niven, Julie can't find her broom."

"I'll help you look for it. Catch you later, Shell. I want to have that parrot tell my fortune."

Olivia hurried off with her student and I wandered over to the other side of the gazebo. About twenty feet away a man and a woman stood, deep in conversation. I recognized the woman at once. Krissa Tidwell. The man I didn't know. Krissa seemed very nervous. Her head bobbed to and fro and her face was quite red. The man appeared to be making an attempt to soothe her. I wondered if Johnny had seen Krissa after all, and this was the aftermath. I debated moving closer to try and overhear their conversation when a hand dropped down on my shoulder.

"Penny for your thoughts."

I jumped, then whirled around and found myself staring into the beady eyes of none other than Quentin Watson. "You startled me," I said.

Quentin shrugged. "Did I? Sorry." He followed my gaze and his lips turned downward. "Well, well, don't the two of them look cozy. I wonder if Johnny paid his former lover a visit?"

"I was thinking the same thing," I murmured. I looked at Quentin. "What are you doing here?"

His fingers fiddled with the strap of the Nikon slung around his neck. "My job. Reporting on this august event."

I lifted a brow. "That's it?"

He chuckled. "I might be hoping to catch a glimpse of Johnny Draco. I understand he's paid a few visits."

I shot the newsman a sharp glance. Had he found out about the meeting between Johnny and Rita? Watson stole a glance Krissa's way and then turned back to me. In a low tone he said, "Draco's planning to stay. To set up roots back here."

"He is? How do you know—never mind. You wouldn't tell me anyway."

"True that." He leaned closer to me. "What I will say, however, is that I have it on good authority that Mr. Draco has designs on leasing the former Alder Dry Goods store."

My mouth dropped open. "You're kidding. That's right across the street from Sweet Perks."

"Indeed. I imagine Rita will be thrilled with her new neighbor. As her friend, you might want to give her a heads-up." Watson inclined his head toward the man. "No doubt Krissa is giving Evan an earful on past history."

"Evan?"

"Evan Hanley. His family owns a good bit of real estate in Fox Hollow, and the old dry goods store is among the properties." He coughed lightly. "Evan's the last of the Hanleys. His brother Ian died in an auto accident five years ago, and the mother shortly after that. The father had a heart attack and died suddenly two months ago. Evan moved here from New York City to take over the business. No doubt Krissa is trying her best to persuade Evan to reconsider. I understand they're very close." He gave his head a brisk shake. "I hope it's not too late. Something must be done. The man must be stopped. We don't need him back here."

The venom in the newsman's tone chilled me. "Stopped? Stopped how?"

But Quentin Watson didn't answer me, just turned on his heel and walked off toward the stores. I glanced back across the street. Evan and Krissa had finished their conversation. Evan took Krissa into his arms and they stood together for a few minutes before breaking apart. Evan turned to the left, Krissa the right. As they walked off, Evan paused to look back over his shoulder. Our gazes locked for a brief moment, and Evan's brows drew together, giving his face a thundercloud expression. Then he gave his head a quick shake, turned and walked swiftly away.

The glance had only lasted a few seconds, but it was enough to send a chill nickering up my spine. What had I done to deserve such a look? Krissa must have mentioned to him I'd considered hiring Draco. I remembered Quentin's remark about them being close. They must be pretty close, indeed, for Hanley to seem so overprotective. I reached in my pocket for my phone. Josh hadn't yet made an appearance and I wanted to apprise him of all this craziness, but before I could press his number on speed dial, my phone beeped with an incoming text: *SOS—Get back here now. The mothership has landed. G.*

Seven

I saw her the minute I stepped inside the store. Of course, it's hard to miss my mother. Clarissa McMillan always dresses as if any moment might be a photo op. She stood off to one side of the checkout counter, drumming her French-tipped nails impatiently on its top. Today she had on an expensive white linen top, khaki-colored twill slacks and sporty, but feminine, flats with perky little bows. Her carefully coiffed, expertly dyed ash-blonde hair rested in a casual knot at the nape of her neck. When she saw me, her perfectly made up lips tilted in the closest thing she had to a smile. She stopped the finger drumming and rushed forward. In a typical dramatic gesture, she enfolded me into her arms and huffed, "Crishell, finally! Thank *God*!"

I pulled away from her and tugged my blue-and-green-striped top down a little farther over the waistband of my jeans. Being around my mother never failed to make me feel frumpish. "Nice to see you too, Mother," I murmured. "It would have been nice if you'd told me what time you planned to arrive. I could have sent someone to meet you at the airport."

My mother threw her head back and gave a throaty laugh. "For goodness sakes, Crishell, you act as if I've never traveled anywhere before." Her arm made a wide sweep, encompassing the store. "I knew you'd be occupied with . . . this . . . today. I'd made arrangements for a private limo. As a matter of fact, I've already had my bags taken to your house. I had the driver bring them around to the back porch. I hope that's okay."

"Fine, Mother." And then, just because I wanted to let her know I could read between the lines, I added, "No one will steal your luggage, if that's what you're worried about."

"Hmpf. Stolen luggage is the least of my worries." She glanced around the store like a queen surveying the peasants. "I must say, you've got quite a crowd of people here. I didn't know Tillie's store was so popular."

"The folks of Fox Hollow love their pets, I told you that." I put my hand on my mother's arm and steered her away from the counter toward the refreshment table. "Are you thirsty? Can I get you something to drink? I've got iced tea and lemonade."

Clarissa looked at the table, and her nose wrinkled. "Nothing stronger, like a Long Island Iced Tea perhaps?"

"Not here, mother."

She rolled her eyes. "Fine. I'll have an iced tea."

I poured iced tea into a large plastic cup and handed it to her. She made a face as she took it. No doubt she'd expected to be served a crystal goblet. "Would you like some cookies too?"

"No, thank you. I had lunch on the plane. Lobster Newburgh. The tea will suffice, thanks."

I wanted to say, *Well, excuse me*, but I restrained myself and gestured toward the storeroom door. "Perhaps you'd like to sit and put your feet up in the storeroom while you sip your tea," I suggested.

She paused, cup midway to her lips. "Why do you want to stick me in a back room? Are you trying to get rid of me, Crishell?"

Yes, my brain screamed, but I said innocently, "Of course not, Mother. What makes you say that?"

Her shoulders lifted in a careless shrug. "I know you, Crishell. You're afraid I'll say something that might offend someone. Darling, I might not agree with what you're doing, but that doesn't mean I'd make a scene. Give me a little credit, please." She angled a glance over at the counter. "I see you've got Gary earning his keep."

"He's helping out."

She sniffed audibly. "And helping himself to free room and board, no doubt."

"He makes up for it by cleaning and cooking," I replied. "He's an excellent cook, as you'll find out this weekend."

She muttered something too low for me to catch, which was probably a good thing. Robbie stepped behind the counter and Gary, after a moment's hesitation, walked over to us. "Hello, Mrs. McMillan," he said politely, extending his hand. "It's nice to see you. It's been a while."

My mother ignored the proffered hand and after a moment Gary wiped it awkwardly on the side of his jeans. "You can call me Clarissa, Gary. I hate being referred to as Mrs. McMillan." She paused to look at her half-empty cup. "I don't suppose you have anything stronger than iced tea lying about?"

"Not here, sorry. We've got a fully stocked bar back at the house, though."

"That's a relief." My mother took another sip of her tea. "I must say, it's quite a little soiree you've got going here. The crowd outside loves that man with the parrot, apparently. I could barely get in the door."

Killers of a Feather

"Adrian and Honey Belle have been a big hit," Gary said with a huge smile.

"Where are they, anyway?" I asked. I'd noticed that they'd been missing when I'd rushed back to the store after Gary's SOS. "On a break?"

"They're not out front?" Gary frowned and stole a glance at his watch. "His break's not for another hour."

"Do you mean the parrot man?" asked my mother. "He probably felt he needed a break after what happened with that man."

Both Gary and I turned to look at her. "What happened with what man?" I asked.

"When I arrived, I saw the crowd gathered and I decided I'd better see what all the fuss was about. Imagine my surprise to see a parrot telling fortunes." She rubbed the side of her jaw. "I watched it for a bit. The whole act was quite cute, actually, until the parrot's owner called out to some man standing on the fringe of the crowd. He said the parrot had a fortune just for him. The other man seemed a bit reluctant to come forward, but the owner seemed quite insistent. I figured they must have known each other."

"And did Honey Belle tell his fortune?"

"Oh, yes. The man's face got quite red when he saw it. He said something like, 'The two of you are frauds.' I thought for a second he might hit the owner, but he just jammed the paper into his pocket and stalked off." She put a finger to her lips. "The owner didn't seem perturbed at all, just laughed and called a teenaged boy up for his fortune. Personally, I thought he seemed amused that he'd gotten the other man upset."

"I don't suppose you remember what this man looked like?" asked Gary.

My mother waved her hand. "I don't know, I guess you could say he looked rather common. Black sweats, sunglasses. He had the hood of his sweatshirt pulled up. It was almost as if he wanted to disguise himself."

Gary and I exchanged a look. "You don't say," I murmured.

"Ms. McMillan?"

I turned around and saw Robbie standing behind me. He handed me an envelope. "Mr. Arnold asked me to give you this. He said he had to leave."

"Leave? He's gone?" I took the envelope from Robbie's outstretched hand.

"Yeah, he came in around one looking for you. I told him you'd be back soon but he didn't want to wait. He seemed in a hurry." He glanced over at the register. "I'd better get back to the counter and help Janine. It looks like we're getting pretty low on almost everything."

Robbie hurried back to help Janine at the counter. I tapped the envelope against my hand. Did his sudden departure have anything to do with his altercation with Draco?

My mother tapped me on the shoulder. "Aren't you going to open it?" she asked. When I hesitated, she rolled her eyes. "For goodness sakes, I'm not going to look over your shoulder while you read it. It's none of my business, after all." She gave her Aimee Kestenberg shoulder bag a sharp tug. "I think I'll look at some of your kitty items. Maybe I'll take Kahlua a little present, seeing as she's the closest thing to a grandchild I have from either you or your sister."

"Better pick out two presents then," I said mischievously. "After all, you have two grandcats."

"Two? Oh, right, Matilda's cat. Yes, I *can't wait* to meet *him*."

I ignored the sarcasm, and my mother moved off toward the display of scratching posts. Once she'd gone, I ripped the envelope open. There were two pieces of paper inside. I picked up the smaller one and gasped in astonishment.

It was a check for Honey Belle's fee.

I unfolded the other piece of paper and read the note, which appeared to be hastily written. Gary looked over my shoulder as I read:

> Ms. McMillan:
> *Unfortunately something's come up and Honey Belle and I won't be able to continue our performance. Please accept the enclosed refund as my sincere apology.*
> Adrian Arnold.

"Something's come up," I said. I looked at Gary. "Something that had to do with Draco, I'll bet." I repeated what Buck Adams had told me earlier about Adrian's other career. "I think they did know each other, though. Maybe they worked together on a deal at some point."

Gary frowned. "It bears looking into. Maybe I should take a quick run over to his place, see if I can find out anything."

"Good idea," I said.

Gary left and I walked over to my mother. She glanced up as I approached. "Which one do you think Kahlua would like better, this blue one with the stick attached or the rust-colored one with the bench on top?"

"Neither. They'd enjoy a catnip stick much more." I pointed to a box containing the gaily patterned sticks and chuckled inwardly as my mother wrinkled her nose. "I know you mustn't have gotten much rest today, what with your flight and all, Mother. Wouldn't you like to go home and take a nap?"

"That does sound good," she admitted. Her hand came up to her mouth and she suppressed a yawn. "I think I'd feel lots better after forty winks." She paused. "But I do so hate to leave you. I came to give my support, after all."

"And I appreciate that. But I'd much rather you relax so you can enjoy the remainder of your time here." *And just how long will that be?*

"Okay, then." I took my mother's hand and led her back to the storeroom. I retrieved my purse and pulled out my car keys and house key. "My car's parked on the side here. You can go out this door."

My mother held out her hand, and I dropped the keys into her outstretched palm. "How will you get home?"

"It's only a short walk," I assured her. "Gary and I will be fine. I'll see you around five thirty." As my mother hesitated, I added, "You needn't worry, Mother. The cats are here, somewhere."

She leaned over and gave me a swift peck on the cheek. "Thank you, dear."

My mother hurried out and I sat back down at my desk, mulling over the day's events. So far it seemed as if every one of Johnny's supposed "marks" knew he was in town, and none of them were happy about it. I knew he'd spoken to at least one of them—Rita. Had he seen any of the others? And how did Adrian Arnold fit in? What was his connection to Draco, because there was one, I was sure of that.

"*Er-oo!*"

My head jerked up as a flash of white and brown raced past me. The kitties were at it again. They screeched to a stop by the back door, and I suddenly realized that my mother hadn't closed it securely after her. It yawned open, and before I could jump up to close it the two cats had dashed outside.

"Great!"

I jumped up and hurried outside after them. In this crowd the two of them could easily get lost, or worse, cat-napped! I ran to the corner and saw the two of them huddled there. "Kahlua, Purrday," I said sternly. "Get back here now."

The cats looked at me, then dashed across the street. I groaned and took off after them. They headed toward a large building in the center of the block, and I realized that it was the former dry goods store, the one Watson said Johnny Draco had leased. The two cats jumped up on the stoop and paused. I hurried over. "Come here, you rascals," I said.

They both looked at me, and then dashed around the rear of the store, leaving me no choice but to follow them. Once around back, I saw no sign of them. Then I noticed the open window. No doubt they were hiding from me inside the deserted store. I hesitated only a split second, then I raised the window and climbed inside. It wasn't breaking and entering when the window was open, was it?

I stood a moment, letting my eyes become accustomed to the darkened interior. "Kahlua, Purrday," I hissed. "Get over here now!"

From a far corner, I heard a loud meow, followed by Kahlua's distinctive wail. I made my way around the wide counter past rows of shelving in that direction. I found myself in a small storeroom. A door on the far side was ajar, and two chairs lay on their sides. Purrday and Kahlua were both seated on top of a glass and wicker table, staring at something on the other side. As I drew closer both cats turned to look at me, and both meowed loudly again.

I felt a sinking feeling in the pit of my stomach, but still I glanced over the top of the table. A man dressed in a black hoodie and sweats lay on his side, one arm twisted at an odd angle. His other arm was outstretched, and there was something clenched between his fingers. I recognized the shock of red hair immediately. Johnny Draco.

In spite of the butterflies churning in my stomach, I walked around the table and leaned over for a closer look. I recognized the black and white object sticking out of Draco's throat immediately—it was the digital instrument he'd shown me. I couldn't tell, though, if that was the cause of death. I bent down for a better look at the object clenched in his hand. It was a piece of blue-tinted paper, the same type of paper that was in Honey Belle's fortune box. I got down on one knee and peered at it. It was impossible to be certain, but it looked to me like a crude drawing of the ace of spades was on it.

The Death card—had that been the fortune Honey had given him, the one my mother said he'd gotten angry over? If so, it seemed oddly appropriate.

I gave the body another quick once-over, looking for a more obvious wound, like a knife or a bullet hole, but saw nothing else. I reached down and pressed two fingers lightly at the base of his throat.

No pulse, but the body was still warm. Rigor hadn't yet set in. He couldn't have been dead too long. Purrday and Kahlua watched me from their perch on the table. "Er-owl," Purrday said. Kahlua let out a mournful Siamese wail.

"I know," I said to them. "We didn't miss the killer by much." I glanced around cautiously. Was he or she still out there, watching? Suddenly I didn't want the cats and I to be alone here, sitting ducks. I pulled out my cell and punched in Josh's number. He answered on the second ring.

"Hey, Shell. I'm sorry I didn't get a chance to answer your earlier calls. I had to stop by the station this morning to finish some paperwork, and it's been crazy busy at Secondhand Sue's. My sister just got back, so I'm getting ready to head over to your store now," he said.

"Better come to the Alder Dry Goods store instead," I said. "This isn't a social call. I need to report a murder."

Eight

The cats and I went around to the back entrance of the dry goods store to wait for Josh. He arrived within ten minutes, followed closely by an ambulance that I assumed he'd sent for. The ambulance parked right in back of Josh's car and two female paramedics alighted. I'd seen the two of them before, in Sweet Perks. One was a shapely brunette, the other a slightly stout blonde with flecks of silver in her hair. They beat Josh up the steps and the brunette pinned me with a sharp gaze. "Where's the body?"

I pointed at the back door and they hurried inside just as Josh came up to me. He didn't say a word, just pulled me to him and gave me a big hug. We stood like that for a few minutes before finally breaking apart. "This isn't exactly how I'd planned on spending today with you," he said.

In spite of the circumstances, I couldn't help thinking how nice Josh looked. He had on dark blue jeans that seemed molded to his muscular body, and a tan polo shirt underneath a beige jacket. The jacket seemed a bit wrinkled around the edges. I figured he kept the jacket in his car for emergencies like this. "You and me both," I agreed.

Josh's face changed, indicating a shift into what I'd once jokingly referred to as his cop mode. He pulled a notebook and pen from his jacket pocket. "How did you happen to find the body *this time?*"

I ignored the emphasis he put on the last two words. "I gave my mother my car keys so she could go to the house and freshen up. She left the back door open, and the cats got out. They came here and went inside an open window. I followed them." I watched as Josh scribbled in his notebook and then I blurted out, "It's Johnny Draco, or at least the man everyone is assuming is Draco. His body wasn't very cold. I don't think he's been dead all that long."

Josh looked up from his scribbling and arched an eyebrow. "You touched the body?"

"I put my fingers to the base of his throat, just to make sure he was beyond help." I paused, then figured it was best to come completely clean. "There's a paper clenched in one of his hands. I didn't touch it, but I did bend down and look at it. It looks like one of Honey Belle's."

"Who's Honey Belle?"

"Adrian Arnold's parrot. She tells fortunes by plucking a paper out of a box. My mother saw Johnny Draco with Arnold and the parrot earlier. He wasn't pleased with his fortune, and I can see why. As far as I could tell, it looks like the ace of spades." I gave a small shudder. "Pretty prophetic."

"More like a grisly coincidence. You can't seriously believe the parrot predicted Draco's death?"

I set my jaw. "Maybe not the parrot. My mother said that Adrian told Draco the parrot had a fortune just for him. But . . ."

"But what?" Josh asked as I hesitated.

"What if Arnold trained Honey Belle to select that particular fortune for Draco?"

Josh's eyebrows rose. "Why would he do that?"

I repeated the incident I'd witnessed between them in the alley, ending with what Buck had told me about Adrian's former occupation. "Couple that with what my mother witnessed," I finished, "and it certainly seems to me as if there could be a history there."

"Maybe so." The corners of Josh's lips drooped down as he scribbled some more in his notebook. "Since I can't pinpoint anyone else who might have witnessed the altercation, I'll need a statement from your mother."

I couldn't stop the groan that rose involuntarily to my lips. I was fairly certain my mother would be less than thrilled to be questioned in a murder investigation.

The brunette paramedic emerged from the shop and went straight over to Josh. "He's dead," she said crisply. "I've called for the coroner."

"Thanks, Tessa." She disappeared back inside and Josh turned back to me, raised his hand to scratch behind his ear. "What was Draco doing in here anyway? It's been empty for weeks."

"He was going to rent it," I blurted.

Josh's eyes widened. "He was? How do you know that?"

"Quentin Watson told me earlier." I left out Quentin's other comment, about how thrilled Rita would be to have the man set up shop across the street from her establishment. "I asked him how he knew, but of course he wouldn't tell me." My neck and shoulders felt stiff, so as I rolled my neck I added, "I saw Draco earlier this morning. It looked like he was headed toward Krissa Tidwell's store." I paused. "I also saw someone following him."

Josh looked up, his eyes alight with interest. "You did? Could you describe him?"

I shook my head. "I was too far away to see much more than a shadow. I couldn't even tell you if it were male or female." I knew I should probably also tell Josh about what I'd overheard between Rita and Draco, but I didn't want to. Not until I spoke to Rita first. "It does make you wonder, though, who Draco might have been in contact with during his short stay here."

"Well, if he were leasing the dry goods store, obviously Evan Hanley," said Josh. "I'll start there." Josh shook his head and slid his notebook back into his pocket. "Listen, Shell, you don't have to hang around. Go on back to your store. I'll come by your house later to take official statements from you and your mom."

Josh started to go inside, but I reached out and touched his arm. "One more thing. I'm not sure if it was the cause of death or not, but he had a virtual instrument jammed down his throat."

Josh paused and stared at me. "A virtual—what?"

I ran my fingers through my hair. "That's wrong. Virtual instrument actually refers to the software program that acts as a sound module to replicate different types of instruments. What's rammed down his throat is the digital instrument he used to play the software. He had it hooked up to a tablet the night he played and sang at my shop." I swallowed. "He won't be singing anymore."

Josh gave my arm a quick squeeze, then disappeared inside the shop. I looked down at Kahlua and Purrday, who'd been quite good, stretched out by my feet during my talk with Josh. "Come on, kids," I said. "Let's go back to Urban Tails." I waggled my finger at them. "Ixnay on any more escapes today, and definitely on finding more bodies."

Purrday and Kahlua both let out low growls.

The coroner's wagon pulled up behind the ambulance just as we were leaving. We walked back across the street and I fought the temptation to turn around for one last look. As we approached the pet shop, I saw Mae Barker leave her tent and hurry toward me. "Shell?" she cried. "I thought I saw the coroner's truck speed by a few minutes ago?"

"Did it?" I hoped I sounded more innocent than I was. News of Draco's death would surely spread like wildfire, and I didn't want to be accused of starting it.

Mae leaned into me. "I have a bad feeling that something terrible has happened." She raised a finger in dramatic fashion and waved it in the air.

"And I think it's happened to Johnny Draco."

I looked at her. "What makes you say that?"

"I had a premonition," she said in a hushed tone. She balled her hand into a fist and pounded it against her chest. "I just felt it, here, you know. When I saw him."

My head jerked up. "You saw him?"

Her head bobbed up and down. "Oh, yes. At least I think it was him. Kind of hard to tell, what with that hood up over his face and those sunglasses, but I'm pretty certain it was him. He was walking over toward the dry goods store. He stopped for a moment to rub at his cheek."

I frowned. "When exactly did you see him?"

She shrugged. "Not too long ago. A half hour, give or take." She paused. "I saw Rita too. She was hanging back a bit, like she was following him." She lowered her voice and added, "Rita's got a lot of pent-up anger toward that man, you know. It doesn't make for a good situation." She touched her breast again. "Trouble's brewing, I just know it."

Mae paused expectantly, obviously waiting for me to comment. I was spared, thankfully, as a woman broke out of the crowd and rushed toward Mae. "There you are," she cried. "You're the fortune-teller right? My friend Emma and I are dying to have our cards read."

"Sure, be right with you." Mae gave me another expectant glance, but when I didn't reply, she turned and hurried back to her tent, the woman trailing along behind her. I walked around to the rear entrance of the pet shop, the cats at my heels. I let myself inside and, as the cats each scattered to their favorite corners, sank down in the leather chair and leaned back, my eyes closed.

I remembered the altercation I'd heard between Rita and Draco this morning. I struggled to remember the exact words. Rita had said, "I can't believe you intend to do this, and with stolen money, no less."

Rita had to have been referring to Draco's setting up shop in the old dry goods store. I wondered how she'd heard about it. From Quentin? Or Draco himself? Had that been the reason for the meeting in the alley?

I remembered Draco's reply: "I'm as much a victim as you." Obviously someone had disagreed with him. But for the life of me, I just couldn't picture Rita as the murderous type. Then again, I hadn't pictured Mazie Madison as a killer either, until it had been almost too late . . . for me. I jumped up so quickly that I startled Purrday, who'd slithered underneath the desk and had been cat-napping almost at my feet.

"Sorry, boy," I said. "But I've got to talk to Rita pronto." I started for the back door. "I'll be back before closing, promise."

But as it turned out, I didn't have to go anywhere. Because when I flung open the door, Rita Sakowski, hand poised to knock, stood there. "Shell, thank goodness," she cried. "I need to talk to you."

I reached out and fairly pulled Rita inside the store. "Come in and sit down," I said. "I'm glad to see you, Rita. I still feel terrible about the other day. I've been calling and texting you."

Rita flopped down into my leather chair and hung her head. "I know. I haven't just been ignoring you, Shell. It's everyone. I've even been curt with Wesley. Johnny's return just upset me so."

I knelt down on one knee beside the chair. "You said you needed to speak with me?" I asked gently.

Rita swallowed. "Yes. I-I just wanted to apologize for ignoring you these past few days. I'd hate for you to be mad at me."

"Rita, I could never be mad at you," I said. I looked her straight in the eye. "But you and I both know that you're not being totally honest with me right now."

Rita's gaze slid away from mine. "I should have known better than to try and fool you, Shell," she murmured. "I know how perceptive you are."

"You met with Johnny Draco today, didn't you?"

Rita looked back at me, and I could see tears starting to form at the corners of her eyes. "Yes," she said softly. "He called me."

"He did?"

Rita nodded. "Yesterday evening. He said that he needed to meet with me, that there was something he needed to tell me. Shell, the first thing that came to my mind was that he was finally going to confess. Fool that I was, I thought maybe he'd gotten religion or something and was going to pay back the money he'd taken from us. Man, was I wrong!

"I met him in the alley behind the coffee shop this morning. He insisted on meeting somewhere private. He wasn't ready to show his face, he said. Anyway, instead of hearing a heartfelt confession, I got more of the same: He insisted he'd been a victim too, that he'd lost his money same as all of us.

"I asked him why he ran off and he said that he just couldn't face everyone after he'd exercised such poor judgment himself. It made him have a sort of epiphany about his life, his career. How could he guide others financially if he himself could be fooled so easily?"

Pretty much the same things I'd been wondering. I nodded and let Rita continue.

"I asked where he'd been all this time. He said that he needed to get away from here. He knew most everyone hated him after what happened. He needed to regroup, so he went to live with some distant cousin in Danielson, out by the Rhode Island border. His cousin was in construction, so Johnny took a job helping him. He worked hard, saved every penny so he could return to Fox Hollow someday." She paused and choked out a bitter laugh. "Then he told me that he'd decided the time was right for him to come back here. He was going to open up a little café slash deli in the old Alder Dry Goods Store—right across the street from me! I was going to have to look at him every day of my life!" She pounded her fist against one knee. "I was so mad I could barely control my temper."

Rita paused and I asked, gently, "And that's when you hit him?"

She looked at me, eyes wide with surprise. "Yes, but how did you know?"

"I saw you," I confessed. "I saw you go into the alley and I wanted to talk to you, but I heard voices so I didn't interrupt. Then a bit later I saw you come out of the alley, and a few minutes later Draco came out, rubbing at his cheek."

Rita's lips curved slightly. "I guess I can still pack a pretty good punch. My brother was on the boxing team in high school, and I used to practice on his punching bag. I pretended it was Miss Adler, my gym teacher," she said, a proud note in her voice. "I didn't even think twice, I just hauled off and clocked him on the side of the jaw. Then I ran off."

I put both my hands on her shoulders. "Okay, Rita. This is important. Was that the only time you saw Draco today?"

She frowned. "Yes. Why?"

"You're positive. You didn't see him later, or follow him, maybe to the dry goods store?"

A shadow crossed Rita's face, and her gaze skittered away from mine. "I don't know why you're asking me that, Shell? I told you the truth. I only saw and spoke to Johnny that one time." Her body shook slightly. "And that was enough." Now she did look me straight in the eye. "You believe me, don't you?"

I want to, my brain screamed. Finally I let my hands slide off her shoulders and I nodded. "Okay, Rita. If you say you only saw Johnny once today, I believe you."

Rita let out a large sigh. "Oh, thank goodness. I'm so sorry you have to be bothered with this, Shell, and on your big day."

"Rita, we're friends. That's what friends do. I recall you helping me out when I was in a bit of a jam, not long ago."

Rita swiped at her eyes with the back of her hand. "That was different. Look, I'd better get back to my own shop. There's still lots of time left in the grand opening, and I've got to make sure we've got enough coffee and doughnuts."

I squeezed her arm. "Rita, you know you can tell me anything. It will go no further."

She gave me a lopsided smile. "I know. Thanks, Shell."

Rita left and I stood by the back door, watching her hurry back to Sweet Perks. She'd just reached the front door when a police cruiser pulled up to the curb. Josh got out of the passenger side and went over to Rita. They spoke for a few minutes, then I saw Rita shrug and motion toward the side door of the store. Josh nodded, then went back to the cruiser. He said a few words to whoever was behind the wheel, and then he joined Rita and they both disappeared inside the side entrance as the cruiser glided away.

I felt sick. Mae must have gotten hold of Josh and told him what she'd seen. I could tell that Rita'd been lying when she said she hadn't seen Draco a second time. And as much as I hated to admit it, the obvious reason for her to lie was because she was the one who'd killed Johnny Draco.

Nine

"Man, was this a great day or what?" Robbie grinned at me as he closed and locked the door behind our last customer. Janine and Sunny had left an hour ago. They'd offered to stay, but I assured them it wasn't necessary and thanked them for the great job they'd done. Gary still wasn't back from his trip to Adrian Arnold's house yet, so it was only the two of us—or rather, the four of us if I counted the cats. Kahlua was snoozing in a cat bed over in the far corner. I bent down and picked up Purrday, who'd been rubbing up against my ankles. "It does seem as if the grand opening was a success," I agreed.

"Success is putting it mildly," Robbie remarked. "Everyone said how happy they were that the store's open again, and quite a few people are looking forward to pet grooming starting up again."

I stroked Purrday's soft fur. "Some folks mentioned it to me too. I should probably look into it."

"I could help out till you find someone," Robbie offered. "I helped my mom and dad groom the puppies, so I know how to clip nails and give baths." His lips curved upward. "I don't know how I'd be with, say, giving a poodle one of those fancy haircuts, though. For that you'd need a pro."

I pictured the saucy haircuts most pedigreed poodles sported and had to agree. "Maybe we'll just offer nail clippings on certain days as a start and take it from there."

Robbie pulled out a cloth, proceeded to wipe down the front counter. "Whatever you say, Ms. McMillan. You're the boss."

Purrday wriggled in my arms, and I set him back on the floor. "Hm, maybe it's time to switch to diet kibble," I said. "You've put on a few pounds, young man."

Purrday inclined his head toward the food bowl display. "Merow."

I shook my finger at him. "You can't possibly be hungry. Not with all the bits of grilled chicken I saw Gary slip to you and Kahlua out of his sandwich."

"Gary wasn't the only one giving them treats," supplied Robbie. "I saw a few people giving them bits of food. One woman actually opened a package of fish-flavored treats she'd bought for her own cat to give to them."

"Hm." I looked at the cats. "Maybe I should put up a sign, *Please do not feed the kitties*. What do you think about that?"

Purrday looked at Robbie and his lips peeled back, revealing his sharp teeth. He made a sound deep in his throat, which I imagined to be the kitty equivalent of *snitch*. In her corner, Kahlua let out a loud snore.

I chuckled. "Don't blame Robbie. He's just doing his job. You and Kahlua won't starve till we get home. Now, why don't you hop up on the window and watch the cleanup on the street while Robbie and I take care of things in here."

Purrday made a sound that sounded like a harrumph but wandered toward the window anyhow. I glanced out, saw that Mae had enlisted the aid of some teens to help her take down her tent. Seeing her made me think of Rita, and I wondered just what might have transpired earlier between her and Josh. I'd tried texting her a few times but so far hadn't gotten a response. I didn't bother texting Josh. Even if he answered, which I doubted he would, I knew he couldn't tell me anyway.

Robbie went outside, returning a few minutes later with the boom box I'd had out front. "Is this yours, or did you rent it?" he asked.

"It's mine. I think I'll keep it here, though. I like to work to music, it's soothing."

"Yeah, music while you work is always nice." Robbie set the box on the floor underneath the counter and I saw him fiddling with the buttons. A few seconds later I heard the familiar one-two, one-two bang of a drum, followed by the whine of a guitar.

I clapped my hands. "'Big Girls Don't Cry.' One of my favorites. I love the Four Seasons."

Robbie was tapping his foot in time to the beat. "Yeah, they're pretty cool." He paused in his foot tapping. "I wonder how Ms. Niven's girls made out at their performance?"

"I'm sure they were fantastic. She said she was having someone take a video so we could all watch it."

"Cool."

Robbie started to walk around the store, straightening up what items were left on the display tables and shelves. I grabbed a box of Wee-Wee Pads and headed for the storeroom. I'd just deposited it in a corner when I heard a knock at the back door. I walked over, looked out, and then opened the door to admit Olivia.

"Today couldn't have gone better," my friend crowed. Her eyes were shining. "My girls gave one heck of a stellar performance, if I do say so myself. That toad Quentin Watson was lurking around, snapping photos. We'd better make the front-page montage or else."

I frowned. "Did Watson stick around for both performances?"

"Hm." Olivia's brow wrinkled as she thought. "Now that you mention it, I'm not sure. I saw him flitting around for a good bit of it. I know I saw him around a quarter to three."

I did a quick calculation in my head. I'd found Draco's body around three, and by my estimation, he hadn't been dead all that long. It wasn't a long walk from the dry goods store to the gazebo, and Quentin was a pretty fast walker. I'd seen him zip from one end of town to the other in his hightop sneakers more than once.

Olivia's voice broke into my thoughts. "Enough about Fox Hollow's favorite newsman. I'm dying to know if your mother ever showed up."

"Yes, indeed. She made her usual dramatic appearance."

Olivia giggled. "I bet Gary was thrilled."

"Not half as thrilled as my mother. She looked as if she were getting ready to receive a death sentence. I finally sent her home to catch up on her beauty sleep, and that's how the cats got out. She left the back door open. I chased them over to the old dry goods store—where we found Johnny Draco's body."

"His *body*?" Olivia let out a loud squeal. "He's *dead*?"

"Ssh." I tiptoed over and cast a furtive glance toward the main store. Robbie was in the window, straightening one of the displays, snapping his fingers in time to the music. Even though he probably couldn't hear our conversation over the Four Seasons' rendition of "Walk Like a Man," I wasn't about to take any chances. I walked over and closed the storeroom door. "Josh was trying to keep it quiet so it wouldn't put a damper on the festivities. I'm afraid, though, that the news might have leaked out somehow."

Olivia rubbed at her forehead. "Well, believe me, it's possible. I'm sure Quentin Watson knows all about it—oh, golly!" Her eyes widened. "Is that why you asked me when I'd seen him? You think—you think Quentin might have—"

I held up both hands. "I'm not speculating on anything at this point," I said. "I only know I found the body around three, and he didn't seem to be dead very long. And that's not all." I proceeded to fill Olivia in on seeing Rita with Draco, Rita's appearance at the store, and finally what Mae had said about seeing Rita following Draco. "I saw Josh go inside Sweet Perks with Rita. I wonder if Mae might have said something to him."

"Mae does love to gossip," Olivia agreed. "And she knows all about Rita's history with Draco. Knowing her, she'd feel it her duty to report what she saw to the police."

"Rita insists that she only saw Draco once, so one of them isn't telling the truth, and I'm afraid it's Rita," I admitted. "I could tell she wasn't being completely honest with me."

"Oh, no," Olivia cried. "You can't really think Rita killed him, do you, Shell? I mean, I know Rita has a temper, but *murder?*"

"You have to admit, she really, really had it in for Draco."

"True, but she's not the only one." Olivia shook her head firmly. "I don't know why she denied seeing him a second time, but you'll never make me believe Rita's capable of killing anyone."

"I don't want to believe it either," I admitted. "I'd rather concentrate on other suspects."

"Like Quentin Watson?"

"I was thinking more along the lines of Adrian Arnold."

"The parrot guy? Why him?"

"I saw him and Draco arguing in the alley yesterday, and my mother witnessed an incident between them earlier today." I repeated what had transpired with the parrot, ending with, "I did see a paper clutched in Draco's hand that looked like one of Honey Belle's fortunes. It was the ace of spades."

Olivia's eyes widened. "Oh, no. You think that Arnold rigged it so that Draco got that for his fortune?"

"Let me just say that it wouldn't surprise me. And if that were the case, well, it could indicate premeditation. There's some connection between the two of them. Whether or not that connection is strong enough to lead to murder is something I can't answer." I glanced at my watch. "Gary went out to his house to see what he could find out. He should have been back by now."

As if on cue, the back door opened and Gary walked in. Before he could say a word, I grabbed his arm and pulled him over to the desk. "Was Arnold home? What did you find out?"

"Gee, Shell. Give me a second, will ya?" He scratched absently behind one ear. "When I got to his house, I didn't see his car. I went up to the door and knocked, no answer. The front door was locked, so I walked around back. The van he uses to transport his birds was there, but that sedan of his was missing. So then I went and checked out the shed where he keeps the birds. That was open, and all the birds were there, except Honey Belle, and Captain Snaggle, of course."

"Great," I said. "So he deserted his birds."

"We don't know that for a fact," Gary said. "I drove about a mile down the road to the nearest house and asked if they knew anything. The woman, Mrs. Jenkins, said Adrian had told her about appearing at our event, and said he might have to go somewhere afterward. He didn't know how long he'd be, but he'd call her if he needed her to look after his birds. She didn't get a call, so she assumed he'd be back later tonight." He paused to peer closely at me. "Is something wrong, Shell? You've got that look on your face."

"Look?"

"Yeah, you know, the look you always get when something's up. So . . . what is it?"

"Well—" I expelled a long breath. "Johnny Draco's dead."

Gary's jaw dropped. "What!"

I filled him in on the recent happenings, ending with, "I'll bet something precious that Adrian's important appointment had something to do with Draco."

Gary shook his head. "So what do you think? They got into a fight, Adrian killed him and took off?"

"You have to admit it makes sense," I shot back.

"You're making a lot of assumptions, Shell. Just because he's not home right now doesn't mean he's skipped town. I know you don't like him, and you're suspicious because of the returned fee, but maybe the guy was just trying to do the right thing."

I let out a snort. "I think Arnold's idea of the right thing would differ a good bit from mine."

Olivia rose. "Well, kids, I'd like to stay while you two thrash this around but I've got to get over to the studio and make sure all the costumes and props have been returned and put back properly. I want to check on that video too. I'll see you later."

Olivia left, and Gary turned to me. "Okay, something else is on your mind. Spill it."

I put my hand on his chest and gave him a light shove so that he fell backward into the chair Olivia just vacated. "Get comfortable," I told him. "It's a long story, and most of it isn't pretty."

Gary listened while I related the afternoon's events. When I'd finished, he leaned back and laced his hands behind his neck. "Okay, I guess I can understand why you're so hot to place blame on Arnold," he said at last. "But I have to tell you, it doesn't look too good for Rita either."

"No," I agreed, "it doesn't. But I can't picture her as a murderer. I'd rather give that honor to Adrian Arnold. Or one of Draco's other victims. I saw someone else follow him this morning. It wasn't Arnold, because it was around the time he came in to sign his contract. And I know it wasn't Rita. So that leaves who? Stanley Sheer, maybe? Quentin? Krissa Tidwell? Lester Babcock? Anyone else out of the dozen or so people Draco swindled?"

Gary stroked his chin. "Here's something else to consider," he said. Maybe Draco's murder isn't even connected to what happened here five years ago. Who knows, maybe he pulled a similar scam on others during all this time."

I tapped my index finger against my chin. "I never thought of that."

"Well, think about it. Maybe he scammed the wrong person, and maybe that's why he came back here. That person could have followed him here seeking revenge. Think about it. The guy was obviously trying to disguise himself. Maybe the people he supposedly swindled in Fox Hollow aren't the only ones he was hiding from."

"Maybe," I said grudgingly. I had to admit Gary's theory did make sense. But if that were true, the suspect pool had just widened considerably. Who knew how many there might be?

Gary reached out and gave my shoulder a pat. "Not to worry, Shell. Your boyfriend's on the job. I'm sure Joshy will do a very thorough investigation. Now, what say we table this for the moment and help Robbie with the cleanup. The kid did a great job today, didn't he?"

"Yes, and so did Janine and Sunny. At the risk of patting myself on the back, I think I did pretty good on staff selection. I'm glad I decided not to open tomorrow. They deserve a day off."

"That's the spirit. Concentrate on what's really important. Once we're done, maybe we can grab a quick bite over at Bottoms Up. I think we've earned it."

I gave him a look of mock horror. "Have you forgotten we have a guest? I doubt the Bottoms Up Tavern would be Mother's cup of tea."

"Oh, sheesh!" Gary slapped his forehead with his palm. "You're probably right. So where is Clarissa, anyway? Out taking in the sights of Fox Hollow?"

"I sent her home to take a nap. Big surprise, she was getting on my nerves."

"Swell." His face morphed into a worried expression. "You don't think she'll want me to cook tonight, do you?"

I reached out and lightly touched his cheek. "Gary, I doubt she'll want you to cook any night. No, we'll get take-out, but let's get it from the Captain's Club or a more upscale place. You can cook to impress my mother tomorrow night."

• • •

By six o'clock the grand opening area had been cleaned up and most of the stores were shut down. A few were still open, Sweet Perks being one of them. "Think we have time for a quick latte before we hit the Captain's Club?" Gary asked after we'd said good night to Robbie. "I could use a caffeine jolt, especially if I have to face Clarissa."

I chuckled. "Sure. Knowing my mother, she probably took a long, hot bath before settling in for forty winks, so we should be good for another hour at least."

There was a good crowd inside the fragrant little café, and I saw Rita's niece Jodie behind the register, taking orders. Gary went and got a table at the rear of the store and I got in line. When it was my turn I ordered lattes for both Gary and myself. Jodie's face lit up when she recognized me.

"Shell, great to see you. Sorry I couldn't get over to your store today. It's been a nuthouse here all day, between inside and the booth outside. I promise to visit you next week, though. McAllister needs a new bowl." McAllister was Jodie's gray and black tabby.

"No problem. My shelves got picked pretty clean, but I think there are still some nice bowls left. Come around Monday." I glanced around the store. "Is Rita here?"

Jodie shook her head. "She's been in and out all day. Between you and me . . ." She leaned over the counter and lowered her voice. "She's got something on her mind. I know she's upset over Johnny Draco coming back to town."

Apparently news of Draco's death wasn't common knowledge yet. "I know," I said. "I spoke to her earlier."

"Can't say as I blame her. Both she and Uncle Wesley lost a good chunk of money to that man. Uncle Wesley isn't too thrilled at the prospect of Draco's being back either. I heard him tell Aunt Rita more than once to calm down, that the guy wasn't worth getting upset over."

"Your uncle was here today?" I knew that Wesley Sakowski, who suffered with crippling arthritis, seldom made an appearance at the store. I was a bit surprised that Rita hadn't mentioned the fact her husband had been here today—then again, when I'd seen her, she'd had other things on her mind.

Jodie nodded. "Yeah, he came around ten, and he left a little while ago. Aunt Rita was surprised to see him too. I don't think she expected him to come, but I think it was good he was here, although he didn't seem to be able to calm Aunt Rita down like he usually does. I tell you, Shell, I've never seen her upset like this. It's like she's, oh, I don't know. Possessed?"

Jodie hadn't mentioned anything about Josh's visit to Sweet Perks and I was debating whether or not to bring the subject up. It was possible Rita had conducted the interview in her back room rather than the café proper, so as not to call any undue attention. In the end I decided that discretion was the better part of valor. Jodie rang up the lattes, and I asked her to have Rita give me a call when she came back. "No matter how late it is," I told Jodie.

I brought the steaming cups over to the table. Gary was hunched over, fiddling with his phone, and he didn't glance up until I'd pushed his cup in front of him. "Nothing on Watson's social media page about the you know what yet," he said in a low tone. "No online bulletins from the *Fox Hollow Gazette* either."

I slid into the chair opposite. "That's probably a good thing."

"Right. I'm astonished our local newshound hasn't glommed onto the story yet, though." Gary took a sip of his latte.

"To be honest? I am too. Rita's not here," I added. "I was hoping she would be. I'm dying to know what went down with Josh."

Gary leaned back. "You know, Rita seems pretty strong to me. I've seen her lifting heavy sacks of flour."

"Yes, she is pretty strong," I agreed. "As much as I hate to admit it, she could have jammed that instrument down Draco's windpipe."

Gary drummed his fingers on the table. "So she had motive, and she's strong enough to have used the means. The police could argue that Rita could have gone across the street, killed Draco and been back in minutes. As far as they're concerned, they've got their man—or woman."

"Therein lies the problem. You and I know that once they home in on a worthy suspect, they tend to overlook other possibilities. We know there are plenty of others with equally strong motives, I'm sure. What kills it for Rita is Mae's eyewitness report. We need to find that other person who was tailing Draco this morning."

"Ah, the one you can't describe because you couldn't see him or her clearly. And just how do you propose to do that?"

Before I could think of an appropriate answer, my phone buzzed in my pocket, signaling an incoming text. I pulled it out, hoping it might be Rita, but instead I saw my mother's name pop up, along with a message: *Crishell, get home now!!!!!!!!!! The police are here and want to question us!!!!!!!!!!!!!!!!!!!*

Ten

A black and white police cruiser was parked in front of my house when we arrived. Everything seemed serene, but I knew better. I looked over my shoulder at Gary. "Ready?" I asked.

He made a shooing motion with his hand. "You go on in."

I made a face at him. "Chicken. Don't worry, my mother won't bite you. She's got bigger fish to fry right now."

Gary chuckled. "As much as I'd enjoy watching an interchange between your mother and Joshy, I think my time might be better spent picking up dinner. After this experience your mother's certain to be famished. Besides, it's a golden opportunity for me to pick up some brownie points."

I couldn't argue that.

Loud meows sounded from the backseat, reminding me of the other two passengers. "They can come with me," Gary said as I hesitated. "No sense springing both them and the police on Clarissa." He stole a glance at the cats. "I think maybe we can rustle up some nice cod for the two of you, what do you think?"

Both Purrday and Kahlua gave loud meows of assent. Purrday's tongue darted out and licked at his lips.

I blew Gary an air kiss. "You know, sometimes you're really not so bad."

"That's what I keep telling you. Give Joshy my best."

I stuck my tongue out at him and slammed the car door. He and the cats roared off, and I squared my shoulders and took a deep breath. Time to venture into the lion's den.

I let myself in the front door and immediately heard voices coming from the parlor. "I understand fully what you want," I heard my mother say. "And I told you I'd prefer to wait to say anything until my daughter gets here." Another pause, and then my mother said in a stiff tone, "I also believe I told you I prefer to be called Ms. McMillan."

Uh-oh. I swallowed and hurried into the parlor, not certain of just what I'd find. I didn't see Josh, and my mother was seated on the couch. I noted that she'd changed out of her earlier outfit and now wore silk printed pajamas under a matching silk kimono. Her eyes lit up when she saw me and she waved an arm in my direction. "Crishell, thank *God*. Where on earth have you been?"

"This is your daughter, I assume?" said a feminine voice.

I turned to see a woman standing in front of the fireplace. She was tall, maybe only an inch shorter than Josh, and she had on flats. She appeared to be lean and well-muscled, with thick black hair, dark eyes and a flawless olive complexion. She was dressed in jeans, a pale blue shirt and a leather jacket. The slight bulge at her left indicated she might have something under there, most likely a gun. I walked over to her and extended my hand. "Yes. I'm Shell McMillan."

The woman shook my hand briefly and then said, "I'm Detective Amy Riser. Detective Bloodgood's been delayed, so I'm going to start taking your statements." She nodded toward my mother. "I'm afraid your mother got a bit upset."

My mother sniffed loudly. "Wouldn't you, if the police showed up on your doorstep without any warning and said they needed to question you regarding a possible homicide?" She jumped up and threw her arms wide. "And while we're on the subject, who died anyway?"

Riser cocked her brow and said in an even tone, "First off, ma'am, I didn't say I needed to question you. I said I needed to take your statement."

My mother scowled. "It's the same thing."

"Actually, it's not."

As my mother stuck out her lower lip in a pout, I looked from one to the other. Amy Riser seemed to be a no-nonsense individual who cut to the chase, the total opposite of my mother. I groaned inwardly. This wasn't going to be pretty.

Riser eased her lanky frame onto the love seat opposite the sofa. She reached into her jacket pocket, pulled out a small notebook and pen, then looked directly at my mother. "All I need to know, ma'am, is just exactly what you witnessed today outside of Urban Tails."

My mother fiddled with the edge of her kimono and didn't even look at the detective. "What I witnessed?" She looked at me and spread her arms out wide. "What does that even mean?"

Amy inclined her head toward me. "Your daughter, here, told Detective Bloodgood that you witnessed an altercation between the deceased and another man. We just need a few details concerning that."

"Oh, you want my *observations*." My mother angled her head toward me. "Thank you for this, Crishell," she murmured under her breath. Then she crossed her arms over her chest and glared at the detective. "Okay, you mean the man with the parrot and the man who had on that ridiculous hoodie and sunglasses. Which one is dead?"

She'd directed the question toward Detective Riser, but I answered. "The man in the hoodie. Since you heard them arguing, the detective just needs some details."

My mother's eyes narrowed. "Details? Why? Is the parrot man a suspect in this man's murder?"

"The police have to investigate every possible avenue, Mother."

My mother frowned, then barked out a short laugh. "To be honest, I would have figured it to be the other way around."

Riser looked up sharply. "Oh? And why do you say that?"

"It was obvious that the parrot man was deliberately trying to get under the other's skin, but the man wearing the sunglasses was the angrier of the two. He came right out and called the man and the bird frauds."

"He did? And how did the other man react?" asked Riser.

Thus encouraged, my mother launched into a vivid description of the argument between Johnny Draco and Arnold, punctuating it with dramatic hand gestures. Riser's expression didn't change, but I could tell from the muscle twitching in her lower jaw that she was more than a little irritated at my mother's flamboyant manner. Honestly, I would have been too if I weren't used to it by now. Midway through her dissertation the doorbell rang, and I excused myself (thankfully) to answer it. Josh stood on the porch. "Sorry, but something came up," he said. "Amy volunteered to come over and start taking your statements."

I couldn't suppress a chuckle. "I bet she wished she'd waited for you."

"Why?" He looked at me searchingly. "That wasn't a problem, was it?"

I swung the door wide and motioned for him to enter. "Not for *me*," I said. "My mother's feathers got a bit ruffled, though. She's used to a bit more notice before receiving guests—and unfortunately, that includes the police. Plus, I'm pretty sure Detective Riser interrupted her beauty sleep."

Josh let out a soft chuckle. "Somehow I think Riser can handle her. She seems pretty tough."

"I'd have to agree with that assessment. Come on in."

I motioned for him to follow me and we headed back to the parlor. Amy's head was bent over her notebook, but my mother glanced up. Her eyes lit up as she caught sight of Josh. "Don't tell me," she said as Josh approached her. "You have to be Detective Bloodgood."

"Yes." He took her proffered hand. "And you must be Mrs. McMillan."

Amy glanced up from her notes. "She prefers to be called *Ms.* McMillan," she said pointedly.

My mother ignored Riser and looked straight into Josh's eyes. "*You* can call me Clarissa," she fairly purred at him. "Being called Mrs. just reminds me of my marriage, and of the husband who left me." She paused and swiped at her eyes. "It's very traumatic for me. You seem to be a sensitive man. Surely you understand."

Amy Riser coughed lightly. She looked as if she were having a hard time keeping from rolling her eyes. Josh slid a glance my way that plainly said, *How do I answer that?* I shrugged. Finally he reached out and patted her hand. "I'm sorry, Ms.—I mean, Clarissa. I imagine it must have been hard on you."

"Yes, it has. Extremely," my mother said. Her gaze swept over Josh, and she moved a bit closer to him. "Well, I can certainly see why my daughter didn't mind being your number-one murder suspect."

I felt my cheeks flame, and I saw Detective Riser shoot me a curious glance. "Mother!"

"Oh, Crishell, really." My mother made a tsking sound in her throat. "Detective Bloodgood knows I meant that as a compliment." She looked up at him almost adoringly, and I blinked. Did she just bat her eyelashes at him? I swallowed, determined not to make a scene. I'd apologize to Josh later—and have a little chat with my mother, too.

Detective Riser rose and cleared her throat, breaking the uneasy silence. She flipped to a page in her notebook. "One last thing. Ms. McMillan, you're positive Adrian Arnold told the man he had a fortune just for him?"

"His exact words." My mother's carefully coiffed head bobbed up and down. Her gaze slid from Amy to Josh. "I have an excellent memory. It comes from years of learning lines, many of them from difficult Shakespearean plays."

"Hm. And this all happened around one o'clock this afternoon?"

"Around then. It might have been a tad earlier." She smiled apologetically at Josh and extended her wrist. "My watch hasn't been keeping good time. I've been meaning to get it fixed."

I looked at Detective Riser. "I watched the parrot tell a teenaged girl's fortune. That was around twelve thirty, and I didn't see either Draco or my mother there, so I'd guess this all happened closer to one."

"Yes," my mother cut in. "That's what I said. One o'clock. A tad means a few minutes, so the earliest is probably five of."

"Thank you," Riser said curtly. I had the impression she was fighting hard again to keep from rolling her eyes. She snapped her notebook shut, totally ignored my mother and turned to Josh. "I think I've got all we need. Do you want me to hang around?"

Josh shook his head. "No, you can go back to the office and type up that report. And file Quigley's too while you're at it."

My ears perked up at that tidbit. Amy nodded curtly to us. "I can show myself out," she announced. Once she'd gone, I grabbed Josh's arm. "Quigley? As in Reynard Quigley, the county coroner?"

Josh let out a breath. "Yes. But you know very well I can't discuss the details of an ongoing case with you."

"Not even the time of death or the method?" I cried. "After all, I found the body, for goodness sakes. That should entitle me to *some* information."

I'd forgotten my mother was standing right in back of Josh until I heard her horrified gasp. "What's that? *You* found the body?" she cried, pointing a manicured nail at me.

Ay, caramba. Here we go! I turned to her. "Actually, your grandcats found it after you left the back door open and they escaped. I was just trying to capture them."

My mother took a step back, turned her hand inward to point at her breast. "So your finding another dead body is somehow *my* fault?" She shook her head. "Crishell, I can't say that I approve of this new hobby of yours. At least you're not suspected of killing this one." She paused and slid Josh a look. "She's not, is she?"

"Of course not, Mother," I said before Josh could answer. "I had no reason to kill Johnny Draco, unlike other people."

My mother's eyes widened. "So you do think the parrot man might have had something to do with it," she cried. She fastened Josh with a wide-eyed stare. "Do you think that as well, Detective Bloodgood? Is that why my statement was so vital?"

Josh's eyebrow lifted, but before he could say anything else, a shadow loomed in the parlor doorway. "Oh, sorry. Am I interrupting?" Gary asked. He didn't wait for an answer and added, "I've got three Cuban spiced pork dinners with sofrito rice just waiting to be devoured." His lips drooped slightly as he looked at Josh. "Sorry, Joshy, I didn't realize you'd still be here. If you'd like to join us, I'm sure we can stretch the dinners. The Captain's Club always gives you enough for an army."

"What a marvelous idea," my mother said. Her eyes sparkled as she looked up at Josh and laid her hand on his arm. "Do stay, Detective. It will give us a chance to get better acquainted."

I saw the side of Josh's neck redden slightly, but he said politely, "As tempting as that offer is, I'm afraid that as soon as I get Shell's statement, I've got to get back to the station."

My mother's face fell. She withdrew her hand from Josh's arm and dropped it at her side. "Oh. Well, some other time perhaps."

Gary stepped forward and laid his hand on my mother's shoulder. "Clarissa, why don't you join me in the kitchen while the detective talks to Shell. I've got a new mojito recipe I'm dying to try out."

My mother hesitated, then nodded. "Sounds divine." She extended her hand to Josh. "Lovely to meet you at last, Detective. Don't be a stranger. Do drop by anytime—hopefully not on business."

Josh smiled politely as he shook my mother's hand. She looked vaguely disappointed as she swept from the room. Gary grinned, shot me a wink, and followed her.

I turned to Josh. "Sorry about that. My mother has never been known for her subtlety."

He reached up to brush an errant lock of hair from his forehead. "If I didn't know better, Shell, I'd think your mother was flirting with me."

I grinned at his obvious discomfiture. "She *was* flirting with you, Josh. She's always done that. It's as embarrassing now as it was in high school. I used to meet my dates on the sly to avoid scenes like this. It's gotten worse since my father left. She wants to think she's still attractive, I guess."

"Well, she absolutely still is attractive. It's easy to see where you got your good looks from." He chuckled. "She's been retired for a while, right?"

"Fifteen years now."

"Personally, I think she misses acting, or at least the attention she got from being in the limelight."

"You could be right," I said. "It was hard for her to give it up, but roles for women in their late fifties are few and far between. I think she figured she'd rather get out while she was still on top." I reached out and squeezed his hand. "I'm sorry if she made you uncomfortable."

"Don't worry about it." He gave my arm a squeeze and gestured toward the sofa. "We'd better get started, though."

I sat on the sofa, Josh next to me. No sooner had he pulled out his notebook than Purrday and Kahlua materialized out of nowhere. Purrday squatted at my feet while Kahlua hopped onto the top of the couch behind my head and stretched out full length. Josh laughed. "Where did they come from?"

"Who knows? Cats are great at hiding, and these two are masters of the art. No doubt they were in the kitchen, but now they've escaped to get away from Mother." Both cats looked up at that remark, and I could swear Purrday's head inclined in a nod.

Josh flipped open his notebook, and once again I recounted the events leading up to my finding of the body. This time, though, I added in the altercation that I'd witnessed between Draco and Arnold in the alley. I did not, however, mention the similar incident between Draco and Rita. I ended by saying, "It's just a hunch, but I think there could be more going on between Draco and Arnold. Buck seemed to think that Arnold might have been in investments before going into the parrot training business."

"I'll definitely check that out." Josh slid his notebook back into his pocket. "Okay, we'll get that typed up. You and your mother could come down to the station to sign them, but I'm betting it will be easier on everyone if either I or Detective Riser drop them off here."

Josh started to rise, but I laid a hand on his arm. "Not so fast," I said. "You didn't answer my earlier question. And don't tell me you can't discuss details, because I happen to know those are the types of details that you can share, and someone from your office probably already has with members of the press."

"Fine," Josh said. "Quigley's preliminary examination estimates the time of death as somewhere between two and three fifteen this afternoon."

I gasped. "I knew he hadn't been dead long," I cried. "Was Quigley able to ascertain how Draco died?"

"Yes. His windpipe was crushed, ostensibly from having that instrument rammed down his throat. You're positive you didn't see anyone else hanging around the dry goods store when you went in after the cats?"

"No, no one." I paused and then decided to bite the bullet. "I saw you and Rita going into Sweet Perks earlier. Mae Barker told you she saw Rita following

Draco, didn't she?"

Josh's eyes narrowed. "Actually, no. I haven't spoken to Mae. Now, though, I guess I'd better get a statement from her too."

I frowned. "It wasn't Mae?"

"No. And that's all I can say. I've said too much already." He snapped the notebook shut and slid it into his pocket. "I've got to get back to the station. I'm sure that Quentin Watson and his minions are sniffing around, and I don't want to leave Riser alone for too long." He paused. "One last thing. I'd appreciate it if you could keep what you saw on that paper clenched in Draco's hand quiet, at least for now."

I nodded. I knew the police never liked to reveal every detail at a crime scene. I wondered if Watson knew that detail. I made a motion of mashing my lips together and throwing away the key. "No one will hear it from me."

"Good." He leaned over and gave me a peck on the cheek. "Good night, Shell. I'm sorry your grand opening day had such a lousy ending."

"It was more of a lousy ending for Johnny Draco than for me, but I get what you mean."

Once the door had closed behind Josh I leaned against it. Purrday ambled in from the parlor and squatted at my feet. He looked up at me with his one good eye. "Merow," he said.

"I agree, it doesn't look good for Rita," I said. "And if things weren't bad enough, it appears someone else besides Mae saw Rita following Draco."

"Merow," said Purrday. I wasn't sure if the cat was agreeing with me or not. He ambled off in the direction of the kitchen.

"Rita's strong enough to have jammed that instrument down Draco's throat, particularly if she was in a rage," I murmured. "She's got a temper, I've seen it. But was she mad enough to kill? It sure sounded that way the other night. It doesn't help that she denies following Draco, either, especially now that it seems at least two people saw her."

I hated to admit it but if I were in Josh's shoes, Rita would be at the top of my list. I had the very bad feeling that the only way to get Rita out of heading Josh's suspect list was to find a better one.

But who?

And as I pondered that question, I heard my mother's horrified shriek from the depths of the kitchen.

"Crishell! Is this Tillie's cat? Good Lord, he's only got *one eye!*"

Eleven

Sundays I liked to sleep in, usually with Kahlua and Purrday curled up next to me. I'd get up around ten and read the Sunday paper in my pj's with my morning cup of java. This Sunday, however, was different. I felt a heaviness in my chest and awoke to find a one-eyed white cat sprawled there, his flat face pressed close to mine. Kahlua wasn't curled up in her usual spot against my hip but lay on the pillow next to mine. Her paw shot out, batted insistently at my cheek.

"Hey, guys," I said sleepily. "Remember, today is Sunday. It's considered a day of rest."

Both cats looked at me, then let out loud meows.

I sighed. "You're right. How can I sleep after what happened yesterday, knowing that Rita could probably be arrested at any moment."

A glance at the alarm clock on the nightstand told me that it was a few minutes past seven. I sat up, dislodging Purrday from his position, threw back my comforter and slid my feet into the gray mules by the bed. I pulled on my robe and went into the bathroom, where I washed my face and brushed my teeth. I went back into my bedroom and looked longingly at the gray sweats thrown over the back of a chair. I rummaged in my closet, finally deciding on a pair of black denim jeans with a slightly flared leg and a crisp white button-down shirt. I sat down at my dressing table and ran a comb through my blonde curls, then tied them back with a black ribbon. After a quick mental debate, I dusted a smidge of pink blush across my cheekbones and applied a peachy pink gloss to my lips. I doubted my mother was up yet, but if she should be, I didn't want to hear a lecture on how I should always come to the breakfast table looking presentable. I'd had my fill of that growing up.

I went down to the kitchen, where it appeared I was the first one up for a change. That honor usually went to Gary. Kahlua and Purrday wound around my ankles making little kitty noises. "I know, I know," I told them. "Starvation is imminent. We can't have that, now, can we?"

Kahlua let out a loud yowl and Purrday pawed at my leg. I bent down, gave them each a scratch behind their ears, then went to get the kibble. While they hunkered down to their breakfast, I put the kettle on for tea and then went outside to get the Sunday paper. I hoped Quentin Watson might have devoted the front page to the Urban Tails grand opening festivities; I should have known better. Front page above the fold was devoted to Johnny Draco's untimely demise. I winced at the headline: *Former Fox Hollow Resident, Suspected of Fraud, Found Dead. Foul Play Suspected.* I took it over to the counter, spread it out and read the story standing up:

> Fox Hollow—John Ira Draco, 42, was found dead yesterday at a property he was considering leasing.
>
> Homicide Detective Joshua Bloodgood responded to a distress call from a citizen who found the body shortly after three p.m. While the exact cause of death has not yet been determined, foul play is suspected. According to Detective Bloodgood, no suspects have yet been identified, but the department is pursuing a number of leads.
>
> John Draco left Fox Hollow under a cloud of suspicion five years ago when an investment he made for several clients went belly up, causing the investors to lose substantial sums of money. At the time Draco protested his innocence, claiming to have also lost funds in the transaction; however, the speed with which he left town afterward caused many to speculate on the validity of the transaction and whether or not Draco might have swindled his clients out of their life savings.
>
> Draco steadfastly maintained his innocence in the affair right up until the time of his demise. He has no surviving relatives. Memorial services have not been planned.

The kettle whistled. I went and fixed myself a cup of tea, then went back to the counter and thumbed through the rest of the paper. At least Watson hadn't forgotten entirely about the grand opening. Page five was devoted entirely to anecdotes about the festivities, and the centerfold had at least twenty black-and-white and color shots of the various booths and entertainers. In the top corner was a publicity headshot of me that had been taken a few years ago at the height of *Spy Anyone*'s popularity. I had on a sequined top and my hair was teased in what was supposed to be a "sexy" style. Underneath the photo was the caption: *Shell McMillan, formerly Shell Marlowe, new proprietor of Urban Tails Pet Shop.* Square in the middle was a large photo of the outside of the shop. I saw a crowd clustered around the left side of the building. Watson, or someone from the paper, must have taken the photo at the time Arnold and Honey Belle were performing.

"Penny for your thoughts?"

Gary leaned his head on my shoulder. "They aren't worth that much," I said. I turned my head and looked him up and down. He still had his pj's on—the ones with the penguins he'd had on the other night. His cowlick was sticking up, and I caught a whiff of morning breath as he passed me. I swatted at the air with one hand. "Don't you brush your teeth before breakfast?"

"Of course. Right now my electric toothbrush is recharging." He ran his finger across the front of his teeth, then paused and looked at me, one eyebrow raised. "You're dressed pretty early. Is there something I should know?"

"I just didn't feel like hearing a lecture from you know who."

"Oh. Gotcha." He glanced at his own attire, shrugged and went over to the Keurig, selected a pod, and set a mug on the drip tray. "I'll be more awake once I have some java. Man, can your mother talk!"

"You didn't have to stay up with her." My mother had seemed especially energized after dinner, or maybe it had been the three cups of espresso she downed with the tiramisu Gary had brought for dessert. Whatever, she'd regaled us with several stories about her last Shakespearean tour. I'd finally begged a headache and escaped to bed.

"Well, you bugged out and she looked so disappointed I didn't have the heart to bail," he grumbled. He picked up the mug, coffee steaming, got some milk out of the fridge and then added two packets of Sweet'N Low. He stirred the coffee slowly, shaking his head. "I never thought I'd say this, but her tales were actually interesting. I never knew she was so chummy with Sir John Gielgud and Michael Caine."

I shook my head. "You do know that ninety percent of what she told you was exaggerated, right? And Michael Caine never came over for dinner while I was living there. I greatly doubt she ever had lunch with Richard Burton. They might have been in the same restaurant, but same table? Doubtful."

Gary took a sip of the coffee. "Oh, sure, I knew that. I've got to admit, she's got a flair for storytelling, though."

"She ought to. She's been spinning tales long enough." I harrumphed. "It used to irritate the heck out of my father. Sometimes I think that's the main reason he left and married Darlene."

Gary nodded toward the paper. "Onto better topics. Did we make the front page, or were we usurped?"

I pushed the paper in front of him. "Draco got dibs on the front-page honors," I said. "At least Watson didn't mention I found the body."

"That's a relief." Gary opened the paper to the centerfold and spread it out on the counter. He tapped at the photo of Urban Tails. "This is a great photo. It would be nice to get a copy and hang it in the store to commemorate the opening."

I looked at the photo again. "Yes, I guess it would," I said. "I wonder who took it. There are no photo credits listed."

"Quentin Watson, I assume. I saw him with his trusty Nikon several times, and he was snapping away."

"True, but there are a lot of photos here. He couldn't have been everywhere at once," I murmured. I leaned closer, studying the photo. It was a bit grainy, but I was pretty certain I could make out Adrian Arnold and Honey Belle in the corner. I tapped Gary on the shoulder. "Get me the magnifying glass out of that cabinet, please?" I asked.

"Magnifying glass? Are we channeling Nancy Drew this morning?"

"Just get it."

"Okay, okay." He went over to the cabinet and a few seconds later handed me the magnifying glass. I put the glass over the photo and leaned forward. I tapped excitedly at the edge of the photo. "See right there! That figure on the fringe of the crowd on the far side. Doesn't that look like Johnny Draco?"

Gary took the glass from me and leaned over the paper. Finally he looked up. "It's hard to tell, the images are pretty grainy. It looks like a dude in a hooded sweatshirt, that much I'll say."

He handed me back the magnifying glass and I peered at the photo more closely. "This must have been taken shortly before the parrot told Draco's fortune. And look here." I tapped at the edge of the photo with my nail. "See this person, just off to the left of the figure we think is Draco? See how the head is turned slightly, like he's staring straight at him."

Gary looked over my shoulder. "Maybe," he said at last. "It's hard to tell from that angle. Hard to tell, too, whether it's a man or a woman."

"You're right," I said as I bent over for a closer look. "It looks like they've got something on their head—a cap or a hood, maybe? Plus, they've got sunglasses on." I turned my attention to some of the other photos. One of Olivia and her girls standing off to the side of the gazebo caught my eye. I reached out and grabbed Gary's arm. "Look here," I directed. "There are two figures standing behind the pagoda."

Gary squinted at the photo. "Hm, it's hard to tell. Looks more like two blobs to me."

"I know. I wish these images were clearer, better yet, time-stamped. It looks like one of them has on a black sweatshirt like Draco's, but I can't be sure." I pushed the paper back and glanced at the clock on the wall. "Do you think Quentin is at the newspaper office now?"

Gary frowned. "It is Sunday, but then again, we're talking about Watson, who has no life. So, yeah, he probably is. Why?"

I was already reaching for my tote bag. "Like you said, it would be nice to have a print of that photo to frame and hang in the shop."

Gary looked at me searchingly. "Uh-huh. And maybe get some prints of other photos for a montage, I suppose? And while you're framing them, check their time stamps?"

I reached out and clapped him on the shoulder. "I hadn't thought about that, but that's a great idea."

Gary rolled his eyes at me, then gulped down his coffee. "Wait. It'll only take me a few minutes to get dressed. I'll go with you."

I thrust out my hand and pushed lightly at his chest. "Oh, no. You've got to be here when Mother wakes up. Someone's got to be here to fix her morning coffee and breakfast."

"Breakfast! Darn! I was going to get the fixings for sweet potato waffles, but I forgot. Do you think she'll be satisfied with eggs Benedict?" He started opening and closing cabinet doors and drawers like a madman.

"Serve a little champagne with it and she'll never know the difference," I said. "Or a nice Chardonnay. Whatever works. Oh, and a rose on her plate is always a nice touch." Then I stuffed my phone into my bag and sailed out the back door, leaving Gary still grumbling and slamming drawers.

• • •

The buildings in Fox Hollow all had the same look: just old enough without managing to look run-down. The *Fox Hollow Gazette*'s offices were housed in a two-story white structure across the street from City Hall. The carved wooden sign out front was shaped like a bell and said in big block letters, *Fox Hollow Gazette*. Underneath, in smaller letters, *Quentin Watson, Editor in Chief*. Parking was usually at a premium, but thankfully today was Sunday. People were either sleeping in or at church. I was lucky enough to find a space right in front of the newspaper office and I backed my convertible into it. As I hurried up the short walkway, I noticed a black Lincoln SUV parked in the driveway. The license plate read QWNEWSMAN. Quentin's car, no doubt. Well, good. At least he was inside.

I pushed open the front door and found myself in a foyer-type waiting area. To my left a cozy arrangement had been set up: a sofa and love seat, a low coffee table covered with magazines. A rack with copies of the most recent edition of the *Gazette* was just to the left of the sofa. Built-in wall shelves held rows of books, and binders which I imagined contained back issues of the paper. To the right was a long table that held various snacks and pitchers of iced tea, covered in plastic wrap. Rows of gaily colored plastic cups sat next to the pitcher.

I moved farther down the hall and saw what had to be the reception desk, a wooden circular affair with a computer and stacks of papers on either side. I was surprised to find a woman seated there. She had black hair that had been teased into a giant pouf and very heavy makeup. I figured her to be late fifties, early sixties. She glanced up, saw me, and gave me a smile that was obviously forced. I noticed she had a smudge of red lipstick on her front tooth.

"Good morning," she said. "Might I help you?"

"Yes, I'm looking for Quentin Watson."

The smile faltered just a bit. "Do you have an appointment?"

"No, but I know he's here. Could you tell him Shell McMillan would like to see him?"

"Wait just one moment."

The woman got up and teetered uncertainly around the desk. I noticed that she had on five-inch bright yellow heels, a match to the yellow suit she had on. She walked slowly down the hall, and I leaned against the desk. I glanced over at the work area. A nameplate that said *June Regan* was pushed off to one side. A steno pad lay open next to the computer, and I recognized Watson's distinctive scrawling handwriting. I started to look away, when one name leaped out at me: Rita Sakowski.

I gave a quick glance around and then walked around the desk. A Word program was on the screen. It appeared that June had been in the midst of typing up some notes for Quentin when I'd interrupted. I quickly read the few lines she'd typed up.

- Draco leasing building. Why? What did he hope to gain?
- Draco visibly upset over fortune told at grand opening. Arnold appeared to be goading him. Any connection?
- Rita Sakowski seen by two people following Draco. How close to TOD did she follow him?

I read the last item and did a double take. Two people saw Rita, as Josh had indirectly confirmed. I knew Mae was one, but who was the other? There were a few more lines but the tap-tapping of heels alerted me that June was returning. I'd barely walked back around the desk when she appeared. She motioned down the long hall. "He said he can give you five minutes. It's the office all the way at the end."

"Thanks."

I walked swiftly down the hall. The door at the end was partly ajar. A gold placard on it read *Q. Watson, Editor in Chief.* I pushed it all the way open and went inside. Watson sat behind a massive cherrywood desk. The top of the desk was cluttered with newspapers and lined pads. There was a laptop on the desk, and Quentin closed it as I walked in. He leaned back in the leather chair and laced his hands behind his neck.

"Well, well, Shell McMillan. And what can I do for you on this fine Sunday? Don't tell me you're displeased with the article on your store?"

"Not at all, Quentin. The article was perfect."

"Good." Watson leaned back further in the chair. His eyes, behind his wire-rimmed glasses, were sharp and calculating. "For a minute there I thought you were a bit resentful that Johnny Draco got the top spot."

"Hardly. I know murder trumps grand opening in the news world."

"I'm glad you're so understanding." He leaned forward, picked up a pencil from the cup on the desk, and tapped the eraser end against the blotter. "I don't suppose you happened to see that little altercation between Draco and Arnold yesterday?"

"No, but I heard about it."

"Too bad you didn't see it. I interviewed quite a few people and got a different viewpoint each time. I need someone's account I can rely on."

I wondered if Quentin might consider my mother someone reliable. I wasn't about to venture that information, though. "I think it's possible the two men knew each other," I said. I repeated what Buck had told me. "If Buck's information is correct, it's possible they might have worked together at some point," I finished.

Quentin arched an eyebrow. "Together, as in that scam?"

"It's something to consider."

"Hm, maybe so." He stared off into space for a few seconds, then shook his head. "I wouldn't rule it out, although I'm not sure that means Arnold is the one who killed him. I'll do some digging." He eyed me. "So you haven't yet said the reason for this little visit."

"I just wanted to tell you how much I liked the article, and the photo montage. I especially like the one of my storefront."

Watson leaned forward, rummaged through the piles of paper on his desk and finally grasped the Sunday edition. He opened the paper to the centerfold and ran his finger down the page. "Ah, yes. That is a good shot. Bill took that one. He took most of the ones on the east side. I was covering the entertainment events at the gazebo area."

"Bill?"

"Bill West. He's a freelance photographer I sometimes use. I have to say, he did a darn good job."

"Yes, he did. I was wondering if it would be possible to get an eight-by-ten print of that photo. I thought it might be nice to frame and display in the pet shop, as sort of a commemoration of the event."

"Splendid idea. I'll see that you get a copy." He gestured toward the piles of paper on his desk. "I trust you can wait a few days. It's doubtful I'll get to it today."

"Oh, I don't want to put you to any trouble," I said. "If you'll just give me a number for Mr. West, I can contact him myself."

Watson shook his head. "No can do. West's a very private person. As a matter of fact, I've never even met him. I hired him on one of those freelance sites, and we do all our corresponding via email. And before you ask, no, I can't give you his email addy. He'd flip if I did and I'd never get to use him again, and the guy's good. I told you, I'll take care of it." He leaned back again and laced his fingers in front of him. "Was there anything else?"

"Yes. Since by your own admission you know everything that goes on, maybe you know who saw Rita Sakowski following Johnny Draco?"

Watson didn't even bat an eyelash. He looked amused, actually. He waggled his finger at me. "Ah, ah, I knew you couldn't resist playing detective."

"Rita's my friend, and you've known her longer than I have. You know that she's not capable of murder."

Watson took off his glasses, rubbed the lenses against the sleeve of his shirt, then plopped them back on his nose before he answered. "Anyone who's pushed far enough could be capable of murder. You know that as well as I do. I mean, look at Mazie Madison, right?"

I shook my head stubbornly. "Not Rita. She hasn't got it in her."

Watson's laugh boomed out. "Are you really that naive, Shell? You weren't living here when Draco took our money and pulled his little disappearing act. Rita was madder than a wet hen. I think if he'd have been in front of her at that moment, she'd have choked the life out of him."

"I'm sure she did feel that way, then. It's been five years. She's had plenty of time to cool down."

"Except she hadn't, had she? She walked out on your dinner when you told her you were considering hiring Draco. She was plenty mad then."

I balled my hand into a fist and placed it on my hip. "More hurt than mad, and how did you know about that?"

He spread his hands and gave me a maddening grin. "I have eyes and ears all over Fox Hollow. You'd be surprised at what I know."

As usual, his smug attitude infuriated me. "If you know so much, then maybe you know who killed Johnny Draco."

"Well, I can't know everything now, can I?" He leaned forward and started to fiddle with the pile of papers closest to him. "I can tell you this: Rita might well have been the last person to see him alive."

"Even so, that doesn't mean she killed him."

"Then why did she lie to the police? She said she only saw Draco once yesterday. She saw him at least one other time, maybe more. The people who saw her are both reliable sources who wouldn't lie."

I wrinkled my nose at him "No offense, Quentin, but I don't know if I'd consider Mae Barker a particularly reliable source."

Both Quentin's eyebrows winged skyward. He picked up a pencil and tapped it against his blotter. "Mae Barker? That busybody? What's she got to do with anything?"

"You know darn well. She's one of your two sources."

Quentin paused in his tapping, then started to laugh. "Well, well, Nancy Drew. Someone's been doing some snooping, I see. Look, when it comes to reliable sources, Mae Barker doesn't even come close. I wouldn't put stock in anything she said." Then he added, "Look, I know you like Rita. Most everyone does. Heck, I like her. She makes great jelly doughnuts. Draco had a lot of enemies, a lot of people who weren't happy to see him back here. Maybe Rita's not the one who killed him. But if it does turn out she is the one who did the deed, heck, I'll be first in line to shake her hand. I might even get her a medal."

"Great. So I take it Mae's not a source?"

He shot me a maddening smile, then gestured toward his laptop. "Now, if that was all you wanted, Shell, I'm really very busy. Newsmen never sleep, you know. I'll make sure you get that picture."

I was tempted to press him on who else had seen Rita, but I figured it would do no good. Quentin could be tighter than a clam when it suited him. "Thanks," I murmured. I walked to the door, paused. "You said that Draco had a lot of enemies. Would you include yourself in that group?"

Watson steepled his fingers underneath his chin. "Is that your oh so subtle way of asking me if I killed Draco?" He barked out a laugh. "Sorry, Shell. I have an ironclad alibi. Ask your boyfriend if you don't believe me. Now, if you'll excuse me, I really do have work to do."

Watson turned his back to me and I left without a backward glance. Back out on the street, I exhaled a deep breath. Quentin was as irritating and uncooperative as ever. I fully intended to ask Josh about his "ironclad alibi" first chance I got. What really bothered me were the two other "very reliable" witnesses to Rita's tailing of Draco. It was apparent Mae wasn't one of them, so who were they?

I went over to my car, plopped in the driver's seat, and pulled out my phone. It was time to google some information on William West. If I could convince him to share the photos he'd taken with me, maybe I could get some insight as to who really killed Johnny Draco.

Twelve

"Honestly, who in this day and age doesn't have a phone? Or a Facebook or an Instagram page? Especially a photographer."

Olivia regarded me over the steaming rim of her coffee cup. I'd spent a good twenty minutes trying to track down William, or Bill, West on every social media outlet I could think of, to no avail. I had finally decided to take my frustrations out on a latte and headed over to Sweet Perks, where I saw Olivia waiting on line. She'd waved me over to join her and now we were seated at a rear table by the window, enjoying caramel vanilla lattes as I recounted my morning encounter with Quentin and subsequent search for William West. "I turned up plenty of William Wests," I groused. "But none of them seem to be the one I want."

"Maybe Watson didn't give you his real name?" Olivia suggested. "He said the guy's a private person, right? And Quentin knows you. Maybe he figured you'd try to find this guy on your own."

I sighed. What Olivia said made perfect sense, unfortunately. "Darn him," I said. "That's probably exactly what he did. So now I've got to figure something else out." I reached up and gave one of my blonde locks a sharp tug. "This is so frustrating."

"Personally, I'd be interested in the other two people who saw Rita," said Olivia. "Quentin said they were reliable, and if Josh is putting stock in their accounts then it must be true."

"It could have been anyone," I said. "The big question is, what time did they see her following him? Mae claims she saw her tailing him shortly before three, which is more in line with the time of death. If these other people saw her with him earlier, well, it could go to establish motive, maybe, but wouldn't necessarily make her the last person to see Draco alive, as Watson was so quick to point out."

"He was pretty quick on the trigger with that," Olivia said. She took another sip of her latte. "So, where's Gary this morning? I thought maybe he'd have accompanied you to the news office."

"He wanted to, but I told him he'd better stick around in case Mother woke up. She'd have a fit if she found out he and I went sleuthing and left her all alone in the house."

"But she's not alone," Olivia said with a mischievous grin. "Kahlua and Purrday are there with her."

"Oy." I rolled my eyes. "Mother got her first good look at Purrday last night. You should have heard her when she saw he only had one eye."

"Did you tell her he lost it in a noble battle?"

"Actually I whipped out his pedigree papers. Thank God Aunt Tillie kept them. She softened a bit once she saw his lineage. She even bent down and told him that he was a fine-looking fellow, even with one eye, then told me I should go out and get him an eyepatch."

"Oh, no!" Olivia burst into a wave of giggles. "Can you see Purrday actually wearing something like that?"

"No, but I wouldn't put it past Mother to actually order one from somewhere."

"How are she and Gary getting along?"

"Better than I expected. They bonded over mojitos last night." I chuckled at the memory. "I think as long as he can keep plying her with liquor, the two of them will be able to tolerate each other."

"Why does she dislike him so?"

"Lots of reasons. For one, she thinks he has a crush on me."

Olivia's eyes popped and I saw the corners of her lips start to droop down. "Really?"

"She's wrong, of course," I hastened to assure my friend. "I explained to her that our relationship is more brother and sister, but she can't see it."

Olivia let out a breath. "I could see where she'd get that idea. You two had real chemistry on the show."

I waggled a finger at her. "Chalk that up to good acting, especially on my part. Also, she thinks he hogged more than his share of the press for *Spy Anyone*. I tried to tell her that it wasn't as important to me as it was to him, but she couldn't see it back then. She still doesn't." I ran my finger idly around the rim of my coffee cup. "She refuses to give up the notion this is just a phase I'm going through, that eventually I'll see the light and want to go back to Hollywood and acting. She still keeps in touch with my agent."

"She just cares about you, Shell. She probably just wants you to be happy."

"An acting career made her happy. It didn't make me happy. Reopening Aunt Tillie's store, catering to the needs of dogs and cats—that makes me happy."

"And so does solving mysteries," Olivia remarked.

"I always did like puzzles," I admitted. "And I have to admit, Draco's death is a real one."

"You have to admit, there are lots of suspects."

"Maybe more than originally thought. Gary brought up a good point. Maybe Draco made more enemies during the time he was away. Maybe that disguise wasn't only for the benefit of the people he swindled here." I pushed away the napkin I'd been fiddling with. "I wish Rita were working today. I'd like to ask her more about what Johnny told her about his time away."

"He could have lied to her about that, you know."

"I know. *Aah!*" I tugged at a curl, then pulled it forward to examine the ends. "I need a trim—oh, wait!"

"What?" Olivia demanded as I grew silent. "You had a thought. What?"

"Stanley Sheer. When I saw Rita go into the alley yesterday morning he popped up behind me. Maybe he saw Rita with Draco and he's one of the two who snitched!"

"Maybe. Taking it a step further, maybe he's the one who killed Draco and he's pointing the finger at Rita to take suspicion away from him."

"That's why I like you," I said, pushing back my chair. "We think alike. I'm going to take a quick walk over to the barbershop. Care to join me?"

Olivia pushed back her own chair. "Miss a chance to watch you in action? Never."

• • •

The barbershop was only a five-minute walk from Sweet Perks, and I knew that Stanley opened on Sundays from ten to two. When we got there, however, the lights were all off and there was a *Closed* sign on the door.

"Darn," I said. "He takes his first Sunday off in months today? Why? I wonder."

"Shell. I thought that was you."

Olivia and I both turned to regard the short, stout man with the head of bushy black hair who stood behind us. "Garrett Knute," I said. "Fancy seeing you here."

Knute was a retired accountant who now served on the Fox Hollow Museum's board of directors. He flashed me a quick smile and reached up to run a hand through his thick mass of hair. "I was going to stop in for a trim, but then I remembered Stanley mentioning at the festivities yesterday that he was going to visit his aunt over in Closter today. It's her birthday."

"How nice," I murmured. And convenient.

"I'm sorry I didn't get a chance to talk to you yesterday," he said.

"You came to the grand opening?"

He nodded. "Of course. Wouldn't miss it. There was such a crowd at your store, though, I didn't go in. I plan to rectify that during the week, though. Anyway, I saw Stanley over by his booth and we chatted for a while. He was pretty upset about Johnny Draco being back in town."

"Yes, I understand he was among those supposedly swindled by the man."

Knute sniffed. "No supposedly about it. Man was guilty as sin. And he got away with it. I never had a good feeling about that man. Stanley urged me to invest as well, but I refused. I told him not to do it, but did he listen? Anyway, Stanley mentioned that he was going to try and speak to Draco, ask him point-blank what he'd done with the money and demand he make restitution. I told him not to waste his time."

Olivia and I exchanged a glance, then I said, "And did he ever manage to speak to Draco?"

Knute shook his head. "I don't know. I had to leave and I didn't see Stanley after that. And now Draco's dead."

"Mr. Knute, what time did you speak with Stanley?"

He put a finger to his lips. "Hm, good question. I'm not really a clock watcher. It could have been one or even two or as late as three." He glanced at his watch. "Well, I've got to get going. It was lovely to see you Shell, Olivia. I'll be sure to drop by later in the week." He started to turn away, then paused. "Oh, by the way, Shell, I heard your mother, Clarissa McMillan, is in town."

Good news travels fast. "Yes, she is. She came in for the opening."

He shifted his weight from one foot to the other. "Ah, well, I hope she stays for a while. Such a talented actress. I'd love to meet her."

Knute walked off and Olivia poked me in the ribs. "Was I imagining it, or was he actually blushing when he asked about your mother?"

"You didn't imagine it," I said with a chuckle. "He's obviously a fan. I wish he could have remembered what time he spoke with Sheer, though," I added. "If it was before three, there would have been time for Stanley to find Draco, maybe even do the deed. The barber definitely bears further investigation.

Why don't you stop by later on? We can discuss the case further, and you can stay for dinner. I think Gary's making some sort of steak dish."

"Sounds tempting." Olivia glanced at her watch. "Right now, though, I've got to get going. My cousin asked me to stop by and give my opinion on a new dress she bought."

I pulled a face. "I should get home too. Mother is probably up by now, and I feel guilty leaving Gary to deal with her alone."

"Well, chin up. She should be leaving soon, right? She was only coming in for the grand opening, right?"

"Why, I'm not sure," I said. It was true. My mother had said she was coming in for the festivities, but she hadn't said one word about just when she'd be departing Fox Hollow.

• • •

I arrived back home to find my mother sipping coffee at the breakfast table and perusing the Sunday paper. Gary was busy loading dishes into the dishwasher and looked up as I entered. "Hey, Shell. Are you hungry? I can make some more waffles. There's plenty of batter left."

My mother looked up from the paper. "Yes, dear. Gary made waffles with a pecan syrup and lovely strawberries and bananas on top. Quite simple but enjoyable. I told him that perhaps he'd missed his calling and I offered to give Gordon Ramsey a call."

I arched a brow. "Gordon Ramsey? Really?"

Gary paused, dish in hand, and remarked, "Your mother thinks that I could be an excellent gourmet chef, with the proper training."

"Ah, well, I understand Gordon Ramsey's pretty busy with all his television shows, so I doubt he'd have time to take you on as his protégé right now," I remarked. "But I hear Rosie's Diner here in town is looking for a good short-order cook."

"Oh, Crishell. Gary's cooking is far superior to diner food." My mother paused a moment and peered at me. "Oh. That was a joke, right?"

"Right, Mother. We all appreciate Gary's cooking here, especially his two biggest fans." I gestured toward the corner, where Purrday and Kahlua were curled up together, fast asleep. I shed my jacket and slid into the chair opposite my mother. "So, Mother. I didn't get much of a chance to ask you yesterday.

When were you planning on returning to LA? Not that I'm trying to get rid of you," I added quickly, "but if you should need a ride to the airport . . ."

"I'm perfectly capable of calling an Uber car should I need a ride, Crishell," my mother said without looking up from the paper. "Didn't I tell you? My friend's jet isn't available for the return trip until next Saturday."

Next Saturday? "So you'll be staying the entire week?"

Now she looked up and fixed me with a stare. "Yes, dear. Is that a problem? If you recall, I did ask you for the name of a good hotel."

"Uh, n-no, not a problem," I stammered. "I was just surprised, that's all. I didn't expect you'd, ah, want to stick around any longer than you had to."

My mother closed the paper and pushed it off to one side. "Really, Crishell. If I weren't going to visit with you for a decent length of time I wouldn't have made the trip. I had nothing pressing going on this week, so I thought it would be the perfect time for me to drop in and see just exactly what you've gotten yourself into." She paused. "I have to say, that little shop of yours seems to have garnered quite a bit of interest. Did you see the page with quotes from the people? Apparently the shop was a big favorite when Tillie managed it, and they are expecting great things from you."

I smiled. "I know, and I have no intention of letting them down."

"Hm. Well, perhaps I'll come down one day and just, you know, casually observe what all the fuss is about. One person mentions handmade sweaters for cats and dogs in your shop?"

"Yes, and that reminds me. I have to call Kathleen Power and get more in. Robbie can pick them up one day on his way in."

My mother leaned back in her chair. "So, since you're not open on Sundays—"

"Not yet," I cut in. "If business demands it, I plan on opening on Sundays from noon to four."

"Well, while you're still closed, what do you usually do?"

"The past few weeks we've been working to set up the store," Gary said. He'd poured himself a cup of coffee from the Keurig and now leaned against the island counter. "Before that, we were working on solving Amelia's murder."

My mother gave a visible shudder. "Like I said yesterday, Crishell, I'm not particularly fond of this hobby of yours, but I think I've been pretty tolerant. So maybe, for today, you can indulge me in one of mine."

"Okay. But I don't believe there are any good plays around here, and the movie theater here specializes in oldies. This week it's Jimmy Cagney. A double feature, *Public Enemy* and *Yankee Doodle*."

My mother waved her hand. "I'm not talking about the theater or entertainment. I'm talking about shopping." She pulled the paper back in front of her, thumbed to a small ad and pushed it in front of me. "That store sells antiques, and you know how I love them. I used to go with Tillie and you all the time, remember?"

I fought the urge to roll my eyes. "You used to go twice a year with us, Mother. Sometimes less if you were in a play."

"Whatever. I still enjoyed it. I've become quite a collector in my old age. Why, just last month I found a Wedgwood Jasperware coffee pot at a quaint little shop in Orange. I got it for a steal, too. Twenty bucks. Do you think this store might have anything like that? Or maybe some antique glassware?"

I looked at the ad. It was for Secondhand Sue's. "Josh's sister owns this," I murmured.

My mother clapped her hands. "That dreamy detective's sister is the owner? Well, what do you know? Talk about a small world."

I looked at my mother. "You do know that Josh probably won't be there, right?"

"Oh, for goodness sakes, of course I know that. Anyway, I see her store is open today, and what's even better, she's having a sale. So what do you say?"

I remembered Josh's remark about Sue arriving back at the shop right around three. Could Sue have seen something? She'd certainly be considered a reliable witness by Josh, despite the fact Draco had also cheated her.

Well, I'd struck out with Stanley Sheer. Maybe I'd have better luck with Sue. "Sure, why not, Mother. Grab your purse and credit card and let's go."

Thirteen

While my mother went upstairs to change into something "appropriate for antiquing," I filled Gary in on my interview with Quentin, then asked him if he wanted to accompany us.

"I'd sooner drive a pitchfork through my eye," he said.

"It could be worse," I informed him. "She could have wanted to go clothes shopping."

He made a face. "My time is better spent here. I'll call Kathleen Power and put an order in for more sweaters. I'll give Arnold a ring as well. Then I'll do a bit of Internet surfing, see if I have any better luck finding anything out about Arnold's financial career and your mysterious photographer."

"Sounds like a good plan. Maybe concentrate more on the photographer right now. Olivia thinks Watson probably gave me a phony name."

"Yeah, well, I'm sure other people must have seen him snapping photos. I'll make some inquiries. It's a small town, after all. Someone is bound to know just who this guy is. While I'm at it, I'll call some of the hotels in the surrounding towns. Draco had to have stayed somewhere, right?"

"Right. Unless he did as Mae suggested, and pitched a tent in the woods."

I left Gary to pick up the slack on the detective work and a half hour later I pulled my convertible into a parking space across the street from Secondhand Sue's. The shop was housed in a redbrick building, situated a few doors up from Urban Tails, just where the street curved. Sue's was a cross between an antique shop and a secondhand store. She sold some antiques, but concentrated mainly on furniture and housewares that had been repurposed from their original use. She'd mentioned to me that she wanted to expand her inventory to include some more upscale items, but right now was strapped for cash. I'd toyed with the idea of becoming a silent partner, but for right now that idea was on hold until Urban Tails was running smoothly. I was pretty well acquainted with Sue's inventory and I doubted my mother would find anything to suit her here, but, after all, pleasing her wasn't my main purpose for coming.

The bell above the shop door tinkled as we entered. It was more like squeezing in, actually. I was amazed at how many people were crammed into the tiny store. Apparently my mother wasn't the only one who loved a good sale. Her sharp gaze wandered around the showroom the second she stepped inside. "Ooh," she squealed, startling me. In all my thirty-eight years, I'd never heard my mother squeal. She gave my arm a squeeze and pointed to a shelf in the far corner loaded with glasses of varying colors, shapes and sizes. "That looks like Italian Murano stemware," she said. "I'm going to check it out."

"Be careful," I cautioned her. "You break it, you buy it." I pointed to a sign near the shelf that displayed that very axiom. My mother gave an impatient wave and hurried over to the display. I went in the other direction, straight to the main counter. Sue's assistant, Iris, was just ringing up a Batman lunch box for a stout woman. "Your nephew will love it," I heard her say. "And you're so lucky to get it on sale today."

"I know," the woman gushed. "You have some wonderful things here. I'll be back, count on it."

Iris made change, then slid the lunch box into a plastic bag that had "Secondhand Sue's" emblazoned on it in bright pink letters. The woman made a few more comments about how wonderful the store was and then left. I wasted no time in sidling over to the counter. "Hey, Iris."

Iris's face lit up when she saw me. "Hey, Shell. That was a great opening party yesterday. And Urban Tails looks great! I love your window display!"

"Thanks," I said, "I'll be sure to tell Gary. He did most of the work."

"I bought Chester one of those catnip chew toys. He loves it." Chester was Iris's Maine coon. "I wanted to get him one of Kathleen's sweaters, but the larger ones were all gone by the time I got over there."

"We should be getting more in," I assured her. "As a matter of fact, Gary should be ordering them as we speak. I'll save you one, if you want."

"Oh, would you? I'd really like a blue-and-white-striped one, but I'll take anything."

I glanced around the shop. "Busy for a Sunday."

Her grin stretched from ear to ear. "Yeah, it's the sale. We were busy yesterday too, but not like this. Sue and I were happy when Josh finally came over to spell us."

"Yes, he said he got down here later than intended."

"Yeah, it was after one, I think. No biggie. We said we wouldn't take too long, but you know how that goes. I guess I got back around two thirty. I told him to go, but we were so slammed he said he'd stay till Sue got back."

"Uh, yeah, he did mention that when I saw him."

Iris clapped a hand across her mouth. "Oh, that's right. Sue said you found the body. That must have been pretty gruesome, huh?"

"It wasn't pleasant," I said. "I could definitely have thought of more fun things to do. My mother—that's her over by the stemware display—accidentally let the cats out and I trailed them to the dry goods store."

"That's your mom, huh?" Iris peered in my mother's direction. "She's pretty, like you. And so young-looking."

"If she ends up buying anything, be sure to tell her that. She thrives on compliments like that." I glanced around. "Is Sue here today?"

"Of course. She wouldn't miss the big sale day. Our Keurig's broken, so she went to get us some coffee. She should be back any sec—oh, here she is now."

The door opened and Sue, bearing a foam tray with two coffee cups, hurried through the door. "Rita wasn't there, so I had to explain to Crystal just what we wanted—well, hi!" Sue's face brightened as she caught sight of me. "Shell! What a nice surprise. I was hoping to run into you—sorry, if I'd known you were going to be here, I'd have gotten you a mocha java latte too."

"No problem, I had a latte earlier with Olivia. My mother wanted to come down and check out your sale."

Sue's grin broadened. "Yes, Josh told me your mother is in town."

"Did he tell you he had to take a statement from her?"

"No!" Sue's eyes widened. "Goodness, what for?"

"She saw Draco and Adrian Arnold having a rather heated exchange during Honey Belle's act yesterday."

Sue pursed her lips. "Adrian Arnold? That jerk?" She shook her head. "What, was Draco making fun of his act and he got hot under the collar? Wouldn't be the first time."

"According to my mother it was the other way around. Draco got mad when he saw his fortune and called Arnold and the bird fakes."

Sue barked out a laugh. "Sounds like someone wasn't pleased with their fortune. I wonder what it said."

I recalled the ace of spades I'd seen in Draco's hand. I was tempted to tell Sue, but I figured Josh's warning about keeping mum on that detail also applied to his sister. I shrugged. "Who knows? It probably wasn't all that bad."

"Say what you want about Arnold, but he does put on a good show with those birds. He did a benefit for my son's school last year. Those parrots were a big hit, although I don't recall fortune-telling being one of their accomplishments."

"So Arnold's lived around here for a while, then?"

Sue put a finger to her lips. "Good question. I'm not really sure. Someone said he moved to Franklin a year or two ago. I guess before that he might have lived in Madison or maybe Hartford."

"Why there?"

"Those towns aren't far from New York City, and he always used to brag his birds were in a few commercials and on TV. He claimed they made an appearance on an episode of *Saturday Night Live*, but no one could ever substantiate that claim."

"Did you ever hear anything about Arnold being involved in investments or banking as a career?"

Sue's nose wrinkled. "You mean before he got into bird training? No, can't say as I have."

The crowd had thinned out a bit. I saw Iris walk over to my mother, who apparently had a question about the stemware she clutched possessively in one hand. I figured this was as good a time as any, so I leaned over the counter and said to Sue, "You know Josh talked to Rita Sakowski yesterday."

Sue looked up, and surprise was evident in her expression. "He did?"

I nodded. "Rita was pretty upset when she learned Draco was back in town."

"So were a lot of people. I started to tell you the story, but then we got interrupted."

"I got filled in later on, by Olivia and Ron Webb and Rita herself. She was definitely angry with Draco, but I don't think she was mad enough to kill him."

"Kill him!" Sue gasped. A stricken look came over her face. "Oh, no. Is that what my brother thinks?"

"It's hard to tell just what Josh thinks, because as you know, he's a stickler for rules and won't discuss the case," I said. "But I think Rita's pretty high up on the suspect list. It seems several people have come forward and told Josh they saw Rita trailing Draco."

Sue bit down hard on her lower lip, then glanced quickly around the store. She crooked her finger at me. "Come with me," she said. I followed her to a small curtained alcove at the rear of the store. Sue parted the curtain and motioned for me to follow her. I found myself in a postage stamp-sized room. There was a small desk in the center, the top cluttered with papers and magazines. A small file cabinet was off to the left, and there were two well-worn chairs also covered with papers. Sue pulled the curtain shut, then cleared both chairs off and motioned for me to sit.

"My office," she said apologetically. "Sorry about the mess, but this is the only place where we can talk without worrying about someone interrupting." She tilted her head to one side and reached up to rub absently at one eyebrow. "I probably shouldn't say anything, but Josh didn't tell me I couldn't. I'm one of the 'several people' you just mentioned. I told Josh that I saw Rita follow Draco. But it wasn't like I planned to squeal on her or anything. It was perfectly innocent."

I could see Sue was upset so I scooted to the edge of the chair and laid my hand lightly on her arm. "I'm sure it was, honey. What happened?"

Sue let out a deep breath. "Josh was kinda late getting here, and Iris and I were psyched to visit Urban Tails and take in some of the sights. I promised Josh I wouldn't be long because I knew he wanted to get over to your store and see you. I went to Urban Tails first, but honestly, Shell, it was so crowded I couldn't get in the door. I decided to walk around, then circle back and try again before I came back here. I went and saw the mime—he was really good—and then I got a chocolate chip ice cream cone at Nelson's Flavors stand. It was starting to get pretty late, about a quarter to three, so I figured I'd better get back. I took the shortcut behind the alley, you know the one I mean. Anyway, I was just exiting and about to cross the street over to my shop when out of the corner of my eye, I caught a glimpse of someone wearing a black hoodie. And about twenty feet behind that person I saw Rita. She had this expression on her face—I don't know."

"Did she look angry?"

Sue shook her head. "No. Actually I thought she looked worried. Anyway, both of them disappeared around the corner near the dry goods store. I came right back to the store. Josh had just finished waiting on a customer. All I said was, 'Gee, I thought I saw Rita over by the dry goods store. It looked like she was following somebody in a hoodie.' And Josh said, 'Really? I wonder why?' Then a few minutes later he got the call from you and he took off."

"I see. And what time exactly was that? Do you remember?"

"It had to be between two forty-five and three, closer to three I think."

I drummed my fingers on the arms of my chair. "The coroner placed the time of Draco's death at somewhere between two and three fifteen. Your sighting does place her in the vicinity at the time of the murder."

Sue pressed her lips together in a slight grimace. "If I'd only known, I would never have said anything. I'd never hurt Rita."

I squeezed her hand. "I know that, Sue. It's best you told Josh, though."

She ran a hand through her hair. "I suppose you're right. I'm sure Rita had a perfectly logical explanation for her actions. The person Rita was following might not have been Draco, anyway."

"Mae Barker claims she saw Rita right around the same time as you did. She was pretty convinced it was Draco."

"Oh, Mae!" Sue's lips twigged downward. "She's such a gossip. She's Rita's neighbor, and she always acts so friendly toward her, but I've always thought she was a bit jealous of Rita. Envied her the store and her success, and her marriage. Maybe Mae just made up the whole thing."

"I'd like to believe that, but I got the sense that she was telling the truth."

"Swell." Sue got up and ran her hands down the sides of her pants. "It has to be a mistake, Shell. Rita hated Johnny Draco, but she'd never kill him. I know that."

"I agree completely." I glanced at my watch. "I suppose I'd better get back out there and rescue Iris. I'm sure my mother has talked her ear off about antique glassware by now."

I reached for the curtain, but Sue caught my arm. Her gaze was troubled as she looked at me. "My brother can't let himself get sidetracked, Shell. He has to find the real killer. You'll help him stay on course, won't you? I know he values your opinion."

I somehow doubted that applied to murder cases, but I raised my chin and gave Sue a smile. "I'll do my best."

"Your best is generally pretty good." She swiped at her brow with the back of her hand. "I'm feeling better already. With you on the job, Rita's as good as cleared."

I smiled, wishing I shared Sue's optimism. I figured Sue was one of the two people Quentin Watson had mentioned as seeing Rita with Draco. Now I needed to track down the other informant. But who could it be?

Fourteen

Gary was sitting at the table reading the paper when my mother and I returned from our afternoon shopping excursion. We'd barely gotten through the door when he tossed the paper aside and jumped up to relieve my mother of her burden. "Looks like your little venture into the Fox Hollow merchant district was successful," he remarked.

"It was extremely successful. I found the most beautiful glassware, Murano stemware, to be exact." Her eyebrows bounced as she added, "I got it for a steal, let me tell you."

Gary set her two large brown bags carefully on the counter then turned to relieve me of my burden. "Geez, these are even heavier," he proclaimed, pretending to stagger under the weight. "Don't tell me you bought glassware too?"

"I didn't buy a thing," I said loftily. "Those are mother's. She bought the entire shelf. Three dozen glasses."

Both his eyebrows lifted. "Did I hear right? Three *dozen*?"

I spread my hands. "Once she got going, there was no stopping her."

"It's true. I know it seems a bit extravagant but I simply couldn't resist," my mother gushed. "They are genuine Italian Murano Venetian Green Art glasses. Let me show you." She reached into one bag and pulled out a hunk of tissue paper. She sat down on one of the stools beside the counter and unwrapped the glass carefully, then held it up for inspection. "See how beautiful? And it's in near perfect condition."

I'm not much on kitchen items, let alone antique kitchen items, but I had to admit the stemware was beautiful. The goblet was about five inches in height with a twisted stem. It was made of emerald green glass with a gold overlay on which was etched a beautiful butterfly design. They were indeed in excellent condition. There were no chips or cracks as far as I could see.

"A dozen of those for eighty-five dollars is a steal, trust me," my mother told Gary. "I almost felt bad, like I should have offered her more money."

My mother bent her head to examine the glass, and Gary winked at me. "But you didn't."

Her head jerked up and she let out a loud laugh. "Heck, no. I'm no fool."

"They are pretty," I admitted. "Too pretty to drink out of."

The expression on my mother's face was one of abject horror. "I'm not going to drink out of these, Crishell! Are you mad! No, these are going in my display case. I have two vintage Murano bud vases that these will complement nicely."

"You must really like them, to buy three dozen all the same," Gary remarked.

"Oh, they're not all this style. I bought a dozen of these, and a dozen tall stemware glasses in varying colors. I've see the same kind sell for over three hundred in an antique shop in LA. These were only ninety-nine fifty. The rest are a mixed bag. There's a few tall green stemware, a few blue optic, and a couple Millefiori wine goblets." She rubbed her hands together. "All in all, I got about five hundred dollars' worth of stemware for less than two hundred. I'd call that a bargain day, wouldn't you?"

"If you say so. I'm glad your trip was so successful." He turned to me with a meaningful look. "It was, right?"

I knew he wasn't talking about the stemware and nodded. "Oh, yes."

My mother started to gather up her bags. "I'll just take these up to my room, and then I think I'll take a little nap. Shopping, especially successful shopping, has a way of tiring me out. And I'm not as young as I used to be, although that nice salesgirl—Iris, right? She told me that I didn't look a day over forty, can you believe it?"

"You are very attractive, Clarissa," Gary said. "And you always dress so beautifully."

My mother ran her hand down the sides of her lemon-yellow pants and then adjusted the collar of her simple, three-quarter sleeve ivory V-necked top. "Thank you, Gary." She bent to retrieve one bag from the floor, and I gave Gary a sharp poke in the ribs.

"Allow me," he said. He reached out to take one of the bags.

"Be very careful," my mother said. She glanced at me over one shoulder and wagged a finger in the air in a playful gesture. "You break it, you buy it."

No sooner had they disappeared to take the bags to my mother's room than Purrday and Kahlua emerged from underneath the sink. "Oh, ho, let me guess. You heard us coming and hid in there."

Both cats let out loud meows. I gave them some extra kibble as a reward for their good sense and had just seated myself at the table when Gary returned. "I didn't know Clarissa was such an expert on antique glass," he said. "Were you aware Murano glass is made on the Venetian island of Murano? Or that Murano's glassmakers led Europe for centuries in the refining and development of technologies such as crystalline glass?"

"She was going on about that in the car, but I tuned her out. I had other things to think about." I shot him an impish grin. "Don't you wish you could hide from her as easily as the cats? They were under the sink."

He shook his head and eyed the narrow cabinet. "I wish I could fit under there," he said. "Did I mention that glassmaking in Murano originated in eighth-century Rome, under considerable Asian and Muslin influence?"

"No. And while all that is fascinating, to be sure, I'm more interested in how successful your afternoon was."

He eased into the chair opposite mine and laced his fingers behind his neck. "All in all, not bad. I got hold of Kathleen Power. Turns out she has about two dozen sweaters on hand, so I called Robbie and asked him if he could pick them up. He's got a dental appointment tomorrow morning, so he said he'd drop them off here later today."

"That works. Remind me, I have to put one aside for Iris. Now, how about *your* detective work?"

"I'm afraid I was a little less successful in that area," he said with a grimace. "Well, first I tried Arnold's number and got voicemail. I left a message for him to give me a call. Then I checked with the Fox Hollow Inn. It just so happens Lester Babcock's been out of town the past ten days, visiting relatives in California. He only just got back last night, so we can cross him off our list. Then I called several other hotels within a twenty-mile radius. No one named Johnny Draco or Ira Draco registered at any of them."

"I didn't think there would be, although that's not conclusive. He could have used an assumed name."

"I thought of that too, so I also emailed each of them that photo you took. No one recognized him." He chuckled. "Maybe he did pitch a tent in the woods after all. Anyway, next I ran a search on Adrian Arnold. That came up a dead end too. There's absolutely nothing about his ever being involved in banking or investments, just bird and small animal training."

"That's odd. I suppose Buck could have been mistaken. He didn't seem too sure about it." I let out a breath. "How about the photographer?"

"No luck there either. I spent quality time online. There are a ton of William Wests, but none of them photographers from around this area."

"I told you that."

"Never hurts to double-check. Anyway, then I went over to Bottoms Up and checked with a few people there. No one noticed any professional photographer other than Watson snapping away with his Nikon."

"I greatly doubt this guy used an iPhone to take those photos," I said. "They looked professional grade to me."

"Apparently he knows how to blend in with a crowd and not be noticed. Fits in with what Watson told you about him liking his privacy."

"Figures." Suddenly I snapped my fingers. "Wait. Olivia told me that one of the mothers took a video of the dance performance. Maybe he was there, taking photos, and we can spot him in it." I whipped out my phone. "She was going to visit her cousin, but I invited her for dinner later. I'll just ask her if she's gotten the video, and if so, to bring it along." I tapped out a quick text. "Maybe we'll get lucky. Of course, it would help if we knew what this William West looks like."

"Didn't you ask Quentin?"

"He was very vague on the subject. I doubt he even knows himself. He hired the guy on a freelance site and he emails the photos in."

"Pretty mysterious. I suppose if we spot some guy with a Nikon around his neck that isn't Quentin, that's our guy."

"Probably," I agreed. "In the getting lucky category, Sue did admit that she's one of the people who told Josh about seeing Rita. She said that she saw Rita tailing someone in a black hoodie, but she couldn't say positively it was Draco."

"Everyone just assumes it was Draco because he was wearing a black hoodie," mused Gary. "But lots of people had similar garb on."

"Mae Barker swears it was Draco, but she attributes that more to a psychic premonition than observation. Sue says Mae's always been jealous of Rita and could be lying. Now, I know you don't want to hear this, but my money's still on Adrian Arnold having something to do with it. Remember, he left early and no one's seen him since. He'd have had time to do the deed and take off."

"I might buy that theory, except for one thing. He'd have to have had the parrot with him. He wouldn't have had time to bring the bird back home and return in that time frame. I think if Arnold were involved, there would have been some sort of evidence that the bird was there."

"You mean feathers." My brow furrowed as I tried to visualize the crime scene. "I don't recall seeing any," I said at last. "That doesn't mean there weren't any, though. *Aah.*" I grabbed a stray lock of hair and twisted it. "I get the feeling we're missing something important, but I can't figure out what it might be."

Gary put up a hand to massage his temple. "I agree. This puzzle is giving me a headache too. It's worse than Amelia's murder." He paused in his rubbing to shoot me a lopsided grin. "At least you're not the number-one suspect this time out."

"Yeah, thank goodness for small favors. Once was quite enough, thank you very much."

The doorbell rang. Gary looked up. "That's probably Robbie. I'll get it." He jumped up, went out to the foyer and returned a few minutes later, Robbie in tow. The lad had a huge box in his arms. He set it on the kitchen island and smiled at me.

"Hey, Ms. McMillan. I got those sweaters from Ms. Power."

"Thanks, Robbie, I appreciate it. Would you like a cup of coffee? Or some iced tea or lemonade?"

He smacked his lips. "Lemonade would be great, thanks."

"I'm up, I'll get it. Want some, Shell?" Gary asked.

"I think I will." As Gary moved over to the refrigerator, I looked at Robbie. "Yesterday went well," I said. "Did you hear any feedback from any of your friends about it?"

"Oh, sure. Everyone I talked to raved about it. A few of 'em came in the store. Some of them even bought stuff for their pets."

I smiled. "That's good to hear. I never asked, did you manage to get out and take in some of the entertainment on your break?"

"Sure thing. I caught a bit of the parrot act before they split. I thought it was pretty cool, and so did Buster."

Gary came over with a tray on which rested three glasses and a pitcher of lemonade. "Buster?" he asked as he sat down. "That's someone's name?"

Robbie laughed as I poured him a glass of lemonade. "Nah, that's my friend Billy's nickname. When he was little his mom used to cut his hair in one of those Dutch Boy styles, it made him look like Buster Brown on those old shoe ads." He chuckled. "He's sure changed a lot since then. He's older than me, in his early twenties, but now he's got a crew cut and he keeps himself real trim. In his line of work he has to look good."

"What does Buster do?" I asked as I took a sip of lemonade.

"Well, he went to school for photography but he got roped into modeling. He's appeared in some national ads. The latest one was for Jockey underwear." Robbie pulled a face. "He likes to keep a low profile on account of the modeling. You wouldn't believe how some women go nuts when they see him." He shook his head as if the whole idea were insane.

Things were starting to click inside my head, though. Billy. Photography. Low profile. I leaned forward. "What's your friend's name?"

"Well, his professional name is Billy Van Sant. I think his agent dreamed up the last name. Said it sounded romantic." Robbie rolled his eyes. "But he'll always be Billy 'Buster' Weston to me."

I looked at Gary and raised an eyebrow. "His real name is Billy Weston?"

"He likes to be called William Weston. Sometimes, though, he shortens his last name to West, like if he's doing a photography gig. He does that on the side, because as he once told me, his looks aren't gonna last forever."

"He sounds like a smart young man," said Gary. "I heard that Quentin Watson hired someone by that name to take photos of the grand opening. Would that be your friend?"

Robbie hesitated, then nodded. "Yeah. He swore me to secrecy, but I guess it's all right to tell you."

"I saw some of his photos when I went down to the newspaper office today," I said. "They're very good. There was one I especially liked, of the storefront. I wanted to get a copy of it to hang in Urban Tails, and maybe some others. Make a montage. Do you think your friend could get me some copies of the photos he took?"

"I don't see why not, just so long as you promise not to tell anyone who he really is."

"Oh, we won't." I made a crossing motion over my heart, and Gary did the same. "Do you think you could get in touch with him today?" I asked, trying not to sound too eager, but it was hard not to let my face fall at Robbie's next words.

"He's on a plane to Hawaii right now," Robbie said. "He's got a photo shoot the next few days. I think he'll be back Wednesday. I can text him, though."

"Would you? The sooner the better." At Robbie's inquiring look, I added, "I'm sorry to sound so impatient, it's just I can't wait to display that photo. It was *so* good."

Robbie beamed. "Buster sure will love to hear that." He pushed his chair back. "I've got to get going. I'll be in right after my dentist appointment tomorrow."

Gary rose as well. "I'll walk you out, Robbie. I just remembered there are a few things I need to pick up at the market for dinner." He turned to me and closed one eye in a wink. "Your mother was very specific about wanting shitake mushrooms with her steak."

No sooner had Gary and Robbie left than my phone pinged with a text message. I picked it up from the counter and looked at it. *Sorry I won't be able to make it over tonite. My cousin asked me to go to dinner and the movies over in Hastings. Here's the video of the girls' performance for you to enjoy. Let me know how you like it. Tell Gary I want a rain check on dinner!*

I knew Gary would want to watch the video too, but I couldn't wait. I settled back and opened the file. Olivia's girls were in excellent dance form, and the girl who performed the musical number had an especially good voice. As she sang the last stanza of the song, there was a sudden jerky movement, and the video camera swung off to the left.

"Mrs. Fein must have tripped," I murmured, then gasped as a fleeting image caught my eye. I sat stunned for a second, wondering if I'd seen correctly. The clip stopped, and I hit the button to replay it, then fast-forwarded to the part that interested me. When the camera dipped, I froze the frame and stared at the image displayed on the screen.

The image wasn't all that clear, but I could make out two figures standing behind the pagoda. They were standing in approximately the same position as the photograph I'd seen in the paper. One was Draco. There could be no mistaking that shock of flame red hair. It was the other man I wasn't too sure of.

I'd only met him once, but I was almost positive the man with Draco was Rita's husband, Wesley Sakowski.

I set my phone down and sat for a few moments, contemplating what I'd just witnessed. Had that been why Wesley Sakowski, who never came down to Sweet Perks, decided to pay a visit? Had he intended to track down Draco, maybe give him a piece of his mind? Or had Draco contacted Wesley directly for a meeting?

I jumped up and went over to the kitchen counter. I rummaged in the drawer, found a pad of paper and hastily scribbled a note:

Went to check out something. Back before dinner. After a moment I added another line. *Entertain Mother till I get back.*

I propped it up where Gary would be certain to see it, then grabbed my jacket and tote. It was time to pay a little visit to the Sakowskis.

Fifteen

Rita and her husband lived over on the north end of Fox Hollow in what was known as the Mayfair section. The first time I'd gone to Rita's house I'd fallen in love with it. Built to resemble an old-time English cottage, it was set far back from the street, surrounded by a wrought iron fence and beautiful shrubbery. The house boasted a sharply pitched roof, cross gables and bow windows. A stone chimney and a corner turret on the second floor added to its charm. I'd gone to England several years ago and toured Anne Hathaway's cottage. This house could be its twin. The mere sight of it brought back memories of hours spent devouring not only Shakespeare but also of reading books like *Anne of Green Gables* and *Little Women*.

I parked my convertible and gave a quick look around. I didn't see Rita's SUV on the street or in the driveway, but it could have been parked in the garage. The rose and white Chinese lamp Rita had gotten at Secondhand Sue's glowed in the window, a good sign someone might be home. I exited the car and hurried up the short walkway to the porch. I'd just started up the steps when the front door opened and Rita peered out. She opened the door all the way and stood blocking the entrance, hands on her hips. "Shell? This is a surprise. What are you doing here?"

I shot her an apologetic smile. "I'm sorry to barge in on you on a Sunday, Rita, but I really need to talk to you."

Rita glanced over her shoulder. "This really isn't a good time," she said. "Wesley is taking a nap. He had a double treatment yesterday, and it really knocked him out."

I laid a hand on her arm. "Rita, we have to talk. Three people have already said they saw you following Draco not long before he was murdered."

She let out a sharp gasp. "Three people! Who?"

"Let me in and I'll tell you."

Rita hesitated, then stepped aside and motioned for me to enter. I stepped into her brick-floored foyer and waited for her to shut the door, then followed her into the living room. Rita went directly to the chintz sofa opposite the brick fireplace and motioned for me to take a seat in the damask chair directly opposite. Once we were seated she leaned forward and clasped her hands in front of her. "Okay. So who claims to have seen me following Draco? Because whoever it is, is lying."

"First answer a question for me. Is the reason Wesley was at the grand opening because he had a meeting with Draco?"

Rita sat quietly for a few moments, head down, and tugged at the wedding band on the third finger of her left hand. Finally she raised her gaze to meet mine, and I caught the glimmer of unshed tears. "Wesley didn't kill Johnny Draco," she said flatly.

"I didn't say he did. But he did meet with him in the afternoon, while Olivia's girls were putting on their recital."

Rita lowered her gaze again. "Maybe," she muttered.

"No maybes about it. I saw them on a video."

Her head jerked up. "What? Whose video? Where did you see it?" Her face flushed red as she rattled out the questions.

I reached out and laid my hand on her knee. "It was on a video one of the kid's mothers took. Olivia emailed it to me this afternoon. As soon as I saw it, I knew I had to talk to you." I looked her straight in the eye. "You weren't lying when you said you weren't following Johnny Draco. It was Wesley you were following, wasn't it?"

Rita scrubbed a hand across her mouth. She was silent for several seconds before she answered. "Yes," she said in a small voice. Now her hand shot out to cover mine. "He didn't do it, Shell. Wesley didn't kill Draco."

"Why don't you tell me what happened?" I asked in a gentle tone. "Draco got in touch with Wesley, the same as he got in touch with you, didn't he?"

Rita nodded. "Yes," she said. "But I didn't know it until later on." She exhaled a long breath. "Let me start at the beginning.

"Friday night I told Wesley all about Draco coming to your shop and asking for us. Wesley was more curious than mad. Wondered why Draco would bother coming back after all this time, unless maybe he wanted to gloat, to lord it over us how he'd gotten away with everything. Then Draco called me. He said he needed to speak with me in person, there was something he had to tell me. I didn't tell Wesley about the call because I didn't want to get him upset. Little did I know that right after he called me, Draco called Wesley and told him he needed to talk to him in person too."

Rita's tongue darted out, swiped across her lower lip. She looked straight into my eyes. "You know how my meeting with him turned out. He told me that he was as much a victim as the rest of us, that he'd spent the past five years getting his life back in order and now he was ready to return. When he told me he was going to lease the dry goods store and turn it into a deli slash sandwich shop, I saw red."

"So then you smacked him in the kisser and the two of you went your separate ways."

Rita nodded. "What I didn't know then was that he'd made arrangements to meet Wesley over near Krissa Tidwell's shop. I guess he didn't want me to see them talking."

My mind flashed to the figure I'd seen tailing Draco right after his altercation with Rita. Could that have been Wesley? "Go on," I said.

"Well, he met up with Johnny. Johnny told him about leasing the dry goods store, same as he told me. He actually had the nerve to ask Wesley to intercede for him, to try and calm me down and make me see that he had no malicious intent. Can you believe that guy's nerve?"

"And how did Wesley react?"

"He was upset, naturally. He told Johnny that he and I would find a way to block him from opening the store. Johnny said that would be a mistake. Then he got a call and told Wesley that he had to leave."

"But they saw each other again, around one thirty."

Rita leaned back against the cushions and stretched her legs out in front of her. "Wesley was fuming over Johnny wanting to meet with both of us. He wanted to try and talk some sense into him, so he set out to find him. They did meet around one thirty, but it was very brief. Johnny said that he had to go, he had an important meeting with someone, something that could change his life and possibly the lives of other people in Fox Hollow."

I frowned. "What an odd thing to say! What do you suppose he meant?"

Rita shook her head. "I have no idea. We were running low on coffee and goodies for the stand outside, so I was helping with that. Then I looked up and I saw Wesley starting off down the back alley that leads to the dry goods store. His nostrils were flaring, and he had this look in his eyes—well, I dropped what I was doing and went after him. I figured it had something to do with Johnny Draco, and I didn't want Wesley to do something foolish." She ran a hand through her hair. "I got to the end of the alley just where it opens up behind the dry goods store. I didn't see any sign of Wesley or Draco. I just stood there for a few minutes. I didn't know what to do."

"Do you remember what time that happened?"

Her brow puckered. "Around two thirty, give or take a few minutes, I think. Then all of a sudden someone wearing a black hoodie came out the other end of the alley."

"Draco? He was wearing a black hoodie."

"But so was Wesley. He'd put one on earlier when he spilled coffee on his denim jacket." Rita frowned. "This person walked with a sort of shuffling gait, like Wesley does. I was positive it was him. I started after him, and then a light wind sprang up and I got something lodged in my eye. I paused for a few seconds to swipe at it, and I got it out. But by then Wesley—or whoever it was—had gone."

"So you went back to Sweet Perks?"

She nodded. "I went in the side entrance and went straight to my office, went inside, shut the door and just sat there for, oh, I don't know. Ten minutes? Fifteen? No one saw me. Then I went out and started making a fresh batch of muffins."

"And your husband?"

Rita started to chew at her lower lip. "To be honest? I didn't see him until I came back from bringing the fresh muffins outside. That had to be between three fifteen and three thirty. He looked tired. I wanted to ask him where he'd been, but he didn't give me a chance. He said that being out today had exhausted him, and he'd phoned the doctor to see if he could give him another treatment. Our neighbor picked him up and took him around a quarter to four."

My mind was racing. "So if that hooded figure you saw was Wesley, that puts him in the vicinity at the time of the murder."

"If," Rita said, emphasis on the word. "Even if it were Wesley, he didn't kill Draco. My husband isn't capable of murder."

I didn't think so either, but there was something else I had to ask. "How are Wesley's treatments coming, by the way?"

Rita's face brightened for the first time. "Very well. This trial seems to be doing wonders. Plus, the doctor started Wesley on a new series of exercises that seem to have increased the strength in his hands."

I hesitated, then decided to ask. "Enough for him to be able to jam something down someone's windpipe?"

Rita's mouth dropped open. "Why—I don't know. Maybe." We sat in silence for several seconds and then Rita looked me straight in the eye. "Okay, I've told you everything, now it's your turn. Who are these three people who claim to have seen me tailing Draco?"

"One is Sue Bloodgood. She was taking a shortcut and caught a glimpse of a guy in a black hoodie with you not far behind. She said you looked worried."

Rita's lips twisted into a wry smile. "And of course she told her brother."

"For what it's worth, it wasn't intentional. She mentioned it in passing when she got back to her shop, and then a few minutes later I called Josh to report the murder."

"And Josh, excellent detective that he is, put two and two together." She ran a hand through her short crop of hair, making the ends stick out. "Who else?"

"Mae Barker."

I saw the sparks flash in Rita's eyes. "That busybody? It figures."

"Truthfully, I'm not sure if she told Josh or not. She told me that she saw Draco, or at least someone wearing a black hoodie and sunglasses, walking toward the dry goods store. Then she said she saw you a few yards back."

"I guess, from the place her tent was situated, she could have gotten a glimpse into the opening to the back alley. But she can't positively say I was following Draco." She shot me a wry grin. "I can't say I was following Draco, or Wesley either, for that matter. I just don't know."

"Mae seems convinced it was Draco. She said she had a premonition of danger concerning him, and then she saw him swiping at his cheek."

"Wow, it still hurt from the punch I gave him three hours earlier?" Rita shook her head. "Trust me, Mae didn't see anything. Oh, she might have seen me, but as for the rest . . ." Rita shrugged. "She's heard all the gossip about Johnny Draco and wouldn't miss an opportunity to fan the flames, if you know what I mean. Now, you said there were three people. Who's the third?"

I spread my hands. "That I don't know. But I'm working on it. All I know is it's someone considered a reliable source."

"Well, that's definitely not Mae."

I let out a soft chuckle, then sobered. "You know, Rita, you should come clean with Josh."

Rita shook her head stubbornly. "I can't give Wesley an alibi for the time of death, Shell. I don't want them looking at him."

"But you'd rather they looked at you."

Rita's chin jutted out. "I'm in better health than Wesley. I can take it better. Besides, I know I'm innocent."

I laid my hand on her arm. "Secrets have a way of coming out, Rita. It's better if they hear it from you than someone else."

She sighed. "Maybe. Oh, it's all such a mess." She looked at me hopefully. "You're a pretty good detective yourself, Shell. After all, you figured out who killed Amelia. Maybe you can figure out who killed Draco before either Wesley or I are arrested."

"I doubt they'll arrest either of you, Rita. In spite of these so-called witnesses, there's no concrete evidence that either of you did it. Right now it's all circumstantial."

Rita twisted her hands in front of her. "I hope you're right, Shell. But you know as well as I do that once they set their sights on someone . . ."

Her voice trailed off, and I rose. "I think I'd better get going. Gary will kill me if I leave him alone with my mother for too long. Just keep your chin up and try not to worry."

"I'll try, but it's easier said than done."

Rita walked me to the door and watched as I got into my car. I saw the resigned expression on her face and it strengthened my resolve to get to the bottom of this. As I started down the street, I glanced in my rearview mirror and saw a police cruiser pull into the very space I'd just vacated. I pulled over to the side and watched Josh and a grim-faced Amy Riser get out of the cruiser and make their way up Rita's front steps. I noticed Riser had her iPhone in one hand, and I had a feeling Mrs. Fein's video might be the reason for this unexpected visit.

My lips thinned as I pulled away from the curb, and I gripped the steering wheel tightly. It was time to get down to business, and that meant dragging out my trusty whiteboard.

Sixteen

The enticing aroma of garlic and onions smacked me in the face as I let myself in the back door. I spotted Gary instantly. He was hunched over his Le Creuset frying pan at the stove, stirring something that could only be described as absolutely heavenly. Purrday and Kahlua lingered not far away, their noses twitching at the delicious aromas emanating from the pan. Gary looked over at me and then glanced significantly at the kitchen clock. "Shell. How nice of you to join us."

I walked over to the stove and bent over, inhaling deeply. "I think you've outdone yourself this time, Presser," I said. "Your skills are really improving. This smells just as good as anything you could order in Taix or Bouchon."

Gary wiggled his spoon in the air. "Usually flattery can get you anywhere, McMillan, but not today. Not after I had to spend the afternoon with you know who, who kept looking over my shoulder and offering me cooking advice."

I clapped my hand across my mouth to stifle a laugh. "Really? I don't think she's set foot in a kitchen to do any real cooking in years other than heating up take-out. What sort of advice did she offer?"

"Excellent advice, for your information."

Gary and I both looked up at once. My mother had come up silently behind us, no doubt aided by the pricey soft-soled Gucci flats she wore. She eased one slender hip against the kitchen island and leaned over, letting one elbow rest on the counter. "I'll have you know, Crishell, that when you and your brother were young I did a great deal of the cooking."

I tore my gaze away from the frying pan to look at her. "Really? I thought that was what we had Daisy and Monique for. Or was I hallucinating all those times I saw them slaving over the kitchen stove?"

My mother let out a snort. "They cooked—under my supervision. There were times when I couldn't be the perfect little housewife. Someone had to earn a living during the years your father was out of work." She straightened and crossed her arms over her chest. "Have you forgotten that when I was on the Royal Shakespeare Tour in Paris I studied French cuisine with Alain Ducasse?"

"I vaguely remember you talking about spending time with some chef but I was what? Five, six at the time?"

"Oh. Well, my point is, while I might not indulge in the actual act of cooking, I do know my way around a kitchen."

"Of course you do, Mother," I said soothingly. "And I'm sure Gary listened to whatever advice you offered him."

"Well, of course he did," my mother said. She sniffed the air. "Can't you tell?"

"Clarissa here was very disappointed when I told her that we didn't have any Hennessy Paradis on hand to add to the steak Diane, but she did approve of the D'ussé cognac I picked up the other day." Gary pointed to the half-full bottle on the kitchen counter.

"It smells wonderful, and I'm famished," I said. "What time is dinner?"

"About twenty minutes, give or take a few minutes to feed these rascals." Gary inclined his head toward the two cats, who were circling around him. "It's nice to know someone appreciates me."

"You might show some appreciation for me too, Crishell," my mother chimed in. "By the way, where do you keep Matilda's Waterford wineglasses. I looked in all the cabinets."

I glanced over at the kitchen table and noticed that for the first time every place had been set with Aunt Tillie's good bone china. "Wow," I said. "We usually don't drag out the good stuff. I just use that nice set of Corelle."

"A dish as delicious as steak Diane calls for special dinnerware, dear." She paused and then added, "I'm not the only one. Gary thought it was a good idea."

I glanced at Gary. He shot me one of his patented *What else was I supposed to say?* looks. "Fine," I said stiffly. "I'll get out the Waterford wineglasses. Red wine goes with steak, right? I do believe I saw a bottle of Hall Darwin in the wine rack."

"You're right, dear. I saw it too." My mother jumped up. "I'll go get it. You do have a corkscrew, don't you?"

"Yes, Mother."

As she hurried off to get the wine, I went to get the glasses, which were in the cabinet next to the stove. I deliberately bumped Gary with my hip as I passed. "I see you lied to me," I said.

He looked taken aback. "Lied? About what?"

"You made it sound like a hardship to be stuck here with my mother," I chided him as I bent to retrieve the glasses. "Sounds more like you two have gotten rather chummy."

"Well, what did you expect?" he hissed. "I had to make nice, I was alone here with her for hours while you were out doing—say, what exactly were you doing, anyway?"

I straightened and laid three glasses on the counter. "I went to see Rita." I gave him the CliffsNotes version about my afternoon, from watching the video to visiting Rita to seeing Josh and Riser pull up as I left. When I finished, Gary let out a low whistle.

"Sounds as if the cat's out of the bag about that video," he remarked.

"Exactly what I thought when I saw Josh and Riser pull up to Rita's house. I sent Josh a casual text, asking how things were going, but so far he hasn't answered me."

Gary looked up from stirring and frowned. "That doesn't sound too promising."

"No, it doesn't. Rita says that she doesn't believe Wesley could murder anyone, but I'm not so sure she believes that."

"You think she'll confess to something she didn't do to get him off the hook?"

"I hate to say it, but yes, I think she would. Who knows what else the police might have uncovered about Draco's movements Saturday? That's why I think it's time we had a meeting to discuss suspects. I texted Olivia and asked if she could get out of going to the movies with her cousin, and to see if Ron were available to come later too. Maybe if we all put our heads together and start narrowing down the field, something will click."

"Now that you mention it, I've been itching to draw on that whiteboard," Gary admitted. "But we're forgetting one thing."

"What's that?"

"What are we going to do with your mother? Unless you plan on inviting her to join us?"

"Heck, no. She freaked out when Riser took her statement, can you imagine her actually trying to whittle down suspects? No, I want my mother to stay as far away from this as possible." I drummed my fingers on the countertop, then reached for my phone. "I've got an idea. If it works, we're home free. If it doesn't . . . have you got any sleeping pills?"

∙ ∙ ∙

Fortunately I didn't need to go hunting drugs. We'd just finished dinner and I'd gone into the parlor with Mother and our wine while Gary cleaned up. No sooner had we seated ourselves than the doorbell rang. I went to answer it, returning a few minutes later with Garrett Knute in tow.

"Mother, this is Garrett Knute. He's on the board of directors at the Fox Hollow Museum, and he's a big fan."

Garrett stepped forward and clasped my mother's hand. "It's an honor," he murmured. "To meet the woman who played Lady Macbeth to standing ovations at the Royal Shakespeare Festival."

My mother preened like a peacock. "You've seen me perform?"

"Yes, and I must tell you, my dear, you were absolutely enchanting! I wonder—would you consent to going out for a cappuccino with me? I know this delightful little place over in Morgan. I'd love to hear all about the roles you've played."

My mother's face brightened and she jumped up from the sofa. "That sounds lovely. I'll just get my wrap." She turned to look at me. "Darling, you don't mind, do you? We won't be long."

"Take as long as you want, Mother."

As she disappeared up the steps, Knute poked me in the ribs. "This is a real treat for me, Shell. Spending an entire evening with your mother. How can I ever thank you?"

I grinned at him. "Hold that thought, Garrett, but it's really me who should thank you."

My mother returned, a rose-colored cashmere sweater draped casually around her shoulders. I walked the two of them to the door and told them to have a good time. As Knute's Cadillac pulled away from the curb, my phone pinged with an incoming text. I saw that it was from Josh: *Hey Shell! Sorry I haven't been in touch. It's been crazy here. I'll touch base w/you tomorrow, promise.*

I texted back: *Busy here too, entertaining Mother. Talk to U tomorrow.*

I looked it over before I hit Send. I thought "entertaining Mother" was a nice touch. It wouldn't do to let Josh know I was doing my own investigating, at least not yet. I needed to find out more about how his investigation was going first. I slid my phone back into my pocket, wondering just what Josh and Riser had been going crazy with. Had they uncovered more suspects, or were

Rita and Wesley the only two under the police microscope? I retraced my steps back to the kitchen, arriving just as Gary opened the door to admit Olivia and Ron.

"We saw your mother leave, so we figured the coast was clear," Ron said.

I smiled at Olivia. "I hope your cousin didn't get too upset with you."

"It's okay. I didn't want to see that movie anyway," Olivia remarked. "I'd much rather be here narrowing down suspects to get Rita off the hook. Oh, and by the way, that was a clever idea, to get Knute to take her out for coffee," she added with a broad wink in my direction.

"Thank goodness I remembered he was a fan. This will either go one of two ways. Either he'll be sorry he ever mentioned wanting to meet her to me, or he'll become even more besotted. Probably the latter. Mother can be charming when she chooses to be. Why, she and Gary are best buds now."

Gary pulled a face. "I wouldn't go that far. Let's get down to business, though, shall we? I set up the whiteboard in the den, just in case the evening turns out to be a bust and Clarissa comes home early."

We all trooped up the stairs to the room that doubled as an office/den. Gary had the whiteboard set up in the middle of the room. In the center of the board he'd drawn a large box and written inside it: *Johnny Draco–Victim*.

We all took seats and Gary walked over to the whiteboard and uncapped a magic marker. "I didn't draw any boxes like I did last time because I wasn't sure just how many to draw," he said. "So we'll do that now."

"First we should put the obvious ones. The people he supposedly swindled," I said.

"Okay." Gary started drawing boxes off to the right of the main box. "Unfortunately, Rita and Wesley's names have to go here." He wrote their names in the top box, followed by Quentin Watson, Stanley Sheer, and Krissa Tidwell in boxes underneath. Below Krissa's name he put a question mark in a box. "For person or persons as yet unknown," he said.

"Draw another box," I directed. "Put in Adrian Arnold. There's some connection between those two, I'm just not sure what it is yet. Plus, right now he seems to be MIA. Not a good sign, if you ask me."

Gary did so, then added a similar box with a question mark below that one. "Just in case Draco's death is not related to the Fox Hollow swindle. Remember he was away five years. Who knows what he might have been up to?"

"According to Rita, he told her that he'd been working for his cousin and getting his act together so he could come back here," I put in.

"Doesn't mean he told her the truth," remarked Olivia. "Leopards don't change their spots. Maybe he went back to his old tricks and conned someone with a phony investment."

We all stared at the board for a few minutes, and then I cleared my throat and stood up. I walked over to the board and picked up a marker. "For now, let's concentrate on the suspects we know. I think we should do a time line too. That might help us make some sense out of everything."

I started to write in the upper-left-hand corner. "Let's start with Friday. A little after noon, I saw Draco and Adrian Arnold having a . . . discussion, for want of a better word, in the alley across the street." I wrote that down, then asked, "What next?"

"Well, Draco obviously called Rita and Wesley and Krissa and set up meetings. For all we know he could have called others too," suggested Ron.

I wrote down: *various times: Draco sets up meets.* "Now we move to Saturday, when it really gets hairy.

"At about nine thirty-five I saw Rita go into the alley behind Sweet Perks. Stanley Sheer came up behind me about a minute later. He hinted I should get back to my store and he left. About five minutes later I ventured into the alley. I heard voices raised in argument and the sound of a slap. I figure it was around nine forty-five when Rita came out of the alley, followed about a minute later by Draco. I considered following Rita to talk to her, but then I caught a glimpse of Draco, heading in the direction of Krissa's store. And someone was following him, but I couldn't get a good look at whoever it was. I saw a line starting to form and it was almost time to open, so I went back to the store."

"And you didn't leave until when? It was around twelve thirty?" Gary asked.

"Right. That's when I saw Buck standing in the crowd, so I went over to him. We watched Honey Belle tell a few fortunes and then we both left. My mother arrived somewhere between twelve forty-five and one and saw Honey Belle tell Draco's fortune. Then shortly afterward, Arnold left the check and note for me and cut out."

Gary took the magic marker from me and continued writing down the time line. "Then between one and three, Olivia's girls performed at the gazebo."

"And Mrs. Fein took that video I sent you, Shell," said Olivia. "At around one thirty you can see two figures behind the pagoda. One is definitely Draco."

"The other looks like Wesley Sakowski, and Rita admits they met," I said. "So for right now we'll assume the other figure is Wesley. Next would be two thirty, when Mae Barker told me she thought she saw Rita tailing Draco. Sue Bloodgood saw Rita too, and a third person who so far is unidentified also saw her following Draco, but I'm thinking it could be Stanley Sheer. He was hanging around the alley in the morning, and he *might* have also seen Draco and Rita arguing then."

"And you found Draco's body between three oh-five and three ten," Gary finished. "Joshy told you the coroner established the TOD as somewhere between two and three."

"Right." I picked up another magic marker and tapped it against my chin. "If Mae, Sue and this mysterious third witness are correct, and they saw Rita tailing Draco, that puts the TOD sometime between two thirty and three. But if Rita was tailing her husband and not Draco, it could make the TOD earlier. Draco might already have been dead."

"You're right," cried Olivia. "That would let Wesley off the hook."

Ron raised a finger. "Unless Wesley killed Draco before Rita started tailing him?"

Olivia plopped back in her seat, and the corners of her lips drooped downward. "Didn't think of that," she muttered.

"Sue couldn't positively identify the person Rita seemed to be following as Draco. Mae's identification is based on her psychic feeling," Gary said, making air quotes around the last two words. "Both Sue and Rita seemed to think Mae could be fabricating the story. Let's concentrate on what we know as factual."

"Okay. We know for a fact, thanks to that video, that Draco was at the pagoda at one thirty," I said. "Rita said he told Wesley he had an important meeting, something that would change people's lives. That remark brings up several questions. Where did he go? Who did he meet?"

Gary inclined his head. "I think we can safely deduce that whoever he met with is our killer. Now we just have to figure out who that might be."

"Wesley told Rita he thought he saw Quentin lurking around when he met Draco the first time by Krissa's store," I mused. "Quentin says he never saw Draco, but he could be lying."

"And what about this Krissa Tidwell?" put in Gary. "It's not the usual method of murder for a woman, but that doesn't mean the killer isn't a female."

"True," I agreed. "And if Johnny was involved in that swindle, who's to say Krissa didn't suspect something, or was maybe even part of it? They lived together, after all."

"I don't know about that," Ron piped up. "Krissa's rather meek and mild. She always trailed Johnny like a puppy dog. If he wanted to keep a secret from her, it wouldn't have been hard. She doted on everything he said. Besides, she lost money too, remember?" He shook his head. "She's not the killer type."

"She's a woman scorned," Olivia cut in. "They're always the killer type, given the right circumstances. Besides, have you ever looked at her hands? Really looked at them." She held out her own dainty hands and gave her head a brisk shake. "She's got big paws. Man hands. I bet she'd have no problem jamming that instrument down Draco's throat."

"It's possible Draco went to see his ex," I said. "She looked plenty upset when I saw her in the square with Evan Hanley. Hanley looked annoyed too."

"Well, that would make sense. Hanley and Krissa are a thing," said Olivia.

My eyebrows went up. "A thing?"

"Involved. Dating. Maybe more than dating. It's been going through the gossip mill for weeks."

"Hm. Well, that might explain the dagger look he shot me. Krissa might have told him I'd considered hiring Draco."

"No doubt she did. And trust me, if Draco did pay Krissa a visit, she definitely told her new boyfriend all about it." She flicked a bit of lint from her sweater and continued, "I bet Evan didn't like the idea of Draco sniffing around Krissa. I hear he's the jealous type. Real jealous." She paused. "Maybe even enough to kill."

"Well." Ron rubbed absently at his cheek. "Looks like we've just discovered two more people who could have good motives for wanting Draco out of the way."

"They definitely bear further investigation," I said. Then I whipped my cell phone out of my pocket, hit speed dial. My call went straight to voicemail, so I decided on a text instead:

Don't stay out too late, Mother. We've got a big day tomorrow. I'm taking you clothes shopping.

Seventeen

"I must say, you never fail to surprise me, Crishell."

My mother and I were in my convertible, driving through the center of town. I had my eyes peeled for a good parking spot near Krissa Tidwell's store. "How so, Mother?"

"Setting up a shopping excursion at an exclusive little boutique. It's something your sister-in-law and I do frequently, but not you and I. I do believe this is a first."

"Well, you know what they say. There's a first time for everything. Ah, here we are now."

As luck would have it, there was a prime parking spot right in front of Ages Past. A little tight, but I managed to maneuver my convertible into it. I'd gotten Gary to agree to open up Urban Tails so that I could venture out on this little excursion. I hoped with all my heart that it would prove to be worth it.

A bell tinkled overhead as I pushed open the shop door. I'd never been in Krissa's boutique before, so I took a moment to look around. The shop was charming. The walls were papered in gray and pink flowers, and light pink curtains graced the windows. The inventory seemed to be varied. Off to the right was what appeared to be modern clothing. Racks of long gowns hung beside circular racks holding silky tops with matching pants. Lacy camisoles nestled in silk lined boxes perched on antique highboys. A tall shelf held a display of strands of opera-length pearls. Beneath them rested an array of bracelets, necklaces and scarves. Glass shelves set into the wall held handbags of supple leather and soft suede. A shoe rack offered designer heels by such names as Louboutin and Choo. Farther down were racks holding airy dresses, elegant tops and slacks.

To the left was what was obviously the vintage clothing section. My mother made a beeline for that. A few seconds later she was holding a striped maxi dress with an Empire waistline and square neck up to her. "Crishell, how does this look?" she asked.

"Lovely, Mother," I murmured.

My mother sighed. "No, it's not." She put the dress back and continued pawing through the selection. I wandered through the racks, pausing every now and then to look at a blouse or a skirt, wondering where the help was. We'd been in the store a good ten minutes unattended, which was unusual. I moved into the modern clothing section and paused before a midnight blue top with matching slacks. I held it up and felt the material. It was silk, and whisper soft. I glanced at the price tag and almost had a heart attack. Five hundred dollars!

"It's pricey, but it's genuine silk and the designer is a popular Italian one."

I whirled, nearly dropping the outfit. Krissa Tidwell had come up quietly behind me. I'd always thought her a bit old-fashioned, but today she looked anything but. She was dressed in an Empire-waisted midi dress in a soft periwinkle blue that brought out the same color in her eyes. Today her hair was down instead of in its usual bun and it flowed freely about her slim shoulders. She coughed lightly and laid a hand on my arm. "I'm sorry, Shell, I didn't mean to startle you," she said. She looked down at her feet, and I saw she wore soft-soled light blue Sketchers. "These things are comfortable, but they're quiet as a mouse on these hardwood floors."

I smiled at her. "My mother is in town, so I thought this was the perfect time to visit your store," I said. I glanced around. "You have some lovely things here."

"Thanks. I try to keep a varied selection. My customers are very specific about their likes and dislikes."

My mother bustled over to us, her arms laden with clothing from the vintage portion of the shop. "Are you the proprietor?" she asked without preamble. "You have some marvelous vintage clothing here."

"This is my mother, Clarissa McMillan," I said. "Krissa Tidwell."

Both women inclined their heads in greeting. My mother's sharp gaze roved over Krissa's slim form. "I love your dress," she said.

"Thanks. It's an Isaac Mizrahi. I just got it in yesterday." She looked appraisingly at my mother. "I've one in a soft coral shade that would look lovely with your coloring."

My mother shifted the bundle in her arms. "Sounds enticing, but I'd like to try these on first. Where is your dressing room?"

"Right over there. I'll show you."

As Krissa led my mother to the other end of the store, I gave the blue pantsuit another longing glance, then put it back on the rack. I wasn't after a new outfit today, particularly one that pricey.

Krissa came back and noticed my empty arms. "You decided against it?"

I nodded. "Don't get me wrong, it's lovely. Just a little too fancy for ringing up cat and dog food," I said.

Krissa let out a light laugh and closed one eye in a wink. "Well, you never know. You might get called back to Los Angeles to do a movie, and it might come in handy."

I shook my head. "No, I'm afraid those days are over."

Her lips twitched. "I've learned never to say never, Shell."

That was my opening. "I guess that's true. I mean, I guess you never thought you'd see Johnny Draco again, right?"

Krissa's back went ramrod straight. "That's right," she said stiffly. "That toad should never have come back here."

"But he did. He came to my shop."

"I know. Mae wasted no time letting me know. Thank goodness you didn't hire him to sing, although he did have a lovely voice."

"He actually came to my shop looking for my aunt. I got the impression they'd been friendly."

"I guess you could say that. Johnny didn't have many friends, male or female. He was a loner." Krissa picked up one of the scarves and threaded it loosely through her fingers. "No offense, Shell, but your aunt could pick up strays faster than anyone I know, and I don't mean animals. She was always fond of taking the underdog's side."

"I didn't realize Draco was considered an underdog."

"He wasn't, not until he lost all our money."

"You had no idea what was going on? Not even an inkling?"

She shook her head. "None at all. Johnny was a smooth talker, and I was quite naive back then." She paused and then added, "He even fooled your aunt. Tillie championed him for weeks afterward. She said that he'd warned us all it was a risk, and she was right." She looked me straight in the eye. "I loved that man, I really did. I defended him when it all happened, and I would have kept on, had he not dumped me like yesterday's trash. No note, no warning, no explanation . . . nothing! And then he shows up here, just as if nothing had ever happened, and wants to make amends."

"So that's why he came to see you? To make amends for leaving the way he did?"

Krissa let out a soft snort. "So he said. I tell you, I was so shocked when he walked into my shop Saturday morning I didn't know what to think. I just stood here, speechless, while he rambled on." She set down the scarf and twined her fingers through the thin silver chain she wore around her neck. "He told me that he was sorry he'd ended things the way he had, but back then it was the only way. Then he said that he'd come across some information that was going to change people's lives, and then maybe everyone would believe that he hadn't intentionally defrauded them, that he was just as much, or more, of a victim as them."

I nodded. That fit in with what Johnny had said to Wesley. "Did he tell you what this information was?"

She shook her head. "No. He just asked me to trust him. I told him that the trust had vanished along with him five years ago. He said he was sorry about that, but soon I'd understand. Then he said he had to go, and he left."

"So he mentioned nothing to you about his plans to lease the dry goods store?"

"No. Evan told me that later. I was so upset I had to go for a walk. I met him in the square." She frowned at me. "You were there too. I remember seeing you, and Quentin Watson. Anyway, Evan told me that he'd shown Johnny the store the day before. He had no idea who he was." She twisted her hands together in front of her. "He told me that if he had, he would never have agreed to the rental. He said he was going to try and find Johnny and tell him the deal was off."

"And did he find him?"

"No, he didn't."

"You're certain?"

Her eyes narrowed. "I'm not sure I like your tone, Shell. Yes, I'm certain. And Evan's spoken with the police. *They* seemed satisfied with his explanation." She gave her head a toss. "Now, if you will excuse me, I have some things to attend to. You can see yourself and your mother out."

With that, Krissa turned and vanished into the back room. I chewed absently at my lower lip. Her reaction spoke volumes. She had no idea where her boyfriend was at the time of Johnny Draco's death. Evan Hanley would definitely bear some investigating.

My mother appeared a few minutes later, empty-handed. "No luck?" I asked.

She shook her head. "The dresses were lovely, just not my style. And the coral one that Krissa mentioned isn't in my size." Her sigh was audible. "It seems this expedition is a bust."

In more ways than one, I thought.

• • •

I dropped my mother off at home and went straight to the pet shop. Urban Tails was crowded when I arrived. Sunny was behind the counter and Robbie and Gary were helping customers. I put my things in the back room and helped Sunny whittle down the line at the counter. I wanted to fill Gary in on the morning activity, but there was simply no time to chat. Business continued at a brisk pace until twelve o'clock. After wrapping up a new bowl for Mrs. O'Hanley's dog Skipper, I sent Gary and Robbie off to lunch. Sunny had just gone into the back room to see if there was any more gerbil food. I happened to glance toward the front door just as it opened and a tall, reed-thin man with light hair entered. His lips thinned as he caught sight of me, and as he drew closer I recognized him—Evan Hanley. He paused before the counter and I could see fire in his eyes. He lifted his hand and jabbed a finger in the air. "You're Shell McMillan?"

It was more of a statement than a question, but I nodded. "Yes. What can I do for you?"

His features morphed into a dark scowl. "For one thing, you can stop badgering my girlfriend."

I stared at him, not certain I'd heard correctly. "I beg your pardon?"

"You heard me," Hanley said. His tone was belligerent, to say the least. "I've just left her, and she was highly upset and indignant at your insinuation that I had something to do with Draco's death, as am I."

I splayed both hands on the counter and leaned forward. "I'm sorry, Mr. Hanley, but I think there's been a misunderstanding."

"There's no misunderstanding," he said crisply. "Krissa told you that I wanted to find Draco and tell him I'd changed my mind about renting to him, and you asked her if I'd found him. When she told you no, you asked her if she were sure." He leaned in toward me, his lips curled upward in a snarl. "I'm no fool, and neither is Krissa. You were hinting at the possibility I'd found Draco and gotten rid of him once and for all."

"I merely asked her a question, Mr. Hanley. I didn't badger her."

"You upset her," he shouted. He ran his hand through his hair and took a step backward. "Krissa went through a lot when Draco left. He absconded with a good deal of her money, money she could really use now. It took her a while to get over him, and then, for him to suddenly show up out of the blue . . ." He spread his hands. "His showing up like that was very upsetting to her, as I'm sure you can imagine. I didn't know him, but I've heard the stories. Draco was bad news."

"I'm sorry if my visit upset her," I said carefully. "I merely wanted to find out—"

"I know what you wanted," Evan Hanley interrupted me. "You wanted to play detective. Krissa told me all about the murder you solved. Well, Ms. McMillan, I'm here to tell you that you're not going to play detective at my girlfriend's expense. Got that?"

Hanley was clearly upset. His cheeks were red, and a vein in his forehead throbbed. He didn't give me a chance to answer but continued, "For your information, I've already spoken with the police. A Detective Riser." His lips curved in a triumphant smile. "It just so happens I have an ironclad alibi for the time of the murder."

"You do? What is it?"

The smile morphed into a sneer. "Oh, I bet you'd like to know, wouldn't you. Well, that's none of your business. All you need to know is that the police are satisfied with it. So now I'm telling you, not asking. Leave Krissa and me alone. If I were you, Miss Detective, I'd set my sights elsewhere. Find some other unsuspecting ex-acquaintance of Draco's to put under your microscope. I'm sure there are plenty."

With that, Hanley turned on his heel and strode out of the shop, slamming the door behind him so hard the bell jangled back and forth.

"Whoa, what's his problem?"

I turned to see Sunny behind me, a box of gerbil food in her hands. I took the box from her and set it on the counter. "Just another satisfied customer," I said, attempting to make light.

Sunny shook her head. "He sounded plenty angry to me. Angry and maybe a little defensive."

Sunny picked the box back up and headed toward the aisle with the gerbil food. I leaned across the counter and plopped my chin in my hands. Now that Sunny mentioned it, I had to admit she had a point. Hanley had sounded the teeniest bit defensive during his tirade. Now, why would that be? One thought popped into my head: maybe his so-called ironclad alibi wasn't so ironclad as he wanted me to believe. I started to turn toward the register when I noticed something on the floor, wedged underneath the parakeet food display. I bent down and picked it up. It was a dirty-looking envelope, and my name was crudely printed across its face. I opened it and withdrew a single sheet of paper. I unfolded it and gasped as I read the words printed in red:

Stop snooping if you don't want to end up like Draco.

Eighteen

The minute Gary returned I pulled him over to one side and showed him the note. "Someone obviously feels threatened."

Gary scratched at his head. "Obviously you've struck a nerve somewhere. Any idea who might have left it?"

"We were slammed pretty much all morning. Anyone could have come in and put it there. I do have one thought, though. Evan Hanley."

"Who? Oh, right. The jealous boyfriend. He was here?"

"Oh, yes, and I have to agree with Olivia's assessment of him." I filled Gary in on my morning meeting with Krissa and subsequent talk with Hanley.

"Definitely jealous, and let's throw in overprotective, too," Gary observed when I'd finished. "I don't suppose he offered any names of these ex-acquaintances we should be badgering instead of him and Krissa?"

"Nope. Probably because there are none."

"Well, the guy bears watching, in my opinion." He pulled at a strand of hair on his shirt. "Are you going to show that to Joshy."

"I suppose I should," I said. "Although I bet whoever left it is too clever to have left any incriminating prints on it."

"Still, it's a threat. Joshy should know about it. Why not give him a call now?"

The door opened just then and a half dozen people came inside. Two of them had small dogs with them. "Later," I said, slipping the note into my pocket. "Right now we've got customers."

• • •

Things got really slow around four o'clock, so I told Robbie and Sunny they could leave early and Gary and I would lock up. Robbie offered Sunny a ride home and I saw the girl's face light up at the offer. Gary noticed we were low on singles and offered to make a quick run to the bank and get some. I was alone in the shop for less than five minutes when the door opened and Josh Bloodgood walked inside. He looked tired as he approached the counter. "Hey," I said. "You look beat."

"It's been a tough weekend," he said. "Today was so crazy I didn't even have time for lunch. Two more guys called out with the flu. I had to commandeer one of the beat cops to help Riser question suspects."

"You know, I haven't eaten either," I said. "I've got a huge tuna sandwich I don't mind sharing, though, if you don't mind eating in the back room."

"Sounds good. I love tuna." He glanced around. "But what about the store?"

"Gary will be back soon. He just ran to the bank for singles."

I flipped the sign on the door from *Open* to *Closed* and led the way into the storeroom. Josh eased into one of the leather chairs and I got the tuna sandwich out of my insulated bag. I split it in half, then pulled out my bottle of Sprite and found two paper cups left over from Saturday's grand opening. I put napkins down on the desk and for a few minutes both Josh and I enjoyed the tuna in silence. Josh finished his half first, picked up his Sprite and took a sip. He set the cup back down on the counter, leaned back in the chair and stretched his long legs out in front of him. "I got a call from Evan Hanley a little while ago. It seems he didn't appreciate your, quote, badgering his girlfriend, unquote."

I resisted the impulse to roll my eyes. "He was here earlier and told me the same thing. I tried to tell him that I wasn't badgering her. I just asked some relevant questions while my mother tried on a few dresses."

A smile quirked at his lips. "You just can't help yourself, can you? You've got to play Nancy Drew."

"I wouldn't call asking a few innocent questions channeling Nancy Drew," I huffed. "If you want to know, Sunny thought Hanley sounded defensive, and so did I. Maybe he's got something to hide."

"He's not hiding anything. Evan Hanley had no reason to kill Draco."

"No? How about jealousy? Olivia said he's the jealous type, and Draco went to see Krissa Tidwell to ask her forgiveness. He might have been afraid Draco wanted to start up their romance again. Plus, he seemed very protective and possessive of Krissa."

"Hanley might be the jealous type, but he's also a shrewd businessman. He wouldn't do anything to put his business in jeopardy. Besides, we checked him out already. He's got an alibi."

I threw my hands up in the air. "Oh, yes. He mentioned his ironclad alibi."

"It is pretty ironclad." Josh reached into the pocket of his jacket and pulled out his notebook. He flipped a few pages and read, "Between two and three on Saturday Evan Hanley was in the Bottoms Up Tavern. He sat at the bar, joked around with some of the patrons, even indulged in a game of darts."

My face fell. "You've got witnesses?"

"Half a dozen." Josh snapped the notebook shut and slid it into his pocket. "So, you can cross him off your list—I'm assuming you have a list."

I leaned back in my chair and crossed my arms over my chest. "Okay, maybe Hanley's off the hook, but what about Krissa? Now there's a woman with a motive. Plus, Olivia was right. I looked closely at her hands when I was in her shop today—she does have large, mannish-looking hands. If you ask me, she'd be more than capable of ramming that instrument down Draco's throat."

"That might be true, but Ms. Tidwell also has an alibi. She's on the store surveillance camera between two and three, helping Jenny Vickers select several antique pins as bridesmaid gifts."

I shrank lower into my chair. "Oh. And while we're on the subject, Quentin Watson claims to have an ironclad alibi as well."

"He does. He was snapping photos of the mime's performance between two fifteen and three, in front of more than two dozen people. Some even have him on video."

I dropped my head into my hands. "Great. I don't suppose you've had time to check out Adrian Arnold?"

"As a matter of fact, I have. Arnold moved to Frederick a little over a year ago. Before that he lived in Hartford, where he was pretty successful with his parrot business. Prior to that, it's a little spotty, but I can't find any evidence that he was ever involved in an investment career, or with Draco, for that matter."

"Of course not," I muttered. "He's covered his tracks well."

"I haven't given up. I've still got Amy digging for more info on him." Josh leaned forward and placed his hand on my knee. "I know you're upset about Rita, Shell. I know that's why you're getting so involved in this."

I sat up straight and shrugged his hand off. "So it's true? Rita's officially a suspect?"

Josh hesitated, then nodded. "There are witnesses who saw her tailing Draco down that alley around three o'clock. And another who heard her having an argument with him earlier that day."

"Stanley Sheer!" I cried out, then clapped my hand over my mouth.

"That's right." Josh's eyes narrowed. "And how do you know that?"

I sighed. "Because I heard the argument too."

His eyebrows lifted. "And when were you going to tell me?"

"I know, I know, I should have said something sooner. It's just, well, it makes her look guilty, and I know she didn't do it."

Josh let out a long breath. I could tell from the set of his jaw he was pretty pissed at me. "What else are you keeping from me, Shell?"

I thrust out my lower lip. "I'm assuming that you know all about the video."

"If you mean the one Mrs. Fein took, then yes. She brought it to us yesterday. We went to question Wesley."

I didn't think it wise to mention that I'd seen him and Riser going into the Sakowski residence. "And what did Wesley say?"

"He was pretty forthcoming. He didn't deny meeting Draco there. As a matter of fact, he saw Draco twice Saturday, but I'm betting you know that already."

"Rita said that Wesley's shown a marked improvement since he started this clinical trial. But you and I both know that sometimes, given the right circumstances, people can perform feats of unusual strength. He's not off the hook either, is he?" I sighed. "There's something else you should probably know." I pulled out the envelope and passed it over to him. "I found this on the shop floor, shortly after Evan Hanley paid me a visit."

Josh opened the envelope, unfolded the note and read it. He shook his head, then slid the note and envelope into his pocket. "Shell, Shell. This penchant of yours for amateur detective work could get you into serious trouble."

"Honestly, Josh, it takes a lot more than a cowardly anonymous note to scare me off."

"This is more than that, Shell. It's a threat."

Josh rose, leaned over, and pulled me up out of my chair to face him. He cupped my chin and raised my face to his. "Look, Shell. I know you care about the Sakowskis. Rita was there for you during the whole Amelia thing. Personally, I don't think either one of them is guilty, but I have to do my job, and that means I have to follow the facts." He started to rub my chin with his thumb. "Doing my job would be a heck of a lot easier if I didn't have to worry about you and Gary playing Nancy Drew and Joe Hardy." He paused in his chin rubbing to look deeply into my eyes. "Promise me you'll cool it with the detective work. Please."

I was spared answering as the door was suddenly flung open and Gary's head popped in. "I put the singles in the register. Why are you back here . . ." he began, then stopped as he saw Josh. "Oh, sorry," he said. "I didn't realize we had company."

"Your timing is excellent, as usual, Presser," Josh said. "I was just about to leave, anyway." He turned back to me. "Remember what I said, Shell. Stay out of trouble. And once this is all over, I'm taking you out for a nice dinner at the Reserve."

"The Reserve," I squealed. I'd been dying to go to the upscale Italian restaurant ever since Gary had taken Olivia there and come back with rave reviews. "I hear the clams casino is to die for."

"So do I," agreed Josh. He waggled his finger under my nose. "So stay out of trouble and let me wrap this up. Deal?"

"Deal," I said.

Josh gave me a wink, then pushed past Gary and left. I flopped back into the chair, and Gary eased himself into the seat Josh had just vacated. "Does this little bargain with Joshy mean you've quit investigating?" he asked.

I raised an eyebrow. "What do you think?"

Gary grinned. "That's my girl. Okay, then, what did Joshy want? I'm sure he wasn't here to give you an update on his investigation."

"No, he came to tell me that he got a call from Evan Hanley complaining about my 'badgering' Krissa."

Gary's eyebrows winged skyward. "Hanley did that, eh? Well, well. That certainly seems suspicious to me."

"Well, don't get hung up on it. According to Josh, Hanley has an alibi. He was playing darts at your favorite watering hole at the time Draco was getting an instrument jammed down his windpipe. Six witnesses saw him there. Krissa has an alibi for the TOD too, and so does Quentin." I shot him a dejected look. "We just lost three good suspects."

"Chin up, Shell. There are others. We just have to keep narrowing them down until we hit the right one."

"Maybe. I'm missing something." I drummed my fingers on the countertop, my eyes slitted as I thought back over the events of the last several days. Suddenly my head jerked upward. "The backpack," I cried.

Gary looked at me. "Sorry?"

Killers of a Feather

"Draco had a backpack with him when he came to my shop. It was pretty stuffed too, probably with most everything he owned." I whirled around. "Do we still have the centerfold with the event photos around here?"

"I put it in the middle drawer under the counter," Gary volunteered.

I walked over, jerked open the drawer. The paper lay right on top. I pulled it out and spread it over the counter. "See here," I cried. I pointed to the photo that showed Johnny on the fringe of the crowd. "I know the photo's not all that clear, but it sure looks to me like he doesn't have the backpack with him. I'm positive it wasn't at the crime scene." I let out a sigh. "If only Bill West would send those darn photos."

"He had the backpack, he didn't have the backpack," Gary said, a note of impatience in his tone. "So what?"

I dragged a hand through my hair, then scrubbed it across my chin. "He was pretty possessive of that backpack when he was here. If he didn't have it on him Saturday, I'm betting he stashed it somewhere he considered safe." I started to pace again, jabbing my finger in the air as I thought. "He had something in that backpack he didn't want anyone else to see, something that he thought would clear his name."

"O-kay," Gary said slowly. "Say that is the case, and he stashed the backpack somewhere safe. Where would that be, exactly?"

I sighed. "A good question. According to Krissa, she and my aunt were about the only two people here who remained friendly to him. I'm positive he came looking for my aunt, hoping she'd offer him a place to stay." I drummed my fingers on the counter. "So, once he found out that wasn't an option, he must have gone somewhere else—but where?"

"Maybe he rented a room from someone," Gary suggested. "I see ads like that in the paper all the time. I doubt he'd have rented one in Fox Hollow, though." He let out a sigh. "There must be dozens of rooms for rent in this area. How do we narrow it down?"

"Simple," I said with a smile. "We just have to ask the right person. And I know exactly who that is."

• • •

A half hour later we pulled up in front of Robbie's house. He answered the door himself, a sweet-looking calico cat bundled in his arms. "Ms. McMillan.

Mr. Presser. Golly, what are you doing here?"

"Paying you a visit," Gary said. He inclined his head toward the cat, who was purring like a locomotive. "Aren't you going to introduce us to your friend?"

"Oh, sorry." Robbie cradled the cat in his arms. "This is Sweetpea. Remember I told you my girlfriend had two cats? Well, this is one of 'em. She had to go visit her aunt, so I'm cat-sitting. I was just about to give this little lady some dinner."

"We won't keep you then," I said quickly. "We just need some information about Johnny Draco."

Robbie looked puzzled. "I don't see what help I could be to you. I never met the guy."

"No, but you told me that he used to rent an apartment from one of your neighbors."

"Oh, yeah, the Collinses. Nice folks. Live on a farm about a half mile from here. They were surprised when he just up and left like that, but he'd paid for the month in full. They liked him."

"I guess Johnny Draco knew this area pretty well, huh?"

"I guess he did. He lived there for a few years."

I looked at Gary, who nodded. I leaned forward and said, "I suppose there are quite a few families in that area who rent rooms out?"

"Oh, yeah. Most of the houses are huge, and once the kids are grown up and off to college, it's another source of income."

"I don't suppose you know the names of some of these families who rent out rooms offhand?"

"Sure I do. There's the McAffreys, and the Joneses, the Collinses of course, and the Freys . . ."

"Whoa, whoa." Gary reached into his pocket and started jotting down the names. "I don't suppose you have phone numbers for these people."

"No, but I bet my mom's got 'em in her address book. If you want, once I'm done feeding Sweetpea, I'll make up a list and email it to you."

"That would be super, Robbie," I said. "Thanks." I reached out and stroked Sweetpea's head. "Nice to meet you, Sweetpea."

The cat gave a rumbling purr in response. As we retraced our steps to my car I touched Gary's arm. "Could it be this easy?"

He shrugged. "I don't know, Sweetums, but I bet we'll soon find out."

• • •

It turned out not to be so easy after all.

True to his word, Robbie sent us a list twenty minutes later. There were fourteen names in total on it. Gary and I went back to the shop and retired to the back room, where we whipped out our cell phones and proceeded to make some calls. About an hour and a half later, we compared notes. Half of the people hadn't rented a room out in months. The other half had, but to college students. Only one person remembered Johnny Draco, and that was his ex-landlord, Marv Collins. "I rented to him for almost three years," the man told me. "He seemed like such a nice, quiet person. It just goes to show, you never know. Still waters run deep, like they say."

Gary crumpled his list and tossed it in the wastebasket. "Now what?"

"We can't give up. We've got to keep searching. Maybe expand our radius. He had to have stayed somewhere."

"Maybe he buried the backpack," suggested Gary. "Or hid it in the gazebo, or in a trash can in the park, or somewhere he could get at it. The problem with us is we don't think like a homeless person. A homeless person would probably know the answer just like that!" He snapped his fingers for emphasis.

"Or maybe he did have another friend, someone Krissa didn't know about," I said. "What about a coworker? Maybe he was friendly with someone at his place of business."

"Hm, you might have something there. Where did he work again? Some investment firm, right?"

"Yep, with a big fancy name. Benson, O-something and Mc-something. Or maybe it was Mac-something."

Gary whipped out his iPhone. "Never fear. The Internet will tell us all we need to know." His fingers flew over the keypad on his phone, and a few minutes later he waved the phone in the air triumphantly. "You were close. It's Benson, O'Toole and McShay. They're located in Wolverton, on Highway 55."

"That's not far from here. Okay, so now we need to talk to someone who worked with Draco five years ago. Any ideas?"

"Yes, as a matter of fact, I do have an idea." He leaned across the counter and I saw a twinkle in his eye. "It will involve a bit of acting skill, however. Are you up to the challenge?"

I puffed out my chest. "I think I can handle it. What do you have in mind?"

"The role of an intrepid reporter, accompanied by his pretty photographer. We're doing a follow-up story on the life of Johnny Draco for the *Fox Hollow Gazette*. We want to focus on the human interest side of John Ira Draco. You in?"

"Try and keep me out," I said. "But Gary, I don't have one of those fancy cameras like Quentin does. All I use for photos is my phone."

He held up a finger. "Not to worry. I happen to know that Olivia has a Canon that will definitely do the job. We'll need some phony press passes. I bet if I pile on the charm, Tricia over at Kinko's would make some up for me."

"Great." I reached for my phone. "You go get them while I call Robbie and ask if he can open for us tomorrow. The sooner we find out this information, the better."

Nineteen

Promptly at nine a.m. the following morning Gary pulled my convertible into the parking lot at Benson, O'Toole and McShay. The building was even more impressive in person than it was in the photos we'd called up online. It loomed seven stories up, and the sides were constructed entirely of glass, giving it a decidedly modern appearance. We parked in the section marked *Visitors* and walked slowly toward the building. Gary paused in the front to admire his reflection in the mirrored glass door. He had on a light tan three-piece suit that molded to his body like a second skin. I had on a comfortable printed maxi dress with gladiator flats. I had Olivia's red Canon camera slung around my neck, and a leather camera bag dangled from my shoulder.

"We look the part, anyway," I whispered to Gary as we pushed through the double doors into one of the most opulent lobbies I think I'd ever seen. Thick, pale rose-tinted shag carpeting covered the floor, and I felt my shoes sink in with every step. We moved swiftly across the lobby to the massive cherrywood desk that stood on a raised dais in the center of the room. Behind the desk, on the wall, the name Benson, O'Toole and McShay stood out in large, shadow-blocked gold lettering. The perky-looking redhead seated behind the desk wore a low-cut blouse and a brass name tag that read *Adelle*. She was frowning at something on her computer screen but glanced up as we approached. The frowny face morphed into a seductive smile the minute she set eyes on Gary.

"Good morning," she purred. "May I help you?"

"I hope so." Gary whipped out the press pass from his jacket pocket and flashed it in front of Adelle's heavily made-up eyes. "Sam Malone. I'm a reporter for the *Fox Hollow Gazette*. This is my photographer, Diane Chambers." He flicked his thumb in my direction, and I hoped Adelle wasn't a fan of the old TV show *Cheers*. "We're sorry to just show up here without an appointment, but we're on a tight schedule and rather pressed for time. We'd like to see someone who could give us some background information on one of your former employees."

She picked up a pen. "Who's the employee?"

"John Ira Draco."

She paused, pen poised above her pad. "Who? I've never heard of him."

"He worked here a few years ago." Gary leaned one elbow on the counter. In a somber tone he added, "I guess you haven't heard. He died rather suddenly Saturday."

Adelle let out a gasp. "Oh, no!"

Gary reached out to pat her hand. "Yes, I know. Anyway, our editor wants to run a story on Draco, seeing as several of his clients were from Fox Hollow. Sort of a 'man behind the myth' piece? So, what we'd really like to do is speak to someone who knew him on the job, a former coworker perhaps?"

She shot both of us a sympathetic smile. "Let me see if I can get someone in HR who might be able to help you."

She turned away from us, picked up the phone and punched in a number. She spoke with someone in a very low tone for a few minutes, occasionally glancing back at us over her shoulder. She hung up, dialed another number, and held another whispered conference. At last she hung up the phone and turned her attention back to us. I noticed the bright smile was gone, replaced now by a somewhat guarded expression. I detected a definite chill in her tone as she said, "Mac Benson will speak with you personally. Take the elevator to the seventh floor. His assistant will meet you there."

Message delivered, she turned back to her computer. Summarily dismissed, Gary and I made our way over to the bank of elevators at the far wall. There was no one else waiting, so we had the cage to ourselves. Once we were inside Gary grinned at me. "It seems we've attracted the attention of the big guns."

"Yes. Let's hope that's a good thing."

The elevator dinged and the door rolled back. We stepped out into more plush, deep carpeting, this a mauve color. The woman appeared in front of us suddenly, like a puff of smoke, and I gave her an assessing glance. Five-six, well-built, platinum blonde hair. She looked poured into the animal-print blouse and pencil skirt she had on. Her voice when she spoke was breathy, like a junior Marilyn Monroe. "Mr. Malone? Ms. Chambers?"

Gary smiled his most dazzling smile. "Yes. You must be Mr. Benson's assistant."

"Yes. Phoebe Grant. Follow me, please."

We fell into step behind her and followed her down a long hallway. We passed several offices, and I noticed some of the occupants giving us curious glances. Phoebe led us into a large room that boasted a mammoth oak table with at least a dozen, maybe more, ergonomically correct leather chairs grouped around it. Off to one side was a smaller table on which rested a large samovar, a platter of fresh fruit and another one of bagels. Phoebe waved us into chairs and then motioned toward the table. "Fresh coffee, fruit and bagels. Please help yourself. Mr. Benson will be with you shortly." With a brief nod and an even briefer smile, she sashayed out the door and shut it, leaving us alone.

I looked at Gary. "What do you make of all this?" I asked.

Gary moved over to the table, grabbed a cup and poured himself a coffee. He picked up a bagel, dropped it onto a plate and brought it over to the conference table. "Hard to say. No doubt they're wondering why the interest in Draco after all this time."

"More likely they're worried that this publicity might uncover some skeletons rattling around in their closets," I observed as I helped myself to a small bowl of fruit.

About fifteen minutes later the door opened and a man that I assumed was Mac Benson strode in. He was tall and well-built, the charcoal suit he wore draping nicely on his frame. He had a firm chin, well-shaped lips and his eyes, a deep blue, looked puzzled as they went from Gary to me and back to Gary again. He stepped up to the table and held out his hand. "Mac Benson," he said.

Gary brushed a crumb from the corner of his mouth and rose from his chair to shake Benson's hand. "Sam Malone, *Fox Hollow Gazette*. This is my photographer, Ms. Diane Chambers." He indicated me with a sweep of his arm. "Thank you for seeing us, on such short notice."

"Not a problem. I understand you're looking for some information on John Draco?"

"That's correct."

Benson eased his frame into the chair opposite Gary's. "The name Draco hasn't been spoken in this company since he up and left five years ago. Now I hear it twice in the course of two days, first from the police, and now you."

Gary and I exchanged a quick look and then Gary said, "Then you're aware John Draco was murdered Saturday."

Benson cleared his throat. "Yes, I had a call from the Fox Hollow police Saturday evening. They wanted to know if Draco had been in touch with me since his return. I told them no. They also asked if I knew of anyone who would have wanted to see him dead." Benson let out a mirthless chuckle. "I told them that after what he pulled, I was pretty sure there were a lot of people who would probably fit into that category, but I didn't know any of them. Draco did that investment all on his own, without any sanction from me or our board. He acted as an independent counselor."

"So I imagine there was a lot of resentment among the people here when it failed?" I asked.

"Resentment, embarrassment. Johnny reported to me while he was working here, and he always struck me as a model employee. I was just as shocked as anyone when all this went down. To be honest, I was amazed that he'd had such bad judgment. He'd always been so fastidious in business deals. He'd lost a great deal of his own money, or so he said."

"You didn't believe him?"

"I did at the time. Now, thinking back on it, I'm not so sure." He let out a sigh. "Anyway, I stuck my neck out for him with the board. I pleaded his case, told them that he was just as much a victim as anyone else. I managed to convince them to reinstate John, and then a week later, he up and quits and takes off for parts unknown. His sudden departure made me look like a fool, to say the least." Benson leaned forward, a gleam in his eye. "Tell me the truth. You two are investigating Draco's death, aren't you? There is no 'man behind the myth' piece, right? You're looking for a much bigger story."

Gary leaned forward and said in a conspiratorial tone, "Well, officially we're researching a human interest story on Draco. But unofficially, I guess you could say we're doing a bit of investigating." He closed one eye in a wink. "Just, please, don't tell our editor. He's already made a point of telling us that our beat is features, not true crime."

"We were hoping to talk to some of Draco's coworkers," I added, "maybe someone he was particularly close to."

Benson shook his head. "If that's what you've come here looking for, I'm afraid you're going to be sadly disappointed. Most of the people who worked with John have left for greener pastures, and I doubt the few that remain would remember much about him anyway. Draco kept pretty much to himself. He didn't forge any deep friendships during his tenure here. He wasn't one to socialize. He just did his job and went home."

"He didn't socialize at all? He wasn't friendly with any of the women?" I cut in. "That seems a bit hard to believe. From the photos I've seen, he was an attractive man."

Benson nodded. "Yes, he was and there were plenty of women interested in him, but he didn't give any of them the time of day." Benson snapped his fingers. "He once told me he was serious about some woman in Fox Hollow. She owned a dress store, I think. Krista something. Maybe you should check her out."

"We have," I said. "She, ah, didn't want to talk about him."

Benson shook his head. "I can understand that. He skipped out on her too, eh?" He slapped both hands down on the table and rose from the chair. "I have a staff meeting to get to. I'm sorry I couldn't have been more help."

"We appreciate your time," Gary said, rising as well.

"I do have one last question," I said. "Mr. Benson, did you ever hear of an investment counselor by the name of Adrian Arnold?"

Benson frowned. "That name isn't familiar. Was he involved with John in some way?"

"We're not sure," I said. "It's very possible."

"Well, I wish you good luck with your investigation. I'll be interested to read your story when it's done." He inclined his head toward the overflowing bagel tray. "Please, help yourselves to something before you leave. If you'd like something more substantial, I can have Phoebe send down for some eggs."

Gary picked up a bagel, split it, slathered some cream cheese on it. "No, this will be fine, thanks."

Benson started to leave, but he was halfway out the door when he suddenly turned and came back into the room. He shut the door behind him and walked over to us. "A thought just occurred to me," he said. "There was someone that John seemed to be close with."

I'd been pouring a cup of coffee, but now I paused, pot in hand. "Who?"

"Bernie Falco. I saw them together once or twice in the cafeteria. It might be nothing, but then again, maybe it could be something."

I set the pot and the cup down. "Great. Where is he? Can we speak with him?"

"He's not employed here anymore. He only worked here a short time—a month or two, if that—in accounting. His personnel record should still be in storage, but I don't know how much help it would be to you. Falco's been gone from here longer than Draco. I doubt any of the information in it is current."

"Hey, any little bit helps," Gary said. "We appreciate it."

"Fine. I'll have my records clerk, Marla, dig it out of storage. It may take a while. You're welcome to wait if you wish, otherwise I can have her email it to you."

"Email's fine," said Gary. He pulled a card out of his pocket and wrote his email address on it, then handed it to Benson. "Thank you for your time."

Benson gave us another curt nod, then left. Gary turned to me with a triumphant expression, then grabbed both my hands and started to do a little jig. "Now we're getting somewhere," he said jubilantly.

"Whoa, down boy," I said, pulling away from him. As he executed a swift two-step, I pulled out my phone. I typed "Bernie Falco" into the search engine and hit Enter. Twenty-five pages of hits came up. "Okay, not so uncommon a name. Let's narrow it a bit."

I typed "Bernie Falco—Benson, O'Toole and McShay" into the search engine. I was rewarded for my effort with one article about the company softball team. "Apparently Falco stayed on long enough to play in a few softball games," I remarked. I tapped on the article and a photo filled the screen. Beneath the photo the caption read: *Benson, O'Toole and McShay beat Oppeneimer Funds 7–5 in last softball game of season. Winning team pictured above.*

Gary leaned over my shoulder as we studied the photo. It was grainy, but I picked Draco out of the crowd right away. He was down on one knee, cap in hand, smiling right in the front row. Falco was in the last row on the far right. He appeared to have a muscular build, but the cap he wore was pulled down low on his forehead, partially obscuring his face. "Not much help, is it?" Gary hissed in my ear.

I squinted at the photo. "No, but . . ." I tapped at the image with my nail. "See here. He's got some sort of decal on his shirt."

Gary leaned closer. "By George, you're right." He took the phone from me and fiddled with it a bit.

"Well," I demanded after a few minutes. "Did you manage to make it larger or not?"

"Oh, yeah." He handed the phone back to me. "See what you think."

I took the phone and stared at the blown-up image of Falco's right bicep. The decal image came across clearly now.

A parrot.

I looked at Gary. "Are you thinking what I'm thinking?" I said. "Buck said that Adrian Arnold used to be in investments. Could it be possible . . ."

"Let's not jump to conclusions. Being an investment counselor is a heck of a lot different than working in accounting," Gary said.

"Maybe he just *said* he was an investment counselor. Like he *said* his name was Adrian Arnold."

Gary's phone pinged. He looked at the screen, then at me. "Well, we'll soon find out. Marla just sent the personnel file."

I leaned my chin on his shoulder as he opened the email. There were three attachments. I pointed to the one marked ID photo. "Open that first," I directed.

Gary clicked on the document and a second later the photo filled the screen. I sucked in my breath. The haircut was a bit more stylish, the hair a shade lighter, and he had on a shirt and tie, but there could be no mistaking that sharp nose, those thick lips, or those penetrating dark eyes.

Bernie Falco was none other than the man we knew as Adrian Arnold.

I felt suddenly jubilant. "So they did know each other," I cried. "I thought so when I saw them in the alley together. Adrian Arnold is Bernie Falco, or maybe it's the other way around. In either case, we've got to find him and confront him."

"And ask him what, exactly? If he killed Johnny Draco?"

"Well, duh, we can't just come out and ask him that," I said. "But I'm betting that Johnny went to him once he found out my aunt had died, and Arnold let him crash at his cottage. I don't know if Adrian is the one who killed him or not, but I'm willing to bet that Johnny's backpack is somewhere in his house. And I'll go a step further . . . once we find that backpack, I'll bet we'll know just who killed Draco, and why."

"Okay, I'm all for that, but we'd better put in an appearance at Urban Tails first. Robbie's alone, in case you've forgotten. The girls have class all day today."

"Ouch," I said. "I did forget. But Robbie's a good kid. He can handle it."

Gary arched a brow at me. "You know that's not fair, Shell. The kid's just starting. We want to keep him awhile, don't we? Besides, Adrian has no idea we know all this," he said. "He's not going anywhere."

"If he hasn't flown the coop already," I said. "He took off right after that altercation with Draco Saturday, remember? And he wasn't at his cottage when you went to check up on him."

"True." Gary stroked at his chin. Suddenly his expression brightened. "I know how we can find out where Adrian is. I could kick myself for not thinking of it sooner." He started to fiddle with his phone. "He's got a website and he lists all his appearances on it. I checked it last week and he had the grand opening scheduled. So let's just see what he's got on tap for today."

A few minutes later a website with pictures of beautiful parrots in various poses appeared. At the top was a bright gold banner that read *Arnold's Performing Parrots*. I recognized Honey Belle in a few of the photos, and Gary pointed out a large yellow parrot wearing a buccaneer hat who was obviously Captain Snaggle. There was a tab for each of the six birds, and any other time I would have relished going through it, but right now my focus was on one tab: the one marked *Coming Attractions*.

Gary clicked on the tab and the page opened. A large photo of Arnold, Captain Snaggle on one shoulder, graced the top of the page. Below that was a small paragraph:

Upcoming events. To schedule an event, please email me at parrotman.net, or fill out the form at the bottom of the page.

Below that was a list of upcoming appearances. Next to Saturday's date was the notation *Urban Tails Pet Shop Grand Opening, Fox Hollow, CT*. Sunday and Monday were blank, but next to today's date was a notation: *Saint Charles School, Annual Carnival, Winnset, CT. 10:30 am.*

I glanced at my watch. "It's ten thirty now. Winnset is only about twenty minutes from Fox Hollow. What say we go back to the shop, see how things are going, and then take a run over there? Maybe we'll get lucky."

Gary shoved his phone back into his pocket. "Or, I could drop you off at Urban Tails and take a quick ride out to Saint Charles School by myself, see if I can find Arnold."

"Oh, no." I shook my finger in his face. "No way are you going alone. We're in this together. Why should you have all the fun?"

• • •

It was a good thing we'd decided to go back. Urban Tails was filled with customers, and I felt guilty about leaving poor Robbie alone all morning. As Gary started to back into a parking space, I suddenly slapped myself on the side of the head. "The cats," I cried. "I totally forgot to feed them this morning." I groaned. "I'll have to run home. You know darn well my mother won't do it. She'll ignore them and they'll probably hide from her anyway."

"Okay. I'll go inside and help Robbie. When you get back we'll leave for Saint Charles School."

Gary hurried inside the shop and I slid behind the wheel. Fortunately I only lived a few minutes away. I parked in front of my house and went up the side entrance to the kitchen. As I opened the door, I was blindsided by a flying white blur.

"Purrday," I cried. "Calm down."

Purrday apparently had no intention of doing so. He kept winding himself around my ankles, making it nearly impossible for me to take more than a half step at a time. Finally I reached down and hefted the cat into my arms. "Purrday, calm down. I'm sorry I forgot about your food, but if you just give me a minute, I'll correct my error."

Purrday squirmed about and finally managed to extricate himself from my grasp. He started padding around in circles, letting out little mewling sounds. Kahlua looked up from her cat bed and squinted her eyes, obviously as puzzled as I was by her brother's strange behavior.

Purrday leapt up onto the counter and started to paw it. I walked over and stroked his back gently. "Purrday, what is the matter?" I really didn't expect an answer, but then again . . .

Purrday turned and swiped at the purse hanging from my shoulder with his large paw. Startled, I stepped back and the bag dropped from my shoulder onto the floor. Purrday jumped down, thrust his large paw inside my bag.

I knelt down. "What are you doing? What's gotten into you?" I demanded.

"Er-*owl*," Purrday growled. I looked down and saw the object he held captive beneath his large paw. My cell phone. I snatched it up, turned it on . . . and saw that I had a half dozen messages from Rita.

I looked at the cat, who'd gotten calmer now that I had the cell phone in my hands. I shook the phone at him. "Is this what you were trying to tell me? How did you know Rita was trying to get me?"

Purrday's shoulders rolled, the equivalent of a kitty shrug, and he ambled over to his own cat bed in the corner, his work obviously done.

I set my purse on the counter and hit the speed dial number for Rita. I got her voicemail. I left a message for her to call me back and then I hung up and dialed Sweet Perks. After five rings a harried-sounding Jodie answered.

"Uncle Wesley called about a half hour ago and said Aunt Rita couldn't come in today," she said. "He didn't say what was wrong but I guess she's got one of her migraines. I'm starting to get one too. Celia's late, and I've got a line out the door, plus one of the oven's on the fritz . . ."

I waited for Jodie to take a breath before telling her I'd try and call back later. I disconnected and stood for a minute, tapping my phone against my wrist, debating my next move, when it suddenly rang. I saw Rita's name on the caller ID so I quickly depressed the Answer button. "Rita! I was just trying to call you."

"It's not Rita, it's Wesley." Rita's husband sounded weak, as if he'd just run a decathlon. "I need your help, Shell," he said before I could speak. "That Detective Riser was here earlier. She took Rita downtown. I think they're going to charge her with Draco's murder."

Twenty

"Charge her with murder?" I gasped. "Wesley, are you sure?"

"Pretty sure." Concern was rife in Wesley's tone. "Riser came here and told Rita that she had to take her downtown. Rita tried to call you, but she couldn't get an answer. Riser didn't say they were charging her with anything, but it didn't sound good. I wanted to go along but Rita told me to stay here and call Tim Boswell, our lawyer. She also wanted me to keep trying to get you."

"Maybe it's not as bad as you think, Wesley. Maybe they just want to ask Rita some more questions."

His voice sounded haggard, tired. "I'd like to believe that, Shell, but I didn't get that impression from Riser. Something's up. I hate to impose, but . . . could you go down to the station, check on her for me?"

"Sure, Wesley. I'll go right now."

I hung up and stood for a minute, marshaling my thoughts. If the police were getting ready to charge Rita with Draco's murder, then they had to have found something, some sort of concrete evidence, linking her to it. What could it be? My lips thinned as I realized why I hadn't seen too much of Josh lately. Had he been avoiding me?

I had no time to worry about that now. I tiptoed upstairs and peeped into the guest bedroom. My mother was sound asleep, her sleep mask firmly in place. I shut the door, tiptoed back downstairs. I put out food for the cats, with some extra tuna for Purrday. Then I sent Gary a quick text: *Don't wait for me to go to the school. Something's come up. Will tell U later.* Then I grabbed my phone and keys and hurried out to my car.

• • •

Police headquarters was tucked into a skinny two-story brick building located in the downtown district of Fox Hollow. I flew into the parking lot, which was located right behind the building, and thank goodness there was a vacant spot at the far end, else I would have slid my convertible into the section marked *For Police Vehicles Only*. I locked my car and hurried around to the front, up the stone steps, and pushed through the plate glass door into the reception area. A policeman stood in one corner, taking a statement from a girl in baggy jeans and an even baggier sweatshirt. Aside from them, the waiting area appeared deserted. I looked over at the wide, walnut wood reception desk and my spirits fell as I recognized a familiar figure.

Quentin Watson saw me at the same time I saw him and he walked right over to me. "So it's true," he said without preamble. "They are charging Rita with Draco's murder. That's why you're here, isn't it?"

"I was just about to ask you the same thing," I said. "I got a message from Rita's husband that Riser brought her in for more questioning."

Quentin shook his head. "Not according to my source." He glanced furtively over his shoulder, first left, then right. Apparently satisfied, he leaned forward and said in a low tone, "From what I've been told, Rita's the best suspect they have. She had a history with the deceased, was heard arguing with him, and seen following him shortly before his demise."

"All of which is purely circumstantial."

"Oh, that's not all of it. I heard—"

He stopped speaking abruptly as a door at the far end of the room opened and Josh came through it. He caught sight of Quentin and me, blinked, then strode purposefully over to us. His expression was not happy. Not at all.

"Quentin, Shell," he said, his voice tight. "What are you doing here?" The question was directed more at me than at Quentin, but Quentin answered.

"My job. I'm here checking up on a report I got that Rita Sakowski is being charged with Draco's murder. Care to comment, Joshua?"

Josh didn't bother to hide his annoyance. "I don't know where you get your information, Watson, but you should vet your sources more carefully."

"So it's not true?" That from me.

Josh's answer was to take me by the elbow and propel me forcibly past the reception desk and through the door he'd just vacated. We walked in silence down a long hallway, and Josh pushed open a door at the end that led into a small conference room. He motioned for me to have a seat and then stood for a few seconds, running his hand through his hair, before flopping into the chair opposite mine.

"I didn't want to talk in front of Watson, who'll probably manage to find out the details anyway," he said. His expression was sorrowful. "I'm sorry, Shell."

I stared at him. "So it's true? You're charging her with murder?"

He shook his head. "I've got no choice. The evidence points straight to her."

I jumped out of the chair. "What evidence? So she argued with Draco—I bet so did a lot of other people, Krissa Tidwell for one! And some people think they saw her follow him, but all they saw was someone wearing a black hoodie. It could have been anyone. It could have been Wesley, for God's sake. He had a black hoodie on!"

"I wish that were all it was, Shell, but there's more."

I swallowed and lowered myself back into the chair. "More? What more?"

He raised his gaze to meet mine. "There's another detail we didn't release. There were prints on that digital instrument. Draco's and another set that we've only just identified."

I put my hand to my mouth. "Oh, no. They're Rita's?"

Josh nodded. "I'm sorry, Shell. But in light of that . . . my captain is pressuring me. We have to make an arrest."

I leaned back in the chair, jutted my teeth out, and worried at my lower lip. "This can't be happening," I muttered. I looked up at Josh. "Don't you see? Someone's trying to frame Rita. They probably knew about her argument and her past with Draco and figured she was the perfect patsy. The real killer, no doubt, wore gloves when he jammed that instrument down Draco's throat."

"It's a nice theory, Shell, but at this stage we need more than theories. We need concrete proof."

"So I guess it's up to me to get it for you," I grumbled. "Because you know as well as I do that once the police have a suspect . . ."

His hand shot out and his fingers dug into my forearm. "You know how I feel about you doing detective work," he said gruffly.

"And you know how I feel about innocent people being arrested."

We stood there in silence for a few moments, and then Josh cleared his throat. "Would you like to see Rita?" he asked.

"I don't know. Is it against the rules?"

"Probably, but I know if I don't let you we'll never get that dinner date," he said with a feeble attempt at a grin.

In spite of myself, I let out a dry chuckle. "No argument there."

Josh left and a few minutes later returned with a haggard-looking Rita. "Ten minutes," he said, before closing the door behind him. Rita walked over and flung herself into my arms. Her shoulders heaved, and I could tell she was trying her best not to cry. Finally she raised her head to look me straight in the eyes. "I didn't do it, Shell."

I rubbed a lazy circle on her back with my fingertips. "Of course you didn't. And neither did Wesley. But Rita, Josh said they found your fingerprints on the instrument that was rammed down Draco's throat."

"I know," she said. She leaned in close to me and whispered in my ear, "Johnny showed me that thing when we were in the alley that morning. He let me hold it. Told me how he played it for extra money. He wanted to give me a demonstration, but I just flung it back at him and told him I didn't want to hear his phony explanations." She huffed a stray hair out of her eyes. "That's the truth, I swear."

"I believe you. Rita, someone's framing you. Someone who knew about your past with Johnny, and who must have overheard your argument that morning. Did you see or hear anything when you were in that alley with him?"

She shook her head. "Nope. I was too focused on him, and too angry. I didn't know you were there until you told me."

I let out a breath. "Well, someone saw you. Someone who wanted Draco dead."

"Gosh, that could be any number of people."

"Okay, other than yourself and Wesley, who was hurt the most by Draco's swindle?"

"Well, Krissa, I suppose. And Stanley Sheer. He almost lost his business because of it. If his cousin hadn't bailed him out . . ."

"Sheer, huh?" I remembered the venom in the barber's tone when he'd spoken of Draco. I knew he'd heard the argument. He'd told Josh about it. And I remembered something else too. The way he'd flexed his hands when he spoke about Draco.

His large, powerful hands.

There was a knock on the door, and then Riser stuck her head in. "I have orders to take Mrs. Sakowski down for more questioning," she said.

I leaned over and gave Rita a swift hug. "Not one word till your lawyer gets here," I whispered in her ear. "And keep your chin up. I'm on this."

I pushed past Riser and back out into the main reception area. I noticed Quentin Watson had gone, and that was a good thing. I wasn't in the mood for his questions right now.

I had other fish to fry.

Stanley Sheer's shop was open, but there was no one waiting for a haircut. The barber was alone, reading a magazine. He glanced up as I came in. "Well, hello, Shell," he said. He gave my hair a critical glance. "Need a trim, I see."

"Not today, Stan. Today I need some information."

He looked wary. "Information? Regarding what?"

"Johnny Draco. What else."

Stanley sighed. "What else indeed? So, has your boyfriend figured out who done it yet?"

"They have a suspect in mind," I said carefully. "However, I believe it's the wrong suspect."

Stanley's eyes narrowed. "Ah, then it must be Rita. For what it's worth, Shell, I agree with you. Rita's not a murderer."

"Then why did you tell the police about the argument between Rita and Draco?"

Sheer shot me a plainly puzzled look. "I was asked if I'd seen anything unusual, so I answered truthfully. It never does any good to withhold information in an investigation, Shell. Surely you've watched enough crime shows on TV to know that. Any nugget of information you give can eventually lead to the apprehension of the killer."

"Yes, except when it leads the police in the wrong direction."

Sheer's eyes narrowed. "I'm sure they have more to go on than just my account."

I frowned. This wasn't getting me anywhere. Time to switch gears. "I understand Draco almost cost you your business."

Sheer raised a hand to rub at the back of his neck. "Someone's been talking, huh? Well, it's common knowledge to folks who were here around that time. I gave Draco every penny I had, mortgaged this building, because he was so certain it would pay big dividends. I guess you could say my greed got the better of me. If my cousin hadn't helped bail me out, why, I'd probably be bagging groceries in Kruger's now."

"And of course you weren't bitter about it."

"Of course I was. Had I seen him, I'd have definitely given him a piece of my mind. But kill him?" He shook his head. "Not my style."

"It was someone's," I said grimly. "Do you remember Draco ever mentioning any friends?"

"Friends?" He snorted. "Johnny was a lone wolf type. He didn't have friends, just acquaintances."

"Was one of those acquaintances Adrian Arnold?"

Sheer's jaw dropped slightly. "The parrot guy? Didn't look that way from what I've heard. Draco got pretty upset with his fortune at your shindig." He chuckled. "Next you'll be telling me you think the parrot guy killed him."

I crossed my arms over my chest. "I'm not ruling it out."

Sheer shrugged. "I did hear him one time on the phone. He was talking to some guy he called Mick. They were making arrangements to meet somewhere."

"Mick? Not Bernie?"

Sheer looked puzzled. "Who's Bernie? No, I'm sure he said Mick. I remember because I thought, is he talking to Mick Jagger of the Rolling Stones?"

"I don't suppose you heard a last name?"

"No, sorry."

"Well, thanks for your time." I turned to go, and then paused. "I imagine you've already been asked, but just where were you between two and three Saturday?"

Sheer laughed. "I was wondering when you'd get around to asking me that. It just so happens I've got one of the best alibis going." He turned and pointed to a photograph hanging behind the register of him standing in front of a long table, shaking hands with Buck Arnold. "I won Buck Arnold's drawing over at the Rialto stand. The drawing was held at two fifteen, and I was there for a half hour, taking photos and chatting with Buck. Oh, and there had to be about thirty people milling around, at least. I've told all this to Josh." He rubbed his hands together. "Not only does it clear me of any suspicion in Draco's death, but there's another benefit. Free movies for two months."

Twenty-one

Fortunately, there were only a handful of people in Urban Tails when I arrived. Robbie was behind the counter, ringing up a sale. I found Gary in aisle three with Geneva Parsons, an elderly lady who lived a few blocks away. As I approached I noticed Geneva held a small bundle tucked into the crook of her arm. The bundle started to squirm, and a little white, lilac and fawn head popped out. A pair of gold eyes fastened on me. "Merow," the cat said.

"Isn't she darling?" Geneva said. Her voice was raspy, probably from years of smoking. "Her name's June Bug, but I call her Juney. I just got her from the shelter this morning. She's a dilute calico."

I reached over to give Juney a pat on the head. "She's darling," I exclaimed. I smiled at Geneva. "I hope you don't mind if I steal Gary away for a moment."

Geneva laughed. "Not at all. He was just helping me decide on a collar for Juney."

I noticed the two collars the woman held in her free hand. One was pink with silver studs, the other bright red with yellow stones. I looked at the rack and reached for one in a pale lilac shade, with pale stones of fawn and lilac. "This one," I said. "It will compliment her coloring more."

"That it will. Thanks, Shell."

Geneva scooped up the lilac collar and headed over to the register. I motioned for Gary to follow me into the storeroom. Once I'd closed the door, Gary placed his hands on his hips and looked at me. "Okay, what happened? It had to be something important to make you put off going to St. Charles School."

"Oh, it was."

I quickly filled him in on what happened with Rita and my interview with Sheer. When I finished, he whistled. "Wow, poor Rita. You can bet now that they've got her prints on the murder weapon, the police won't be doing any more investigating."

"Which is why we have to," I said. "Sheer mentioned that Johnny was friendly with some guy called Mick. I wonder if that could be another of Adrian's aliases?"

"Maybe. And speaking of our boy Adrian, after I got your text, I called the school. It seems he didn't show up for his appearance today, and he didn't phone them to tell them so. The principal is plenty pissed, let me tell you. She tried calling him several times but the call went straight to voicemail. I tried myself. Same thing."

"So he's taken off," I said. "Flight is considered evidence of guilt, right?"

"Usually. But we don't know he's taken off for sure. Maybe something came up."

I let out a snort. "You don't believe that, and neither do I."

"You're right," Gary admitted. "I hate to say it, but it looks like Adrian could be the killer. So, what shall we do? Call Josh, tell him what we suspect?"

"That won't do any good. We've no proof, only a theory. We need to get proof, and there's only one way to do that." I flexed my fingers. "Ready for a little housebreaking?"

Gary groaned. "Would it matter if I said no?"

"Absolutely not. Let's go."

• • •

Adrian lived in a tiny bungalow on the outskirts of Frederick, down a winding dirt road that seemed endless. The cottage was set in the center of a clearing, with thick blankets of trees on either end. Gary pulled my convertible all the way up to the edge of the driveway, which ended abruptly less than two feet from the sloping front porch.

"Well, it's certainly . . . secluded," I said.

"Adrian told me he liked it because it gave him a lot of privacy with his parrots," Gary said as he switched off the ignition. "Okay, where do you want to look first? The house or the shed?"

"We'll take the house first, but then I do want to check on the parrots. If he took off and never called Mrs. Jenkins to look in on them . . ." I shook my head as my voice choked up. I couldn't abide animal mistreatment in any shape or form.

Gary reached over and squeezed my hand. "Don't worry. If that's the case, we'll see they get taken care of." He released my hand and opened his car door. "How do you plan to get in?"

"Don't know. I'm making this up as I go along."

Killers of a Feather

We exited the car and walked up the rickety steps to the front porch. I took a moment to peer through the large picture window. The interior was dark, but I could make out a sofa, love seat, a wide-screen TV mounted on the far wall. The floors looked to be hardwood, with throw rugs scattered about. I walked up to the front door and rang the bell. It echoed eerily through the house. When no one came to the door, I tried the knob. Locked.

I looked at Gary. "Is there a side entrance?"

"There's a sliding door around back. I tried that too, no luck."

"Let's try that one first."

We walked around to the back of the bungalow. Sure enough, there was a sliding glass door at the back of the house that overlooked the shed. I walked right up to it, grasped the handle, pulled—and let out a squeal as the door slid back.

"Well, I'll be damned," Gary cried. "It was locked up tight Saturday, which can only mean . . ."

"Adrian . . . or someone . . . has been here," I said. I started to enter the house, then stopped. I looked at Gary. "What if he's inside?"

Gary frowned. "I didn't see his car anywhere. The parrot van's still here." He gestured with his arm and I noticed the large truck parked near the thicket of trees. *Arnold's Performing Parrots* was splashed across the van's side in bright blue lettering.

"He must have come back for something. Maybe he notified someone to take care of his birds." I exhaled a deep breath, then stepped over the threshold and into the house. I saw at once that we were in the kitchen area, and a nice one at that. There were granite countertops, and a stainless steel stove and refrigerator off to the left. Ahead of us was the living room. At the far end of that was the front door. A long hallway led off to the right.

"So?" Gary spoke close to my ear. "Should we split up?"

I shook my head and pointed to the hallway. "No need. Let's start down there. I'm betting there's at least two bedrooms, Adrian's and a guest room."

We made our way slowly over to the hallway. Sure enough, there were three doors. Two were closed, and one was slightly ajar. I could see enough through the thin crack to know the open door led to the bathroom.

Gary looked at me, his hands on his hips. "Okay, Ace. Which one first?"

"Eeny, meeny, miny . . . moe," I said. I placed my hand on the doorknob to the right and twisted it. The door opened, and we stepped inside. A king-sized bed took up most of the room, and it was neatly made. There were two nightstands—one held a small clock radio, the other a lamp. There was a low-slung bureau directly across from the bed, and a small wide-screen TV rested on top of it. There was a set of double doors along the wall, ostensibly the closet. I walked over and flung open the doors.

The closet was empty, save for a few lonely-looking wire hangers and a pair of scuffed-up bedroom slippers lying side by side on the carpeted floor.

We stood just staring for a minute or two, and then Gary found his voice. "Guess you were right after all, Shell. Looks like he took a powder."

"Sure does. There's got to be some clue here somewhere as to where he might have gone, Gary. We can't let him get away with murdering Draco and letting Rita take the blame."

"*If* that's indeed what happened," Gary said grimly. "But I'll admit, it doesn't look too good for Adrian, or should I say Bernie Falco, right now."

I made a sweeping gesture with my arm. "You look around in here, make sure we didn't miss anything. I'm going to check the other room. I'm betting that's where Draco was staying."

I exited the master bedroom and went directly to the door across the hall. I touched the knob, and the door swung inward at my touch. This bedroom was much smaller than Adrian's, and had obviously been used as a combo office slash bedroom. There was a bookcase on one wall filled with books, both hardcover and paperback. I walked over to inspect some of the titles: *Parrot Training made Easy. Amazing Facts About Parrots. Guide to Quaker Parrots.* I spotted a few children's books about parrots as well. Practically every book was about parrots in some shape or form. The guy wasn't too obsessed with the birds, now was he?

I tore myself away from the bookcase and glanced around the rest of the room, looking for some clue that Johnny Draco had been here. There was a small desk over by the window, and a laptop was on top of the desk. I walked over and booted the laptop up, grimacing as it asked for a password. On a hunch, I typed "parrot" into it. Unfortunately, that didn't work.

A small futon was positioned between the bookcase and the desk. I figured that this might be where Draco had slept. I bent over the futon and ran my hand along its sides and in between the cushions. Nothing.

There was a door on the far wall. I opened that and saw it was a tiny closet, which was just as bare as the one in Adrian's bedroom. I started to shut the door when I noticed that one section of the rug seemed to be a bit higher than the rest. I got down on my hands and knees and felt around. There was a small section of loose carpeting that came up easily when I pulled at it, and I was looking at hardwood floor. I ran my hand along the grain and stopped as my questing fingers felt a slightly raised section of wood. I wiggled it a bit with my nail and it popped up slightly. One sharp tug and the block of wood came away in my hand, revealing a cavity beneath. I reached in and let out a small cry as my fingers touched something hard. Another two tugs and I was staring at a dirty gray backpack. Draco's backpack.

Heart pounding, I pulled it all the way out of the hole and carried it over to the desk. I pushed the laptop off to one side, unzipped the backpack, and spilled out the contents. There were two faded pair of jeans, four T-shirts, a few pair of jockey shorts, two pair of socks, a toothbrush, a pair of dirty sneakers, and a plastic bag. I pushed the clothes onto the floor and dumped the contents of the bag onto the table. There were a few tabloid magazines and a few issues of the *Fox Hollow Gazette*. In yet another clear plastic bag were some articles that looked like they'd been clipped out of newspapers. I dumped them on top of the desk too and started going through them. After a few minutes I realized they were all articles on Draco's swindle.

The door opened and Gary poked his head inside. "Nothing of interest in Adrian's bedroom," he reported. "How about in here?"

"I think I've found something," I said. I held up the baggie with the articles in it. "Draco was carrying around old articles about the swindle he was involved in."

Gary came over to my side and bent over to look at the clippings. "There are quite a few here," he said at last. "I wonder why Draco carried them around with him? As a reminder of his past, perhaps so he didn't make the same mistake twice?"

"Or as a reminder that one day he'd have to return to settle a score," I murmured. I rubbed at my chin thoughtfully. "Remember Rita said that he told her he was just as much a victim as anyone else. As Bernie Falco, we know he was an investment counselor too. What if . . . what if that investment was his idea? What if Adrian/Bernie was the true mastermind, the one who defrauded John Draco and all those people?"

"I guess it's possible, although if Arnold were a criminal mastermind and had stolen that money, he'd probably have had it laundered and he'd be in some mansion somewhere, not this little bungalow out in the sticks."

"Maybe so," I agreed reluctantly. "But he was involved in that scam in some shape or form, I'll bet my last dollar on it."

"If you ask me, it's a better possibility he got taken in, same as Draco. The whole thing just might have been what it was, a very bad investment. Those guys saw dollar signs, a way to make easy money, and it backfired on them."

"I might agree with that, except for one thing: Draco told both Krissa and Wesley Sakowski that he'd found out information that would change people's lives. I think whatever he'd found out would clear his name, and someone didn't want him to do that."

"And you think that someone was Adrian?"

"Well, right now I can't think of anyone else," I said. "If he's anywhere in the vicinity we've got to find him, Gary. If he didn't kill Draco, I bet he knows who did. I can't let Rita go to prison for a crime she didn't commit."

"Okay, fine." Gary threw up both hands in a gesture of surrender. "I know better than to argue with you. We'll go out and look in the shed, see if there's anything out there that might tell us where he went."

"Thanks." I looked at the jumble on the desk. "I thought for sure the way Draco guarded that backpack that he had something valuable in here. I guess I was wrong about that." I picked up the backpack and shook it, then thrust my hand inside and felt around. "Nope, nothing else . . . oh!"

"What's the matter?" Gary looked at the expression on my face. "Did you find something?"

"I-I think so." My fingers had slid inside a hole in the lining. Now I pulled out what I'd found, a long scrap of paper and a photograph, and laid it on the table.

"Those were inside the lining?" Gary peered at the contents. "Rather odd."

I picked up the paper. It was a crude drawing, with lots of slashes and lines. If one stretched their imagination, it could resemble a floor plan—but to what? The right end was jagged, as if someone had torn a piece off.

I decided to examine it more closely later, and turned my attention to the photograph. It was of two men. One was definitely Johnny. He looked a lot more dapper in this photograph, clean-shaven in his three-piece suit, and his hair—what appeared to be a dark brown—clipped in a short style. The other man was tall and a bit paunchy around the middle. He had a round face, a pointed nose and wore dark-framed glasses. His most arresting feature, though, was his hair, or rather, lack of hair. This man was totally bald. I flipped the photo over, but there was nothing written on the back that would give me any sort of clue as to his identity.

Gary peered over my shoulder at the photo. "Tough-looking customer," he said, pointing to the bald man. "At least we know it's not Adrian."

"Well, it's someone Draco knew. He had these items with him for a reason." I was pretty sure the paper and photo might have been the reason he'd acted so protective of the backpack, and why he'd secreted it underneath the floorboard. He was keeping it safe, but from who?

I peered at the photograph again, then tapped at the image of the bald man with my nail. "You know, something about this guy does seem a bit familiar, but I can't quite place it."

"Someone like that would stand out. I haven't noticed many bald men hanging around Fox Hollow."

I started to slide the photo into my pocket, then stopped. "Wait. Stanley Sheer said Draco was friendly with someone named Mick. Maybe this is him."

"Mick, you say? Sounds more like a nickname. It's not much to go on."

Gary handed me back the photo, then glanced at his watch. "It's getting late. Let's check out that shed and get back to the store. Then you can call Joshy—or not."

I slid the photo and paper into my pocket, then hastily shoved the clothes back into the backpack and slung it over my shoulder. Gary and I made our way out of the bungalow and over to the shed. As we approached the worn-looking structure, I paused.

"Did you hear that?" I asked Gary.

Gary shook his head. "I didn't hear anything."

"It's coming from the shed," I said. I quickened my pace, and when I got to the door I paused and pressed my ear to the wood. "There it is again," I cried.

Gary had come up behind me, and now he also pressed his ear to the door. "You're right," he said after a minute. "What is that sound?"

My face had morphed into a grim expression. "I hope it isn't what I think it is." I pulled on the door. "It's stuck," I said.

Gary and I both put our shoulders against the aging wood and pushed. Finally the door groaned inward, and the two of us nearly toppled inside. The sound we'd heard was louder now, accompanied by another sound . . . the flapping of wings.

"That's definitely a bird," Gary said. "Maybe one of the parrots got out?"

I didn't answer, just moved slowly forward. That particular sound, I knew, didn't belong to just any parrot. It was the honking sound native to eclectus parrots—the same type of breed as Honey Belle.

"Didn't you say Honey Belle was missing when you were here Saturday?" I called over my shoulder.

"Yep. The other cages were full, but hers and Captain Snaggle's were empty."

"Well, it sounds to me like Honey Belle might have come back."

I'd turned the corner and now could see the rows of bird cages lining one wall. As I drew closer, I felt my heart skip a beat. All the cages were empty. "Gary," I called. "The birds are gone."

"They are?" He was next to me in an instant. He peered at the empty cages, scratching at his head. "They were all here Saturday, I swear."

"Maybe one is still here," I murmured. "Hear that?"

The sound of flapping wings was a bit louder now. "It sounds like it's coming from over there." Gary pointed to the far end of the shed.

Slowly I moved forward, Gary right behind me. When I got to the end of the aisle I peered cautiously around the corner. I sharp gasp escaped my lips as I caught sight of Honey Belle. The bird was sitting on a large stand positioned off to the left of an oak door. Her head was cocked, and she was flapping her wings back and forth.

I moved toward the bird slowly, so as not to frighten her. "Honey Belle," I whispered. "Girl, what's wrong?"

The bird let out another mournful honk. "Trouble," she croaked. "You're in big trouble, kiddo." Her head bobbed toward the door, and I noticed it was slightly ajar.

Behind me I heard Gary mutter, "I don't have a good feeling about this," and I agreed, but we'd come this far. I, at least, had to see it through. I walked slowly over to the door and gave it a shove. Instead of swinging open, the door creaked open a couple inches and then stopped, as if something were blocking it. Through the small opening I could make out a workbench and some tools, so this was obviously a workroom of some sort. I leaned forward and poked my nose in, trying to peer around the edge of the door. I looked down, then gasped and put my hand to my mouth.

Adrian Arnold was sprawled awkwardly across the floor. His hair was matted with blood, and his hands were covered with what appeared to be bloody defensive wounds. There could be no doubt he was dead.

Behind me, Honey Belle's wings flapped insistently. "Big trouble," she croaked. "You're in big trouble, kiddo."

I took a step backward and bumped full tilt into Gary. His brows knit together as he noted the expression on my face. "Don't tell me," he said. "You found Arnold."

I exhaled slowly. "Yep. Better call 911," I said.

Gary reached for his phone, paused as we heard the sudden crunch of tires on gravel outside. He walked over to the door, peered out, then slid his phone back into his pocket.

"Not necessary," he said. "They're already here."

Twenty-two

We walked outside the shed just as Amy Riser and a uniformed policeman alighted from the cruiser. Amy's eyebrows raised slightly as she caught sight of us, but she kept her expression neutral as she approached. "What are the two of you doing here?" she asked bluntly.

"We came looking for Adrian Arnold," Gary answered. "We had a few questions for him."

Her eyes narrowed. "You did? What sort of questions?"

Gary shrugged. "Sort of a moot point now. He's dead."

Now her eyebrows winged skyward. "Dead? Are you sure?"

I nodded. "Oh, yes."

Her lips thinned. "Where's the body?"

"There's a workroom inside. He's on the floor."

"Don't move, either of you," Riser barked. She turned to the other officer, a middle-aged guy with a slight paunch. The name tag on his shirt read *Brennan*. "Watch them. Bloodgood should be here in a few minutes."

Riser disappeared inside the shed. Gary and I walked a few feet away from Brennan and huddled together. "She's a real pleasant individual," Gary muttered under his breath. "Does she even have teeth? I don't think I've ever seen her crack a smile."

"She is a bit on the stiff side," I admitted. "I think she's just very intense about her job."

"She's not even on the Fox Hollow force. She was just supposed to spell Joshy for the weekend, wasn't she?"

I shrugged. "Yes, but Josh has been working shorthanded. He told me he had to get one of the regular patrolmen to help interrogate suspects. His captain probably asked Riser to stick around and help out too. She's probably just trying to make a good impression so Josh will give a good report back to her superior."

Gary wiggled his eyebrows. "Or maybe she's just trying to impress Joshy, period. Ever think of that?"

I had, actually, but I'd sort of tabled that thought due to recent events. Amy Riser, in spite of her no-nonsense attitude, was an attractive woman. She hadn't really displayed any interest in Josh other than camaraderie, but I had an idea she was a master at keeping her feelings under wraps. Further discussion on the subject was spared as another police cruiser came down the gravel driveway and pulled up behind Riser's. Josh and another officer I recognized, Tim Riley, alighted. The two of them made their way over to us, and the surprise on Josh's face was evident as he looked at me. "Shell? What are you and Gary doing here?"

Before either of us could answer, Riser emerged and walked right up to Josh. "Arnold's dead," she said flatly. Her thumb jerked in our direction. "They found the body."

"Actually Honey Belle found it," I said.

Josh looked at me. "Honey Belle? The parrot?"

I nodded. "She was on a perch near the workroom door. She kept honking and flapping her wings."

Riser looked puzzled. "I didn't see a bird in there."

"She's upset. She's probably hiding somewhere," I said. I turned to look at Josh. "We should look for her. For all we know, she could be a witness."

Riser let out a snort. "What? That's ridiculous."

"Not so much," Gary put in. "Arnold had Honey Belle with him Saturday afternoon. It's not beyond the realm of possibility the bird was with him when he died, which would mean . . ."

"It's possible Honey witnessed Adrian's murder," I finished.

Riser shook her head. "So you're telling me this bird could identify the killer?"

"That depends," I said. "When I was in there before, Honey kept repeating a phrase 'Big trouble. You're in big trouble, kiddo.' It's possible she could have heard the killer say that to Arnold."

Riser frowned. "So how would that help us identify the murderer?"

I shoved my hands into my jacket pocket. "Right now, I have no idea. Maybe she heard the killer say something else. We won't know until we find the bird."

Riser muttered something under her breath and looked at Josh. "Arnold doesn't appear to be dead very long. It doesn't look as if rigor mortis has even begun to set in. I've already called Quigley."

"Good. You, Riley and Brennan secure the area and wait for him." Josh jerked his thumb at Gary and me. "You two, come with me."

We followed Josh around the side of the shed. He stopped abruptly, almost causing me to run full tilt into his back. "We can talk here," he said. He folded his arms across his chest and his features settled into his cop face. "Okay, what were the two of you doing out here? You first, Shell."

"We were following up on a lead," I said. I paused and then added dramatically, "Adrian Arnold wasn't who he appeared to be."

"I know. He also went by the name of Bernie Falco."

I felt color rise to my cheeks. "So you know about that."

Josh folded his arms across his chest. "Mac Benson had his file clerk send me a copy of Falco's personnel file earlier. He explained in the email with the attachment that he didn't want to be accused of withholding evidence in a murder investigation. He also mentioned the two crime reporters who'd paid him a visit earlier."

I felt my palms start to sweat. "Two crime reporters?"

"My first thought, of course, was Quentin, but it seems he was at City Hall all morning covering an important council meeting. I checked with Watson's assistant, who told me they hadn't hired any new reporters recently, and no one named Sam Malone or Diane Chambers. Once I heard her description, though, I had a good idea who they might be." He focused his laser-sharp gaze on me. "I thought you were going to cool it with the investigating."

I shifted my weight to my other foot. "I don't recall exactly promising I'd do that," I hedged.

"No, you didn't, did you? Honestly, Shell, I wish you would have some faith in me."

"I do, Josh. It's the legal system I have a problem with."

He sighed. "I came here hoping to grill Arnold on his past with Draco, maybe get a confession out of him. No chance of that now."

My eyes popped. "A confession! So you thought he might have killed Draco?"

"I was willing to consider that possibility. I told you, Shell, I don't think Rita is guilty."

"They definitely knew each other," I said. "I found evidence."

"What sort of evidence?"

I slid the backpack off my shoulder and held it out. "This was Draco's backpack, the one he seemed so possessive of when he was in my shop Thursday night."

Josh took the backpack, unzipped it, and shoved his hand inside. "Looks like he traveled light," he said.

My hand tightened on the pocket where the scrap of paper and photo rested. I could feel Gary's eyes on me and I studiously avoided looking at him. "Yep," I said. "I didn't see the backpack on Johnny in any of the photos taken on Saturday, and I didn't recall seeing it with his body either. He was holding on to it so tightly that I figured he wouldn't just leave it anywhere, so we started figuring out who he might have stayed with. Once we found out that Arnold was really Bernie Falco, and that he and Draco knew each other . . ."

"You came out here to confront Arnold," Josh finished. "Once again, you took some chance."

"Hey, I'm here too," Gary protested, waving his hands back and forth in front of Josh's face. "Between the two of us I bet we could have handled Arnold."

"Maybe. But what if you'd come across Arnold and his killer? Could you have handled that?" He reached out and put his hands on my shoulders. "This isn't an episode of your old TV show, Shell, where justice prevails and you save the day. This is real life."

"I know the difference, Josh," I said. "But surely the fact that Arnold and Draco knew each other counts for something?"

He slid the backpack onto his shoulder. "Not much, I'm afraid. With Arnold dead, all we have is supposition, and the DA's not interested in that."

"No, he's more interested in Rita's prints on the murder weapon. With that exception, all the evidence against her is circumstantial."

"True, but he thinks a jury will buy it," replied Josh.

"But what about this?" I cried, swinging my arm in the direction of the shed. "Rita couldn't have killed Arnold. You've got her in jail."

"Yes, but there's nothing that proves Arnold's murder is related to Draco's," he replied. "We're not certain they even knew each other, and now both of them are dead. The DA will say it's unrelated."

"But you don't believe that, do you?" I asked.

"It doesn't matter what I believe, Shell, it's what the evidence points to. And right now, unfortunately, those fingerprints point straight to Rita."

"Honk!"

We all looked up as a red blur flew out of the shed. Honey Belle flew over to a nearby tree, settled on a low-hanging branch. "*Honk. Honk.*"

"The poor thing," I murmured. "She must be frightened to death."

Gary turned to Josh. "If I were you I'd put that bird in protective custody," he said. "She might utter a phrase at any time that could lead us to Arnold's killer."

Honey Belle cocked her head. "*Honk.* You're in big trouble, kiddo! Big trouble! *Honk.*"

Gary pointed to the parrot. "See. Out of the mouths of babes—or parrots."

The corners of Josh's lips turned down. "Reaching a bit, aren't you?"

"Hey, I hate to break it to you, but there are documented cases of parrots as valuable witnesses in murder cases. I read about one recently where a parrot repeated the phrase "Don't shoot" and mimicked an argument between a husband and a wife before the husband was shot dead. Family members believed the parrot had witnessed the event. There was a lot of controversy as to whether the parrot could be called as a witness."

"I read about that as well," said Josh. "The parrot's words were ruled inadmissible."

"But still, he was considered a witness," Gary said. "Parrots are darned smart. I wouldn't take the possibility of Honey Belle as a potential witness lightly if I were you."

"I'd like to know what happened to all the other birds," I said. "Did Arnold take them somewhere? Or did the killer get rid of them, and he missed Honey Belle?" I pressed a hand to my stomach. The thought of what might have possibly happened to the other parrots made me ill.

"I'll give animal control a call," Josh said. "I'll have my men make inquiries about the other birds too. I don't suppose you could give me descriptions of them."

"No, but there's a page devoted to them on Arnold's website, with photos," said Gary. "That should help."

Josh looked at me. "I could use some help getting that parrot into her cage," he said. "Any ideas?"

"Maybe," I said. I unzipped the top of my crossbody bag and removed a small package of saltine crackers. "Lucky for you I always carry a snack with me."

I unwrapped the package, removed a cracker, and walked slowly toward the bird, my hand with the cracker extended out. "Honey Belle," I said softly. "Are you hungry?"

The bird cocked her head, then flapped her wings. In one swift motion she flew over and perched herself on my shoulder. I held the cracker up, and she nibbled at it.

"Honey Belle hungry! Good grub! Good grub!" she croaked.

"Poor thing. When did you eat last?" I looked at Josh over my shoulder. "If you get her cage, I can crumble these crackers up and try to entice her inside."

"I'll be right back." Josh turned to go, then paused and pointed a finger at Gary. "You wait right here."

Josh disappeared inside the shed and Gary hurried over to me. "You didn't give him what you found in the backpack," he said. It was a statement, not a question.

I patted my pocket and shook my head. "Not just yet, but I will."

Gary clucked his tongue. "You're setting yourself up for another lecture, you know. And isn't it a crime to withhold evidence in a murder investigation."

"It is, but there's no proof that these articles are evidence of anything . . . yet."

Gary's eyebrow twitched. "Draco had them hidden in the backpack's lining. They're evidence of something."

"Maybe. Or maybe they were just things he couldn't bear to part with." My hand dipped into my pocket and I pulled out the photograph of the bald man I'd found in Johnny's backpack.

Gary rolled his eyes. "You can't be serious."

"Why not? Animals recognize faces. Besides, I remember reading an article once about a study some college did with wild pigeons. They recognized faces and weren't fooled by a change of hair color or clothes. Parrots are just as smart if not smarter, I think Honey Belle's proven that. It's worth a shot."

Gary made a sweeping gesture. "Fine. Go ahead."

I held the photo up in front of the bird, who was still nibbling on the cracker. "Honey, look at this. Do you know him?"

The bird's head rose, and her beady eyes fastened on the photo. She looked at it for a few seconds, then went back to her cracker.

I held up my hand. "Don't say it," I cautioned Gary. "Please." I turned and waved the photo in front of Honey Belle again. "Come on, Honey. Have you seen this guy? Did he come here to visit Adrian, or maybe Johnny?"

Gary's mouth opened to say something, but I shot him a withering look and he shut it again. Honey Belle's head lifted. She stared at the photo, and this time I swore I saw a gleam in those beady eyes. "*Honk. Mick, you old devil. What did you pull? Honk.*"

Gary let out a low whistle. "Well, what do you know? You were right, Shell."

I couldn't resist throwing him a smug smile. "Maybe next time I make a suggestion you won't be so quick to doubt me."

Honey Belle resumed eating, and I slid the photo back into my pocket. "So now we know this is a photo of the mystery man Mick who Sheer told me about," I said. "If Honey recognized him, it's a good bet he knew, or at least was acquainted with, Arnold as well as Johnny." I balled my hand into a fist. "He's the key to this, I know it. Now all we have to do is find him."

"How do you propose we do that?" Gary asked. He started to tick off on his fingers. "We have no name, no address, no past history with either victim, other than Stanley Sheer overhearing Draco calling someone Mick on the phone. Kind of like looking for a needle in a haystack, doncha think?"

"Maybe, but we've got to give it a shot. With Arnold dead, our best suspect is gone, and I don't fancy seeing Rita in jail for a crime she didn't commit."

Josh emerged from the shed. He had Honey Belle's cage in his arms. He came over to us and set the cage down on the ground. I took the remaining crackers, held them up to show Honey Belle, then crumbled them and scattered them on the cage's floor.

"There's food, Honey Belle," I crooned at the parrot.

Honey Belle cocked her head at me, her beady eyes fastened on the cage and the treasure within. Then she flapped her wings and flew over to the cage. She thrust her head inside, looked around. She seemed to hesitate just inside the door. Hunger won out over caution, though, and she stepped inside the cage and started hungrily snapping up the bits of cracker. Once she was all the way inside, I hurried over, knelt down, and before the bird could do anything, I'd closed and locked the cage door. Honey Belle paused in her eating to look at me through the bars of the cage. She blinked twice, then gave her head a shake and went back to devouring the cracker bits.

"Sorry about that, Honey," I said. I glanced up at Josh. "What are you going to do with her?" I asked.

Josh frowned. "I never thought I'd say these words, but Gary has a point. The parrot might be considered a witness. I'll take her back to the station and talk it over with the captain."

"If you need a place to keep her, I'd be happy to look after her," I volunteered. "And the other parrots too, when you find them."

Josh's lips twitched. "Thanks, I'll keep that in mind." He looked back at the shed and shook his head. "There is the possibility, you know, that this was a robbery."

"A robbery?" I said. "How do you figure that."

"Parrots in general are pricey birds, and Arnold's are even more valuable because of how well they've been trained. You said that Arnold wasn't around much this weekend, so someone, maybe even a few someones, might have come here to steal them. Arnold might have come back and surprised them. A case of being in the wrong place at the wrong time."

"That would tie everything up nice and neat," I remarked. "Too much so, perhaps. I'm not buying it."

The crunch of tires on gravel alerted us to the fact another vehicle was approaching. We looked up to see the coroner's wagon coming to a stop behind Josh's car.

Josh turned to us. "You two can go, for now. I'll probably have some more questions for the two of you later."

"Don't leave town, right?" Gary quipped. That remark was met with a frosty stare from Josh.

"Something like that," he said. He hefted the cage in his hands and started back toward the shed. I saw Quigley exit the wagon and hurry over to him. The two talked in low tones for a few minutes, then both vanished inside the shed. A few seconds later Tim Riley and Officer Brennan emerged and stood in the shed's doorway like two guard dogs.

"I guess that concludes any further snooping on our part," Gary remarked, inclining his head toward Riley and Brennan. "So what now?"

I looked at my watch. "It's three thirty. If all's well back at the store, I'd like to go back to Benson, O'Toole and McShay. If both Adrian and Johnny knew this guy Mick, maybe he's also connected to that firm. Maybe we'll catch a lucky break and Benson, or maybe someone else there, might recognize him."

"Okay. What have we got to lose except time."

I called the store and Robbie assured me that he and the girls were all fine and had no problem working straight through till six if need be. "I can close up, no problem," he said. "Besides, we all could use the overtime."

"Thanks, Robbie. I'll take you up on the offer. I owe you guys one."

"No problem, Ms. McMillan."

Gary chuckled as I disconnected. "You feel guilty, don't you?"

"A little," I admitted. "But if we can get a lead that will clear Rita, it will be well worth it."

We flipped a coin for driving privileges and Gary won. He pulled into Benson, O'Toole and McShay's parking lot a little after four, and as luck would have it, found a prime parking spot right near the front entrance. I looked on that as a good omen as we once again pushed through the glass door into the lobby. Adelle had apparently left for the day, replaced by another girl, a honey blonde in a skintight sweater. She raised her heavily mascaraed eyes as we approached, and I saw them light up with interest as Gary leaned an elbow on the counter. "Good afternoon," he said, tossing the blonde a dazzling smile. "Could you ring Mr. Benson and tell him that Mr. Malone and Ms. Chambers are back and would like to see him?"

"Sure thing." She picked up the phone and punched in a number, her eyes never leaving Gary's face. "Hello, Phoebe? It's Sara. Could you tell Mr. Benson there's a Mr. Malone and a Ms. Chambers here to see him?" She put her hand over the receiver and smiled at us. "It'll just be a few minutes," she said.

"No problem—Sara," Gary said. "That's such a pretty name. With or without an *h*?"

"Without." Sara giggled, then abruptly turned back to the phone. She listened for a few seconds, then gave her head a brisk shake. "What? Really? Well, okay." She hung up the phone and looked at us, her expression puzzled. "Phoebe said that Mr. Benson isn't in to Mr. Malone and Ms. Chambers, but he could spare a few minutes for Mr. Presser and Ms. McMillan?"

Gary and I looked at each other, then laughed. "Busted!" we both said at the same time, which earned us an even more puzzled look from Sara. Gary leaned across the counter. "Thanks. We know the way."

Phoebe met us when we stepped off the elevator. She shot us both a sheepish grin as she said, "I could just kick myself. I caught your old show once or twice on cable when I'd get home a little early." She lowered her lashes and shot Gary a shy smile. "I almost told you I thought you resembled Gary Presser but I thought better of it. Some people get upset when you tell them you think they look like someone they've seen on television."

"True," Gary said and laughed. "The trick is to tell them that they look *so* much better in person."

She laughed. "I'll remember that."

We went down the same hall as before, past the conference room we'd been in that morning, to an oaken door at the end of the hall. A brass nameplate on the door read *Mac Benson, Executive VP*. Phoebe pushed it open and motioned for us to enter. Mac Benson was seated behind a massive cherrywood desk, typing away on his computer. He barely glanced up as we entered. "Thank you, Phoebe. Mr. Presser, Ms. McMillan, please have a seat. I'll be with you in just a second."

Gary and I seated ourselves in the buttery soft leather chairs in front of Benson's desk. He typed for a few more minutes, then abruptly swung away from the computer to face us. He folded his hands on the desktop in front of him. "Well, well. I should have made the connection as to your real identities sooner. It's been awhile since I've seen a *Cheers* rerun. I used to like that show." He looked at me and his lips curved upward in a smile. "My teenaged son has a poster of you in his room, Ms. McMillan. I'm sorry, I never watched your show but he loved it. He was extremely annoyed when it was canceled."

"All good things must end," Gary said. He shifted a bit in his chair. "So how did you find out? I guess Detective Bloodgood ratted on us, huh?"

"He was very diplomatic about it," Benson said. "He said that you two were apparently carrying your fictitious roles a bit too far. I do believe he was concerned for your safety." His eyes narrowed and he leaned back in his chair. "That said, I can only assume the good detective has no idea you're here now, does he?"

"No, but rest assured we intend to share any pertinent information with the police," I said quickly.

"I see. So the reason for this visit is more questions about Johnny Draco?"

"Just one, actually." I pulled the photograph out of my pocket and laid it on the desk in front of Benson. "Do you recognize that man?"

Benson flicked a glance at the photograph, then picked it up to scrutinize it more closely. "Yes, I recognize him," he said finally. "He met with John here a few times." His hand shot out and he tapped at Mick's face. "He was an executive with Tandor Industries, the company Johnny urged those people to invest in."

Gary and I exchanged a swift glance. "And is his name Mick?" Gary asked.

Benson shook his head. "Mick? Oh, no. His name is Kruse. Charles Kruse."

Twenty-three

Disappointment arrowed through me at Benson's answer. "Charles Kruse? Are you sure?"

"Positive. John gave me one of his business cards." He opened the middle drawer of his desk, started to rummage in it. "I think I might still have it somewhere around—ah, yes. Here is is."

He passed the cardboard square over to us. Gary took it and we both looked at it. It was a plain white card with a tiny picture of a computer in the corner. The words *Tandor Industries–Software Specialists* was embossed in gold across its face. Below that in bold black letters was *C. Kruse, OCN*.

Gary laid the card on the desk. "What does OCN stand for? I've never heard of that."

"I believe it's Open Computer Networking, or something like that. John was rather vague. I don't think he knew either."

I peered at the card and pointed with the edge of my nail to Kruse's name. "There's only an initial. Are you certain his name is Charles?"

Benson shrugged. "I admit I'm guessing at that. I did hear John refer to him as Chuck, which I know is a nickname for Charles."

I picked the card up. "Would you mind if we kept this?" I asked.

"Not at all. Now, if there's nothing else, I do have a report I have to get ready for a meeting at five thirty."

"I think we're done here," Gary said, rising. "No need to bother your assistant. We can see ourselves out."

We exited the office and made our way back down the hall to the bank of elevators. There were a few others waiting there, so we rode down to the lobby in silence. Once we were outside, though, Gary turned to me. "Well, I guess that blows Honey's ID skills," he said.

"I'm not so sure," I remarked. "And I'm not so sure about this guy's name. I think it's an alias." I pulled a notepad and a pen out of my purse. I printed out C KRUSE on one line, then OCN next to it. "You've heard of anagrams, right?" As Gary nodded, my pen flew across the paper. C KRUSE became SUCKER. OCN turned into CON.

Gary looked at me, a glimmer of admiration in his eyes. "Not bad, Shell. Pretty good, in fact."

I took a small bow. "Thank you, thank you. So, I think we can assume from this clever anagram that this Mick person used a phony name. He definitely had something to do with what went down with Tandor Industries." I tapped the card thoughtfully against my chin. "How much you want to bet he's not even connected with that company."

"I'm not taking that bet. You're on a roll."

I looked at the photo again. "I can't shake the feeling of familiarity I get when I look at this guy's picture, though. It's like a sense of déjà vu, like I've seen him somewhere before."

"We need to regroup, attack this from a fresh angle." Gary looked at his watch. "It'll be after six by the time we get back. What say we stop, feed the kitties, and then head over to Bottoms Up for a good meal. My treat."

"That'll work," I said. "Mother texted me earlier that she was going to have dinner with Garrett Knute. He was going to pick her up at five thirty, so we don't have to worry about running into them."

"Unless Knute takes her to Bottoms Up."

I chuckled. "No worries there. They were going to some Portuguese restaurant in Franklin."

Gary whistled. "Knute's really pulling out all the stops to impress her, it seems."

"He's impressed with her Shakespearean career, and of course she's playing that card to the hilt. Garrett's walking around with stars in his eyes, and she's taking full advantage."

"All the better for us," Gary remarked. "Give Garrett time, though. Eventually he'll come around."

"Not too soon, I hope."

This time I won the coin toss, and we got into the car. Gary pulled out his iPhone as soon as I backed out of the space. I'd just gotten to the highway entrance when he said, "I was right not to take that bet. I pulled up everything I could find on Tandor Industries. There's no mention of a Charles Kruse being one of their executives."

"So he lied."

"About being an executive, at least. He might have worked there in a lower capacity. I googled Charles Kruse as well, and I've got to tell you, the ten guys that came up aren't a match either. For one thing, they all have hair."

I giggled. "They could be wearing toupees."

"True, but none of them are the right age. Most of them are either in their early or late twenties, and three of them are over sixty. Our guy looks to be around Johnny's age, early forties."

"So another dead end. For now, at least," I said glumly.

"Don't worry." Gary reached over to pat my hand. "Everything will look better over a Broadway Babe Burger. You'll see."

• • •

Purrday and Kahlua were in the front window, noses pressed to the glass, when I pulled up in front of the house. They jumped down as soon as Gary and I got out of the car and greeted us at the back door, both meowing loudly. I bent down to give each of them a pat on the head. "Did you two rascals really think we wouldn't feed you? How could we forget you?"

The two of them wound in and out around my ankles as I made my way to the cupboard where I kept their food. I spooned them each out a generous helping of tuna and turkey while Gary got out their favorite dry food and filled the large bowl they shared. I set their bowls down on the place mat and the two cats hunkered down, side by side, to enjoy their meal. I turned to Gary. "Ready to go?"

He was fiddling with his phone. "Yeah, my battery's low. Let me just get my charger and we can take off." He smacked his lips. "I can taste that burger now."

As Gary hurried upstairs, I reached into my jacket and pulled out the scrap of paper and photograph of Mick. I sat down at the table and laid them both out in front of me. I pushed the photo off to one side and concentrated on the paper. Something caught my eye, and I held the paper up to the light and peered closely at it. I could discern very faint marks on the top and side, as if something had been written there and then erased. I got up, walked over to the drawer near the sink and rummaged around until I found a pencil. I went back to the paper and moved the pencil over the paper, lightly shading the area, then peered at the paper again. Now I could see two numbers, and eight and a five. I looked more closely and realized there was a small *x* in between the numbers. Eight by five. Measurements? To what?

A loud knock on the back door broke my concentration. I ignored it. Whoever it was knocked again, louder and more insistently this time. I sighed, set the paper down, and went over to the door. I peered through the curtain, and let out a sharp breath. "You've got to be kidding," I grumbled, and flung open the door. I stared at the long-haired man in the scarred black motorcycle jacket and well-worn baggy jeans who stood on my stoop. "Elvin Scraggs," I cried. "What are you doing here?"

Elvin offered me a lopsided grin. "Evenin', Ms. McMillan. I stopped by your store, but Robbie said that you were gone for the day. I took a chance you'd be here." He held out his hand, and I saw a white envelope clenched tightly in it. "It's for you. It's your deposit," he said. "I've been so busy the past few days, I forgot to mail it."

Truth be told, I'd forgotten all about the deposit. "Thanks, Elvin," I said, accepting the envelope. I could hear Gary's voice in my head: *Make sure it's all there*. I hesitated only slightly, then lifted the flap. I saw a bunch of bills inside.

"It's all there," Elvin said. "But you can count it if it makes you feel better."

I figured I'd let Gary do the honors on that. I shook my head. "No need. I trust you, Elvin."

He laughed. "Lots of folks around here would tell you that's a mistake."

"Hey, you gave me the deposit back, didn't you? And by the way, how is your grandmother?"

His brows drew together. "My grandmother?"

"Yes. You canceled on me because she took a spill, remember?"

His expression cleared and he nodded. "Oh, yes. My grandmother. She's much better, thanks for asking. It-it wasn't too serious."

"Nothing that would interfere with her daily power walk, I assume."

He looked at me blankly for a second, then chuckled. "I see word's gotten around, eh? Yeah, Granny likes her power walking. It takes more than a little slip and trip to slow her down."

"Well, good."

"She really did slip," he added. "She was taking her morning walk and some girl had a pit bull on a leash, but the dog was restless and broke free. She ran off and hit my granny in her hip. Went down like a sack of potatoes, but nothing was sprained or broken, fortunately. She was up and about again in a few days."

"It was good of you to go down there to check on her."

Elvin's face split in a wide smile. "Granny paid my airfare and I stayed at her bungalow. It was like having a little vacation. Fishing's good there this time of year."

I drew my brows together and put just the teeniest bit of bass in my voice. "Her bungalow? I thought she was in a nursing home."

Elvin's cheeks reddened. "A nursing home? Did I say that?"

I folded my arms across my chest and gave him my best *Don't you lie to me* stare, the one that always worked on countless bad guys on my old show. "Yes, you did."

Apparently I hadn't lost my touch. Elvin's shoulders slumped, and he hung his head. "I'm sorry. I guess I'm just used to telling that story," he admitted. "Most people don't believe me when I tell 'em my granny's eighty-eight but still lives on her own, jogs, takes yoga, and is one heck of a ballroom dancer." His smile faded a bit as he added, "I did feel bad about cutting out on you, Ms. McMillan. I was looking forward to performing at the event. Honest."

He sounded sincere and I found myself believing him, even though I could hear Olivia's voice calling me a sucker. I hesitated, then said, "Would you like to come in, have something to drink? I think there's a pitcher of iced tea in the fridge."

Elvin's eyes lit up. "If it's not too much trouble. I am a little thirsty."

I waved him over to the table. "Have a seat. Would you like a sprig of mint in your tea?"

"No mint, but I'll take lemon, if it's no trouble."

I got the iced tea out of the refrigerator and poured some into two tall glasses. I got a lemon out of the crisper, cut it into quarters, then squeezed lemon into both glasses. "Do you take sugar?" I asked.

No answer.

I turned. Elvin was hunched forward in the chair. He'd picked up the photograph of Mick and was turning it over in his hands. I walked over and set one glass of iced tea in front of him. "Elvin, do you recognize that man?" I asked.

He set the photo down, picked up the iced tea and took a long sip. Then he looked up at me. "Why, sure I do," he said. "That's Ian McBride."

Twenty-four

My heart was pounding so hard in my chest I thought it would explode. "Ian McBride? That's his name? You're certain?"

He looked at the picture again and then nodded more emphatically. "Yep. It's him all right. It's been awhile, but I'm good with faces. Why? You thought he was someone else?"

"I was under the impression his name was Mick."

"Mick?" He started to laugh. "You're not far off. Mick was his nickname. Short for McBride, get it?" His gaze wandered over to the photograph. "How did you happen to get hold of that? I'm just curious."

"It's Johnny's photo. It, ah, fell out of his backpack the night he came to my shop. I never got to return it to him."

Elvin nodded. "That makes sense. They were friends."

"They were?"

"Well, maybe friends is too strong a word. They knew each other though. I saw 'em a few times in the Watering Hole. That's a dive over in Frederick."

"I see." I paused. "I don't suppose you know how I could get hold of this Ian? Maybe he'd like the photo."

"He prob'ly would, but it'd be of no use to him now." Elvin leaned back in his chair and laced his hands behind his neck. "He's dead. Killed in an auto accident not long after Johnny left town."

"Oh." My face crumbled. Another good lead shot down.

Elvin leaned forward and reached for his iced tea. "That was something, huh, how you found Johnny's body. That must have been upsetting."

"It wasn't pleasant." I took a sip out of my own glass of iced tea, then sat down opposite Elvin. "I don't suppose you know anyone who might like this photo. Perhaps a friend of either Johnny or Ian? Or a relative?"

"I don't know too much about Ian. Johnny . . ." Elvin's brow furrowed and his lips scrunched up as he thought. Finally he shook his head. "Johnny was a bit of a loner. He didn't have many friends. As a matter of fact, I think he only knew Ian through Arnie."

"Arnie?"

"Arnold Collins. Folks called him Arnie. He wasn't from Fox Hollow. I think he moved here from somewhere in New York. Rented a bungalow out in the sticks. Sometimes he'd be at the Watering Hole with Ian, and Johnny would join them." Elvin shook his head. "He liked animals, that I remember. Birds in particular."

"Birds, you say?" I felt my pulse quicken. "Any particular type of bird?"

"He had a parrot. Snaggle Puss, I think he called him. Trained him to do tricks. I don't know what happened to him, though. Arnie, I mean, not the parrot. I'm pretty sure he cut out right after Ian's accident."

My mind was racing. I reached for my phone, called up my email. Gary had sent me a copy of Falco's personnel file, and I opened it so that his photograph filled the screen. I handed my phone to Elvin. "Is this Arnie?"

Elvin gave the screen a casual glance, then did a double take. "Heck, it sure looks like him. Where did you get this?"

"From Johnny's old firm. This man's name is Bernie Falco."

Elvin scratched at his ear. "Bernie Falco, huh? Wow, he's a dead ringer for Arnie."

Dead being the operative word. "Gary and I think he also went by the name Adrian Arnold. As a matter of fact, he was at the event Saturday. He also trains parrots. You've never heard of him?"

Elvin shook his head. "Nope. He was never booked at any of the same gigs as me. I do mainly weddings and bar mitzvahs. Not much opportunity for a parrot trainer at those." He pointed at the photo. "It's some coincidence, though."

"I don't think it's a coincidence. I think Arnie Collins, Bernie Falco, and Adrian Arnold are all one and the same person."

Elvin let out a low whistle. "That's weird. If it bothers you, maybe you could just ask him?"

"I would, except for one thing. He's dead."

Elvin's eyes popped and then he raised his hand to scratch at his forehead. "Yeah, I can see where that would be a bit of a problem." He scraped back his chair. "I've got to get going. I just wanted to make sure you got your deposit back."

He picked up his glass, drained it, and I walked him to the door. "Thanks, Elvin. And if you should remember anything else about either Arnie Collins or Ian, give me a call."

I'd no sooner shut the door behind Elvin than Gary appeared. "Sorry it took me so long. Apparently Purrday and Kahlua were playing a game of hide and seek with my charger." He inclined his head toward the door. "Was someone here? I thought I heard a male voice."

"You did. It was Elvin Scraggs. He came to return my deposit in person."

"Yeah? That's a surprise." He saw the envelope on the table and walked over, picked it up. "Is it all here?"

"It looks like it is. I figured you could do the honors."

Gary pulled the bills out of the envelope and started counting. I walked over and stood next to him. "I had rather an interesting talk with Elvin."

"That sounds like an accomplishment." He laid the bills down on the counter. "All here. Okay, I can tell you're dying to tell me. What was so interesting about your talk?"

I quickly hit the highlights of my conversation with Elvin. "I wonder which name is the real one, Arnold, Falco or Collins," I finished. I whipped out my phone and typed Arnold Collins into the search engine. Over two million hits came up, including one on Wikipedia about an Arnold Collins who was a chemist at DuPont.

Gary took the phone. "Let's narrow this down a bit." He typed in "Arnold Collins" and then, after that, "Criminal Records." "Just a hunch," he said, and hit Enter. I gasped as "Arrest Record—Arnold Collins, Spartanburg North Carolina" flashed on the screen. Gary clicked on the article, which detailed the arrest of one Arnold Collins for fraud in the small town. No details were given about the exact nature of the crime. Collins spent three days in the local jail, and was then released on bail. The charges were dropped shortly afterward.

"Well, that's a good reason to want to change your name, your whole identity even," I remarked.

"Let's not get carried away just yet," Gary said. "We don't know if this is the same Arnold Collins Scraggs knew. There's no photo of him, nothing to indicate it is the same man."

"There's nothing to indicate it's not the same man, either," I said.

"All right, let's assume it is the same man. He moved here, changed his name to Bernie Falco, and worked at McShay, O'Toole and whatever for a while, and then changed his name again to Adrian Arnold and went into the parrot training business. Now, why would he do that?"

"It all comes back to the money." I took the phone back from Gary and called up the original article I'd found about Johnny Draco. "See here: *the fact* that Draco required the participants to give him their share in cash should have been a red flag. He claimed that doing it that way cut through a lot of red tape and would enable him to 'get in on the ground floor' faster."

What if that wasn't Johnny's requirement, but Collins's or maybe even this Ian McBride's? Johnny was friends with both men. What if they convinced Johnny this scheme was on the up and up? Remember, he told Rita he'd been hoodwinked too. What if he'd given the money to them, and then when the news of Tandor Industries biting the dust hit, they'd taken off with the loot, leaving Johnny in the lurch?"

"That's a nice theory, Shell, but you're forgetting one thing. Arnold Collins, or Adrian Arnold, has been hanging around here the past five years, making a pretty good living with his trained parrots. If he were in on that scam and had all that money, he sure as heck wouldn't be doing this."

The thought drifted into my head, unbidden. I started. It was a long shot, to be sure, but when one thought about it, it made perfect sense. I turned to Gary and said, "But what if he wasn't the one with the money!"

Gary looked at me. "What are you suggesting? That the other guy, McBride, made off with it?"

I leaned one elbow against the counter, my eyes gleaming. "Hear me out before you scoff at my idea. Do you remember season three of *Spy Anyone*, episode seventy-five?"

Gary's eyelids lowered in concentration. "Episode seventy-five. Was that the one with the three brothers who stole the diamonds?"

"Yes," I cried. "Remember, they were going to split up until the furor about the diamonds died down, then they were going to split the loot. The older brother was in charge of hiding the diamonds, but he got killed before they could rendezvous. So the other two . . ."

"Spent time looking for them in different places while still maintaining an aura of respectability," Gary finished. "And it was our job to smoke out the diamonds' hiding place."

"Right. So, if they could hide diamonds, why couldn't someone hide money?"

"Sure they could," Gary replied. I heard excitement in his tone as he continued, "That could be why Johnny insisted everyone pony up their share in cash. It wasn't to cut down on paperwork, it was so they'd have it all, neat and tidy, to split up."

"Right. So they wait a few weeks, then split up the money and vanish and no one's the wiser. Except this Ian went and got himself killed, and I'm betting he was the one in charge of hiding the money. I'm also going to go out on a limb and suggest that maybe Johnny was telling the truth, that he wasn't in on it. He left town for the exact reason he told Rita. He'd had an epiphany and he wanted to change his life around.

"Meanwhile, good old Arnie hangs around here, looking for the money. That has to be why he started that parrot business. Gave him a lot of opportunities to get into lots of places where this Ian might have hidden it."

"And Arnold hangs around here, keeping a low profile with his bird business. Probably still hunting for the money, maybe tracking down leads as he uncovers them."

"And then Johnny comes back to town. He hooks up with Arnold. Something happened—I'm not sure what—but Arnold thought Johnny knew too much."

"Maybe Johnny found the money," suggested Gary. "He hinted at something that would change lives, remember? Maybe he stumbled upon the cache of money and wanted to repay everyone what was taken from them."

"That would certainly have upset Arnie," I said. "Maybe they fought over it, and in a fit of anger Arnie shoved the digital instrument down Johnny's throat. Then he frames Rita for the crime."

Gary clapped his hands. "Nicely done, except for one big flaw. If Arnold is the mastermind, who killed him?"

I arched a brow. "Are we certain that Ian McBride is really dead?"

Gary waved a finger in the air. "Ooh, faked his death. Good one. Let's find out."

We plugged "Ian McBride—obituary—Fox Hollow" into the search engine and hit Enter. A few minutes later a short article appeared on the screen. Gary pointed to the photograph. "Sure looks like the guy in the photo," he said.

I read the article out loud:

> A Fox Hollow resident was killed Thursday, March 8, when he lost control of his vehicle while driving down his own driveway to get his mail.
>
> The County Sheriff's Office received a call at 3:41 p.m. that an unconscious driver was in a ditch on

Cumberton Road, about two miles northwest of Fox Hollow in Pike Mills Township.

The Sheriff's Office said Ian McBride, 42, had been driving down the road when another car came out of a side road and sideswiped him into the ditch, where he hit a road sign.

He was transported to St. Gabriel's Hospital and later died at the hospital. The County Sheriff's Office was assisted at the scene by the CT State Patrol and Gold Coast Ambulance.

"Not much there," Gary said as I paused. "It's pretty straightforward. Doesn't leave much chance that he walked away from it. So, another dead end."

I reached out, gripped Gary's arm. "Not exactly. You didn't finish. Read the last paragraph."

Mc Bride is survived by his stepfather, Angus Hanley, and his stepbrother, Evan Hanley, of Fox Hollow, Connecticut.

We both looked at each other. "Holy crap," Gary said.

I picked up the photograph of Ian McBride again and tapped at it with my nail. "That's why he seemed so familiar to me," I said. "He's got the same cleft in his chin as Evan. He's got that same pointy nose, too."

Gary put his hands on my shoulders. "Okay, Shell, I know you. I know how your mind works and where you're headed with this. A word of caution. Just because they were brothers doesn't necessarily mean Evan knew anything about what Ian was involved in."

"Half brothers," I amended. "And just for the record, he didn't necessarily have to know about the money to want to kill Johnny. You're forgetting his oh-so-jealous streak. And his temper. He certainly displayed it in full force when he came into the shop."

"You still can't just go off half-cocked and accuse him," Gary answered. "You need more. The police will need more. And don't forget—"

The rest of Gary's sentence was cut off as my phone beeped, signaling an incoming text. I looked at the screen and my heart started to race. "Gary," I cried excitedly. "Look at this."

The message was from Robbie: *Buster lost your email address. He sent me the photos. Here they are.*

"I can't believe it. What a break," I said as I called up the email. There were two dozen attachments. I scrolled through them and bit back a jubilant cry as I saw one labeled *Parrot Show*.

I looked at Gary. "Moment of truth," I said and clicked on the attachment. The photograph filled the screen, and I saw it was indeed the same photo of the person in the cap watching Johnny. I had to admit, Buster Weston was an excellent photographer. The photo was sharp, the image crystal clear. There was no mistaking that pointed nose, or the cleft in his chin.

The man looking daggers at Johnny was Evan Hanley.

Twenty-five

Leave it to Gary to burst my bubble. "Okay, take it easy," he cautioned. "Before you start celebrating Rita's release, let me finish my earlier thought. Didn't you tell me that Josh already checked Hanley out, and he's got a good alibi?"

"Yeah. He was at Bottoms Up, supposedly drinking and playing darts in front of several witnesses."

"Supposedly?"

"Well, it wouldn't be the first time a witness was wrong," I said. "Maybe they were all drunk. Better yet, maybe Evan paid them off to say he was there."

Gary clucked his tongue. "Now you're really grabbing at straws."

I reached for my purse. "Let's go down to Bottoms Up. We were going to have dinner there anyway, right? Maybe we'll run into some of these so-called witnesses and kill two birds with one stone."

Gary grabbed my purse out of my hand and thrust it behind his back. "Oh, no. We're not going anywhere until you promise me you're not going to do anything stupid. There's a killer out there, Shell. He's killed twice and probably won't bat an eye at killing a third time. You are going to call Josh, tell him what we've discovered, and let him handle it."

"Okay, fine," I hissed. "I'll call him right now."

I hit the speed dial number on my phone for Josh and a few seconds later his voicemail kicked in. "This is Josh Bloodgood. I'm unavailable to take your call right now. Please leave a message and I'll return it as soon as I can."

"Josh, it's Shell. Gary and I have something very important to show you, something that could change everything in Johnny Draco's murder case. Please, please call me as soon as you get this." I disconnected and glared at Gary. "Happy?"

"Immensely." He cocked his head and put a finger to his lips. "Maybe we should go somewhere else for dinner."

"What, you don't trust me? You don't think I could handle this discreetly?"

"To be honest . . . no, I don't." He reached out and took my hand. "Lots of people would have my head if I let something happen to you. Joshy, Olivia, Rita, Ron . . . your mother. Face it, you're not a trained investigator, Shell, and neither am I—at least, not yet. You've gotten one threatening note. This person might be keeping a close eye on you. I'm not going to let you endanger yourself."

"Fine." I held up my hand and said in a singsong tone, "I swear on a stack of Bibles that I will not track down these witnesses at Bottoms Up and cross-examine them. I'll let Josh handle it. Happy?"

He sighed. "My yearning for a Broadway Babe Burger is probably clouding my better judgment, but . . . I'm going to trust you, Shell."

I smiled demurely. "Thanks, Gary." *Sucker.*

• • •

Bottoms Up was packed full when we arrived. A country tune was playing in the background, there was a line waiting for tables, and the bar was jammed. "What, are they giving away free lottery tickets or something?" Gary asked the pretty blonde girl who was at the door, taking names. "I've never seen it so packed."

"The Connecticut Huskies are in the semifinals," she replied with a big smile. "Everyone's first two drinks are on the house. And tonight's karaoke night. That always draws a big crowd."

"I can see that," I said, glancing around. My stomach let out a loud growl. "How long a wait for a table?"

"Shouldn't be too much longer. Fifteen, twenty minutes." She gestured toward the bar. "You can get your complimentary drink and help yourself to some snacks."

Gary looked at me. "Your call. We could go somewhere else."

I shook my head. "No, I know how much you wanted to eat here. We'll just wait at the bar."

We made our way over to the crowded bar. I could see at once most of the patrons were college students. "Josh's sister would probably like bartending here," Gary remarked. "She'd make good tips, that's for sure."

I nodded in agreement. Josh's younger sister, Michelle, worked tending bar part-time while she studied law at the University of Connecticut. "I'm surprised she isn't here," I said. "She must be working tonight."

Two guys wearing Yale sweatshirts pushed back their stools and dropped twenties on the bar. We wasted no time in claiming the vacant stools. The bartender, a middle-aged balding man who looked to be in his early sixties, came right over to us. "Hello, there," he boomed. "Your first two drinks are on the house, in honor of the Huskies! So, what'll it be?"

"What's on tap?" Gary asked.

"Coors, Heineken, Stella, Blue Moon. We just got in a nice little IPA. Prairie Madness." He jerked his thumb at me. "The lady might like it. It's got Mosaic and Simcoe hops layered over a rich base of American, German and English malt. Makes for a nice fruity but clean taste."

I held up a finger. "Sounds good to me."

"I'll have a Heineken," Gary said. He turned to me. "I have to visit the facilities. Save my seat, if you can."

I set my purse down as Gary threaded his way through the crowd toward the restrooms. The bartender returned and set two frosty mugs down. He pushed my glass in front of me. "Take a sip," he said.

I did and was pleasantly surprised. "It's good."

"Told ya. Most folks listen to me when I tell 'em an ale is good," he said with a satisfied smile.

He seemed to be a chatty sort. I saw a name tag pinned to his shirt. "Well, Bud," I said, taking another sip of the IPA. "Have you worked here long?"

Bud snorted. "I worked here when it was Guido's. The owner joked that I came with the place."

"So you work a lot, I'm guessing?"

"Every chance I get. Since my wife passed on and my daughter moved to New Orleans with her husband, it's what keeps me going."

I decided to take a chance and leaned in closer. "I don't suppose you were working here this past Saturday?"

"As a matter of fact, I worked all day Saturday. The other bartender called in sick." He tossed a towel over his shoulder. "We were busy too, what with the pet shop's grand opening celebration and all."

"Yes, I can imagine," I replied. "It certainly turned out to be an eventful day."

"Ah, you must mean the murder," Bud said instantly. "That was something, huh? Guy comes back after all this time and gets iced. Pretty sad."

I took another sip of my IPA. "Yes, it was."

Bud leaned closer to me and said in a conspiratorial tone, "They questioned me, you know. The police. Wanted to verify some guy's alibi."

"You must mean Evan Hanley."

"Yeah, that's the guy." Bud reached up to scratch at one ear. "He was here, all right, but to be truthful, I couldn't swear absolutely he was here between—what time was it again? Oh, yeah, two fifteen and three. There were a lot of people here at the bar Saturday. It was crowded just like this. I saw him over by the dartboard and the pool table, but I couldn't swear he stayed there."

My pulse quickened. "Is that what you told the police?"

Bud let out a harumpff. "I might have, but once I said I remembered seeing him here, that female officer didn't seem interested in anything else I had to say. It was like she was just checking off something else she had to do, ya know."

"Really?" I frowned. "That's kind of hard to believe. Detective Riser strikes me as being very thorough."

Bud shook his head. "No, that wasn't her name. She wasn't a detective, either, just a regular police officer. Said she was helping out. Adamson, I think her name was."

I bit down on my lip. I knew Carla Adamson. I'd gone to high school with her too. She'd been a bit of a shirker back then, always looking for the easy way out. Apparently she hadn't changed. Josh must have really been hurting to send her out interviewing witnesses.

Bud inclined his head over toward an alcove off to the left. "Ronnie Sanna's back there playing pool. I know she talked to him too."

Someone at the far end of the bar held up a mug. Bud excused himself and hurried off. I took a quick glance around. No Gary yet. I laid a ten on the counter for Bud, picked up my half-full mug, and made my way toward the alcove. It wasn't as crowded back there. There were two pool tables, and there were two men at each, brandishing cues. I walked casually up to the first table, giving it what I hoped was an interested look. "I'd go for the nine ball in the corner pocket," I said casually. "It looks easier than getting the five in."

The blonde man wearing a Huskies T-shirt turned and gave me an appraising glance. "Play much?" he asked.

"I had to learn for a TV show."

He looked at me with more interest. "You an actress?"

"I used to be. Now I just run the local pet store."

He banged his cue against the side of the pool table. "Of course. You're Tillie's niece, the actress. I should have recognized you, I've seen your photo often enough. Tillie'd whip it out every chance she got. Shell Marlowe, right?"

"Actually it's Shell McMillan. You knew my aunt?"

"Oh, sure." He set down the cue and held out his hand. "Sorry. Ronnie Sanna. I did some plumbing for your aunt. She was a real nice lady. I was sorry when she passed."

"Thanks."

He picked up his cue again. "Must be quite a difference for you, living here in Fox Hollow instead of out in Hollywood with all the movie stars."

"It's different, all right, but in a good way. Hollywood isn't all it's cracked up to be."

"So the gossip rags say," Ronnie proclaimed with a laugh. "That was some nice celebration on Saturday. It was a shame it had to be marred by, well, I'm sure you know."

"Yes. I understand the police questioned you about one of the suspects."

"Oh, yeah." Ronnie shifted the cue to his other hand. "Officer Adamson showed me a photo, asked if I remembered seeing him in here between two and three."

"And you said yes?"

Ronnie leaned over, took his shot, missed. He swore softly under his breath, and as his partner lined up his shot, turned back to me. "I told her I seen him in here, but I couldn't swear positively he was here all the time. But I remember around two fifteen he went to the men's room."

I looked at Ronnie. "How do you know that?"

"Because he brushed past me on his way and made me miss my shot. When I glared at him he said, 'Sorry. Restroom.' And he took off in that direction." Ronnie shrugged. "I never saw him after that, but when you think about it, where else would he be?" He let out a snigger. "It's only one stall. Sometimes you can wait on line forever."

Ron's companion missed his shot and banged his cue against the end of the pool table. "Your turn, Ron," he shouted.

Ron tipped his hand to me. "Nice to meet you, Shell McMillan. I have a golden retriever named Millie, so it's very likely you'll see us at your shop."

"I look forward to it. We always keep treats for dogs and cats available."

I left Ron Sanna sizing up his shot and retraced my steps back to the bar area. Gary hadn't returned and now two girls wearing tight jeans and even tighter T-shirts had taken our stools. I saw Bud at the end of the bar and went over to him, raising my now-empty mug to catch his attention. He came over to me immediately. As he refilled my mug with my second free drink, I asked, "I know this is going to sound odd, but is there a way someone could get out of the restroom other than the conventional door?"

Bud handed me my mug, and I took a sip. "Not really," he said. "Of course, there are windows in each restroom, but they're pretty small. You'd have to be a skinny Minnie to fit through 'em."

I thanked Bud and took another sip of my ale. Gary was still nowhere to be seen. I figured, considering the crowd and amount of beer probably consumed, there was a long line for the one-stall restroom. I noticed a side door just in back of the bar area and I made my way over there. The lighting, I noticed, was pretty poor, and the door was only a few feet from the alcove bearing the sign *Rest Rooms–This Way*. It was possible someone could sneak out without anyone noticing. I set the mug on the end of the bar and pushed through the door. I walked around the left side of the building. There were two windows, sure enough. Bud was right. They weren't large, but they weren't super small either. I was betting with a little creative maneuvering, Evan Hanley could easily fit through the window with no problem.

I shoved my hand into my pants pocket and pulled out the drawing. I turned it left, then right, studying it. I wasn't an architecture student but it looked to me as if someone had drawn a crude floor plan, but of what?

"Hard to tell with half missing," I grumbled. I turned the paper over in my hands. "Johnny was killed in the dry goods store," I murmured. "He wanted to lease the dry goods store. Why that store? There are other, probably more affordable storefronts in Fox Hollow that would have served his purpose. What was so special about this particular one?"

I fished my phone out of my pocket and dialed Elvin Scraggs's number. It rang about ten times and I was just about to hang up when I heard Elvin's voice. "Hallo?"

"Elvin, it's Shell McMillan."

"Hey, Ms. McMillan." Elvin sounded wary. "Is everything okay? All the money was there, right?"

"What? Oh, yes, the deposit's fine. Listen, I wanted to ask you a question about Ian McBride. You mentioned he died in an auto accident?"

"Yeah. Darn shame. He was on his way back from overseeing renovations to a rental property. Car sideswiped his little roadster out of nowhere. He never stood a chance."

"Overseeing renovations?"

"Yep. There was a fire in the building that Claude Alder leased, that's why they gave him a break on the rent. Ian knew a bit about architecture, so he helped the guy with designing the interior. You know, shelving, cabinet placement, that sort of thing. He was heading home from there when the accident happened, I guess. It sure shook Alder up. He felt guilty for weeks."

I thanked Elvin, reassured him once again that the deposit was fine, and then looked at the drawing again. I supposed it could be a crude sketch of a building interior. I smoothed the paper out. One of the slashes looked like half of a small *x*. "X marks the spot," I murmured. "Could this possibly be—a treasure map? A map indicating where something valuable might be hidden? Something like a sack of money, maybe?"

The more I thought about that, the more logical it seemed. Ian had studied architecture, and was helping to renovate the store. Johnny must have known that, and somehow acquired the map. He'd put two and two together and figured out that Ian had hidden the swindled money somewhere in the dry goods store. Someone had killed him over it. Adrian? Or Evan, maybe to avenge his dead brother?

"Only one way to find out," I muttered. I shoved the map back into my pocket and went back inside. Still no Gary, but the girls were still perched on our stools, chugging down beers. I called Bud over and slid him a twenty. "Keep those girls drinking," I said. "When my friend comes back, introduce him to them as Gary Presser, the former star of the cable show *Spy Anyone*."

Bud took the twenty. "O-kay," he said. "What if he asks about you?"

"I've got an important errand to run," I said. "With any luck, I'll be back before he even realizes I'm gone."

I left Bottoms Up and headed to my convertible, giving thanks I always kept a spare set of keys to the car in my purse. I slid behind the wheel, and just as I was about to turn the key, a soft merow sounded from the backseat. I turned around and saw Purrday. He was on the floor, curled up in a ball. He lifted his head and his one good eye looked at me balefully. "Merow," he said again.

I shook my finger at him. "You little stowaway," I cried. It was too late to take him back home. I turned the key in the ignition. "Okay, you're coming with me," I told the cat. "But you stay in the car like a good kitty, okay?"

Purrday raised his paw and blinked his good eye. I took that for a yes.

I drove swiftly to the center of town and found a parking spot directly across from Alder's Dry Goods. I cut the motor and the lights and sat there for a few minutes, drumming my fingers on the steering wheel. The crime scene tape, I noticed, had been removed. The door was probably locked. Perhaps one of the windows might still be open enough for me to crawl through. I hesitated. The smart thing, of course, would be for me to call Josh and share what I knew with him, and let the police take over. But Josh was so overworked and still hadn't returned my earlier call, and this was only a theory. Far better to call him after I had actual proof, and I couldn't think of any better proof than finding a sack of stolen money.

I was just about to exit the car when I saw another car approaching from the opposite end of the road. Instinctively I ducked down in my seat, low enough so that I couldn't be seen but could still see over the dashboard. When it was about ten feet away from me, the car cut its headlights and rolled to a stop. A few seconds later a figure swathed in a long overcoat and a cap exited the car and started toward the store. The moon came out from behind a cloud, and its white rays shone down on the figure just as it removed its cap. I sucked in a breath as I recognized Evan Hanley! He glanced furtively around, then hunched his shoulders and started straight for the store.

Purrday let out a loud meow, almost like a warning, but I didn't listen. Without a second's hesitation, I pocketed my car keys and followed him, Purrday's loud yowl of protest ringing in my ears.

Twenty-six

Evan Hanley didn't head for the front door of the dry goods store. Rather, he made an abrupt turn and headed for the north side of the building. In his dark overcoat and cap he melted right into the shadows and I had to strain to keep him in sight. He rounded the corner of the building and I saw him pause and lean against a patch of ivy growing along the building's side. Before I could do more than blink, he'd vanished!

"What the . . ." I stopped, flabbergasted. Where the heck had he gone? I moved cautiously forward, to the exact spot where I'd seen Hanley last, and looked around. The ivy appeared to be knotted in a cluster at chest level on one section of the wall. I reached out and pressed my fingers against the knot, then jumped back as the wall swung slowly inward, revealing a set of stone steps leading down. I hesitated only a brief second before stepping through the entryway and descending the steps. When I was about a third of the way down I heard a loud creak. I whipped my head around and saw the wall snap back in place, plunging me into total darkness. I felt in my pocket, whipped out my phone and called up my flashlight app. The bright circle of light cut through the inky blackness, and I continued my descent.

Finally I reached the bottom. Two doors loomed in front of me. I did a quick eeny, meeny and grasped the knob of the door on the right. It swung inward, revealing another flight of steps. I went up those and came to another door. I twisted the handle, and the door opened easily. I stepped out and paused. I recognized my surroundings at once. I was in the storeroom, about ten feet away from the spot where I'd found Johnny's body.

I made my way over to the glass and wicker table, pulled out the map and spread it out on the table. Without the rest of the map it was hard to tell, but I was fairly certain it was a crude markup of the main floor. I tapped at a large square on the right. The letters *SR* were written in the square—storeroom? I flashed my light out across the main floor. If that was a correct assumption, then the spot where the *x* was marked would refer to the stone fireplace at the far end of the room. I picked up the map and made my way over to the fireplace. In a mystery story I'd read as a young girl, two detective sisters had found a valuable cache of jewels hidden in a fireplace. But where to start?

I angled my face, studying the map more closely. The notation "8 x 5" seemed to jump out at me. I'd initially thought it referred to some sort of measurement, but what if it were a direction instead? I decided to start with eight bricks up, five over and moved to the hearth. Dropping to my knees, I started on the far end and counted eight bricks up, then five over. The stones all seemed solid, so I moved over a row and tried again. On my third try, the fifth stone shifted slightly underneath my touch. I held my breath and pressed on it again. It was loose, all right, but not loose enough for me to grasp and pull out. I looked around and spied a crowbar over in one corner. I picked it up and wedged it underneath the stone. One jerk, two, and on the third the stone moved enough for me to get a grip and pull it free, revealing a dark crevice. I was just about to stick my hand in when I felt something touch my leg. I jumped and looked down.

"Merow." Purrday squatted there. He blinked his one good eye at me.

"Purrday! How on earth?" I bit my lip. I'd had my window rolled down, and in my hurry to follow Hanley had forgotten to roll it up before I exited the car. Purrday, no doubt, had jumped out and followed me. I bent down and gave the cat a reassuring pat. "Okay, but you have to be quiet," I whispered. So far I'd seen no sign of Evan Hanley. He must have gone through the other door and was probably in the basement. I had to find out what was in this crevice and then get out of here!

I thrust my arm into the dark hole and felt around. My questing fingers touched something rough and stiff. I grasped it and pulled. A second later I was looking at my prize: a bulging burlap bag. I took it out, lay it down on the floor, then worked to untie the knot. My efforts paid off, and I pulled the string free, opened the bag and shone my light into the interior. Piles of tightly bound bills stared back at me.

"Oh my gosh," I breathed. "I was right. That's what must have happened. Ian McBride was in on it with Johnny and Arnold. He was in charge of hiding the money so he hid it when he was doing the renovations on this building. They probably planned to meet, split the money and take off and then Ian was killed. And he never shared where he'd hidden the money."

I was just about to press Josh's number on speed dial when suddenly the room was flooded with light. I glanced up, saw that an overhead light had gone on. Then a voice from behind me said, "I wouldn't do that, Ms. McMillan. I'm afraid you're in big trouble, kiddo. Big trouble."

I froze. Slowly I turned my head. Evan Hanley was just closing a door on the other side of the room. I caught a flash of blued steel and knew he was carrying a gun. Before I thought, I blurted out, "You killed Adrian Arnold!"

His eyes widened. "Yes. How did you know?"

"Honey Belle saw you do it. She repeated that phrase about big trouble."

Evan shook his head. "I knew I should have killed that bird," he muttered. "Arnold, like you, thought he was pretty darn smart." His eyes narrowed as he approached me. "How did you get in here?"

"I followed you," I said coolly. "That's a rather cleverly concealed entrance. Designed by your half brother, the late Ian McBride, no doubt?"

His lips twisted into a half sneer. "That's right. Ian was almost as good an architect as he was a con man. As a matter of fact, that whole Tandor scheme was his baby, start to finish."

"Really?"

He thrust his other hand into his jacket pocket and whipped out a sheet of paper, which he dangled before me. "It's all here, in a letter Ian wrote to Krissa. I saw Johnny reading this the day of the grand opening. He'd just come from seeing Krissa. I followed him. I wanted to know what he was up to. The letter fell out of his backpack and I scooped it up. Ian was a real stickler for detail. He wrote everything down about his scheme except where he'd hidden the money." Evan tossed the letter on the counter. "Once I read it, well, I knew what Johnny was going to do, why he wanted the dry goods store. He was going to hunt for that money."

"Johnny wanted to return the money, didn't he? But you wanted your brother's share, that's why you killed him?"

Evan's brows drew together. "I didn't kill Johnny," he said.

I frowned. "You didn't? But if not you, then who did?"

"Can't you guess? I'm afraid I'm guilty of that."

I glanced up. Krissa had appeared, walking so softly on her thick-soled sneakers I hadn't heard her. I stared at her. "You, Krissa? But you couldn't have? I've been able to punch some holes in Evan's alibi, but you're on tape helping a customer at the time of the murder."

Krissa chuckled. "Yeah, that was a nice touch, wasn't it? It's easier than you'd think to reset those security camera clocks, so after I got back I reset for mine two hours earlier. When that Officer Riser checked my tape, it showed I was helping that customer between two and three, not four and five. They never interviewed Jenny Vickers, but it wouldn't have mattered. She never wears a watch." She walked closer to me and I saw the insane gleam in her eyes. "Between two and three, I was jamming that ridiculous instrument down Johnny's throat. He never saw it coming."

I stared at her. "B-but why, Krissa? I thought you loved him?"

She shrugged. "I did, at first. But Johnny was so wrapped up in his work, some days he hardly noticed me. And then Ian came along. Johnny invited him for dinner one night, and the attraction between Ian and me, well, it was like fireworks! We saw a lot of each other. It was easy, because between soliciting investments for Tandor and work, I hardly saw Johnny at all." She paused for a breath. "We'd planned to elope the day Ian was killed. I was heartbroken, but I had to pine away in secret, because no one knew about our affair. When I read that letter, it hit me. Ian had never loved me. He was going to take his share of the money and blow Fox Hollow without me."

"The letter? The one Johnny found?" I asked. "That had to be the information he told Wesley Sakowski he'd come across. He said it would change lives."

"Oh, yes. It would change lives, all right," Krissa said. She moved closer, and I could see the madness in her glittering eyes. "He'd found it in a secret drawer in the dry goods store, along with a map. He figured the money had to be somewhere in the dry goods store, but he wasn't sure just where.

"He said he was going to find that money and make restitution. He wanted to get that cloud of suspicion off his head once and for all." Her hands balled into fists. "He accused me of cheating on him, and knowing all about Ian's scheme. I told him I'd found out after the fact, but he wasn't buying it. He said that he'd return everyone's money, except mine. That he was going to donate to charity, and if I made any move to oppose him, he'd give the police that letter. No one would believe I didn't have some idea about what Ian had planned. He told me that I should think about what I'd done and try to see the light and become a better person." She reached up and pounded one fist against her breast. "Imagine, him lecturing me! I begged him to reconsider. He said he might. It all depended on how sincere I was about turning my life around. Then he said he wasn't mad about me cheating on him, because he'd never loved me all that much. Can you beat that? And I gave him five years of my life!"

"That made you angry. You followed him?"

"I didn't need to. I knew darn well where he was going. I got the key from

Evan and I was waiting inside when he got here. I tried to convince him once and for all that I had nothing to do with Ian's scheme and not to call the police. He said he couldn't make that promise. We had rather heated words, and when he turned his back I grabbed that stupid instrument he loved so much and I jumped on him." She flexed her hands in front of her. "I'm stronger than I look. He wasn't expecting it. I picked up a rag that was lying nearby so I wouldn't leave fingerprints and then grabbed that stupid instrument of his and jammed it down his throat as hard as I could." A faraway look came into her eyes as she added, "I stood there and watched him choke, watched the life drain out of him, and then I left. I saw Rita's husband in his black hoodie skulking around the back alley and I also noticed Rita a little distance behind him. I figured she'd mistaken her husband for Johnny. I saw Mae look in that direction, and I knew she'd seen them too. And knowing Mae, I had no doubt she'd waste no time in blabbing to the police."

"You knew the police would suspect Rita."

"I knew about Johnny's earlier argument with Rita, because he told me. He said that she'd sure as heck forgive him now. I knew Rita would be an excellent choice to take the rap for his death."

I turned to Evan. "And Arnold? Why did you kill him?"

"Arnold had followed Johnny to the dry goods store as well. He'd also planned on killing him, but Krissa beat him to it. He saw the whole thing, and was blackmailing her. Arnold was a greedy bugger. His demands would never have stopped, they would only have gotten bigger. I had to put a stop to it."

"So you went to his house, found him in the shed and killed him, and then you took the parrots to make it seem like a robbery."

"Yep. They're in Krissa's garage. They'll bring us a tidy sum too, I'm sure." He looked at Krissa. "Told you I should have killed that other parrot. She's repeating what I said right before I stabbed Arnold."

"So what?" Krissa said with a shrug. "No one would ever trace that back to you. Only Miss Smarty Pants here. Well, she won't be smart for much longer."

She looked downward. I followed her gaze and noticed for the first time two red gasoline cans. "What are they for?" I asked, although I had a sinking feeling I already knew.

"What do you think?" Evan laughed hollowly. "We planned on tearing this place apart tonight until we found that money. Then we intended to make sure there could be absolutely no way it could ever be traced back to us. This building was always an eyesore, renovations or not," he added with a sniff. "No one will miss it."

My tongue snaked out, slicked across my lower lip. I thought about Purrday and glanced quickly around. There was no sign of the white cat. I heard a distinct click, like the hammer going back on a gun, and then I felt something jab into the small of my back—hard.

"Be a good girl, now, and toss your cell phone on the floor," Krissa hissed in my ear.

I laid my phone down on the floor. Krissa snatched it up, then tossed it carelessly into a far corner. "Now raise your hands above your head. *Do it,*" she commanded.

I raised my hands, my eyes darting around the room. No Purrday. Where had he gone?

Evan pulled a length of rope out of a nearby drawer. He stepped forward, jerked my hands down in front of me and started to tie them up. Krissa stood off to one side, gun pointed right at my heart.

"So, what's your plan?" I managed to croak out. "Kill me and skip town with the money?"

"The country, actually." Evan finished tying up my hands and then he bent down to retrieve the sack of money. "We've got two one-way tickets to Costa Rica waiting at the airport." He motioned to me. "Sit. I'm sorry we have to do this to you, but we can't leave any loose ends, and I'm afraid you, Ms. McMillan, are a gigantic one."

I sat down on the floor, and Evan bound my ankles. Then he dragged me over beneath the window. "It won't be long now," he said. "Hopefully the smoke inhalation will kill you long before the flames lick and tear at your flesh."

"Yes," agreed Krissa. "And I'll be far away with the money."

Evan looked up. "You mean we'll be far away."

"No. I said it right the first time." Like a snake uncoiling to attack, Krissa's arm lashed out. She clocked Evan on the side of the head with the butt of her gun, and he slumped forward with a little moan.

"Fool." She looked down at Evan and shook her head. "I'm sure he would have found a way to dump me too, just like his brother and Johnny." She smiled at me. "You really can't depend on men, Shell."

I ignored that remark and said, "So you're going to douse the building with gasoline and leave us here to burn?"

"It's nothing personal, Shell. Well, maybe it is a little. I really didn't like the way you talked to me the other day."

Krissa undid the ropes around my ankles, then whipped a scarf from her sweater pocket and stuffed it into my mouth. Then she pulled out another one and covered my eyes. She raised me up and gave me a push. "Walk," she commanded. I stumbled forward a few steps and then I felt her hand clamp down on my shoulder. She spun me around like I was a sack of potatoes. I could hear her fumbling with something, and then she gave me another push, one that sent me sprawling forward. I landed on something that felt like a hard cushion.

"Don't get too comfortable," she sang out. "I need more gasoline. Don't worry, I'll be back to say goodbye."

I heard a door slam and then . . . nothing. I leaned forward and, working my head against the hard cushion, managed to dislodge the scarf around my eyes. As they adjusted to the darkness, I could see that I was in some sort of storage closet. I looked down and saw the hard cushion was actually a case of toilet paper.

Stay calm, I told myself. *Don't panic. First things first. Get this scarf out of your mouth!*

I worked my tongue back and forth and relaxed all my muscles. Fortunately Krissa hadn't jammed it in too hard and I was able to work the piece of cloth out of my mouth. I leaned back and closed my eyes, willing myself to relax. After a few minutes I opened my eyes and rocked back on my heels to assess my situation.

Screaming at the top of my lungs would do no good. I looked around the walls of my prison. Was it my imagination, or did one wall seem to be shorter than the other? I saw a broom in one corner and grasped it, aimed the pointed handle at the center of the wall. Thunk. Thunk. Solid wood. I gripped the handle again, aimed at the far corner. This time I heard a different sound. A softer, hollow sound.

Plasterboard?

I gripped the broom handle and charged forward, aiming at the midway point of the wall. A crack not unlike a rifle shot sounded, and then half the broom disappeared through the hole! I punched it through again, making the hole wider, and then I dropped the broom and dragged the case of toilet paper over and positioned it beneath the hole. I climbed atop the carton and pressed my eye to the newly formed hole. Suddenly the area was flooded with light. I could see the glass and pewter table, and feet scurrying about. I pressed my mouth to the hole and screamed as loudly as I could. "Help! Police! Help!"

I stopped screaming as a familiar blue eye appeared on the other side of the hole. "Purrday?" I cried.

"Merow!"

Purrday's blue eye vanished and was followed by another familiar pair of eyes. "Shell?"

"Josh!" I cried. I spoke so fast that my words all ran together. "It was Krissa! She killed Johnny, and Evan killed Arnold. She knocked Evan out and shoved me into a storage closet, and now she's getting away."

"We know, Shell. I've got Krissa."

"You do?"

"Yes." Josh's eyes disappeared, replaced a few seconds later by Gary's. "Shell! Hey, Josh has Krissa, and we found Evan too. They're both in police custody."

"That's great," I cried. "So, then—*can someone get me out of here?*"

Twenty-seven

It was Friday night, and Gary, Olivia, Ron, Rita, and I were all gathered around a table in Bottoms Up. Gary raised his mug of beer. "To the successful conclusion of a very baffling mystery," he said, "and to Rita's exoneration."

"Just like my fortune," I said with a wide grin. "I did solve a complex problem, didn't I?" Gary cleared his throat. "With help from Gary, of course."

"Hear, hear," Everyone chorused. We all raised our mugs and drank.

Rita set hers down and said, "Thanks, everyone. I'm really blessed to have such wonderful friends like all of you, but especially Shell and Gary. If not for them . . . who knows what might have happened? Krissa and Evan might have gotten away with it."

Ron shook his head. "I still can't believe Krissa was part of it all." He shot Olivia a laconic grin. "You were right about that woman scorned stuff."

"Told ya," Olivia said with a satisfied smile.

The tavern door opened and Josh walked in. He stood for a minute, looking around, and his face lit up when he spotted our table. He made his way swiftly over. "Hey, everyone," he said. "Room for one more?"

I gave Olivia a swift poke in the ribs. She moved over and I did too. I patted the empty section of bench. "Sure is." Once Josh was seated I asked, "I imagine you got a full confession out of both Evan and Krissa?"

Josh chuckled. "Evan couldn't wait to roll over on her. Guess he was still a mite upset about that conk on the head. Krissa lawyered up. Bud Colton. I think he might be planning a defense of temporary insanity." He shook his head. "I'm not sure that will stick, though. She knew what she was doing, every step of the way."

Our waitress appeared just then. She took Josh's order for a Heineken and once she'd gone, Olivia leaned forward. "Okay, Josh. Don't keep us in suspense. What did Evan have to say?"

Josh leaned forward and laced his hands in front of him on the table. "According to Evan, his half brother, Ian, had zero interest in the family business. He was always looking for, as Evan put it, 'a big score.' Evan left and went to New York because he and Ian had a disagreement. Ian claimed their father favored Evan."

"So Evan knew nothing about Ian's scheme?"

Josh shook his head. "No. Fortunately, when we searched Arnold's house, we came across a journal he'd written. It detailed everything."

The waitress returned and set Josh's drink in front of him. We waited impatiently as Josh took a long sip. He set the mug down and said, "Seems Ian met Arnold Collins one night at a bar where they both hung out. By then he'd changed his name to Bernie Falco, and had gotten a job in the accounting department at Tandor Industries. He discovered the company was on the downswing, and one night he told Ian about Tandor's financial problems. Ian got the idea for the swindle and he fingered Johnny as the perfect patsy to line up investors for it. Falco got a job at Johnny's firm and cultivated a friendship with him. Apparently it didn't take much on his part to convince Johnny Tandor was a surefire investment. Johnny was anxious to make a big killing as well, so that he could ask Krissa to marry him. Johnny got everyone to give him cash, which he turned over to Ian. Then, of course, Tandor went belly up. Johnny was ashamed of his poor judgment in the matter and a few weeks afterward, quit his job and left town. He went to his cousin's, just like he told Rita, and worked hard, determined to come back one day and clear his name."

"In the meantime Ian had charge of the pilfered money, right?" I asked.

Josh nodded. "Yep. Ian and Arnold decided to lay low for a while and then split. They didn't want to call any undue attention to themselves. Ian told Arnold he had the money hidden in a real safe place, and he did. He'd been overseeing the renovations at the dry goods store and he inserted that secret opening in the fireplace. Arnold was harassing him, trying to get him to tell him where he'd hidden the money, but Ian didn't trust him not to run off with everything and so he kept mum."

"And then Ian was killed in that auto accident," cut in Gary.

"Yep. Arnold decided to stick around, hoping to get some sort of a lead on where Ian had stashed the cash. He changed his name again, this time to Adrian Arnold, and with the small amount of money he had left, he invested in the one thing in life he cared about—parrots. And, as fate would have it, he actually managed to eke out a pretty good living with it."

"He did really seem to care about them," I murmured.

"In the meantime, Krissa was cleaning one day and accidentally dropped a cigar chest that Ian had left there," Josh continued. "A secret drawer popped out, and she found part of a map wedged inside. She knew Ian and Arnold were friends, so she went to him. Arnold ended up confessing the whole scheme to her. Krissa offered to help him locate the money in exchange for Ian's share. Apparently there had been a bit of, ah, trouble in paradise before Ian's death and she felt she was entitled to it."

Olivia let out a snort. "That figures."

"Then Johnny came back to town. He went first to your store, Shell, hoping he could convince your aunt to rent him a room while he figured out his next move. He got a little concerned when you told him Tillie was dead, but then when you mentioned Arnold and his parrot act he had a feeling he might be Bernie. He contacted Arnold, who did feel a bit guilty over what they'd done to Johnny, because he'd really liked him. So he told him he could crash at his place. Johnny told him it would only be for a week or so."

"So Johnny didn't have a clue about the hidden money?" asked Ron.

Josh shook his head. "Not at that point. He'd saved up his own money and he wanted to start over, just like he told Rita. He didn't know Ian had died, so when he went to the real estate office Evan was the one who assisted him. He showed Johnny the dry goods store, not realizing at the time who he was. While looking over the store, Johnny apparently found the letter and other half of the map in a secret drawer underneath one of the cabinets. When he read it, he realized he'd been set up. He decided that the money must be hidden somewhere in the store and he was determined to find it, return it to the rightful owners, and clear his name." Josh looked at me. "He contacted Krissa, went to see her, and I believe you know the rest."

"Yep. Poor Johnny." I shook my head. "And Arnold saw Krissa kill him."

Josh nodded. "Yep. Johnny had read him the riot act too, that was what they were arguing about the day you saw them. Arnold pretended to go along with what Johnny wanted, but in actuality he planned on killing Johnny as soon as he found the money. Krissa killing Johnny resulted in a change of plans. Arnold went to her, told her he'd seen everything, and vowed silence in exchange for money—lots of it. Krissa wasted no time confiding in Evan, who went out to Arnold's cottage and tried to reason with him. According to Evan, Arnold laughed in his face, and he lost it and killed him. Then he made off with the parrots, hoping that the police would think it was a robbery gone bad."

"Except he left a witness behind—Honey Belle," I said. "The minute that phrase was out of his mouth, I knew he'd killed Arnold." I reached out and touched Josh's arm. "What will happen to the parrots now?"

"We've contacted a breeder down in York who's very interested in them," Josh said. "He said he has a client who trains animals for movies and commercials."

"That's wonderful," I said. "Will he take Honey Belle as well?"

"Honey Belle was the main one he wanted," Josh said with a chuckle. "I think that bird's got a definite future. You might see her on the big screen sooner than you think." He cleared his throat and looked straight at Rita. "There's more good news, too. Everyone's money was intact in that bag Shell found. Right now it's evidence, but as soon as the trial is over, you and Wesley will receive your money back. As will Quentin, Stanley Sheer, and the others. Everyone except Krissa."

Rita's jaw dropped. She started to fan herself. "Oh, my goodness. We're getting our money back? All of our money? Goodness, I can't believe it!"

"What will they do with Krissa's share?" Olivia asked.

"It's not all that much, but there's a possibility it might be divided up among the other investors, you know, to make up partially for the interest you've lost these last few years. A court will have to decide that, though."

"I have no doubt a court will do the right thing," Rita breathed. "Wait until I tell Wesley!"

"Thank goodness everything turned out all right," I said. I looked straight at Josh, folded my arms across my chest and said in a stern tone, "But you know, this case might have been solved sooner if Officer Adamson had been a tad more thorough."

Josh winced. "I know. She's been severely reprimanded, trust me."

"I'm surprised she still has a job," remarked Gary.

"It was a close call," Josh said. "But in the end Davies took most of the blame. It was his decision to have her assist in the investigation, and he admitted he should have watched her more closely. But believe you me, it'll be a long, long time before her assistance is requested on a murder case."

"If nothing else, this little debacle should have proved to Davies that you need to hire another detective," I put in.

"You're absolutely right, Shell." Josh cleared his throat. "Davies did realize that, which is why he's offered Amy Riser a full-time position with our department, and she's accepted. We're going to be partners."

"Oh. Well, that's . . . great," I said. I avoided looked at Gary. Truthfully, I wasn't quite sure just how I felt about that yet. But time would tell.

"Partners, huh? Maybe now she'll crack a smile once in a while," Gary quipped. "But seriously, that is good news, Joshy. It means you might actually get a night off once in a while. I know that would make Shell happy."

Josh looked at me. "Would that make you happy, Shell?" he asked softly.

I felt color rise to my cheeks. "It wouldn't make me unhappy," I answered.

There was a bit of an awkward pause, and then Olivia raised her mug. "Here's to Shell and Gary. Without them, Evan and Krissa might have gotten away with the money and be on a plane to Costa Rica right now."

"Merow."

Purrday thrust his head out from underneath the table, his whiskers flecked with tuna. "Merow," he said again.

I laughed. "I think he's trying to tell us we're forgetting the real hero of the piece. If Purrday hadn't come back here and gotten Gary and Josh's attention, it might have been too late for me."

"That's true," Josh agreed. "I came here to double-check Evan's alibi after what happened with Adamson. I found Gary at the bar, and he told me what the two of you had found out when we saw Purrday at the window. He was scratching and hopping around, frantic. We decided to follow him, and he led us to the dry goods store just as Krissa was getting more gasoline out of her trunk."

"Well, as Shakespeare says, all's well that ends well," I said. "And speaking of ending well, my mother is supposed to fly back to LA tomorrow."

Olivia gave me a wide-eyed stare. "Oh, so soon?"

Gary squirmed a bit in his seat. "Speaking of your mother," he said, "I may have forgotten to mention that she's joining us tonight."

I almost dropped my mug. "What? Why? I thought Garrett took her out for one last hurrah?"

He shrugged. "She asked me where we were going to be tonight. Said she had something very important to tell us."

Olivia clapped a hand across her mouth. "Oh, no. Don't tell me she and Knute are getting married."

I laughed. "I greatly doubt that. Divorce has soured my mother on not only marriage but men in general. And Knute is a confirmed bachelor, I think."

Rita scraped back her chair. "I've got to get home to Wesley. Keep me posted on your mother's announcement though." She reached out and grasped my hand. I could see tears forming in her eyes and her voice had a catch in it. "Thank you again, Shell." Rita reached out her other hand and snagged Gary's. "Thank you both."

Josh rose. "I should be going too. Unfortunately, the paperwork doesn't file itself." He caught my hand and squeezed it. "I'll call you tomorrow, Shell. Riser's going to be working the whole weekend, so keep Saturday night open. We have a dinner date at the Reserve, remember?"

I grinned up at him. "Absolutely!"

The door had no sooner closed behind Rita and Josh than it was pushed open again, and my mother stood framed in the doorway. She was attired in a flame red dress and matching Louboutins that I knew cost a small fortune. She spied us and made a beeline for our table. "Good evening, everyone," she said. She plopped down in the seat Rita had just vacated. "I've got the most amazing news!"

I leaned forward. "So do we, Mother. As it turns out, Evan Hanley and Krissa Tidwell killed Arnold and Johnny Draco. And all the people Johnny supposedly swindled will get their money back."

"That's nice, dear," my mother said. She looked me straight in the eye. "Like I said, I've got the most amazing news as well. First off, let me just say that I will be leaving for LA tomorrow."

"Oh, Mother. Really?" I reached across the table and grabbed her hand. "You will come back and visit, right?" *Please, God, let her say no.*

My mother's eyes were actually sparkling. "Well, now, that's the thing. I'm just going back to LA to make a few arrangements, then I'm flying back here."

"Huh?" I slapped at my ear with the palm of my hand. "I'm sorry. Did you say you're coming back to Fox Hollow?" I slid a sidelong glance at Gary. Yep, the color had all drained out of his face too.

My mother threw up her hands. "Really, Crishell. You are so dramatic. Garrett's been telling me about the local theater group and all the problems they've been having. He's found a theatrical manager, but she won't be able to take over here for at least three months, and they have a production coming up in a few weeks." She paused. "I volunteered to help out in the meantime."

I narrowed my gaze. "Help out?"

"Yes. That's one of the reasons I'm going back to LA. I have extensive connections, as you know, and the production is desperately in need of a good director."

Garrett Knute had no idea what he was letting that poor troupe in for. Aloud I said, "That is exciting news. Congratulations."

"Thank you, dear, but that's only part of the exciting news," my mother said.

I almost choked on my beer. "There's more?"

"You know that charming shop, dear? The one your detective beau's sister owns? Garrett told me she's been looking for a silent partner. She wants to expand, go into more upscale antiques than lunch boxes and velvet paintings."

I felt my stomach plummet right down to my toes. "Mother? Are you saying what I think you are?"

My mother made a fist and pounded lightly on her chest. "Yes, Crishell. You're looking at the new, silent partner to Secondhand Sue's."

Oh my God. Why didn't I make Sue that offer when I had the chance. "That's great," I heard myself say. "I know Sue has wanted to expand her business for a while. So, what are you going to do? Manage it from out on the West Coast? Take care of scouring all the stores out there?"

My mother clucked her tongue. "Don't be ridiculous, Crishell. Sue needs hands-on mentoring. She needs someone by her side with a vast knowledge of antiques, someone who can teach her the ropes about what and what not to look for. Eventually, we can split up and I'll take charge of the West Coast, but for now, considering my theatrical obligations, I think the smartest thing for me to do is take up residence here."

My stomach lurched. "Oh, so you want to stay with me for, what, another few weeks?"

"Oh, no, dear, I wouldn't dream of imposing on you. I've already booked a suite at the Fox Hollow Inn for an indefinite stay. After all, who knows how long training Sue will take?" She drummed her long nails on the white tablecloth. "I might be able to inject a modicum of class into this sleepy little town. Better yet, we'll get a chance to reconnect, you and I. Isn't that wonderful?"

Out of the corner of my eye I could see Gary duck his head. It was evident he was trying hard not to laugh. My mother turned her head, and I made a face at him. Maybe having my mother close by would turn out to be a good thing. What was that old saying? *If you can't beat 'em, join 'em.*

My mother touched my arm. Her gaze was earnest as she said, "Well, Crishell. You're so quiet. What do you think of my news?"

What could I do? I slid my arm around her shoulders and gave her a squeeze. "Yes, Mother. It's wonderful news. I-I'm looking forward to your returning here."

She beamed at me. "I hoped you'd feel that way. Now, I hope you all can excuse me. I've got *so* much to do before I leave. See you all real soon."

My mother rose and strode regally out of the bar. I looked around the table. Gary, Olivia and Ron were all studiously avoiding my gaze. "Not one word," I hissed. I eyed Gary. "Not from anyone. This will all work out. It could even turn out to be a good thing. You'll see."

I felt something furry against my ankle and looked down. Purrday's head poked out from underneath the table. I shook a finger at the cat. "Not a meow out of you either," I cautioned.

Purrday lifted his head, and his lips parted in a wide, unlovely cat yawn, showing plenty of sharp fang. Then he ducked back underneath the table, but not before he closed his good eye in a *you'll eat those words* kind of wink.

Acknowledgments

Once again, many thanks to my agent, Josh Getzler, and his assistant, Jon Cobb, who do a great job of keeping me calm when writer's block sets in. I cannot express enough thanks to my wonderful editor, Bill Harris, who catches all of my mistakes and generally makes everything I write better!

And heartfelt thanks to those who have embraced Shell, Gary, Purrday and Kahlua! More to come!

About the Author

While Toni LoTempio does not commit—or solve—murders in real life, she has no trouble doing it on paper. Her lifelong love of mysteries began early on when she was introduced to her first Nancy Drew mystery at age ten—*The Secret in the Old Attic*. She and her cat pen the Urban Tails Pet Shop Mysteries, the Nick and Nora mystery series, and the Cat Rescue series. Catch up with them at Rocco's blog, catsbooksmorecats.blogspot.com, or her website, tclotempio.net.